THE HEALER

Book 1: The Phantom Limb

Ja Man

Mutant Horse LLC
Nashville, Tennessee

THE HEALER
Book 1: The Phantom Limb

First printing January, 2009

Published by Mutant Horse LLC

For more details on the healer's world visit
www.mutanthorse.com

ISBN 978-0-9816678-0-5

Layout by Joshua Blevins
Copyediting by Jamie Chavez
Cover art by J. William Myers

In memory of Andre Norton,
Friend and Mentor

PRELUDE

I remember everything. Some things I have chosen to forget and others . . . to re-remember.

Though few of us can recall it in adulthood, our birth sits at the foundation of our consciousness. Floating peacefully in a water world, surrounded by the drum of a mother's heartbeat—nothing else exists. Given the choice, we would never leave her, fed and protected for eternity.

Then the veils hiding reality reflect away, and a hidden sun appears, burning away our utopia like morning mist. The universe squeezes us in waves and expels us from paradise into a cold world full of pain, fear, and the unknown.

From that moment, our life takes on a singular mission—to never again experience the trauma of our beginning. Fear of that recurrence secretly influences all we do—and don't do—in our brief life.

Yet a few of us embrace the shock of that first moment of awareness, realizing that without its scarification our life would never have begun. So we seek out pain and suffering, in the hope that with each experience we might peel away another layer of the ignorance that encapsulates true awareness, hiding it from our conscious minds. I am such a one.

For the rest of you, fear burns at your heels, threatening to overtake at any moment. It whips your back when you stop to rest, chasing you through life until death.

What I say here follows, as closely as the prejudices of recounting personal history allow, the unlayering of my consciousness through the pain and suffering of a lifetime of births and deaths.

I: TRAINING
ONE

"We are lost, Master." I looked down at the scanner's blank screen, slapped it several times against the palm of my hand. A topographic map flickered on, backlit in green.

"Are we?" Master Yeh stood at the edge of a cliff, precariously peering down at something out of sight.

I moved to grab him before curiosity overwhelmed common sense and he plunged over the precipice. Just as I drew him back, a strong musk carried on a sudden breeze caught my attention. Turning quickly, I scanned the dense scrub behind us but saw nothing. I listened carefully as the wind subsided. "Did you hear that?"

"No."

"It sounded like a snort."

"My allergies have been troubling me of late. The floridon is blooming again, my boy. See there?"

Master Yeh pointed to the fields below us, rising and falling to the horizon, a sea of lapis blue flowers that shifted with the winds, a migrating slash of dark green stems revealed with the moving air currents. I gave their beauty a passing glance and eyed the hedge behind us that hid the stark moor of lichen-blotched gray rocks and purple heather over which we had wandered for half a day.

"Not your allergies, Master," I insisted, pointing into the thicket. "It came from back there." I switched the display, whacked it against my thigh, and stared at the data refreshing on the screen. "Two creatures called *yu-te-aks* and something tagged C-342-unk are trailing us—or tracking us."

"Good," Master Yeh replied. He had migrated back to the cliff edge.

I retrieved him, this time holding onto his shoulder. "Not good, Master. We are lost and three creatures of unknown intent are closing on us. What does C stand for?" I surmised that *unk* meant unknown, a previously unidentified species.

"Carnivore," Master Yeh said absently.

Fear triggered my latent survival instinct, and I immediately remembered our positional lock: the small display secured to my chest by an elastic strap confirmed our location in relation to the institute's central compound. "East along this escarpment for a kilometer, then down the face, north by two and then east again along a service road."

My master turned slowly to me. "You know where we are?"

"No, Master," I repeated, unable to hide my irritation. "But I know how to get us back to the compound. And I suggest we get moving now."

Master Yeh enjoyed walking the grounds of the healing institute on the planet Cristoth. I would have chosen to spend my days in the library studying or in the simulation chamber practicing my healing skills. However, my master had gotten lost on the grounds before—went missing for days one time—and as a result I was strongly admonished by the institute's administration to ensure his safety in whatever manner I deemed appropriate. That subtle but well-worded order eliminated my first choice—administering a strong sedative and leaving him in his quarters would not be *deemed appropriate* under any circumstance—and forced me instead to follow him like a hawk on his random jaunts. Unfortunately, the institute grounds covered a third of the principal continent on Cristoth, and the institute had yet to identify all the species living in every dark corner of their planet-wide experiment in guided evolution.

"Good, boy. East you say?"

"Yes, Master."

Master Yeh promptly swung left and began walking.

"No, Master. That is west. Other way."

Though my master demonstrated a profound lack of geographical sense, he possessed an uncanny ability to avoid the most interesting parts of the galaxy. I had followed him for eight years without experiencing the excitement the universe surely offered, or so I thought as his apprentice. With the blind eyes of youth I missed the miracles he performed on quiet planets with plagues and natural disasters. Mind you, I *learned* what I had to learn regarding technique, the harnessing of one's talent and the directing of one's power toward healing the pain and illness of another sentient being. However, I didn't, at the time, understand the myriad subtleties of the actual process—of the relationship between healer and healed, of the moments so important before the healing ever begins, before the healer, in fact, ever touches the patient—that enable one person to draw out the suffering of another. Having all the tools to build a ship doesn't mean you can do so.

I spent my days as his apprentice honing my healing techniques on patients with ailments of the digestive tract, painfully infected digits of all sizes and shapes, or arthritic appendages of various sorts; my nights I spent studying the anatomy and physiology texts of the major galactic sentient species. I was spared little time for anything else.

However, in the rare moments when our paths crossed those of other healers, I devoted my attention to every detail of the lives of my fellow apprentices. Like myself, the majority spent time on hospital planets, some in the service of galactic relief agencies, and a few on roving medical ships; invariably, though, they had all experienced life on worlds caught in turmoil, exploding in the violence of civil wars, bids for expansion, or rebellion against colonial power structures.

Many told me of healing the victims of interplanetary conflicts brought to them from war zones, and some even described spending brief periods in cities near areas of conflict. A few—a very few— took me aside, far from the sharp eyes and sharper ears of our masters, and told me of working among soldiers on the battlefields and the feeling of imminent death pressing in around them.

My only consolation lay in the fact that every other healer we met paid deference to my master. His honor was my honor, I learned. I assumed the respect for Master Yeh was due to his age: when I first joined his service I couldn't imagine that such an ancient-looking humanoid could live so long and considered what I was to do when he died, which I was certain would be in a matter of months. I was mistaken, of course, and quickly came to recognize his resilience. But youth burns away pleasure faster than age and experience does. So the pride and honor I felt at being my master's apprentice would quickly fade, and I would fall back into the desire for adventure.

I directed him down the face of the cliff toward the fields of floridon, keeping a close eye on the scanner for evidence of ambush or attack. "Master, we have spent months on Cristoth. Perhaps we should consider another venue."

"We have explored only a small section of this planet, my boy. Why would you have us off?"

"It has been ten solar days since you have healed anyone. Your services are certainly needed somewhere in the galaxy."

"Adventure again, is it? That's what you want."

"No, Master."

"Every healing is an adventure into new territory, a place you've never been before—the mind and body of another soul. Running about in the midst of wars no more constitutes adventure than cooking cryptoc stew every day and wondering each time if you left any of the neurotoxin intact."

"Master, I have heard that saying before."

He looked at me with mild surprise. "Who have you heard that from before?"

"You."

"Oh, of course," he laughed.

I navigated us safely into the healing institute's secured central station and quickly put my master to bed. I lay in my own cot thinking of battle-healing, but when I fell asleep, I dreamed of Master Yeh stirring an enormous pot of cryptoc stew with me bobbing up and down in it.

My com unit buzzed me awake in the middle of our designated sleeping time.

"Master Yeh?"

I didn't recognize the Cristothan's voice. I sat up and squinted in the darkness at the unit. "This is his apprentice." I wanted to say *you know that Master Yeh carries no com unit, and every time you have buzzed for him in the last six months I have answered.* Even half awake I managed to maintain an acceptable degree of propriety—a characteristic attributable to my master's instruction.

"We have an emergency request for a healer."

"I will take care of it."

After a pause, the official answered. "All right. Be ready to leave on a shuttle in one hour."

"You misunderstand—" The com unit had already dropped back into sleep mode. What I had meant to say was that I would take it up with Master Yeh, not that I would answer the call for a healer. But then I lay back and considered the opportunity: had providence offered me a chance to prove myself?

Youthful excess arises from miscalculation more often than from a conscious effort to do wrong. In the galaxy there exists a planet I visited years later whose sentient race has a saying: *youth is wasted on the young, and the duty of the young is to waste it.* I understand now what they meant—that the young are charged with the task of making mistakes and then learning how to fix them. Through adversity we grow.

So at that moment I did what my age dictated: I decided to leave my master.

★ ★ ★

By the time the door monitor clicked, letting me know that someone requested admission, I had loaded my small pack with the few personal items allowed an apprentice. For an instant, as my finger hovered over the door release stud, I worried that I would find Master Yeh standing on the other side, his expression blank except for his penetrating eyes. Logic and experience prevailed over neurotic fears, though: Master Yeh never left his quarters early; he always waited for me to come to him.

The door slid away, and a young Cristothan agent of the healing institute bowed to me. "My apologies for disturbing your rest, healer."

It was the first time that I had experienced respect directed at me and not through my master. A smile pulled at my lips despite my resolve not to show pride. "There is no blame," I answered, and he smiled, relieved.

"You must leave immediately. I will escort you to the transport."

As the door to my cell closed and I followed the young Cristothan, a great washing out ran through me, like a rising tide suddenly flooding a dry pool at the edge of an ocean, clearing away a lifetime of debris. Freed from the restricting sediments of tradition and duty, my mind and body shifted, as though I were a jewel with only one facet facing the sun, and, with a single twist, a thousand hidden facets revealed themselves. Sharp, cold, clear—my new mind was alive with fear, hope, apprehension, guilt, and determination. I had made a choice—my very first choice—not bound by propriety, by my training, or by the dictates of my master or the Healing Order, and the overriding exhilaration of freedom balanced out the daunting fear of uncertainty. One can learn by degrees, but one grows by leaps. Or so I thought.

I caught the shuttle to the medical ship—a small cruiser class built and equipped for short trips between solar systems. As we neared the vessel, I grew tense. My experiences had always been within the context of Master Yeh's work; he provided an anchor, a constant I could rely upon if I ventured beyond the range of my abilities or the extent of my training. Cristoth shrank in the transport's global projection monitor and with it my certainty that I was doing the right thing.

The shuttle docked, and the access doors hissed open. I stepped in: a single malish medical officer waited for me at the airlock, rocking nervously side to side on his feet.

"You're the healer?" he asked, inspecting me skeptically. He was older than me and the Cristothan who had showed deference to me.

My apprehension soared, but I saw no chance to retreat. The shuttle had already disengaged and was heading back to the planet. "I am."

He nodded both as a cursory greeting and as a sign for me to follow him down the hallway. "The Chief Medical Officer regrets that he could not welcome you aboard: the current medical crisis requires his immediate attention." He recited the words accurately and without a hint of sincerity. We halted where another corridor intersected our own and waited as a pack of medical personnel rushed across our path, all of them talking at the same time, blending the words into an incoherent mash.

My nameless guide watched them sweep past us and then continued on. "I have been assigned to tour you through our facilities." Said with a minimum of enthusiasm.

I don't recall much of the tour, as little of it interested me. I found technologically advanced facilities quite boring without patients lying in them, moaning and bleeding onto them, screaming or pleading into the air, without nurses and doctors running about, security guards restraining combative individuals, and healers, radiating a strange calm in the midst of the chaos, trying to provide a center, a fulcrum on which the confusion could attach itself, revolve and slowly brake to a stop.

Near the end of the tour, my guide received a com signal: the whispered voice on the other end I couldn't hear, but his answer was clear enough: "I will bring him up." He looked at me. "They want you on the bridge."

I took in the controlled chaos of the bridge with an eagerness that muted my previous apprehension. My guide walked through the storm of alarms and crew running back and forth to stand beside two older malish calmly talking to each other in the midst of the mayhem. One I recognized as the chief medical officer by his uniform, and the other I guessed was the captain. The CMO turned to my guide, leaned over to listen to him, then looked at me.

He waved me over, and I approached. He bowed slightly. "Welcome, healer. I am sorry for the informal greeting but we are faced with an emergency."

"Can you tell me what has happened?"

"A Llastok vessel exploded with one hundred fifty aboard," the captain answered, pointing to the holographic image floating above the console over which they stood.

I examined the hologram. A large hole gaped in the ship's midsection with a sunburst blast that blurred the shape and lines of the hull. "Was it attacked?"

"The explosion came from within the ship," the captain replied. "Perhaps an unstable fuel cell or a leakage in the lines. As you can see, the aft section—the engines and engineering—remain untouched."

"We have contacted the nearest medical facilities," the CMO said. "Unfortunately, the ship lies in a remote corner of the Llastok solar system, and Llastok Prime possesses no credible mobile aid units. They have requested immediate assistance, and I have relayed a message that we are on our way. We are the closest ship with an advanced medical unit."

"Is there anything I can do at this time?"

The CMO shook his head. "We will find you quarters and will call you when we need your services."

Master Yeh would have counseled me to spend the transit time meditating. However, twenty years hardly constitutes an age of wisdom or of patience. Without Master Yeh's moderating presence, I could not remain calm and centered as he had taught me.

Had he control over the energy and drive raging through me at that moment, he certainly would have banked it in some central spiritual repository for future use in healing. Instead, I spent it freely, cruising the hallways, injecting myself into every nook and crack of the ship, imposing myself as gently and generously as possible into the preparations by the medical staff for the inevitable onslaught of wounded. In this way, I learned quite a bit about the mechanics of the medical teams; by the time we left hyperspace and entered the Llastok system, I felt confident that I could participate as a useful member of the ship, though I had done little to prepare myself for healing. Reality has a way of hiding from youthful eyes.

I chose to attach myself to one of the younger physicians, thinking that he would both appreciate and tolerate my presence more readily than the older ones. "They've established a containment field around the ship," he answered my question about how a ship so badly damaged could survive long enough for us to arrive. "The field can temporarily stabilize the hull and restore breathable atmosphere."

We headed for the triage deck, an open arena with portable voice-activated medical units stored in the walls. We turned a corner, and the corridor ended in a doorway. My companion quickly waved his hand over the access panel and plunged through the opening door without breaking stride. I followed closely, and the triage deck exploded over me in sensory waves—first, the awful reek of burning clothes, charred flesh, and smoldering ship parts; the nauseating, oily smell of ship fuel; and intermingled within that stifling fume, the sickly sweet aroma of disinfectant rising through the stench like a lotus through a swamp.

Then the screaming stabbed knives into my ears, rising sharply over the rhythmic hum of moans and cries for aid that reached me beyond their alien tongue. Everywhere I looked, showers of blood jetted through unnatural holes, pumped desperately by hearts trying to fix the unfixable. Bodies lacked symmetry, missing appendages and sides of faces.

The universe contracted suddenly into a gruesome abstraction, a brutal caricature of life. Terror, fear, pain, anguish—they form a universal language, a commonality deeper than words or cultures or traditions—and I felt them all around me as I wandered through the triage deck.

A hand grabbed my wrist and gently directed me toward a humanoid who had lost the lower part of his body. The young malish victim looked at me calmly, watching me as I drew up to his side. For a moment I was distracted by the almost street market atmosphere swirling around us—scattered clots of people shouting across the room, others answering from afar, their words lost amidst the endless clamor and the streams of personnel weaving back and forth. I looked back down at him, and slowly everything else dialed down into a background murmur.

He spoke to me, a foamy, bloody burbling in which I imagined that I heard familiar words in CombineSpeak. I took his hand and nodded my head. "Relax. I am going to heal you of your pain."

He closed his eyes, and I felt him release the tightness, the fearful grip on life characteristic of the dying. I let him go, and looked up at the silent faces witnessing our communion. "Find me another."

Fear gave way to determination. I had no time to question my abilities, and so I used them with greater depth and intensity than I had thought possible.

I don't recall most of those first healings, whether because of my inexperience with the process or simply the intensity of the circumstances. What I do remember is the profound exhaustion, the abiding weight that I carried around, a bit heavier with each healing.

Someone dragged me into a quiet corner of the triage deck and left me there. I don't remember how long I sat on the floor, but I do remember waking up with my head cocked painfully to the side. I heard fewer cries, although the stench of burnt flesh and metal still lingered. I rose and rubbed out the stiffness in my shoulder and neck. The deck had emptied except for a few staff members tending to individuals on stretchers or sitting in small groups talking. Here and there I saw force shields, oblong and opaque: I knew that within them were the deceased, preserved and prepared for transport. I walked up to one of the medical staff who stood apart from the others, punching codes into a small vis-screen.

"Are there more to heal?"

He turned from his hand held console, inspected me briefly, then went back to his screen. "We have finished here. They may need you on the surgery deck."

"Thank you," I said, and headed for the entrance.

Just as I reached it, a klaxon sounded. I whipped around and watched as the rear wall of the triage deck turned translucent. Through it I saw a small shuttle heading straight for us. Before I could cry out a warning, the pod broke through the invisible envelope of the containment field and dropped onto the deck, skidding in a flash of flame and smoke and catching up against the hull. The far wall turned opaque again as the remaining crew ran for the shuttle. The ship's access panel swung back, and an officer jumped out.

"We need help here now!"

For the briefest moment I considered slipping out, but instead, I ran over to the shuttle. When I got there, crewmembers were pulling out a Llastokian malish from the rear hatch of the ship.

"I've contacted the surgery team," one of the staff said.

"He's in a lot of pain," the shuttle pilot replied. "You've got to do something now."

A few of the crew looked to me. Someone said, "*He's* a healer."

The pilot turned to me. "Get to it, then. Heal him."

"Lay him down here," I commanded. The pilot ripped open the victim's coat and shirt, and I knelt down beside him. The right half of his abdomen was missing; I identified intestines, part of what was the liver-equivalent, and the primary blood vessels serving the lower extremities. These were intact, so far as I could see, but there was a lot of blood filling the abdominal cavity and pouring slowly onto the deck; part of the adjacent rib cage was blown away, the lung collapsed on that side, right upper extremity missing above the elbow, blast marks across the right face, and a right orbital fracture with a ruptured globe. Agonal breathing—shallow, intermittent, labored.

"I cannot save him," I murmured.

"That's not your job," someone replied from behind me. "Just ease his pain."

I nodded, closed my eyes, and laid my right hand over his left abdomen. I formed an image of the Llastokian in my mind, and then I tried to enter it . . . enter him. At first I couldn't feel anything, just a sense of blankness. Then I realized that I was breathing normally. His breathing came infrequently, in sharp, sudden gasps that racked his entire body. I ceased my breathing and followed his. I felt something then, something vague, like seeing a shape forming as it approaches in the darkness. I headed for it and felt myself upended and pulled into his supine body, strange and different from my own. Suddenly, blinding pain exploded from my right side; I felt my right hand and my right arm melt away in a burning wind and a searing splash across my face. I reeled backward but kept my feet.

Shaking off the heat and the horror, I managed to right myself. Opening my eyes, I saw the young malish lying in front of me, looking up into my face. He mouthed words I couldn't hear, then stopped. His mouth gaped open, and his eyes widened in fear.

A second sun seemed to rise from inside of me. I yelled and fell back as a liquid fire rushed upward through my middle and exploded through my skin.

★ ★ ★

Something cold suspended me from below. It rose in gentle waves around my sides. I lay on my back, yet I couldn't seem to feel it, to consciously touch it. A wave would rise and my hearing would change, become hollow and indistinct. Opening my eyes changed nothing: all I saw was blue, uniform and unmoving. Voices and sounds vaguely resembling words fluctuated through the liquid atmosphere to my ears.

Master Yeh appeared. Every direction I turned to hide from him, he was there. His gray eyes stared into me and illuminated my insides, their determined light reaching into all the hidden places I thought impossible to find. He said nothing. I tried to ask forgiveness, but my mouth wouldn't open. He came to my side and stared down into me. Then he laid a hand on my chest. After a moment, I felt a great suction drawing into my chest, concentrating at a spot just under his hand.

I closed my eyes and woke up. I lay on a hard flat surface. My eyes opened, and this time I could see. A mobile mechanical arm held an oblong scanning device suspended over the middle of my body. Two medical personnel—one a malish humanoid, the other a gender unknown amphiboid—stood at the foot of the table speaking to each other in low voices. My vocal cords were paralyzed: they refused to move, to respond to my desire to speak.

The two disappeared through a doorway on the left without looking back at me. As my body and mind slowly awoke, I ventured to sit up and then rose tentatively, finally stumbling out of the recovery room in search of help, an explanation, food.

Finding by chance a small room with nutrient dispensers, I sat down alone in the middle of the rows of tightly squeezed tables. Soon after, a falish entered the room. She stopped short when she saw me. She looked vaguely familiar, but I put her out of my mind as I nursed my tentative stomach and considered the option of eating or not. When she dropped a tray of food onto the table across from me and sat down, I stared at her until recognition lit my mind.

"The shuttle pilot," I said aloud.

She nodded. "Lieutenant Therador," she answered in a rough voice just a bit deeper than I expected from a falish.

I took a moment to inspect her, as she did me. Humanoid, perhaps even Earthling, of medium height for falish of my species. She wore her black-almost-blue hair short and watched me warily with her light green eyes and a stern, brow-wrinkling look that I am sure intimidated many. Her one-piece jumpsuit fit her tightly, and I could see from her curves that she maintained a well-conditioned physique. Her smooth, tanned face belied her age, which I gauged at older than myself by at least ten standard solar years. A strange oval formed of punctate dark spots marked her left cheek. I couldn't tell if they represented an injury or an intentional scarring.

"You brought in that last victim—the young malish."

She nodded. Her green eyes remained fixed on me.

"I failed to heal him, I'm afraid. I cannot say what happened, though. My memory of the healing is vague."

"I will tell you then," the pilot said, sitting back and crossing her arms over her chest. "You killed him."

The bitterness unveiled across her face, and I felt the blush of anger warm my cheeks in response. Recalling my training, I let Therador's words wash through me, and in their wake, my emotions. I focused my attention on something symmetric—a Nuruvian chanting palindrome—and watched as both inciting words and incited anger intertwined and consumed each other. As I rose from out of the palindrome, the logical, detached answer presented itself: "I am a healer," I explained calmly. "I don't kill people. I try to help them."

"You touched him, and he died."

"That doesn't mean I killed him. You saw his wounds. He was going to die anyway."

"Is that your reason for killing him? To shorten his torment?"

"I did *not* kill him," I repeated, letting frustration enter my voice.

"I see things as they are, not as I would wish them to be," she countered.

"Are you accusing me of self-deception?"

"Yes."

I stood up, leaned across the table. Tension tightened the muscles of my face and my arms. My entire body felt like a spear.

Lieutenant Therador stood up as well, straight and hard. In the corner of my eyes I could see her hands flexing. She looked past me, and her expression softened. She stepped back, her body loosened, and she bowed her head.

I turned my head and looked over my shoulder. Master Yeh stood in the doorway.

He looked exhausted, but he still managed to fix his burning eyes upon me. He gave Therador a cursory nod and pointed a single index finger at me then flicked it at the door. He turned around slowly and headed back through the entrance.

I had done many wrong things in the eight years that I had followed my master, but none of them intentionally. Therefore, I had never really incurred my master's wrath. Among apprentices there is a saying, held as an unwritten gospel: *those who punish readily, punish weakly; those who punish rarely, punish deeply.* My master certainly tolerated much from me, which put him in the latter category of punishers.

"What have you done with that Nuruvian palindrome I taught you?"

"I lost it, Master."

Without eying me, he snorted. "Well, find it. And don't lose it again—or your temper, for that matter."

"I will not, Master," I replied, while the anger boiled up again. I waited for a few moments and then continued in the meekest voice I could muster. "Master, I ask forgiveness for my behavior."

He said nothing in reply, just kept gliding down the corridor faster than I had ever seen him move; I had to jog in bursts to keep up with him.

"Master, Lieutenant Therador called me a killer."

He halted and turned on me. "I suppose you had to learn sometime." He shook his head, looking at me sadly. "Perhaps it was best this way. I would have kept you from it for as long as I could." He started again down the hall. "The first time is always traumatic—a shock to the mind," he assured me, still shaking his head.

"The first time for what, Master?"

He stopped a second time, looked up and down the corridor to make sure that we were alone, and turned to me. "The first time you kill someone by healing them. Always difficult."

I opened my mouth and felt the hollowness of space enter.

Master Yeh watched me for a time, waiting patiently. "I shall explain," he said finally.

I nodded.

"I will tell you, but remember this: trials of faith come to all of us. Do not expect a time when you have passed beyond temptation or suffering. You have just experienced your first trial. Understand that they are not meant to undermine our faith, but to strengthen it." He paused and then smiled. "Trials will come again, and ones far worse than you can imagine. If you fail to learn from this one, you cannot hope to survive those waiting for you in the future."

"You have had such trials?"

"Certainly," he said calmly. "I am having one right now." He looked old and frail and demanding and calm and at peace, all at the same time.

"How can you look so unconcerned?"

"Shall I fall on the ground and wail? Would that convince you of my suffering?"

I shook my head.

"Obstacles require knowledge and wisdom, not emotional turmoil, to resolve them."

"Master, I still don't understand what happened when I healed the Llastokian."

"Rebound shock at first," he replied. "You failed to accommodate for it, but then you know nothing of such things because you have never healed someone mortally wounded. For those suffering from complex pain, both physical and mental, one must approach the process gingerly. You must heal gradually, stepping slowly into the patient's pain like easing into a raging river, else its force will overwhelm you—as you learned. The sudden intensity of experiencing his pain shocked your system and threw you into unconsciousness—an ingenious mechanism of self-preservation, much like a fuse."

"That's not all of it, though, is it?"

He pursed his lips and bobbed his head slightly, a trait signifying that he prepared to approach a difficult task. "As healers, we collect the pain and illness of those we treat. For now, your lack of experience limits you to the healing of pain. In time, though, with discipline and practice, you may develop the skills to remove illness and disease as well. Pain and infirmity exist in many subtle forms; we can categorize them, define them, subdivide them, in more ways than there are stars. But truly, we can reduce them to two types: natural and unnatural. The natural arises from the native course of life—its creation, its maintenance, its gradual dissolution, and its discontinuation. All life arises, exists, and then ceases to exist. The unnatural exists only because sentient creatures exist." He shrugged. "I have wondered over the years whether even this distinction truly exists; as healers, we recognize the differences only because of how we handle the two forms we collect, but then if we were not to exist, would the distinction cease to exist as well?"

He looked at me, and I shook my head because I didn't understand the question.

He waved his hand absently. "No matter. The lesson: natural pain and disease, when collected, dissipate with time. You gather them, and eventually they dissolve. The unnatural forms never deteriorate. You will keep them forever, unless you encounter the being who created them, either through his action or inaction. Then, if you heal that person, that which you collected returns to him without effort, like water running downhill. You can do nothing to impede or expedite the process." He stopped, and lowered his voice. "The Healing Order keeps that small detail as secret as they are able—and so, too, must you. Your life may depend upon it, and the lives of all healers and the entire mission of the Order as well. But do not trouble yourself with this knowledge. It is very rare in our profession as we practice it to encounter the perpetrators of crimes and atrocities. We, by nature and design, find ourselves immersed in the consequences of those actions, not in the creation of them. And as so often is the case, once the fire is lit, the arsonist runs away—often never to be found."

"That Llastokian—he caused the pain of the others? How?"

"The captain explained after I arrived to recover you. It seems that the Llastok system finds itself mired in a conflict only newly discovered by its people, although germinating for many years, I would guess. The Llastok governance council recently targeted for expanded colonization one of the system's lesser planets, terraformed two hundred years ago primarily by an indentured Llastokian sub-race at great cost in lives. The government wants to annex a large portion of the best lands to develop a highly advanced recreation continent that will service not only the Llastok population but neighboring systems as well. The government by law holds the right to do so and has made several proposals for compensation and resettling of the current population." He sighed. "Naturally, the citizens living there, mostly the descendents of the original terraformers, refuse to leave. Protests throughout the system have remained peaceful, for the most part, but without definitive movement toward a solution. Tensions among the disputing parties continue to rise. The authorities informed our captain that they have monitored extremist groups on both sides of the conflict for some time now."

My master paused for a moment, thinking upon something. I could see the strain in his eyes, in his brow wrinkling more than usual. Shaking his head, he continued: "It appears that the young Llastokian you healed was a member of this sub-race and carried an explosive device. The transport he blew up was en route to the planet in question."

"You mean he meant to blow up the ship?"

"I don't know whether he intended to detonate it onboard or whether he was simply transporting it to another destination for another purpose."

I closed my eyes and saw the young Llastokian—entered him again—but then, without the direct connection, the sensations remained distant, more tolerable. My master described them as afterimages, residue from healings, the memories of our experiences— *the legacy of our actions*, as he put it. I felt his pain distantly, his shattered right eye and the throbbing in his chest and the strange sensation of the absence of his right abdomen. I felt and experienced nothing of his thoughts—of his purpose or motivations, his anger or hatred or fear.

"When you healed him, the pain you had collected from the

victims of the explosion returned to him. The impact of that pain coupled with his injuries killed him instantly."

"He deserved it, then," I said with finality.

"Listen and remember." Master Yeh touched my shoulder with the tip of one finger, and it felt like a stone column pressing down on me. "First: judge not. Never take upon yourself the task of correcting the perceived wrong actions of others. That is judgment, and neither you nor I will ever see with a purely objective eye and therefore will never qualify as impartial judges. Act upon your own convictions, your own understanding of right and wrong. None of us will ever fully understand the reasons for or consequences of our own actions; how then are we to know the reasons for or consequences of another's actions? Tell me, apprentice, do you know your own mind fully?"

Immediately I opened my mouth to answer but realized I didn't have one.

"I will answer for you." My master cut into my thoughts. "No—you do not fully know your own mind, nor will you ever. Many more years have I lived than you and still I have not dug down to the ultimate wellspring of my own mind. We catch glimpses of the processes behind our thoughts and sometimes those of others, but even the most skilled at perceiving will only get an incomplete view."

"But, Master, you cannot tell me that some actions are not inherently wrong."

An eyebrow rose. "Can I not? Tell me, then, is not killing a wrong action?"

"The Healing Order condemns killing by a healer," I recited.

"And have I not agreed with Pilot Therador that you killed the young Llastokian?"

"But Master, I did not mean to. I would never kill by design."

"Ah, so you know that for a fact, do you? What did I ask you before? Do you know your mind fully?"

He looked at me, and I shook my head. "I do not."

He held up two fingers. "Second: defend not. Avoid defending the actions of others, for to defend another presupposes that one has judged their actions well or ill. If you agree that one cannot adequately judge another's actions, then one can hardly defend those actions. Act from your conscience; defend your conscience. That is all." He turned and started walking again.

"But, Master, surely we must consider his action as evil. He killed innocent people."

Master Yeh looked over his shoulder at me. "The first lesson, apprentice?

"Judge not," I recited.

"Yes, judge not. Killing is wrong, my boy, but avoid placing labels on those who act. We do not know what his intentions were, or what the consequences of his actions will be. He killed the other passengers, certainly. And he died as a direct result of your actions, certainly."

"I was trying to save him, Master."

"What is the First Law of the Order?"

"Do no harm."

"How then must you judge your actions, if you were to judge them? Your actions led directly to his death. There can be no argument with that."

"But, Master, I did not intend to kill him."

He nodded. "Do you think those labeled evil consider themselves so? I think not. Across the galaxy and throughout time, good intentions have often led to the commitment of atrocities. It is not enough to do the right thing for the wrong reasons, nor is it excusable to do the wrong thing for the right reasons. One must strive to do the right thing for the right reasons. Remember that."

"By your way of thinking, nothing, then, is evil or good."

"It does seem that way—on the surface—does it not? But I don't believe that any more than you do. The difference between us is that I have an idea of why the world is so and you do not. You want to know that good and evil exist in the world, and you want to recognize their faces, like the faces of friends and enemies, so that you can identify them whenever and wherever you meet them. On the other hand, I have come to realize that they wear the same face. Evil and good do exist, my boy, in all of us. Right action. Wrong action. What then would you say of your face and that of the Llastokian? Both of you have killed. Both of you wear the face of evil, do you not?"

"He intended to kill," I insisted. "I did not."

"Do you hear nothing, or do you hear everything and forget everything? Intentions are not sufficient. Do you think the good and the evil in this world will announce themselves to you?"

"Clearly, Master, there are some who cannot be redeemed."

Master Yeh leaned forward and pointed a bent finger at me. His eyes lit and his brows furrowed. I had seen that look before, but never before had it been directed at me.

"No sentient creature is ever beyond redemption, boy," he said slowly. "When you turn your back on someone, you make a judgment that you will have to live with for eternity. Judgments do not mar the judged: they mar those who do the judging."

I understand now at least part of what my master said at that time, but only after years of experiencing the grayness of life, where the majority of life as we live it exists, without the benefit of absolutes. But at the time I lived and understood as an apprentice, whose life was to a certain degree a fantasy, composed of many absolutes and only a few grays.

"My boy, to kill is wrong," Master Yeh continued, "whether you mean to or not. Certainly there are degrees of action, a spectrum of right and wrong. So killing innocents deliberately one might reasonably consider far worse than killing someone accidentally. Nevertheless, the results of the two actions remain the same—the death of one sentient being through the actions of another sentient being."

He raised his arms and spread them wide, palms up: "Today, you and the young Llastokian malish shared the face of evil. His life passed before his opportunity for redemption. But you? Tomorrow, perhaps you will wear the face of good, of selflessness. Today you shall be condemned; tomorrow, perhaps you will be praised. For good or ill, galactic society will judge you. When will you have them do so? Today—or wait until tomorrow? And if you do evil again tomorrow? What then?"

He paused. "I see and understand your confusion. The truth always demands more of us—more of our time, more of our effort, more of our conscious selves—than lies. Herein one finds the paradox of life: most often, the truth appears as a complex machine while lies disguise themselves as simple machines. Make the effort to look deeper, though, and you will find the truth composed of simple parts and lies, of complicated ones."

I expected the Llastokian incident to represent the last of my adventures with my master. Rather, it became the first of many. From that moment my life changed dramatically. As though realizing that I was behind in my training and there wasn't much time remaining, Master Yeh rushed me into a new world. The moment we returned to Cristoth, he instructed me to pack again. "This time, choose what you will need and what you do not mind leaving behind. We will not be returning."

He insisted on no more than one case, and normally I would have protested, saying that eight years of accumulated anatomy and physiology data cubes, along with items of personal significance could not remain behind—that to leave them would be tantamount to leaving the greater part of myself.

"If you require external objects to remind you of who you were and who you are, then there is something inherently wrong with you," he said with a smile that let me know he didn't believe his words applied to me. "Learn to remember, to incorporate experiences into yourself, and rely less upon the crutch of tangible, external things. These things never change, never grow with you. Experiences, if utilized correctly, provide the foundations of your future existence— use them rather than collecting them in a useless pile of souvenirs."

And this time, I obeyed without argument. Why? As I look back, I realize that I understood that my master planned on leading me into a new place, a new realm, where I could not take anything that was not already a part of me—that the tools and souvenirs of my past would prove useless, perhaps even appear ridiculous, like wearing the clothes of childhood as an adult. So I abandoned everything that I held dear.

In the following year I never once asked my master where we headed, although we traveled more in that year than all the previous eight. I am not certain if he ever had a particular destination in mind. I watched him transform into a wanderer, comfortable living in any situation, existing solely in the moment, content with what the vagaries of circumstance brought us—as comfortable sleeping in a hole dug into the massive carcass of a Luthian bog trudger as living in the Wazian Overlord's personal city globe floating in the third cloud layer of the gas giant Wazia.

The discovery that the ease of his adjustment came not from the excitement of new experiences but from returning to the familiar ways of a past life astounded me. By that time, however, I was too busy absorbing every new environment to either care or comment.

"Expect nothing from this world," he said to me, "and you will never be surprised by what it offers you."

TWO

We learn. We live. We forget.

I listened to all of Master Yeh's teachings, although I cannot attest to having heard everything he said—and certainly I remember even less. Yet, these lapses constitute mistakes of youth and innocence committed by all apprentices and, therefore, do not sit upon my shoulders alone.

Condemn me, though, for lack of judgment—for the poor eye not to recognize the truly singular lessons and commit them to memory but rather to lump everything together as valuable and forget the whole lot. Some lessons are vital to a particular time and circumstance—we would not have survived without them—but their importance quickly fades with time. Others seem of tantamount importance but with the wisdom of hindsight become insignificant. And a very few hold the intensity of the universally applicable—to all times, all places, all circumstances. My master's instruction about not expecting anything from the universe—that lesson fit into the third category. I forgot that teaching for a time.

And then, sometimes luck overcomes ignorance.

We had entered the edge of a wide disc of systems colonized by an ancient and gradually degenerating race. The rest of the galaxy knew them as the Ardri of Condresarc—Condresarc referring to their home planet, of which no current knowledge exists, leading experts in galactic history to assume that the Ardri themselves were transplants.

On the rim colonies, we watched millennia-old monuments to the Ardri thrown down, statues defaced, places renamed in native tongues. We slowly spiraled inward along the standard trade routes, watching a countercurrent of military personnel and their weapons flow outwards to repel the gathering wave of dissolution—to quell it, or simply to temporarily inhibit its progress.

We healed the wounded as we moved with the currents of

displaced civilians driven toward some central destination of hope and security.

Despite my limited experience with galactic dynamics, I correctly surmised that the fragmentation or consolidation of cultures and societies rarely occurs without considerable violence, whether through the force of natural phenomena or of sentient beings.

"Master, why does decay always seem to arise at the edge of things?"

"Does it?"

"It does here, with the Ardri."

He nodded. "Do you know of Gzosash Syndrome?"

"Yes, Master."

"How does it manifest?"

"A disease of reptiloids, it first appears as a slight discoloring of the scales, most commonly on the dorsum of the hands and feet. Such discolorations are often ignored as signs of premature aging or stress, both of which can cause aberrations in scale pigmentation."

"What do the color changes represent in Gzosash Syndrome?"

"The first signs of liver and kidney failure, which eventually kill the sufferer if not treated early in the disease process—"

"—and it is rarely diagnosed in the early stages because initial manifestations mimic benign processes," Master Yeh finished.

"Yes, Master. Usually significant, widespread organ degeneration accumulates before it is diagnosed correctly, and then the damage is often irreversible."

"Gzosash victims look like they die from the outside in, but in fact the disease begins and ends in their very core, appearing initially at the extremes of their bodies where the poison collects first to then slowly spread back in on itself."

"Yes, Master."

"The Gzosash Syndrome mirrors a similar phenomenon on a cultural scale. Essentially, the Ardri suffer from Gzosash Syndrome. It is common that disease attacks the core, with the first signs appearing distantly—remotely—apparently unconnected. For this reason, often disease spreads insidiously before detection. Always be aware of the connectedness of the universe, of parent to child, of master to slave—of your hand with your heart. Why?" He caught my eye. "Because what happens to your hand may be the first sign of something that has been affecting your heart for a much longer time. Do not ignore small things at the edges of your conscience, your moral and ethical periphery—compromise there represents decay in your core." He tapped his sternum with two fingers. "Life flows from a peaceful center, contagion from a diseased one."

"So the current civil war in the Ardri Empire could have been predicted?"

"Perhaps, but the important point is that the fragmentation we are witnessing at the edges represents the long-standing weakening at the center—of the Ardri themselves. Never lose sight of the moral and ethical core taught by the Healing Order. They are the blood and oxygen sustaining your spiritual existence. Lose sight of them and you will decay, and then"—he swept his hand around the transport shuttle in which we stood, swept his hand over the wretched crowd of refugees of a dozen races from two dozen systems crammed together, swept it past the viewing ports in which one could catch glimpses of other transports or the occasional fleet of assault cruisers passing us in the opposite direction—"you will dissolve from the edges."

★ ★ ★

Order takes far more energy and time to develop and maintain than disorder takes to progressively destroy.

The dissolution of the Ardri of Condresarc overtook us like a silent wave gathering from behind, rising above, and then crashing with hidden fury before us. There was no question of it when we entered the spaceport of a stable planet on our journey to the central systems. From Master Yeh's description of the planet and its natives—he had visited many years before—I expected to find refuge amidst an educated, sophisticated, and technologically advanced race.

What I witnessed was the true dissolving of the cultural fabric, leaving only naked instinct: the surest evidence that sentience evolves is watching it devolve. Looting, slavery, indiscriminate killing—anything one could think of to distinguish primitive from advanced—we witnessed. I had a mind to reboard our ship and leave the presentient madness, but my master refused.

"You cannot hide from suffering," he said as we stood under the pillared entrance to the spaceport and watched the streets seethe. A phalanx of heavily armored military ground transports formed a secondary wall around the compound; in front of them a double line of soldiers stood with laser pistols and thermal cannons pointed beyond the defenses, where masses of people swarmed against the barrier. Intermittently, the wave turned back on itself, roiling and swirling, gathering again to crash against the secured gates. Flashes and lines of blue randomly arced out from the soldiers, cutting deliberate, unnaturally clean lines through the crowds, leaving black smoking streaks on the ground. For a moment the masses would retract, and briefly I could make out the tracery pattern created by the laser and thermal cannon volleys, surreal etchings using the ink of burned bodies. Then the face of death scribed on the road would disappear beneath the curtain of people as they descended again on the wall of soldiers. "You can no more leave behind suffering and pain than you can walk away from one of your arms."

"Master, can we not do something?"

"Do what? Stop the killing?" He looked over at me and raised his eyebrows. "Would you have me go down and tell the soldiers to halt the massacre?"

"No, Master."

"Why not?" he replied. "I want to go down there and stop the killing. What we want to do and what we are capable of doing often never meet, but there is no harm in wishing for the former while acting on the latter. If I cannot prevent individuals from falling then at least I can pick them up. We are wake riders, apprentice: our power comes from mitigating suffering, not preventing it."

"Can we not use our influence to convince others not to commit atrocities?"

Master Yeh's eyes narrowed. "Convince—or coerce? How does one distinguish the two? Better to not try convincing than to find oneself coercing. Small steps lead both to heaven and to hell."

"But if we have the power to stop wrong acts, are we not obligated to do so?"

Master Yeh shook his head vigorously. "Power should not be wielded if the threat of its misuse is too great. We hold the potential for tremendous power, my boy. We can collect the suffering created by others, and the threat of returning it we could utilize as an unequaled motivating force. Nothing moves the sentient mind more easily than the fear of pain. Not even hatred so quickly propels us. Remember, judge not. We—all of us—are too weak-minded, too morally feeble, to wield such power without it warping us. It would break you—it would break me—and then you would be lost."

Only police and profiteers—and fools—walk through a war zone without fear. As we were neither the first nor the second, I labeled us the third, although I kept my thoughts to myself. The authorities had cleared away most of the dead, and many of the wounded too injured to protest, before Master Yeh and I managed to convince our way past the lines of soldiers to reach the market. Family members searched through those left on the streets, scurrying nervously from one dark pile of clothes to another, a head popping up frequently to scan the area for approaching danger.

I followed my master through the streets, healing any that the police and military had missed. "They will return soon enough," Master Yeh said, standing up from a dead body and looking about for another victim. He stepped around the dead, never stepped over them, and hobbled toward a jumbled pile at the mouth to a small alley. "We must work quickly to help as many as we can."

"Master, I think we should look for the hospital facilities. We can do more good there."

"You think the military took them to hospitals?" he asked, bending down slowly, touching one body, then another and another. I turned back over my shoulder, noticed that the line of soldiers had contracted to squads that began to move out from the spaceport. "Where else would they take them?"

"All dead." He stood up more slowly, and I lent him an arm. He slapped me gently on my face. "Wake up, boy. The first thing to evaporate in war is justice, although ironically it is the one thing all warmongers vow to preserve by their actions." He shook his head and smiled. "War—such a funny thing."

I heard it before I saw it. Instinctively, I reached an arm around my master and herded him back from the street, just as a cruiser shot around the corner, blasting through the space into which we had prepared to walk. It jammed to a halt ten meters away, and two large amphiboids hopped out, made more bulbous by elaborate weapons shielding. Both held blasters and carried thermal cannons slung on their backs.

I guided Master Yeh away from them, and for their part they seemed uninterested in two humanoids. My master stopped suddenly and changed course heading up the street and back toward the new arrivals. "Master, I believe it is wise to stay clear of them. They look like independents."

"They are profiteers," he said sharply. "Gauging the value of death and destruction." I had never heard my master speak so forcefully, and the shock temporarily distracted me. When I shook off the torpor, I found him walking deliberately for the two mercenaries. I grabbed him and pulled him away, but he resisted.

"Master. Master!" I hissed at him, hoping to avoid the attention of the two amphiboids.

"Leave me be!" he rebuked me loudly.

I actually ignored my master's wrath, eying the two profiteers over his shoulder. They had stopped speaking together and had turned their large lidless eyes to examine us. "Master, we should not provoke anyone with weapons. What of the Nuruvian palindrome?"

He stared at me in silence, and I watched the fire slowly simmer. Without a word, he spun around to face the profiteers. They sniffed the air in our direction, trying to gauge our intentions by the pheromones we emitted. No one made a move. Then, as I felt the stress begin to churn my stomach, one of the amphiboids bowed to my master, after which they jumped back into their cruiser and shot off.

He turned back to me. "I did not lose the palindrome. I chose to ignore it for a time." A smile slowly shed the anger from his face, and he reached up and patted my cheek. "Sometimes we must register our displeasure with the tides of war and commerce."

An Ardri transport spied us wandering through the rubble of the street and picked us up—officially, to ensure the safety of two members of a highly respected order; unofficially, to prevent further embarrassment, as we were sorting through the dead and wounded of a government military action, not a rebel operation. Without a word to us—but a lot of smiles and deferential posturing—they flew us to a secure section of the city and dropped us in a high walled compound surrounding the regional governor's residence.

"Secure means no one to heal," my master commented as guards armed with blaster rifles led us into the main building. "No one to heal. No opportunity for us to highlight the Ardri's excessive use of force, extrajudicial killings and their deployment of mercenaries to erase unsightly displays of personal freedom and representative government."

I had nothing to say in response. Never during my eight years with Master Yeh had I heard him speak with such vehemence—or passion. A switch had been thrown, a hidden trap sprung, that transformed him into someone unrecognizable, possessed of a fire and a reckless disregard for personal safety. He acted like a young healer only recently elevated from apprentice—unbalanced, volatile, zealous. All the characteristics he had worked hard to eliminate in me he now displayed.

"Wake up, boy!"

I nearly ran into a wall, stopping inches away with my master's voice. The passage we walked down ended in a T, and my master stood in the hall on the right. I quickly turned and fell in behind him as we continued through the maze of passages.

"Focus, boy, or you'll run into worse than just walls."

"I was thinking, Master—" I didn't know how to approach the question hounding me.

"Yes?"

"I was thinking—I was thinking that I am puzzled by your behavior toward the profiteers."

Master Yeh nodded quickly. "Sentients are complicated creatures," he said after a lengthy pause. "None of us are simply one person, a static amalgam of emotion, logic, knowledge and experience. We evolve, and our ancestral natures sometimes resurface."

I wanted to ask him more about whether I had witnessed his ancestral nature, but at that moment the guards brought us into a small windowless room. We stood before a desk behind which a tall, thin, bureaucratic-looking humanoid sat. He wore a bland gray outfit with no distinguishing features as to his rank or position.

His long, emaciated face leaned over a small screen on which symbols flashed too rapidly for me to recognize or to follow. A short wire snaked from each of the six fingers on his left hand and the five on his right, each one terminating in a different colored micro-bulb, mimicking an eye on stalk. I noticed that as his large vertical-irised eyes roved over the screen, the lights on his fingertips flashed. A neuro-ocular link, I thought, connecting visual targets to nonoptic neuronal output.

One of the guards stepped forward. "The healers," he announced and stepped back.

The Ardri raised his right eye to quickly inspect us, while the left continued to peruse the screen, sending signals to flash over the fingertips of his left hand, while the ones on the right darkened. The thin, nearly transparent lids curtained the top half of his eyes, as though members of his species were perpetually half asleep. "No more healing in my city," he commanded in a metallic voice, all sharp edges and geometric vocalizations. The right lid retracted so the fullness of his right eye could emphasize the point before the curtain dropped again. Then it returned to the screen, and the right hand lights revived. Interview over.

Surprisingly, my master made no comment and seemed satisfied to follow the guards back out of the room without protest. They installed us in an upper suite of rooms with a view down the hill and over the city. "Why, Master?" was all I could get out after the guards left.

"Why is a futile question," Master Yeh cut me off, "when it addresses the motivations of sentient beings." He spoke no more of it, and we spent the remainder of the day in silent meditation, at my master's insistence.

The next morning I woke up early. Master Yeh was gone. For an instant I panicked, thinking that he had left me. I quickly recovered my composure, dressed, and searched for him. I met a guard as I wandered.

"The other one?" He nodded and pointed over the compound wall. "Went to the market. Commerce day today." He shook his head. "Very crowded. Best stay here."

He gave me vague directions when I insisted on leaving, and I ran down toward the city, wondering how I might find Master Yeh if the press of people was as dense as the guard described. Luckily, my master chose to walk leisurely, stopping to speak with strangers. The calm and peace that flowed from him naturally attracted others, which worked in my favor. As I ran—and got lost—I saw through a side alley a large crowd in a street parallel to the one I was on. Thinking that it was part of the market, I made my way over and found my master deep in its midst.

I pushed my way through to his side and bowed weakly because of the anger building inside of me.

He smiled pleasantly, and turned to the natives reaching for him.

"Master, we were ordered not to heal."

"I am not healing. I am just being."

I grabbed his hand and pulled on him. He didn't resist, letting me lead him down the street with the crowd scattering back in a long tail. "It is best if you don't *be* right now. It is too dangerous." He shrugged and smiled. "Then we shall visit the market."

"That would be good."

As the guard had warned, the market strained the confines of the plaza in which it was set, pushing out into the streets that fed into it. We managed to slip into the main square because of my master: people bent on their own designs and destinations deferentially moved aside for him, and as soon as he had passed, they fell back into their personal struggles for advancement.

Master Yeh looked at every stall and bought nothing. He didn't need to, though. Whenever he approached a stand, the hard, wary stares of the hawkers evaporated with a word or two from him. My master never left without something gifted to him, and he always accepted it as though it were the most valuable offering in the galaxy. The moment we walked away, he gave away the gift to the first stranger that approached him.

I felt my anger disappear as I watched him move through the market like a light cutting through darkness. Witnessing the reverence of strangers reminded me of what I had overlooked—of what I couldn't see because I stared at it everyday. I felt my own respect for my master returning.

"It is midday," Master Yeh said to me. "Why don't you find us some food? I will stay here and wait for you."

"Don't move from here, Master," I emphasized by describing a circle over our heads. "This place is too crowded for me to ever find you again, if you move."

"I promise: you will have no problems finding me." He smiled and waved me off.

I can't say how long I was gone. A few minutes at the most. I remember realizing, to my chagrin, that even if my master didn't move, I had lost all sense of direction and would not be able to find him again anyway. I set aside my foolishness for having not marked his location by some visual landmark and decided to first find some food. I caught a drifting aroma of something interesting, and as I moved toward it, I felt a strong vibration, repeated once, and then the entire population of the market shifted backward, as though hit by a sudden swell.

I twisted about and tried to stand still, to listen for something to indicate what had happened, but the tide of movement picked me up and moved me. I was in a current that was taking me in one particular direction. Ahead of me, people slid left and right around the edge of a large immovable mass of bodies, everyone straining to see something hidden in front.

Something propelled me forward, and spectators moved aside as I pushed through the crowd.

I reached the front, found a small open space around a lone form lying on the ground. My breath caught, and I quickly dropped down beside Master Yeh. Two flowers of red were blossoming on his chest, growing with each beat of his heart. The petals of blood grew from two round, perfect blaster wounds.

When I reached down and grasped his arm, he opened his eyes and smiled as though I were waking him up from a nap. He raised his hand, and I took it. The pull was so sudden and so intense that I thought I had been sucked out of my skin.

I stood on a thin spine of rock, on either side a black precipice whose bottom I couldn't see. Ahead of me, Master Yeh struggled step-by-step up the narrow way heading toward the summit where a red fire burned. On his back he carried a sling of black rocks—coal, perhaps, for the fire. He took a break from his efforts and turned to gaze back down the path just as I reached him. He looked worn and ancient—his cheeks hollowed out, his eyes retracted into their sockets, his hair thin and broken.

I raised my hands, silently asking him to give me the sling. Ash dusted his face and hands, running down in black rivulets where his sweat dripped. He hesitated. Then with pain twisting his face, he swung the sling around from behind and held it out to me. I grasped it with both hands and felt its sudden weight as Master Yeh released it. Far heavier than I imagined, the sling unbalanced me, and I fell over the edge.

THREE

"**E**arth."

The word, or perhaps just the sound, awakened me. It is the first thing I remember after Master Yeh's death on the planet whose name I never learned. The captain of the cruiser stood patiently in front of me.

"Thank you," I said slowly, as though having to remember how to speak. "When will we arrive?"

"We have. We are orbiting the planet."

"I will need to contact the Healing Order."

"A delegation is on its way up. I will greet them if you like."

"No, that is my duty."

The Healing Order's galactic center sits on a high plateau in the mountains of what was once called the Asian subcontinent. Winter had set in, which normally would make no difference whatsoever: climate-regulated domes enclosed most cities on Earth. Healers, however, eschewed any technology that divorced them from the natural order. No domes, no climate-controlled environment—no tube-shuttle link to the closest lowland population center. Only one thin, winding paved road for ground transports and multiple unofficial footpaths snaking up through the mountains for the fanatical pilgrims willing to risk heat exhaustion in the summer and frostbite in the winter. Pressure from the Galactic Council forced the Order to build a landing pad for airborne transports carrying dignitaries, but the treacherous storms closed it in the winter. And it was winter.

Balance—that one concept rested at the center of the Order's teachings, if any single concept did. Across the galaxy, humanoid species shared one trait—a flagrant rebelliousness that often opposed balance. We chase pleasure and run from pain with a religious fervor unmatched by any of the other sentient races.

Balance—it is as alien to humanoids as sentient amphiboids are to Earthlings. In honor of my master, I refused to take the transport carrying his body up through the mountains to the Healing Order's

Center—the Tumrac. Instead, I chose to climb one of the footpaths to the top. I expected to walk alone, as the snows had reached down into the lower valleys, which meant that blinding blizzards encompassed the higher elevations. To my amazement, the path I chose was crowded. A continuous line of pilgrims stretched upward as far as I could see. And they were not only humanoids: members of all the major races set out with me, hopping, crawling, rolling, however they might ambulate up the steep shoulders of the mountains.

"I should have taken a different route," I said to myself as I waited in a line at the trailhead for my turn to begin the journey.

An insectoid ahead of me turned back. "All the paths are so filled, humanoid," he lisped.

"Why?"

"Did you not hear? The Healer of Zaidon Five has returned. Is that not why you make the pilgrimage?"

"No." I had no more words to explain my presence, but my companion's news at least served to distract me from the emptiness I felt. I wondered at the coincidence of my master's final journey with the appearance of some renowned healer. The Order eschewed the seeking of exultation or the accumulation of adulation by any healer, which in part drove their policy to keep us moving. Without a home, we could neither form strong bonds to a certain people or species nor sow the seeds of personal glory. Nevertheless, on rare occasions, a healer performed with such singular bravery and compassion that legend was born from extraordinary but not divine circumstance. As my master always emphasized, "You may wish to live in a hovel, but you cannot stop others from building you a palace."

I thought on my master's words and knew as well that he rejected coincidence, believing that since everything in the universe was connected, events occurred for natural reasons, not because of random chance. This is not to say that he believed in predestination, Fate, or designs elaborated by some divine authority. He explained natural reasons this way: "Are you surprised when your head and your hand reach the same destination at the same time? Your head is not your hand, but they are connected. Now remember the galactic snake, of infinite length. Sometimes two parts of the body meet and at other times they will be a universe away. Yet, they are still part of the same single entity, so if they appear together at one time, why all the fuss and amazement?"

So, in deference to my master, I let my sorrow wash away and considered the good omen that two such important segments of the Universal Snake—Master Yeh and the Healer of Zaidon Five—had come together at that time.

The trek took two days, and I was wholly unprepared. Like a fool, I had brought no food or water—or even clothes warm enough to keep me from dying of exposure. None of that proved necessary, though. As I climbed, a miniscule part in the body of a snake of uncountable segments, an outer jacket appeared when I shivered; gloves materialized when I had forsaken my blue fingers to frostbite; hot food and water were presented to me at the end of each day when the snake stopped moving, and, as one, we all sat down for the night. Our positions never changed in that grand, unified entity: the insectoid ahead of me remained just ahead of me, just as I kept two steps above the humanoid falish below me.

No one spoke. Needed items were silently passed up and down the line, so that I never knew who saved my life by providing the essentials that kept me from freezing and starving to death. The snake dispersed piece by piece as we reached the plateau on which the Tumrac stood. I never again met the insectoid or the falish with whom I shared that journey.

While the snake of pilgrims filed into the walled complex, I stood for a time facing the triple archway of the entrance, gazing at the tall central doors of black wood on which beaten copper discs were arranged in a sweeping left-handed circle ending in an arrow at the apex driving straight down to point at the center—the symbol of the Healing Order. That very image the Order tattooed on my right palm on the first day of my apprenticeship.

Only twice do healers pass through the tall central arch—once in leaving, upon elevation to healer, and once in returning, upon one's death, in order to seek a resting place among the others of our Order. But neither of those moments had arrived, so, after bowing deferentially, I stepped into the Tumrac through the lesser door on the right.

When I named myself at the entrance to the walled city, an escort of apprentices quickly appeared and led me to the main citadel, the Dome of the Sky. I passed along the halls on which artists from across the galaxy depicted the history of the Healing Order and entered the cavernous main hall. Under the central dome of lapis-blue stained glass, Master Yeh lay on a simple wicker palette set on a low, circular stone dais. My boots echoed through the round hall, its edges hidden in the darkness of infinite space. Master Gogee squatted beside my master's head.

He looked much older than when last I saw him, eight years before, when he'd put a large suckered hand on my shoulder and led me before Master Yeh, giving me into apprenticeship. His large amphiboid eyes had clouded, and his once smooth shining skin now appeared blotchy and peeled in places. I bowed to him, and he squatted lower in response.

I helped him back up. "You are ill, Master," I said.

"I am old," he laughed. "That is not an illness either you or your master could cure." He braced himself on my shoulder and turned his cataract-fogged eyes to me. "We waited until you arrived."

"Waited to do what?"

"To admit the pilgrims."

"Master Gogee, the pilgrims have come to honor the Healer of Zaidon Five."

He patted my shoulder. "Master Yeh was the Healer of Zaidon Five."

★ ★ ★

For ten days the pilgrims filled the Dome of the Sky, circling the dais on which my master lay, moving around us like a river. I remained by Master Yeh for the entire ten days, sleeping on the stone floor and eating whatever the apprentices brought me. Eventually the river slowly dried to a stream and then a trickle, returning the Central Dome to the echoing expansive silence that had greeted me on my arrival. Only then did I leave my master's side, searching through the Tumrac for Master Gogee.

I found him in a dark, frozen corner of the encircling wall, squatting with his back against a wind-worn pine tree giving instruction to a small group of attentive apprentices sitting cross-legged on the hard, cold dirt. I waited for him to complete his lesson before I approached, bowing and lending him a much-needed hand to rise.

"Why are you still here?"

"I have questions, Master."

"Speak."

"I want to know about my master. About the Healer of Zaidon Five."

"I noted your surprise when I told you. Did Master Yeh never speak to you about his past?"

"No, Master."

"Then he must have had a reason. I will not speak of it."

"Master Gogee, I can search the information libraries about the Healer of Zaidon Five, but you know that information nodes can be notoriously unreliable, including hearsay and unsubstantiated claims. I would prefer to hear the truth from you."

He smiled, his gum ridges still gleaming white. "So long as you realize that the truth will be as I see it."

"I understand, Master."

We entered the living quarters shared by the elder healers and went straight to Master Gogee's room. I opened the door and warm, humid steam billowed over us. A pool took up the principal space in the small square block, with steps down to the water's edge wide enough to serve as seats. I led him carefully down into his sleeping pond and settled on a top step. He sank under the water for several minutes, my only indication that he remained there the occasional bubbles of his exhalations drifting to the surface and popping with a subtle plink.

Eventually his eyes appeared from within the murky depths, then his flat face and mouth. He looked much younger in the water, with the liquid sheen smoothing away all the blemishes so obvious when he was out on land. In a burbling liquid voice he began.

"Zaidon Five is the site of one of the worst cases of genocide in recent galactic history. Over a period of three standard solar decades, the Sacror of Zaidon killed thirty percent of Zaidon Five's population: five billion lives summarily executed. Most of them came from politically underrepresented sub-races and from the universally oppressed third sex, a recent evolutionary stem from the rapidly evolving Zaidons' main line.

"After the planetary system was liberated by the Galactic Counsel, Healer Yeh, just a young member of the Order at the time, was assigned there. When his replacement came a year later, he refused to leave. This went on for nearly twenty years: the Healing Order would send a healer to relieve him, and Yeh would send him back."

Master Gogee laughed. "I, too, was young at the time, although senior to your master; he was a good friend, and though quietly I admired his will and determination, officially I opposed his personalization of healing. We must avoid crusades; too often they become corrupted by outside influences or co-opted by political or religious forces for their own designs.

"Personal feelings aside, in that time your master healed one million Zaidons of the physical and emotional pain the genocide caused—a feat unequaled by any healer in history. He became a regional saint, universally revered by Zaidons. Naturally, the Healing Order neither approved of nor supported Yeh's singular efforts. They chastised him and nearly expelled him from the Order. Our leaders at the time were afraid of the precedent he was setting: healers are supposed to be humble, simple, and as far from the light of celebrity as possible. Above all, we are never to consciously seek power, authority, or influence over others. I knew your master was not acting out of personal desire for power or to exert coercive influence over others. This I argued strongly in front of the Council, and I believe that enough of the elders agreed with me that they chose not to officially condemn him. They simply charged him with disobedience and demanded that he leave Zaidon Five.

"To me they gave the duty of persuading your master, and I was certain that I could convince him." Master Gogee shook his head, flicking steaming droplets of water off his face. "Stubborn humanoid. He saw his work as an opportunity to further peace in the universe and formally broke from the Order. For a time I lost face because of his actions; many blamed me for failing to control him, and some even accused me of encouraging his rebellion.

"He began traveling around the galaxy like one of the mendicant monks of Earth's ancient history. Other healers flocked to him and for a time he taught them how to live alone as nomadic healers. Eventually, as his reputation spread beyond the sector and across the galaxy, the Healing Order was forced to acknowledge his achievements. They officially recognized his work on Zaidon Five and gave me the opportunity to redeem myself. I found him and persuaded him to return to the Healing Order. He abandoned his wandering life and became a traditional healer."

★ ★ ★

Master Gogee's revelations did not surprise me, but they angered me. During my apprenticeship, I was wise enough in my general ignorance to recognize that my Master's depth far exceeded what he revealed to me. Even if one has never before witnessed a tornado, one cannot help but recognize its inherent power when faced with it. My anger stemmed from the perception that my Master hid his past from me because he thought me unworthy of the knowledge and experience he had accumulated. *If he saw little potential in me*, so I thought, *then why bother teaching me at all?*

My anger slowly simmered to self-doubt, and I wandered through the Tumrac debating whether I should leave the Order. Who better to judge my skill and potential than the Healer of Zaidon Five? Self-doubt eventually cooled to pragmatic resignation: I had no other abilities or inclinations. I could only be a healer, and if I was to be a mediocre one, then so be it.

I waited for the Healing Order to assign me to a new master, but they did not. It was not my place to ask; it was my place to accept their choice. When they never chose, I realized with growing anxiety that they had no intention of finding me another master. I was no longer to be considered an apprentice, but so too I was not a healer until I had passed the elevation ceremony. And to do that, I was expected, as all apprentices were, to stand alone before the Masters' Council and argue the merits for my elevation.

Briefly, I considered protesting. Perhaps they had meant to assign another master but had forgotten. The Tumrac, normally bathed in solitude, had been in turmoil for the month since my master's arrival; in the confusion and the press of pilgrims, they could easily have overlooked the fate of a lone apprentice.

This I rejected out of hand. I was the apprentice to the Healer of Zaidon Five. More than likely they assumed that my master would have prepared me adequately to go out on my own, assumed that there could be no better instructor. I wondered if they actually discussed finding me another master; perhaps no one was willing to take on the task of further instructing Master Yeh's apprentice.

Whatever the reason, I waited patiently for another month. The elders greeted me warmly and mentioned nothing about continuing my apprenticeship. I set a date for myself; when it came and went without a response from the Council, I sat down beside the small rough, unadorned stone marking the site where a handful of my master's ashes were buried, and I meditated for a day.

On the following morning, I stood before the Masters' Council and sued for elevation. In no moment since then have I felt more certain of my inadequacy. Had they challenged me at all to justify my elevation, I would have folded like paper in a breeze. Unanimously they accepted my plea. That very day the Healing Order's symbol was erased from my hand and tattooed on my right forehead. Then, without ceremony or celebration, I walked through the central gateway of the Tumrac as a healer and boarded a ground transport.

II: THE TERRAFORMERS
ONE

After my elevation to healer, I spent five years working on medical ships, healing planets and in the midst of one natural disaster or another, following as closely as I could the path that I envisioned Master Yeh would have chosen for me.

Yet something wasn't right. Even now I struggle to describe the sensation—not pain or imbalance; rather, a tightening or a twisting that set all of me, physically and mentally, at an odd angle. A stone in the boot—such a small thing, but it forces you to accommodate it, misaligning body, altering mood, stance, and gait. Only, in my case, the stone rested somewhere inside of my mind, and I couldn't simply pull off a boot and remove the offending object.

Ridding myself of that hidden discomfort through the routine of a healer's traditional life failed, and as I jumped from one institution to another in a futile attempt to relieve my unease, I slowly drifted into a nomadic life.

I envisioned wandering as a temporary state, an in-betweeness, when I could rest, think and gather myself—when I could recover from Master Yeh's death and regain the path to becoming the healer he had expected of me. Instead, I found myself more comfortable in the twilight regions of the galaxy. Or perhaps I remained there too long—long enough to become comfortable with something to which I should never have grown accustomed.

All the major galactic races knew of and respected the Healing Order. Our reputation preceded us to every system like an invisible entourage, affording us not only the basic necessities of living but also guaranteeing us work: pain extends into every corner of the galaxy; there isn't a place in the universe that hasn't felt its touch. But healers worked on vast ailments, suffering on large scales—natural disasters, planet-wide epidemics, continental droughts, and, of course, war—not on personal pain except as it applied to the larger context.

Those traditional venues were closed to me because I worked outside of official avenues, leaving me to mine for work, digging into dark corners and hidden cracks for bits and pieces of pain forgotten under the shadow of majestic tragedies. Those early years wore on me mercilessly; starvation and the imminent threat of death provided strong motivating forces for learning to adapt. Over time, I became a skilled persuader, a talented manipulator of reality—and, when needed, a pathetic beggar.

Using all three of my newly acquired talents, I eventually found myself with the perfect job, hiring on with a terraforming crew as an adjunct to the company physician, a biped insectoid named Cra'taac. The company provided excellent compensation for the prospect of doing little work. My first encounter with the physician proceeded as I had anticipated: Cra'taac spoke bluntly.

"Are you defective?" he asked me when the captain, an insectoid of a different race, introduced us.

"Cra'taac, there's plenty of food in the storage containers. No need to chew on him," the captain laughed—a rasping vibration I assumed was laughter—before leaving us in the medical bay. Whereas the captain was mostly body—large, heavy, oval-shelled, with four lower ambulation appendages, two upper task-oriented limbs, and a round head on a retractable neck stalk—Cra'taac was mostly limbs: a small, triangular head, all eyes and large-jawed mouth atop a thin, long body with four large, spiked, task-oriented upper limbs whose segments tapered to small joints and two long heavy walkers or ambulation limbs.

"Please, elaborate, Dr. Cra'taac," I asked formally, knowing that insectoids regarded communication as no less intimate than sex: one respected boundaries and didn't overstep them unless invited.

"Why do you not work with a medical ship or on a planet for healing? You work alone. Are you defective—deficient?"

I shook my head. "Neither defective nor deficient, Doctor. I work alone by choice. I assure you that I am fully competent in my duties."

He nodded. "I have read the company report on you. High recommendations. You will find this a boring job, healer. Little work for me; even less work for you."

I shrugged. "The company pays me. I am here—if needed."

The ship manifest listed the captain, the terraformers—a hodgepodge of rough, scarred humanoids and insectoids—Doctor Cra'taac, myself, and a humanoid malish named Traevis. I knew nothing of terraforming and quickly realized that I had entered an entirely different world from any I had yet experienced. The ship, whose name I could not pronounce, and which translated incompletely in CombineSpeak to Colossus Impendor, consisted of a small crew section of five levels attached to a bulbous cargo and staging section that seemed large enough to contain part of a city.

Soon after leaving orbit I stopped the captain in a hallway by the medical bay. "Captain, you have a large ship here. Surely you don't run it by yourself? Where is your crew? I have yet to see them."

For an insectoid, he possessed an amazing array of facial expressions: his look undeniably said *perhaps you* are *defective.* "The terraformers serve as my crew, healer."

"I am sorry, captain, I did not realize—"

His face softened, his mouthparts pouting downward. "Come, take a look around. Meet them. We have never had a healer as part of the crew before. This project will not tax you, so I will assign you other duties as well." He leaned in on me suddenly. "Everyone on board does more than his standard assignment."

I understood his meaning and nodded. Then I followed him from the medical bay on the third level through the crew quarters on the fourth level and down to the engineering and terraforming stations on the lowest level. We found four terraformers—two insectoids and two humanoids—monitoring a wall of holographic displays.

"You four!" the captain yelled as soon as we stepped into the room. "This is the healer. Teach him something." Just as quickly, he stepped out and disappeared.

The pair farthest from me—an insectoid of the captain's race and an attractive, brown-haired falish humanoid with small, almond-shaped multifaceted eyelets lateral to a pair of humanoid eyes—rose and nodded to me. "I am Arthen," the insectoid said, then raised an appendage, indicating the falish, "and this is Jesel."

I bowed. I looked at the other two, both malish, who remained seated, eying me distastefully.

"The arrogant two," Arthen continued, "are Borthax and Anders." Borthax, a biped insectoid, similar in appearance to Dr. Cra'taac but with a green and red mottled carapace, finally nodded. Anders—smooth black eyes without pupils and a dimpled albino hide—scowled and turned back to a hologram of a sleek ship with wings along which were attached numerous oblong canisters.

"An odd-looking ship," I said casually.

Anders turned on me. "It's a dusting cruiser, healer, and I pilot them. So does Borthax. Best that you be wary of what you say." When he spoke, I noticed his blood-red gums and sharp, serrated teeth.

"Anders, put away your hormones," Jesel said.

"I have never seen anything like it," I replied calmly. "It looks like a difficult ship to maneuver."

I sensed the anger boiling over in Anders. Borthax gripped his shoulder before the humanoid could reply. "The captain ordered us to teach him."

The rage melted away from Anders' face, replaced by a cruel smile. "Ever flown a ship, healer?"

"Once—a small rescue pod from a medical transport."

Anders shook his head. "No, I mean one built for planetary atmospheres."

I shook my head.

"Anders, the captain did not want us to teach him how to fly dusters."

"Shut up, Arthen, you can't read the captain's mind. Watch your precious engines. Healer, have a seat here." Anders punched Borthax who immediately rose, leaving his place vacant.

I sensed the tension among the four terraformers. It was still too early to know whom to trust. So I retreated from Anders' and Borthax's challenge. "No, thank you. Your dusting cruiser appears too sophisticated for a novice like myself."

"If you don't know how to do something out here, you learn," Borthax said.

"Or you die," Anders continued.

"Terraforming is dangerous business," Arthen said. "Each of us can pilot the Colossus Impendor, service the engines, and run or repair all of the terraforming equipment on board."

Jesel nodded. "Terraformers' code: rely on the specialists to do the job; rely on yourself to stay alive."

"I am not a terraformer."

Anders laughed. "And you never will be. But this is our world, healer. Our rules apply. Want to live? Then learn." He nodded to Borthax, then got up, and the two pushed past me and disappeared down the corridor.

I looked at the two remaining terraformers. "Have I done something to offend them?"

Jesel shook her head as she turned back to her hologram. "No. Just standard terraformer greeting, healer." She eyed me. "We're like animals—establish dominance hierarchies, mark territory, you understand?"

I nodded. "So where do I find myself?"

"At the bottom," Arthen replied. "Except perhaps for Traevis; he may be below you."

"What is Traevis' position?"

"He's a spy."

Arthen clicked his claw at Jesel. "He is not a spy."

"That's what the captain says."

Arthen turned to me. "By spy, the captain means a bureaucrat—representing the Phelaan insectoid desire to oversee all actions in hyperdetail."

Jesel shook her head behind Arthen. "No, I think the captain meant spy."

"You humanoids thrive on paranoia," Arthen chided his falish companion. "You challenge authority, question order and logic; I am amazed that you have achieved anything resembling a cohesive social structure long enough to evolve."

Jesel laughed. "It amazes me as well."

The two turned on me. "Ask the captain," they answered in unison.

"If I must learn how to operate one of your craft, then perhaps you can start me on something a little simpler than a dusting cruiser," I offered.

"We shall do that," Arthen said. He nodded at Jesel. "Jesel oversees the maintenance of the transport shuttles; we have four of them. Jesel, will you train him?"

"Not now, but after we set course I will find the time."

"Thank you, Terraformer Jesel."

She smiled. "I am not Dr. Cra'taac, healer. Leave the formalities for him. Call me Jesel."

Twenty-three terraformers manned the ship, and I met them all, half of them humanoid, the other insectoid. Self-exiled from the mainstream of galactic society, preferring to live on the frontiers, most of them chose to avoid me like the carrier of some dread disease. And I suppose I was just that: I represented civilization—everything they hated and took the pains to avoid by living at the edges.

The only ones that didn't avoid me were the first four I met—Arthen and Jesel because they accepted the captain's charge to teach me; Anders and Borthax because of some twisted pleasure they derived from tormenting me. The only other terraformer I spent any time with was an Earthling named Dal Broca.

"I am the neobiologist," he explained after introducing himself while I sat in the library unit—little more than a closet with two chairs crammed back-to-back facing holographic displays.

"I am the healer."

"Ah, yes, our tagalong," he replied squeezing into the other chair. Dal Broca was an odd-looking Earthling, and I wondered at that moment if he truly looked odd or if my own eye, having accustomed itself to alien forms for so long, had grown odd in its view. His sharp wedge-like nose stretched his face, drawing the skin tight across his minimal cheek bones and pulling his small brown eyes too close to the nasal bridge; his contracted, almost lipless mouth was squeezed between the hanging nose and a ship prow's chin. Dark brown hair cropped short stood up evenly on his pale scalp. His body seemed an afterthought—thin-limbed, large-jointed, spindly—as though all effort went into forming his head.

"I thought Traevis was the tagalong."

"Oh, right. You're the defective." He laughed at the library holo-gram emerging on the display in front of him.

"Yes, I am the defective."

He slapped his leg. "God! It's good to fly with another Earthling. Finally someone who appreciates my humor."

"I understand it."

He laughed louder. "How considerate of you to trash my humor so politely."

"Would you rather I trash you?"

"You wouldn't if you knew me."

"Well, then, tell me about yourself."

"Nothing to tell. I'm the neobiologist."

"I don't know what neobiologists do."

He twisted around in his seat and looked at me briefly. "In this case, I run the show—the entire show."

I looked at his partial reflection in my wavering hologram. "It must be a great honor."

His reflection turned back to his own console. "It's the only rea-son I signed on for this job—a chance to finally lead a terraforming team. It's rare to find a terraforming unit with humanoids, let alone an Earthling, so—" He shrugged.

"It was an opportunity you could not overlook."

"That's right," he nodded.

"Well, I still don't know what a neobiologist does."

"We choose what xenobiotics—flora and fauna from other worlds—to introduce into the biosphere of a terraformed planet. If successfully done, they will grow and flourish and evolve into new species—neoflora and neofauna—unique to the terraformed planet. If poorly done, they will fail, taking the biosphere with them."

"Quite a responsibility. You have a difficult task ahead of you."

"Not this time. Our target planet is A-grade, the easiest to terraform—already possessing a usable atmosphere and a complex, self-sustaining biosphere. It will only require some minimal tweaking—sculpting, in terraformer lingo—to prepare it for colonists."

"If it already has a biosphere, why not just use it?"

"We will, but the survey units identified a number of plant and animal species toxic to the Phelaan."

"Who are the Phelaan?"

He looked over his shoulder at me and shook his head. "How do you stay alive, not knowing anything? The Phelaan Syndicate hired us."

This time I turned around and stared at him evenly. "Hired you. The company hired me."

"A minor point. The Phelaan are a humanoid-insectoid species conglomerate that holds license over Sigma Tau Beta, the fallow planet we are terraforming. All STB needs is a basic cleansing operation to rid the continents and seas of toxic flora and fauna. That's where my work begins—deciding on which plants and animals stay, which go, and manufacturing the genetic and reproductive poisons we'll use to eliminate them."

"What kind of poisons do you use?"

"Chemical or biologic agents, whatever suits the planet—and the neobiologist." He smiled. "I'll make up my soups, anywhere from one to a dozen different types, then we'll load them into the delivery canisters on the dusters—the dusting cruisers."

"Yes, I have met two of the pilots."

"Which ones? We have ten dusting pilots aboard. I told the captain we'd only need five for this job, it's so straightforward, but he didn't want to take any chances." He leaned back in his chair and clasped his hands behind his head. "Fine with me, as the leader, my pay is fixed; the others will just have to split the rest of the contract over twenty instead of ten."

"I met Borthax and Anders."

Dal Broca shook his head. "Those two I wanted to leave behind. Good pilots, but too aggressive and unpredictable—even for terraformers."

"What do your soups contain for Sigma Tau Beta?"

With a bored shrug that seemed to ripple onto his face, Broca answered in a lazy drone. "A mishmash: both chemical and biologic. I prefer biologics, though." He dropped his head to the side and stared at me. "That's my specialty—what I'm known for." He gazed up at the ceiling and sighed. "There was this terraforming nightmare. The company—our company, actually—cleared a planet for colonization. Ships had landed, population centers established, and then they find a rogue—can you believe it, a year after clearing it?"

"A rogue?"

"Oh, yeah, sorry, I've been in the business too long—think everyone understands terraformer speak." He sat up and leaned toward me, as though preparing to reveal either a secret crime or a profound gem of spiritual truth. I, of course, hoped for the latter, but assumed it would be the former. I have little interest in hidden transgressions of planetary proportions, even though these are the seeds from which grow the trees of pain I prune. But that's another story. I returned my attention to Broca, and he continued.

"A rogue is a native biologic that poses a threat to colonizing species. In this case it was a rare lichen confined to a very specialized niche on the native planet. The original neobiologist overlooked it as unimportant and failed to eradicate it. After the company completed the terraforming operations and approved colonization, they never initiated regular progress surveys—you know, to make sure the introduced species were thriving and intact native species hadn't turned rogue. Well, a year later a plague hits the colonists in the outlying areas. The company sends a team, and they discover the rogue: this minor lichen, with its competitors eradicated during terraforming operations, had spread across the planet. Turns out that it secreted a nephrotoxic, aerosolized natural insecticide. When inhaled by the colonists, even in small doses, it irreversibly shut down their kidney equivalents."

"What happened?"

"They called me in to clean up their mess—offered me a lot of money to leave their competitor and come work with them. They brought me samples of the lichen, and I studied it." He rubbed his chin, propped his feet on the holographic console's base, and stretched out his legs, propelling his seat into the doorway of the cubbyhole we shared. He looked away from the ceiling to me. "You see, a great neobiologist has to be an engineer and an artist. You need the talent to take two dissimilar biologic machines—complex life forms evolved and adapted to fundamentally different environments perhaps on opposite sides of the galaxy—and figure out how to integrate them. The art lies in the actual merging of the two into a unique species."

"Did you solve the problem of the rogue?"

"Of course, but you first have to understand the dilemma: the planet had already been colonized, so we couldn't re-terraform; and a biologic or chemical agent might turn on us, creating a new, more deadly plague. I had to be precise—and absolutely certain of its safety. I chose the Thuruvian moss beetle: highly specialized, it exists solely on one species of moss; I shortened its mandibles and reengineered its digestive tract. The new species lived solely on the rogue. I remember watching the dusting cruisers releasing them into the atmosphere, black clouds spreading and descending over the planet."

"It must have been satisfying to witness your success."

"That's not the end of it: the beetle worked wonders; their

numbers exploded because none of the native fauna fed on the lichen. And of course, I had accelerated their breeding and reproductive capacities. However, the lichen spread to higher latitudes and to environments harsher than the beetles could tolerate. Our initial success evaporated and the project headed for failure. I considered alternatives—use another biologic or go with chemical poisons: I didn't have the time to develop a completely new species, and the chemicals available were nonspecific and likely to kill other flora as well as the rogue. I chose the only reasonable option—to modify the existing biologic."

Dal Broca tapped his forehead with a crooked finger. "That's when my Earthling heritage turned to my advantage. Ever heard of the alternative oxidase?"

I shook my head. "I have studied the anatomy and physiology of a dozen sentient species, and that does not sound familiar."

"Well, that's because it's found in nonsentient plant species from Earth. It's an enzyme—a protein—found in certain plant species that generate heat. It's located in the mitochondria—the energy generators of cells. Instead of gathering and storing energy in a stepwise fashion from substrate molecules, the alternative oxidase drops them from highest to lowest energy in one step, releasing all that stored energy as heat. So, I spliced the AO gene behind a temperature-sensitive promoter and introduced it into the beetle DNA and—" He paused, expectantly.

"It worked," I guessed.

"Of course it worked! As the beetles headed into higher latitudes and the temperature dropped, the AO gene activated, and the beetles warmed up! We rid the planet of the rogue in less time than the company allotted us. Then, soon after the lichen disappeared, so did the beetles—without a trace. The colonists thought it was one of those seasonal infestations. It was brilliant."

"I am sure the colonists appreciated your work to save their planet."

Dal Broca laughed. "The colonists? Hah! They didn't know a thing about the rogue or our mission."

"The company kept it all secret?"

"Of course. Only the executives, a few of the terraformers I worked with, and I knew the story. The company rewarded me well, though. Only right—I saved their asses."

I nodded, considering his words.

"How do you think I got this job, eh? Company bonus—a thank you. I am the first Earthling to lead a terraforming unit."

"Congratulations."

He nodded. "A big step, although the job itself is rather mundane. No flora or fauna to introduce; just a few plants with toxic leaves to eliminate—and the fauna that feeds on them. Some bugs and a few insectivores—they incorporate the plant toxins into their carapaces and skins, quite ingenious really. They probably could even remain, but I don't want to take a chance that their stool will spread some plague to the Phelaan colonists."

Something occurred to me then, but I hesitated to ask the question that had formulated in my mind lest it insult my companion. I returned Dal Broca's smug smile, without the smugness of course, and realized at that moment that I would never, under any circumstances, consider Broca trustworthy. Just a feeling, but a very strong one. Thus convinced of the likely arc of our relationship, I asked my question without concern for hampering a future friendship. "Tell me, Dal Broca, when you eliminate these native species to make room for the colonists, what happens to them?"

He frowned. "I don't understand what you mean."

"What happens to those species? Do you eliminate them just from this planet? Are they found anywhere else in the galaxy?"

I sensed the change immediately, as though I had opened a door into a forbidden room. Broca's eyes narrowed, and his perioral muscles tightened subtly. "What are you implying, healer? That I'm a murderer? You know as well as I that the species on fallow planets tend to be unique—not found anywhere else in the galaxy. So, yes, I cause the extinction of certain species, but if it weren't for me and other terraformers, a lot more species would be lost. Left to the colonists, every native species would be eradicated or crossed with xenobiotic cousins, truly of no real genetic relationship, to create horrible sterile chimeras." His staccato, sharp-edged laughter stabbed the air repeatedly, as though he were assaulting an enemy. He stopped abruptly, perhaps expecting me to answer, maybe to apologize.

I said nothing, and he turned on me a sneer quivering with hate. "Out here, healer, you can choose your friends, but you can't choose your enemies. Let me give you a hint: I'm not a good enemy." Then he got up and walked out.

TWO

I gathered with the rest of the crew during mealtimes, but otherwise kept to myself and asked no questions. The bulk of my time I spent in the library, tapping both the official and the independent micro information nodes for galactic chatter on terraformers, reviewing the history of terraforming, and studying the drive and navigation systems of the transport modules our ship carried in its enormous hold. When my brain felt soft and my senses dull, I would leave studying to wander through the ship, familiarizing myself with the emergency secure rooms, the locations of the auxiliary generators, and the inventory of supplementary provisions.

The crew module required three days for me to scour in a relatively random series of overlapping excursions. The staging deck, in size and shape similar to a small asteroid, I divided into a three dimensional grid for ease and efficiency. Halfway through completing my sixth grid, I discovered an anomaly—an extra space not present on the library's design scheme of the staging deck. I stood before a sealed doorway that should have opened into space.

Bulkhead reinforcements augmented the portal like a thick frame projecting from the wall. Running my hand along the fusion points, I could feel the sharp edges of a crudely fashioned design. Beside the door handle a small hole had been cut into the frame and from it protruded a handful of wires, and below them, like a head severed from its neck, an access panel lay on the deck floor. From my eavesdropping on information node traffic, I knew that terraformers excelled at making low-tech modifications to all their equipment; *low tech means low maintenance*, went the thinking. Whoever had added the extra unit—which from space probably appeared as no more than a dimple on the vast surface of the staging module—obviously considered security a secondary issue, having left installation of the locking panel for another time. For that reason, I felt no hesitance in looking inside.

The locking bars retracted readily, and I pushed through the heavy metal door into a short narrow hallway with a pair of sealing panels on either side. Only one was open: inside the small utility compartment hung a row of personal action suits. Terraformers used them routinely for their nearly universal functionality, attaching self-motivated arms for tasks in space, applying shielding skins to protect the wearer against hostile atmospheres, and adding neurolinked microlimbs for precision work otherwise unachievable if one relied on the relatively crude fine motor skills that evolution provided most of us.

These suits were bulkier than the light, flexible suits with which I was familiar. Heavy plating covered the universal attachment points, creating an armored suit, in appearance like the scaled bodies of some reptiloid species. Shoulder, chest, and neck scaffolding on several suits secured mobile arms neatly folded into the vests. Searching the floor of the compartment I found three stacks of long cases. I slid one of them halfway into the corridor, unlatched its cover and swung it open. A thermal cannon rested inside—too bulky and heavy to carry, but perfectly suited for a mobile arm supported on a personal action suit.

As I closed the case, a blade of cold fire slid through my right shoulder and lifted me off the ground. With the pain arching me backward, I caught a glimpse of the captain's dark reflective eyes. "I—" was all I could squeeze out of my gaping mouth.

"What are you doing, healer?" Without waiting for an answer, the captain dragged me out of the corridor and onto the staging deck. A tearing sensation shuddered my body as he raised me to my feet. Tipping my head to the side, I saw the captain's claw pincered through my shoulder like a giant hook.

"What is your purpose here?"

I shook my head, watched my vision dial down to a black tunnel with the captain's armored head a distant light. The swell of pain overwhelmed me, and I sighed, gratefully awaiting unconsciousness. The excruciating burn peaked sharply and then rapidly dissipated to a dull throbbing ache punctuated by lapping waves of stabbing pain. Blissful unconsciousness passed by—so close. I opened my eyes. The captain leaned over me. "I have released you." To support his claim, he raised his task appendage, the claw tip stained with my blood.

"Thank you," I moaned.

"What is your purpose here?" he asked a second time.

I reached up and gingerly inspected the wound with my left hand. Surprisingly little blood oozed from the puncture site; initially I'd suspected that he had lanced my subclavian artery or vein and that I would bleed out soon. "Familiarizing myself with the ship," I managed to whisper.

"Restrict yourself to the crew module," the captain ordered in his clipped, hammering voice. "Except when accompanied to the staging deck by one of the crew for the purpose of training. Do not meddle in terraforming activities, healer."

I nodded, and he waved his task appendages in a gesture unfamiliar to me. "Find Cra'taac and get yourself healed."

I waited for him to leave and slowly worked my way back to my feet, but I refused to follow the captain's orders completely: I refused to give Dr. Cra'taac a valid reason for calling me defective, so I waited until the insectoid doctor left the medical bay to eat, then I walked in and fixed myself, packing the wound with dermasynth and coating it with a generous layer of long-acting topical anesthetic to mask the pain and permit close to normal use of my hand and arm. Drawing attention to my wound would lead to questions and then the necessity of telling the truth—and the truth in this case would be more painful than the lie I would refuse to tell.

While my shoulder healed, I suspended my investigation of the staging deck and restricted myself to the library and the medical unit, content to keep my hands and eyes out of terraformer business.

★ ★ ★

Halfway to Sigma Tau Beta, Jesel approached me in my quarters. "Time to learn to fly," she said, and disappeared before I could protest. I followed her down through the crew module to the engineering deck, catching her when she stopped to access the service tube, an umbilical connection to the staging deck.

"Why not use the lift?"

Jesel punched out her security code and turned to me as the door slid into the wall. "You need to know what we need to know."

"I don't think the captain expects me to know everything," I replied as she pushed me into the flexible tube. The narrow passage forced me to bow down, limiting movement to a creeping shuffle.

Jesel's finger poked into my back. "Come on, move faster. If the ship blows up and the lift generators shut down, how are you going to escape?"

I chuckled. "If the ship blows up and I'm in it, there's no need for escape routes."

Jesel kicked the back of my right knee, dropping me to the floor of the passage. As I attempted to rise, Jesel crawled over my back to take the lead.

"Watch and learn," she said, curling her head down to look under her body at me. Pressing hands and feet against the curving walls to suspend her body horizontally, the Phelaan humanoid rapidly skirted forward, coordinating movements of her upper and lower extremities much like I imagined Arthen or the captain would glide through the tube.

Imitating her, however poorly, helped me achieve a more efficient passage through the auxiliary access tunnel to the staging deck. When I finally squeezed out of the exit port, Jesel grabbed me without a word and pushed me across the vast open arena scattered with dusters and shuttles resting on their landing gear like combatants waiting for the signal to fight. Arthen patiently waited for us beside one of the transports.

I bowed to Arthen and addressed them both: "I will embrace the knowledge that you can impart to me, but I will not practice in the use of weapons. It is against the tenants of the Healing Order."

Jesel frowned, and Arthen's antennae fluttered. After eying each other for a moment, Jesel shook her head and laughed. "This is a terraforming operation, healer," she said, walking away, "not a military one."

Arthen's fanlike antennae nodded in support. "Terraforming rarely requires the use of weapons, and we do not carry any on this ship."

"That's not true," I responded defensively.

Jesel whirled around and marched back to me. She tightened her jaw and closed her humanoid eyes—small actions that transformed her into a predatory insectoid, gauging the quality of a prey specimen. That subtle shift—like the trick of light that turns a crystal's shining facets black—fascinated me and briefly subdued my initial fear.

"Show me," she hissed, staring at me with her iridescent black multifacets.

I retreated a step and a twinge in my right shoulder reminded me of the captain's warning. "I cannot."

"That's because there are no weapons aboard." She opened her humanoid eyes, which did little to soften her sharp, angular features. "Understand?"

A muted, barely discernable odor wafting from Jesel pricked my nose: I quickly recognized the hormonal surge that often serves as a prelude to fabrication. Jesel had lied to me and insisted that I accept it. Arthen stood by silently, his antennae fixed and immobile, leaving me with no hint as to his thoughts.

I dropped my head in supplication and nodded for forgiveness.

Jesel snorted, grabbed my arm, and with a cruelly intense grip dragged me toward the shuttle. "You need to stop hallucinating and occupy your time with useful activities."

I promised myself to be more cautious and to temper my curiosity, but at that moment I still wondered—*who else on the ship knows about the captain's illegal store of weapons?*

We entered the transport, and the two terraformers led me to the cramped piloting bay. "You will start me on a simulator, correct?"

Jesel laughed. "Simulator? What do you think this is, healer? A recreation ship?"

"We have no simulators," Arthen said simply. "You will learn by flying the transport."

If I'd had the opportunity, I would have backed out, but my companions blocked the only exit. Jesel smiled cruelly and pointed to the middle seat of three. "Sit."

I twisted around and sat down. Before I could move, she grabbed a tangle of harness straps and bound me tightly to the chair. "There," she said, pointing to a rigid pair of gloves suspended above the console in front of me, palms facing each other as though grasping some invisible object. "Stick your hands into them."

The gloves looked considerably larger than my hands, and when I looked more closely, I realized there were only three finger holes— a central one, flat and broad, and a pair of vestigial ones to either side. I looked up at Jesel to ask her the obvious question, and she cut me off before the words had formed.

"Just put your hands into them."

I shrugged and stuck them in easily. Upon contact with my skin, the gloves reconfigured themselves, swarming around my fingers and palms until they fit my humanoid hands perfectly.

"Virtual control gloves," Arthen explained. "They have no physical substance."

"They itch."

"Microcurrent sensors to gauge movement," Jesel replied. "Get used to it."

"What do I do?"

Arthen said, "Activate piloting array."

A voice responded from the console. "Identify."

"Arthen, terraformer tech," the Phelaan insectoid replied.

"Confirmed."

"Enter simulation mode," he added.

"Confirmed."

"I thought you said there are no simulators?"

I looked at Jesel just as she gazed at Arthen and rolled her eyes. She saw me staring at her and laughed, shaking her head. "Healer, can you be so gullible? Do you think Arthen and I would risk our ship to train you to pilot?"

"Well, that's what concerned me."

"No chance," Jesel replied. "This isn't our transport."

"But you said it was."

"I lied." Jesel again pointed to the console. Discussion had ended.

I nodded and announced, "Activate piloting array."

Between the gloves a red holographic sphere coalesced.

"Pick it up."

I reached in with the gloves and felt my fingers contact the surface of the piloting sphere.

"Say activate ship's icon."

I repeated the words, and a transparent holographic image of the transport's external hull appeared within the sphere, with the layout of the interior visible. Colored heat signatures indicated the occupants—blue for me, the pilot; green for Jesel, who stood over me; and red for Arthen, sitting in the navigator's chair. The ship itself was boxy, with no true wings, only atmospheric stabilizing fins on either side; two large engines aft with another pair along the midsection; and multiple small thrusters along the ship's spine and keel.

"Say illuminate lines of control," Jesel instructed me.

I did as she asked, and fine tendrils of yellow-white energy appeared, running from the tips of each of my fingers to key locations along the ship's hull.

"Your thumbs control the primary engines, aft; your forefingers, the mid-engines; your third and fifth digits, the bow and keel thrusters; and your fourth digits manipulate the risers—the stabilizing fins."

I shook my head. "I cannot control all these different systems and fly the ship at the same time."

Jesel patted my shoulder. "Those are manual controls in

emergencies—in case you lose an engine and need to operate them separately. Normally all the systems are integrated, and you pilot the ship simply by rotating the sphere in the desired direction. Piloting array, deactivate lines of control."

The lines of control disappeared.

"I think it would be helpful to have those present," I said, trying to hide some of the fear welling up from my middle.

Jesel shook her head. "You don't need those. Rely on your skill and training."

"I have no skill and no training."

"Yes, but I will train you."

"No offense meant, Jesel," I said, "but you will find me difficult to train—my master did. I could use whatever aids are available."

"Listen, healer, you learn by trying, not following someone around. Jump out of the nest if you want to learn to fly."

"I am liable to crash to the ground."

Jesel sneered. "If you prove to be such a terrible pilot, the lines of control will not keep you alive, right, Arthen?"

Arthen nodded obediently. "Correct. Only a skilled pilot can manage to use the lines of control and not crash at the same time. If it comes to using them, likely the rest of the crew are dead and you are the only one remaining alive."

I nodded. "How do I know where to go?"

"The navigator will plot a course for you," Arthen answered. "It will appear as a tube in front of the piloting sphere."

"So all I need to do is move the ship down the tube?"

Jesel patted my shoulder and chuckled. "Yeah, that's right—it's simple. Arthen, cook up a few simulated navigation trajectories for the healer."

After crashing a dozen times on planetary landing, spearing the Colossus Impendor three times on attempted docking, and twice overloading the engines on atmospheric entry—the first time blowing up the transport and the second time somehow managing to fry the heat-shielded hull—I successfully piloted the simulator from takeoff, through the atmosphere to planetary landing, then re-docking in our ship's bay.

I did crash the transport onto the staging deck, but Jesel discounted that: "You got everyone back alive—that's what matters in your case. You don't need to do things right, you just need to do things well enough to minimize casualties."

Jesel worked me mercilessly for the remainder of the journey. The training sessions helped me avoid Borthax and Anders, which I appreciated. I continued to encounter Dal Broca because he poked and prodded everything and everyone. However, we had no further confrontations, and he treated me well, as though our initial encounter had never occurred.

The captain proved difficult to approach alone, as he appeared only during meals, and the control deck was off-limits to me except during a medical emergency. I had no idea why—and was doubtful that the prohibition applied to any of the others—but I chose to remain silent and not argue. When I did pass him in the hallway, invariably he was busy and could not spare the time to talk with me. He never brought up our encounter on the staging deck, and I tried to suppress the influence of the memory on my behavior around him.

★ ★ ★

Somewhere in the center of failure lies the seed of success, Master Yeh used to say. *Have patience. Search for it long enough, and you will find it in your hand.* My growing fear of Borthax and Anders drove me to spend more time strengthening my piloting skills, and as a consequence, I impressed Jesel enough that she let me pilot a transport—just to take off, rise above the staging deck, and land again, giving me a true sense of the power and feel of the real ship.

The late hours before my designated sleeping shifts I spent alone in the library unit, and it was during one of these quiet moments that I encountered Traevis for the first time.

"We have not had a chance to speak," he said from behind me.

I jerked at the surprise voice and turned on him. He leaned

against the doorframe, his hands hidden in the pockets of the long SOS jacket he wore. I had heard the terraformers discuss the Phelaan humanoid. With no clear duty on board, he walked about the ship loosely clad in a jacket normally used in emergencies only: in case the crew deck lost atmosphere, the ship broke apart, and all the life pods were destroyed, the SOS jackets, when properly secured and inflated, served as individual life preservers, providing a short duration of breathable atmosphere at a livable temperature even in the void of space. They also emitted a location beacon to aid rescuers.

The crew had made a game of conjecture surrounding Traevis' role, leading to the circulation of an assortment of bizarre stories— some humorous, all of them crude—to explain his odd behavior. I had my own theory, which I kept to myself, centered on the feeling that if any member of the crew ever discovered his true purpose on the terraforming project they'd throw him out of the nearest airlock without delay. On the other hand, I couldn't deny the logic of Arthen's argument—that Traevis' presence represented nothing more than Phelaan bureaucracy combined with the nepotism rampant throughout galactic governing bodies: he was a young, probably unemployed relative of some Phelaan dignitary who wanted to get Traevis out of his hair . . . or segmented appendages, whichever the case might be.

I looked up from my thoughts and found him watching me intently, hands still in his pockets. Like all Phelaan humanoids, his facial structure was longer and more angular than that of Earthlings: his eyes formed a composite, the central core humanoid, with light blue irises and circular pupils, and two lateral multifaceted eyelets clearly insectoid in nature. His split chin and ocular ridges also strongly favored his insectoid heritage, as did the long antennae-like hairs of his eyebrows.

"I am the healer."

"Yes, I know. Dr. Cra'taac mentioned you."

"In that case, I am the defective."

He smiled with an easy looseness. "The doctor is a very insect insect, if you understand me."

"I do."

"Then you know not to take his bluntness as arrogant dismissiveness."

"Well, I am not so certain with the doctor."

"He is disparaging about everyone on this ship." He took one hand out his pocket and brushed back thick cords of blue-black locks, at least three times the thickness of human hair. He closed his humanoid eyes and stared at me with his multifacets. When he opened his primary eyes again, I noticed the sudden, subtle wash of tightness flush across his face. "Keep tight, healer."

I shook my head. "I don't understand."

"Terraformer speak. It means stick to your job and keep your arms close to your sides. Those who stick their hands into other people's machinery get them cut off."

"Wise advice," I nodded. "Thank you."

"You live on the very edge of existence here. Frankly, you are lucky that the captain hasn't killed you yet."

"How did you find out?" I asked, thinking of my encounter with the captain at the utility closet.

Traevis frowned, and for a moment he seemed unsettled. "You know?" He stood up straight and closed his humanoid eyes again, staring at me with his black reflective multi-facets.

"I underestimated you, healer," he said after a long moment of silence. "You are braver than I thought, to remain on a ship with a captain who has murdered two humanoids. But just remember," he laughed quietly. "No one will risk himself for you, even those you save with your talents. Good and evil—they don't exist out here. Only life and death." He retreated from the doorway and disappeared before I could ask him about the murders.

Shortly after our encounter, the ship reached the Sigma Tau Beta system.

THREE

The entire crew crowded onto the small navigation deck on the upper tier of the crew module. I stared out of the view port at a planet that looked uncomfortably like Earth—the captain had invited me to attend—while the others laughed and joked or talked terraformer business. Standing apart from the others, I considered the moral dilemma of working for a company that specialized in species extinction.

Dal Broca had made it clear that he had no intention of saving the species of STB destined for his chemical and biological chopping block. For him, time and efficiency superseded the value of species preservation. Certainly without his work, Phelaan colonists would probably exterminate even more native species through indiscriminate clearing and the introduction of unsanctioned xenobiotics. Nevertheless, I could not get out of my head Master Yeh's lesson after I killed the young Llastokian malish: *Remember this: to kill is wrong, whether you intend to or not.*

That conflict had clouded my thoughts since the conversation with Broca. But then, standing on the deck of our ship, orbiting this planet that looked like my home-world—white swirls of clouds and the greens and browns of continents broken up by the smooth deep blues of oceans—I felt the tightness of self-doubt constrict my throat.

"Hey, wake up!"

Jesel stood beside me, Arthen a few paces away. The Phelaan humanoid slapped my back. "Smile! Finally, the good stuff! You're coming with us."

I resisted as she tugged on my arm. "I am a healer. I should remain on the medical deck—in case Dr. Cra'taac requires my assistance."

Jesel's fimbriae danced chaotically. "Require your assistance?" She laughed. "Arthen, wasn't Cra'taac the one who called him defective?"

"I did not actually hear the doctor use the term, but yes, that is my understanding."

She pulled on my arm again, and this time I allowed her to lead me to one of the lifts. "Listen, I convinced the captain to permit you to come down with us to the surface."

"Why do you need to go to the surface? I thought the dusters will take care of the whole process?"

Arthen answered as the lift doors closed and we dropped downward in the ship's artificial gravity. "We will need to monitor the progress and efficacy of the agents prepared by Dal Broca. Jesel and I, along with three other terraformer pairs, will establish biologics monitoring stations around all the major continents and oceans."

"They will collect data on temperature, wind speed, agent concentration, and kill rate," Jesel continued. "The information will allow us to target areas missed by previous duster runs and will give Broca a chance to reformulate his soups—"

"—to more efficiently kill the intended species," Arthen explained.

"What do you need me for?"

Jesel smiled. "You're going to pilot our ship down there."

I tried to protest, but she quickly clapped her hand over my mouth. "No excuses, healer. You need the practice, and what better time to try, right, Arthen?"

Arthen gazed in our direction. I was never certain where exactly he was looking; I assumed with his multifaceted eyes that he could look at me and nearly everywhere else at the same time. "I would prefer that Jesel or I pilot the ship, as I witnessed your training simulations." He shook his head. "But Jesel speaks truthfully. You need the practice."

"How did you convince the captain?"

Jesel winked. "I have my ways."

Arthen clicked his mouthparts. "Jesel, I insist that you stop making lewd references bearing no resemblance to the truth."

"Arthen, it was a joke. Work at picking up on them. Besides, no lewd comments were made. They were only imagined—which means you better clean up that dirty insect mind of yours."

"Your jokes are not worth picking up on, and the dirt in my mind comes from your verbal pollution—and from the rest of the moles on this ship."

By moles Arthen meant humanoids—that I had learned from the incessant but friendly bickering between the two terraformers.

Without turning his head, Arthen addressed me. "Do not listen to her molish nonsense, healer. The captain told me he did not care what you did. He said he could not understand why the company hired you in the first place."

Jesel kicked Arthen hard enough to break a humanoid's legs. The blow, of course, had little effect on the insectoid's carapace. "Smelling engine fumes again? You just insulted him."

"How could I insult him by telling the truth?"

By the time we reached the staging deck, five dusting cruisers already sat by the exit ports. Dal Broca ran back and forth among the terraformers, busily monitoring the loading of the under-wing containers. He saw us and waved us over.

"Healer, the big event!" He grabbed my shoulder and turned me to the ships, pointing to them. "The soups are ready for tasting," he said, laughing. "Hey, why don't you ride down with one of the dusters? Watch it as it happens. Borthax and Anders mentioned you."

Before I could reply, Jesel stepped up. "He's piloting our transport, Broca," she said, nodding at Arthen.

Broca shrugged. "Won't see much from planetside, but if you don't mind missing the show . . ."

"He won't mind. Besides, we're just going to plant the biologics monitors, then we'll be back shipside to see the fireworks." Jesel smiled with exaggerated enthusiasm.

Broca eyed her with a downward turn to his lips. "You're not remaining planetside with the monitors?"

"What for?" Jesel shot back.

"What if something goes wrong?"

"Like what, Broca?"

Broca hesitated, lips pursed with no words coming out. He avoided Jesel's direct stare. Then, suddenly, with a sharp intake of breath, he met her gaze and set his jaw. "The dusting runs require data from the monitors. If they fail—"

"They won't fail!" Jesel cut in, stepping into Broca's personal space.

Reflexively, Broca retreated a step or two, and Jesel let a satisfied smile curl her lips. Broca's eyes narrowed. "How do you know?"

Jesel leaned forward as though to advance, then stepped back and crossed her arms casually. She inspected Broca, up and down. "I know my work, Broca." She raised her chin at him and turned away to join Arthen.

Broca snorted as she left. He nodded to me. "Keep them all in one piece—the monitors that is. They are valuable." The last statement he announced for everyone to hear. Then he walked off to join one of the duster crews.

I wandered back to my two terraformer companions, and Jesel turned on me with blazing eyes. "Arrogant Earthlings! The Phelaan should put you all on the endangered list."

"We are not all like Dal Broca," I offered quietly.

"Enough of you are to make me want to blast the whole species!" She pushed me aside and left the staging deck.

Arthen and I watched her go. "I guess she doesn't care for Dal Broca," I said, laughing gently.

Arthen nodded seriously. "She says that he loves himself too much."

"The Healing Order teaches that one cannot care for others without caring for oneself."

Arthen stared ahead yet addressed me. "I have come to realize that humanoids possess a limited capacity to love. You often spend it on yourselves first, giving to others only what remains, if any. We insectoids have the opposite problem: our nature is to love others to the exclusion of ourselves. Sacrifice comes as naturally to me as self-preservation to you."

I understood and reluctantly agreed. "It always amazes me that insects and moles ever find common ground."

"I, too, find it fascinating." He leaned toward me and continued. "Despite our seeming insurmountable differences, we manage to find—what did you call it?—yes, common ground."

"Your confidence inspires me, Arthen."

"Not confidence, healer—experience."

I nodded because I knew exactly what he meant. "The Phelaan Syndicate's success to unite such disparate elements gives us all hope."

"Certainly, but I referred to personal rather than societal experience. It is something Jesel has struggled to teach me—to think in terms of myself rather than my society."

"You mean working with a diverse terraforming crew?"

He shook his head, his eyes on me, staring but not staring, my own image reflected a dozen—two dozen, perhaps more—times in the mirror-like blue facets. I shook my head: "I am sorry, Arthen, I don't understand."

His mouthparts clicked rapidly in what I had come to recognize as nervousness. In a hissing whisper he said, "Jesel and I are lovers."

The news stunned me, but before I could voice the first of an endless stream of questions, he waved to me and took off after Jesel. He moved surprisingly fast, and I caught him only as we reached our transport, two decks below the staging area. Jesel waited for us there, and I knew that she would not appreciate Arthen telling me of their relationship.

"We're wasting time," she said gruffly as we approached. She eyed me sullenly and nodded over her shoulder. "Ship's internal checks completed. Get inside and prepare for liftoff. I will finish the external checks. Go!"

The levator—a tubular shaft running through the hull to an

antechamber just inside the main hold's bulkhead—sucked me up the moment I stood under it and spit me out at maximum velocity. I hit the hard floor and rolled away, just in time to avoid Arthen's spiked arms as he followed me through the quick-entry port.

"Jesel still functions under the influence of her confrontation with Dal Broca," Arthen offered as we picked ourselves up off the dimpled surface.

I nodded to Arthen. "Of that I have no doubt. She's set the levator high enough to suck up a Tuvian seed whale."

Arthen clicked his mouthparts, agreeing. "I am unaffected by the strength of the vacuum, given the nature of my carapace. I believe she endeavored to make a point."

I flexed a bruised elbow. "Point well taken."

We donned flight suits in the unlikely event of a hull breach—it was protocol, and Arthen followed protocol to the letter—before making our way to the control bay. While I strapped into the pilot's seat, Arthen took up the navigator's place and began making calculations. We had a few moments before Jesel joined us, so I took the opportunity to satisfy my curiosity. "How does it work? I mean, your parts can't be similar in any way."

Arthen continued his calculations, running his finger-equivalents over a 3D holographic flight path from our ship to a landing site on the eastern edge of the largest continent in the northern hemisphere of Sigma Tau Beta. "To what do you refer?" he asked.

I looked around to make sure Jesel had not quietly slipped in behind us. We were still alone. "Arthen, you cannot possibly think I would leave the revelation that you and Jesel are lovers without a single question."

He paused in his trajectory plotting and inclined his head slightly toward me. "Why would you find our mating practices interesting?"

Why indeed? We don't show much interest in how other species eat, or in most cases what they eat. So why so much attention to the mating practices? My own reasoning was quite simple. "I have never mated with another individual."

"Why not?"

"The Healing Order discourages it, although they expressly prohibit it only for apprentices. The period of training aims to develop our skills, test our talent, measure our abilities, and ultimately determine if we are worthy to enter the Order. Distractions of any kind, the Order believes, will limit an apprentice's training and impede his or her progress. I have not been long out from under my master's guidance, so the thought—and, of course, the opportunity—has never arisen."

"So your question comes from lack of experience?"

"Not completely. Earthlings are curious by nature—especially about things beyond our understanding."

Arthen nodded. "How does my relationship with Jesel reach beyond your understanding?"

"It's the mechanics. As a healer, I have studied the anatomy and physiology of most major galactic species extensively. I am not specifically familiar with Phelaan anatomy, but I have studied various insectoid and humanoid races: I have yet to come across any that resemble each other in any way, and I know of no successful interspecies mating."

"It depends on how you define successful," he replied.

"Medicine defines successful mating as the production of viable offspring that are also capable of reproducing."

"Quite limited and narrow in scope," he said, turning his attention back to the navigation panel.

"How, then, would you define it, in a broader sense?"

"When two or more individuals engage in consensual behavior, considered intimate, for their mutual benefit."

"But that is my point, Arthen. Based on my studies of anatomy, I cannot conceive how insects and moles can engage in such behavior—the mechanics defy my understanding."

"Ah," he sighed, "the mechanics—now I understand. You say you have not studied the Phelaan Syndicate?"

"Correct, but I have extensive knowledge of multiple insectoid and humanoid species."

"The Phelaan Syndicate is inherently different from other races. Our insectoid and humanoid ancestors evolved jointly over the last six millennia, some natural, some directed. We suffered through many internal conflicts, much killing between insects and moles, even some extinctions of subspecies. Unfortunate but necessary. We have evolved into what you now see." He waved a hand over his shining carapace.

"And what is that, Arthen? What have you evolved into?"

"Symbiotics," he said simply. "Insect and mole need each other to reproduce themselves."

"How?"

"How what?" Jesel's voice broke over our conversation.

Arthen readdressed the navigation console, his finger equivalents flashing over the holographic displays, refining entry parameters and identifying other monitor sites, while I furiously worked to activate the piloting hologram.

"What's going on here?" Jesel came around my left side. I could see her in the corner of my eye, staring hard at me.

"I am just preparing the piloting controls," I said. I looked at her briefly, then back to the holographic sphere blossoming before me.

"It takes seconds to activate it, and you have been here for ten minutes."

"Actually, we have been present only for five minutes," Arthen responded.

"Precision is not important here, Arthen," she snapped, walking around behind me and accosting the insectoid, much to my relief. "*Two* minutes is more than enough time to start up the piloting array."

The image of our transport appeared in the middle of the piloting sphere. I secured my hands in the piloting gloves, thrust my thumbs aft, and felt the transport shudder just as a glow appeared at the rear of the holographic ship. "Aft engines powering up," I called out, as Jesel and Arthen had taught me.

"Hold up a minute," Jesel said.

I pressed my thumbs inward against the sphere and the glow of the engines rose.

"Hold up!" Jesel bellowed over the rising din.

I pressed my forefingers inwards and announced "Midsection thrusters powering up!"

Jesel cursed and took the seat to my left. She leaned toward me and grabbed my left ear, pulling me the rest of the way over to her. "You can try to keep things from me, but Arthen has no hope. No hope." She released me, and I refocused on the piloting array.

"Course plotted," Arthen called to me.

"Load navigation trajectory." The hollow tube appeared in front of my piloting sphere.

"Let's go," Jesel said, and I nodded.

With one deep breath, I pressed the sphere just slightly with my thumbs, lifted it gently and turned it down into the tube. I felt the ship lurch up with a heavy-handed thrust from the aft engines, slide forward through the lower hanger and then plunge through the exit port and into the void.

"Next time, use the mid-engines for takeoff," Jesel suggested.

"They are smaller and better for finer thrust adjustments," Arthen added.

I just nodded, hearing them only distantly because this was no longer a simulation. I glanced at the global projection monitor surrounding the piloting sphere and watched the Colossus Impendor gradually shrink.

"Keep tight! Concentrate on the navigation tube!"

Immediately I focused on the sphere and realized that it had begun to drift out of the tube. I took a deep breath, steadied my hands and slowly corrected the course, bringing us back into the projected navigation cylinder.

"Good work, healer," Jesel said. "Better than I expected. I was waiting for you to overcompensate and throw us out completely."

"Is that not an insult?" Arthen asked.

"Yes, of course it is," Jesel replied.

"Why, then, can you insult the healer but not I?"

"Mine was constructive, and yours was not."

I chose not to put in my own vote for when and how to insult me, deciding instead to keep my eyes riveted to the navigation tube. Surprisingly, I piloted our shuttle through the atmosphere and down to the designated landing spot without any significant errors. The landing nearly knocked Jesel out of her seat, and I fully expected to hear about it.

Instead, as soon as I powered down the engines and locked the landing struts, my two companions flipped out of their restraints and attended to the mission. I had completed my only task, so I made a point to stay out of their way, helping as I could to load the biologics monitors onto the utility sleds. In an hour we had finished the preparations and headed out to the first planting site.

I asked how they had chosen the sites, and Arthen answered. "Before arriving here, the initial terraforming inspection team launched environmental and atmospheric probes that have been collecting data for the last ten years on weather patterns, jet streams, major and minor ocean currents and seasonal variability in temperature from the poles to the equator. Broca collected and assimilated all the information and then assigned each of the terraformer teams a region to monitor."

"We'd better hope he gave us the correct information," Jesel growled.

"I am sure he was thorough in his evaluations," Arthen replied.

"So he tells you where to place the monitors?" I asked.

"No—we analyze the data he gives us," Jesel snapped. "Not that I don't trust him—which I don't—but if I am planting monitors, I'm going to put them where I see fit. If he or anyone else wants them in specific locations, they can come down and plant the probes themselves."

"We are terraformers, healer," Arthen continued. "Trained in all aspects of planetary restructuring. We are not grunts—to use a mole expression—just following orders without thought or input."

"I understand, and I apologize if I offended you."

"No offense taken," Jesel responded. "I don't expect you to understand the terraformer world—but others, like Broca, should."

In my brief association with terraformers I had come to recognize that they lived in a shadowy world of hidden conflicts riddled with minefields of speech and action. Had I been a terraformer I would have been killed long ago for unforgivable transgressions of which I had no idea. My ignorance—and possibly my status as a healer—protected me for the moment, but the longer I remained with them, the more was expected of me—and the less forgiveness I could expect.

"Broca assigned us the transition zones for this continent," Arthen cut into my thoughts.

I looked confused, and he elaborated: "Coastal zones reaching two hundred kilometers inland and another two hundred into the oceans. The wide variability of weather patterns in these regions requires a greater number of monitors than deserts and polar areas."

"We have a lot of work to do," Jesel commented. She piloted our sled, leaving the conversation to Arthen.

"You can help us if you like," Arthen said.

"I would be honored."

"There's no honor here, healer," Jesel laughed bitterly. "Just work."

We planted thirty monitors that day—two-meter–tall, sleek black cylinders. Some we sank into rock—"fault zone, to measure and monitor seismic activity," Arthen explained—while others we suspended in the lower atmosphere with antigravity rings. Another set we submerged in the coastal waters, tethered to the ocean floor by low frequency sonic lines.

The bulk of the time we spent in a coastal forest that seemed endless. The trees around us grew densely—slender but exceedingly strong, with flexible trunks rising branchless for thirty to sixty meters to crowns of bright yellow and blue frondlike leaves. Clusters of blood-red fruits hidden beneath the canopy reminded me of the coconuts of Earth—and the trees as well. Winged quadrupeds looking similar to monkeys alternately flew and leaped between the treetops. Insects buzzed and crawled everywhere. Occasionally, as I watched the ocean through the trees, I'd see a large sea animal breach the surface and plunge back into the water. Despite having no duties on the main terraformer vessel, I hadn't managed to review the data logs on the flora and fauna of the planet, something I truly regretted.

Leaving Arthen and Jesel to set the monitors, I wandered off into the woods, using a compact sensory capture device to record the animal and plant life I encountered—a small way of compensating for my failure to research the planet's biosphere. As I kneeled down to collect the sounds of an eight-legged insectoid predator and the odor of the prey on which it was feeding, a breeze gently pressed on my back. When the breeze grew steadily, nearly pushing me into the ground, I braced myself on all fours and looked over my shoulder.

I simultaneously felt and heard a concussive explosion—a dull rather than sharp sound, as though the source was hundreds of miles away but nevertheless enormous. A wall of pressurized air struck me, throwing me to the ground, followed by a rush, a gradually diminishing whistle, and then nothing.

Waiting for a second wave, I lay on the ground for a few moments, and when nothing came, I stood up, tucked away the SCD and headed for a clearing I had passed earlier.

I knew immediately that something was wrong. Above me I saw a small nidus of black in the otherwise clear sky. That spot of darkness grew rapidly, casting outward across the atmosphere. Within it a kaleidoscope of colors flashed, like small metallic slivers flashing in the light. The dark canopy seeped across the entire sky like a thin veil, the normal sky partly hidden behind it. Then, slowly, it descended, a curtain of black set with sparkling gems, dispersing gradually as it fell.

I sought out my companions for an explanation of the strange phenomenon I had just witnessed, but before I could speak, Arthen's com link buzzed. Jesel had just completed drilling a fifty-meter hole at the base of a large hill in a forested region of coastal lands—"to measure plate tectonics," she told me—when Arthen motioned to her for quiet. She cut the laser drill's motor and leaned back against an outcropping of rock.

Arthen focused on the com link, and after a few moments he raised his head in Jesel's direction. "Dal Broca wants an update." He pulled the link off his chest and handed it to Jesel.

The Phelaan humanoid refused it with a determined shake of her head. "You can give him the update as well as I."

"He asked for you."

Jesel raised an eyebrow and shrugged. "I am busy. He can speak to you, or he can wait." She hefted the laser drill over her shoulder and disappeared into the forest.

Arthen watched her leave, then stared at the link for a few moments. "Yes, Dal Broca," he said aloud. "Jesel has disappeared. Speak to me."

Arthen nodded several times, adding a "yes, Dal Broca" or "no, Dal Broca" once in a while. Finally, he nodded and replaced the link on the right shoulder of his jacket.

"What did he want?"

"He said the other monitoring teams have reported in, and the dusters have nearly completed their first run. He said he would like us to finish today so in the next few hours he can complete data analysis for the second run."

"Will we finish in time?"

"Certainly not," Arthen said calmly. "Broca knows that we have the toughest job. We must plant two to three times as many units as the others in order to adequately cover the transitional zones of this continent and its surrounding oceans."

"What do you plan on doing?"

"We will cross this continent tonight, set up camp on the western coast tomorrow and deploy another thirty monitors just as we are doing today."

"Then we'll go back to the ship," Jesel cut in, reappearing from the woods, "right on schedule—the schedule we submitted to Broca before we entered orbit." She looked at me and shook her head. Her thoughts projected at me like a spear—*damned Earthlings.*

Based on Jesel's mood, I thought it wise to ask about the explosion and the dark sky later. Of course, I soon forgot it as we worked Broca's impossible schedule. With my meager aid, Arthen and Jesel set up the remaining monitors along the eastern coast of the continent. The planet's sun had already passed our longitude and twilight had set in when we reached the transport.

Jesel waved us off as we pulled up behind the ship. "I'll load the sled and the gear into the hold; you two find a nice spot on the west coast and start up the engines. As soon as I come up I want us out of here!"

"Who will pilot the ship?" I asked.

"You, of course," she replied. "You're nearly useless for everything else, so . . ."

She didn't finish her statement, just pushed me away from the sled and nodded to Arthen, who had just disappeared into the levator. "Give him a moment," she said. "He's slow to move out of the way. I've watched more than a few soft-bodies like us get impaled on his spikes." She chuckled, recalling some memory with a distant look. "He calls them ornamental but they hurt like hell when you fall on them."

She looked up sharply at me, and I noticed the subtle flushing of her face. "Get going! Warm up the engines!"

I nodded and quickly stepped under the levator, which whirred a warning to me before drawing me up more gently than the first time. I landed on my feet, which I appreciated much more than being spit out in a mass on the hard deck of the hold. Arthen had already left for navigation. I made my way up to the control bay, planning on inquiring again about the mechanics of insect-mole intimacy, but found the cockpit empty.

As ordered, I activated the piloting array and started the engines, announcing it over the shipwide com for Jesel and Arthen. They entered together, and I wondered if the insectoid terraformer was avoiding encounters alone with me. Arthen had already plotted our next stage, so he only needed to activate the panel. Immediately a navigation tube appeared before the piloting sphere.

"Takeoff," I called, and the two terraformers quickly strapped themselves into their seats.

We crossed at maximum velocity and at night, so I saw little of the continent's interior.

"Why do you care what the planet looks like, healer?" Arthen asked.

"I am not certain," I said. "Perhaps because it will be lost after we complete the terraforming process: it will never be as it is now."

"Nothing remains the same," Jesel replied. "Everything changes, everything dies—get used to it. If you try to remember how everything was, you'll leave no space in your brain for how things are."

"Part of my duty lies in remembering," I responded.

"How so?"

"I remove the pain that others experience. In some circumstances, I collect it. But in all cases, the pain provides the singular link between myself and others. We share something that no one else does."

"So?"

"Pain leaves an aftertaste—an afterimage—in the sufferer's mind and body. A reminder of what was experienced. In most cases it fades over time, and people forget. But I never forget the link with someone I have healed. Seeing them, or touching them, or hearing them speak—I can remember a few instances when I smelled them—brings back the memory of the healing. To remember pain is to avoid it in the future. Sometimes I must remind them of the pain they once experienced so that they will not require my services again for the same or similar reasons."

Jesel snorted. "And do you find that people listen to you? Take your advice?"

"I don't know—some perhaps do."

"Don't lie to me. Have you never healed someone repeatedly for the same pain?"

At first, I refused to answer, but Jesel read it on my face. I sighed and nodded.

"Hah! See? You waste your time, healer. Sentient beings throughout the galaxy are attracted to pain—attracted to it like . . . like Loso bees to Kanjeer pollen."

I would be lying if I said that I had never contemplated Jesel's premise—and I was little more than ten years from under my master's protection. The Order calls futility the greatest challenge of the healer. I remembered asking Master Yeh when he had come to truly believe in the value of his work. He said he was still waiting. Then he patted my shoulder, looked into my dejected eyes and said, "Futility follows us like our shadow. A sobering thought, but remember this as well: futility no more represents who we are than our shadow illustrates what we truly look like. It distorts the truth just like a shadow distorts our body."

While I considered Jesel's sobering words, Arthen rescued me. "Do you not find our work futile at times, Jesel?"

"Of course not," she shot back, releasing me from her hard eyes to challenge her lover. "Why should I? We produce something lasting—at least more lasting than the healer's work. Our terraforming will outlast us, and I don't care beyond my own death. If it survives for eternity or one minute longer than I do, it's all the same to me."

"I do not believe you care for nothing beyond yourself," Arthen countered. "Whether you do or do not is unimportant for my point, though. Do you not find our work at times ironic? We terraformers, who universally shun the constrictive nature of planet-based cultures, work harder at spreading their influence than anyone else; our work benefits those we do everything we can to avoid. We will never live on any of the planets we terraform, and someday, eventually, we will cause our own extinction, having terraformed away all the frontiers."

"If that ever happens it will be millennia after you and I cease to exist."

"Nevertheless, do you not find it futile that we choose to risk our lives, devote our lives, to those who consider us inferior, strange, and who would never willingly associate with us?"

"I get paid for my work. What do I care if they won't sit down next to me?"

Arthen shook his head. "Sometimes I cannot talk to you. You say things you do not believe just to argue with me."

"Not to argue—just to be contrary," Jesel laughed.

"Can you explain this predilection for conflict, healer?"

I smiled at Arthen. "In my experience, most humanoid species share this trait of sometimes saying the opposite of what they believe. In most cases I don't believe that it represents a desire for conflict as much as it reflects a strange taste for turmoil."

"Turmoil? Do you mean chaos?"

"No, no, not chaos—nothing so extreme." I paused because I struggled to explain Arthen's observation, which I had made years before. "Humanoids like to challenge—challenge convention, authority—"

"Keep tight! You're losing the navigation tube."

I gently guided the piloting sphere back into the middle of the trajectory tube.

"Sometimes, Arthen, I just enjoy driving you crazy," Jesel said after I had brought us back on course.

"That I recognize, even if I do not understand it."

"You understand a lot for an insect."

"What I understand has come with your help. You are quite generous for a mole."

Jesel unlocked her buckles and got up from her seat. "You are doing very well, healer. You can set the ship on autopilot, and it will alarm when we near the landing site. However, you will need to monitor the flight path in case an emergency course change is required or if the autopilot goes off-line."

"I do not believe I am the best candidate for piloting this vessel in emergencies."

Jesel shook her head, dispelling my concerns. "I have run you through emergency simulations."

"Nevertheless I would feel more comfortable with your presence. Will you rest in your quarters?"

"No. I will recheck the biologics—make certain they are prepared for deployment." She stared at me overly long, then tentatively reached out a hand for Arthen's shoulder. "Why don't you come with me?"

Arthen twisted around in his chair and stared at Jesel. Then the insectoid got up quietly and followed the humanoid out of the control bay. My guess was that they didn't check anything, but I did not dwell on their personal interactions, focusing instead on the piloting sphere as the computer's invisible hands guided it across the planet's major continent.

Five minutes before the autopilot signaled that we approached the landing site, my two companions reappeared. I noticed that both of them smelled fresher: they must have cleaned themselves. I suspected they appeared before the autopilot alarmed so I would not go searching for them.

Jesel patted me on the shoulder and dropped into the seat on my left, while Arthen took his place at the navigator's post to my right. I quickly donned the piloting gloves and commanded, "Disengage autopilot." I caught the piloting sphere as it dropped and gently guided it back into the center of the navigation tube: we felt only a subtle pull of negative gs before I took over.

"Well done, healer. I fully expected you to drop the sphere and ram my head into the ceiling." As if to emphasize the fact that the danger had not disappeared, Jesel promptly strapped herself into her seat.

"Why do you insult the Earthling?" Arthen asked.

Jesel remained silent for a moment, gazing first at Arthen, then at me, then back to Arthen. Finally, she nodded. "You are right. I apologize, healer. I only meant to compliment you on a transition as smooth as any experienced pilot's."

"Thank you, Jesel."

"You are welcome. Now concentrate on guiding the ship to the landing site, or you'll kill us all."

I nodded and watched the navigation tube head gently downwards. As I tilted the piloting sphere forwards, I could see a holographic image of the planet's surface, and the navigation tube ending far above the landing site. A moment of panic hit me, and I turned to Arthen.

"There's something wrong," I said quickly. "The navigation tube terminates prematurely."

"It does not," he replied.

"I can see it dangling above the landing site."

"Yes, I know. That is how I programmed it."

"For what reason?"

"So you can learn to pilot the ship manually," Jesel answered. Before I had a chance to reply, she leaned over and said, "Piloting array authorization override, Jesel 5QTX—illuminate lines of control, drop to manual."

Suddenly the energy lines appeared out of my fingertips, and the aft engines roared as I inadvertently pressed my jittery thumbs deeply into the piloting sphere. The ship shot forward out of the navigation tube.

"Hey! Calm down!" Jesel shouted over the thrusting engines.

Arthen grasped my shoulder gently. "Ease up on the sphere, no need to hold it so tightly, it will not fall out of your grip. Start with your thumbs."

I relaxed my grip on the sphere, and the engines quieted. Our forward acceleration decreased but did not stop.

"You must reacquire the navigation tube in order to find the designated landing site. Use the risers to turn the ship around slowly."

I felt the ship tip to port.

"Run the bow of the ship along the horizon. It will turn us around without losing altitude."

I did as he asked, and ahead of us I saw a shimmering gold snake with its head bowed down. "I see the tube."

"Good. Now ease back on the aft engines and move us forward with the mid-engines. Remember, they are smaller and therefore better for subtle maneuvers."

After several tense moments and Arthen's encouragement, I forgot about the lines of control and watched the ship reenter the navigation tube. I cut the aft engines, slowly recoiled the mid-engines while increasing power to the keel thrusters, lowered the landing gear and watched the horizon slowly, steadily rise. I felt a heavy jolt, cut the thrusters and released the piloting sphere.

I looked at Arthen, and he nodded. I turned to Jesel, and she shrugged. "You can kill us another day. Time for work."

"What would you like me to do?"

"Rest," Arthen replied. "Thank you for watching the autopilot and landing the ship safely. Jesel and I will set up the monitors farthest from here and work our way back to the ship. When we ready the nearest monitors for placement, we will contact you, and you can join us then."

I don't recall making my way to one of the resting chambers; nor do I remember falling asleep. I only recall the jolt from my com badge. At first, in the hazy confusion of sudden wakefulness, I thought something had stabbed me in the chest. In the darkness I ran my hands over vital areas first using the systematic trauma survey taught to me by Master Yeh—one of the many survival skills for hostile environments he drilled into me during the years of my apprenticeship. I had completed my primary evaluation when the com shocked me a second time—an electric surge running from the left fourth intercostal space overlying my heart upward along the left carotid sheath, following the external carotid to the maxillary artery then turning anteriorly, creating the prickly sensation I felt along my left jaw.

"Yes?" I got out as I stood up slowly from the narrow bed.

"Fire up the engines," Jesel's distant voice ordered directly into my left inner ear. "Arthen and I have deployed all the monitors. We're ready to head back."

I rubbed the warm spot over my heart where Dr. Cra'taac had hastily installed the temporary receiving and transmission unit of the com I was required to have as part of a terraforming unit. The receiver stimulated the afferent nerves of the mandibular branch of my left trigeminal cranial nerve, warning me of incoming transmissions; those signals directly stimulated my left auditory nerve and were translated into sound without the need for an audio-speaker, while outgoing receptors over my larynx translated vocal patterns into electric signals sent back to the unit situated over my heart. Since the company planned on removing the unit after I completed this assignment, Dr. Cra'taac hadn't bothered to install a shield, causing the device to heat rapidly with extended use. The com only linked me to Arthen and Jesel—my designated terraforming unit— and luckily, I had spent most of my time in the presence of my two companions, minimizing its use. At this particular time though, the unit boosted their distant signal and began to overheat, burning my skin.

"I thought you wanted me to help you set up the nearest monitors?" I said quietly, searching the room for something cool to place over my chest.

"We decided to let you sleep," I heard Arthen say.

"Arthen decided to coddle you is what he means, healer," Jesel cut in sharply, but she laughed as well.

"Are you close by?"

"No, Arthen and I are at opposite ends of the western coast."

I nodded. Having located the food dispensing unit, I was trying to figure out how to order some ice. "I'll have the engines powered up by the time you get back."

"It will take us three hours to reach the ship," Arthen said.

"Power up in two and a half."

I couldn't get the ice, but I knew from conversations with Arthen that Phelaan rataan soup included a certain type of cold-water fish whose skin absorbed heat. He told me that to prepare it the cook first skins the fish, cooks the soup, then throws in the skin to absorb the heat, finally removing the skin and serving the soup cold. I ordered a bowl of it with the skin, and rather than throwing the slimy mass of silver scales into the steaming bowl of thick gray soup, I folded it up and placed it over the growing red circle on my chest.

"Arthen and Jesel—please use the com as little as possible," I said, relieved to feel the burning fire start to cool as soon as I covered it with the rataan skin. "My com unit is burning a hole in my chest trying to boost your signals from so far away."

They never replied, which was fine with me. The fish skin worked perfectly, except for the indelible smell it left on my chest. I spent the better part of the two and a half hours trying at first to eliminate the odor, then—realizing the apparent impossibility of the task—trying to mask it. Finally, I gave up and activated the engines. Thirty minutes later Jesel and Arthen returned.

Jesel stepped into the command center and immediately turned to me, sniffing the air suspiciously. "What have you been doing? Cooking rataan soup? Poorly I should say. You're supposed the throw out the skin and eat the soup, not the other way around."

I started to explain, but then Arthen appeared. "It smells like rataan soup in here," he commented.

"The healer kept the skin and threw out the soup," Jesel explained.

"I didn't make rataan soup," I said, but the two terraformers ignored me.

"You discard the skin after it absorbs the soup's thermal energy and serve the soup cold."

"Yes, I told him that but he didn't seem to understand."

"The skin is poisonous when heated."

"Well, obviously he didn't eat it or else he would be dead."

"Perhaps Earthling physiology metabolizes the inert compounds to their toxic derivatives more slowly."

They both turned to me. "Did you eat the skin?" Arthen asked.

I shook my head. "No, I didn't eat the skin."

Jesel looked at me. "Then what did you do with it?"

"How do you know I kept the skin and threw out the soup?"

"Phelaan metabolize some of the soup's ingredients into aromatic compounds released in our sweat or in the exoskeleton lubricants. The odor is quite pleasant—almost intoxicating to Phelaan—and completely neutralizes the malodorous nature of the fish skin."

Then I understood. "So you smelled the fish skin and assumed I hadn't eaten the soup."

"Precisely."

"Well, I made the soup only for the skin." I pointed to my chest where the redness overlying the com unit had subsided. "I needed something to cool off the com unit, and couldn't program the food dispenser to give me ice."

Jesel laughed. "So you put the rataan skin on your chest?"

"Yes I did," I replied somewhat indignantly. "And it worked."

"And you may have permanently embossed yourself with the smell of rataan skin."

My only thought was how I could continue healing, smelling so abhorrently.

"Do not listen to Jesel," Arthen said. "She will walk you to the edge of sanity and watch you jump off."

"Quite poetic," she said, "for an insect. Go fix him while I get us back to the Colossus. Healer, you'll have to practice docking in space another time."

"Will this smell come off?" I asked Arthen after we left the command center and headed for the emergency pod adjacent to the hold.

"It will require a molecular scrubbing agent," he said, "but it should work. I will have you odor-free before we reach the Colossus Impendor."

Good to his word, Arthen concocted a thin paste, which he applied to my chest and then wiped off several minutes later. Two reapplications and the smell had completely disappeared. We finished up and hurried to join Jesel just as she synchronized orbit with the main terraforming vessel and began manually piloting us into the staging bay.

FOUR

While Arthen and Jesel focused on post-flight maintenance and repairs, I decided to check in with the ship's physician.

"I have no time for you," Dr. Cra'taac said, busy evaluating something he refused to explain. "Your services are not required here. If I have need of you, you will be contacted."

Anders caught me in the hallway as I left the medical unit, moving to block my passage when I tried to pass him.

"Anders, I don't want any trouble." To acknowledge his dominance and avoid a confrontation, I spoke softly with my head bowed.

"Good, I found you first," he replied quietly.

I looked up and noted the hesitance in his half-opened mouth. His black pupiless eyes roved nervously across the hallway and into the open doorway of the medical unit. When he turned to me without the sneering grin that usually cowed me like a raised fist, I lost both fear and caution.

"What's wrong with you?" I blurted without thinking.

"I didn't want to ask the doctor," he said, gazing quickly at the medical bay's door. "I don't trust Cra'taac."

Neither do I, I wanted to say but laughed instead. "Since when do you trust me?"

"I don't, but you I can kill without much trouble—" The hardness had returned to his black eyes and in the tautness of his cheeks, and I was reminded not to take my encounters with him lightly.

I composed myself without backing away in fear. "What do you need?"

Obediently, he reached down to his right wrist and slid away the sleeve of his coat, then pulled off the thick glove from his right hand. The burns stood out clearly, deep erosions spilling across the dorsum of the hand and streaking down the back of his forearm, running away in rivulets to the elbow. The underlying subcutaneous tissue had flared up bright red, within which rose irregular islands of green and yellow pus.

"Splash burn," I commented, gingerly supporting his arm at the elbow and palm. I inspected the wound closely, noting an odd creeping nature at the trailing edge of the burn near the elbow. "What did you drop on your arm?"

"Nothing," he protested. "There was no liquid."

Still holding his arm, I gazed up at the duster pilot: no anger wafted off his skin, only a strange fluttering confusion of feelings—emotional static, like a power unit loosely connected. Anders knew that I recognized his lie, and perhaps he also knew that I lacked the strength or authority to force out the truth. What he didn't know was that I could find the truth without his confession or even his knowledge.

Nevertheless, I hesitated. Information sometimes demands action, while innocence poses no ethical dilemma; it is knowledge that injects morality into our lives. Discovering the reason for Anders' lie might embroil me in terraformer politics that I wanted to avoid. Both the captain's and Jesel's warnings had left their mark on me physically and mentally. And yet the sweetness of the mystery beckoned to me. I weighed caution and curiosity before answering.

"I would suggest that you have Dr. Cra'taac examine your wound."

"No." The word was final.

I gently guided Anders' arm to his side and nodded. "We should find somewhere quiet—if you don't want me to heal you in the medical unit."

"Your quarters will do."

Strangely, I felt more comfortable with the commanding Anders than the fluctuating, uncertain one. I led him to my resting cell, and in his impatience either to get inside or to avoid inquisitive eyes, the imposing terraformer pushed past me to squeeze through the door as it slid open. He walked straight to my bed and sat down, presenting his arm to me.

"Heal it," he ordered.

I slid over the one chair in the room to face him closely, sat down, took his injured arm and closed my eyes. All trepidation and reluctance dissolved as I fell into my professional being. Anders was a patient with a wounded appendage that needed healing. Nothing more.

"Close your eyes and slow your breath."

"What?"

"Try to relax. Take even, slow, natural breaths."

"Taking slow breaths is not natural for me."

I opened my eyes and stared calmly at Anders' grinning serrated teeth and blood red gums. "Breathe in your natural rhythm then—and close your eyes."

The grin transformed into a grimace, but after a moment he closed his eyes. I shut mine again and reached down to carefully place my right palm lightly over the main focus of his wound, seeing the splash burn in my mind. I felt the initial tug and then the sucking vacuum pulled me into him.

I stood on the staging deck under the wing tip of a duster, its long curving leading edge suspended just above my head. Despite the shadow cast by the deck's ceiling illumination, I could still make out tiny divots and trailing grooves along the undersurface of the wing—the tattoos from countless atmospheres of uncounted, nameless planets scattered across the galaxy. I reached up and ran my fingers over the raised edges of one scar, then down into the trough of the gouge. Something acrid burned my nose. I turned abruptly and saw Borthax wheeling a trailer toward me; on it were two sealed wing canisters.

Something felt . . . odd. I opened my mouth and spoke but heard no words. Borthax's mouthparts clicked silently in response. No sound—none at all, not even my heart beating or the rasp of my alien breath. The light cut off suddenly. I looked up: Borthax passed me with the trailer, heading for the opposite wing.

I pointed up to the scars and said something, but Borthax continued on. Whether he heard me and answered I couldn't tell.

The scene tilted suddenly. Reflexively I tried to slow my breathing to accommodate—a rebalancing move healers commonly use when a patient's mind recoils from the intimate connection to another consciousness. Anders' mind fought back fiercely, though, screwing the image into a flailing coil that whipped back and forth across my vision. I released my hold, and the staging deck uncoiled then snapped away into blackness. Giving in was the only way I found to maintain contact with a rebellious mind. *Evaporate into air*, Master Yeh advised. *Invisible yet present. Without a body or form, you provide no focus for challenge. All resistance quickly dissipates.*

Anders' mind reasserted itself, pushing through me easily. His breathing returned to normal. Almost immediately I felt the tension disappear and, like an ebbing wave, I caught the retracting feelers of his mind and was subtly pulled back in, saturating his consciousness without protest.

My vision opened up again: *I was standing under the opposite wing of the duster with Borthax in front of me. He had set the trailer under the wing such that the first canister sat directly below its wing receptacle. Borthax reached into the central hole of the connection unit and pulled down a reinforced flexible metal tube with a large bolting cap on the end. This he fit over the discharge nozzle of the canister, pushed down and brutally twisted clockwise in a sharp snapping motion. He briefly looked up at me, and I noticed his mouthparts clicking away in a silent, continuous monologue. He quickly hooked anterior and posterior locking clips onto the canister, reached up and punched in his access code and stepped back just as the bulbous container retracted up into the wing base.*

The insectoid crept out from under the wing, poked two task appendages into my chest, another down at the remaining canister, and his fourth across the bow of the ship to the other wing.

I protested—or so I think, since I could not hear a thing—and Borthax snapped his head down, working his sharp facial pincers within a finger's breadth of my eyes. Then he straightened up and marched away.

The scene shifted abruptly, and I was back under the left wing, reaching into the hollow attachment port feeling for that familiar ice-cold bolting cap. By instinct, I reached for it and flipped off its retaining collar, and yanked it down from its housing. Just as I prepared to secure it to the canister, I noticed something on the discharge nozzle—a small bubble. I patted down my uniform searching for my gloves, remembered that I had left them in my sleeping quarters and peered more closely at the nozzle: a small droplet bulged from the opening. With my right forefinger I grazed the surface, collecting a small wet patch of green. The slick substance grew surprisingly hot as I rubbed it a few times between my fingers and then lifted it to my nose. I flung away my hand and shook my head to throw off the painfully acrid odor that clung to my nasal passages, searing down into the flesh.

After quickly wiping the liquid remnants onto my pants, I grabbed the locking bolt and slammed it down onto the discharge nozzle. Tears welled up through my eyes as the pain in my nose grew unbearable. I leaned my head back, letting the tears run down my face and into the upper caverns of my nasal passages. Surprisingly, as the tears seeped down through my nose, the burning subsided to a raw throbbing.

I pushed back the pain, reached into the wing receptacle and activated the retractors. Nothing happened, and in frustration I kicked the dispersal canister. That's when I noticed that the locking bolt sat canted on the nozzle. I grabbed the neck of the connecting ring and tried to shove it upright. It refused to move. I used both hands without effect, and then stepped back, defeated by my own aggression that had misaligned the locking bolt in the first place.

An uncontrollable urge to destroy gathered in my middle and surged upward, overwhelming all reason. Looking around, I saw a tightening bar lying in the trailer. I picked it up, raised it back over my head and swung it down.

The metallic crack of the heavy metal bar against the locking bolt exploded through the silence and shattered my vision, leaving me in a black void. I could hear the regular bellows movement of my lungs, but I couldn't sense the air entering or exiting my nose. I thought of reaching up to touch my face but couldn't seem to feel either hand or cheek.

Broca snapped into view, screaming silently into my face. For a moment I was stunned, shocked by the sudden return of vision. My right sleeve was rolled up above the elbow, and I was calmly wiping off a warm oily sheen with a cloth. When I had completed the task, I turned on the Earthling and leaned over him.

Broca bent back like a blade of grass in the wind. It was then I felt my vocal cords moving—hard, hammering movements. Broca wilted as my tirade continued. Then, I stood up, balled up the rag and hurled it into his face. Broca recoiled, desperately wiping at the small wet spot on his left cheek and nose where the soft missile had struck. He stepped away from the cloth and jabbed a finger at me at the same time trying to wipe away the smudge from his face.

My mouth gaped in a hollow laugh, I shot him a parting sneer and turned to walk away.

The scene shifted again, and I stood in miniature on Anders' elbow, looking down at the lake of pain spreading across his forearm. Something moved within it, rippling the surface. I waded into the pool and reached down with both hands, netting pain as I moved to the center and deepest point. Quickly gathering as much of the suffering that floated there, I forced it into a manageable ball, molding it like a wad of clay, until it was too dense to compress any more. Then, unceremoniously I tossed it into my mouth and swallowed.

In the next moment I was sitting again beside Anders. He opened his shining black pupiless eyes and turned to me. Nodding—a silent thank you, or just acknowledgement of the healing?—he stood up and left my quarters.

★ ★ ★

Later, I reunited with my terraforming companions in the meal room. The other transport pairs sat in isolated pockets. None of the dusting crews were present. I picked out my food—an array of Phelaan dishes spanning the insectoid and humanoid palate—and sat down beside Arthen and across from Jesel. "What do we do now?"

Jesel looked through me, absently stirring her food with a fork.

"The dusting crews have already started their third run," Arthen said. "The data from our monitors will help Dal Broca reformulate his soups to optimize elimination of the target species."

"So we wait," I said.

Arthen nodded. "We wait."

A flash of movement focused my eye: on my plate, dark segmented lengths of my insectoid dish slowly consumed short trails of my humanoid food.

"Our job is done for now," Jesel offered, still staring into some other place or time.

"Why are some parts of my meal eating other parts of my meal?"

"We can fine tune the sensors on the monitors," Jesel continued, "even move those suspended in the atmosphere or on the surface if needed. Right now we just collect information and let that idiot Earthling analyze the data as he likes."

"Am I supposed to let half of my food eat the other half, or I am supposed to eat them both?"

"I swear, if once Dal Broca complains about the locations we chose for the monitors, I will—"

Arthen reached across the table and clapped a large claw across her mouth. Jesel stopped immediately and stared at her lover. Finally, she nodded, and he removed his claw.

"We should rest until the dusters return from their runs."

At least a third of my meal had already been consumed before I had touched it. Jesel leaned forward and stabbed one of my hungry pieces of food three segments behind its mouth. It stopped immediately, and she lifted it up off the plate, spiked on the end of her fork.

"Do you like sweet, sour, or salty?" She asked me, dangling over my plate a long, brown-scaled worm with a pale underbelly.

"Salty, at the moment," I replied.

Jesel promptly put the dead creature in her mouth and crunched on it. "Eat them quickly then," she advised me between chews. "They'll process your food to something sweet, and if you leave them even longer, it will turn sour."

I ate quickly, then retired to my quarters until Jesel and Arthen called me. Although exhaustion overwhelmed me, I found it impossible to sleep. Something bothered me that I could not pinpoint. After spending an hour unsuccessfully running through half a dozen relaxation techniques, I got up and went to the medical bay. As before, Dr. Cra'taac examined a specimen, this time using a molecular sorter.

"What are you trying to identify, doctor?" I asked out of routine rather than actual interest.

"Confidential," he said bluntly, not bothering to turn to me, although it may have been unnecessary with his multifaceted eyes.

Some of Jesel's boldness had rubbed off on me because I refused to drop my inquiry: "Specimen from one of the crew I suppose."

"No."

"If the specimen wasn't from a crew member, then how could it be confidential? There's nothing out here."

That brought Cra'taac's head up, whether out of curiosity or because of my impudence to challenge him, I am not certain. Either way, I had a difficult time reading his expression. "From the planet," he said simply, but continued to stare in my direction.

"I didn't know you were interested in plants," I said, yawning. I marveled at how just the briefest conversation with the doctor could bore me so thoroughly as to induce sleep. I wanted to thank him, but I knew that such a statement was universally insulting. I got up, nodded respectfully to him and headed for the door.

"I am not," I heard him say.

"What, doctor?"

"I am not interested in plants," he said.

I nodded and left. When I lay down on my bed, sleep promptly took me.

★ ★ ★

First I felt something sharp, then something shook me. I opened my eyes with the lingering remnants of a dream floating across my vision. Arthen was standing over me; he held my left arm in one of his claws.

"Get dressed and come down to the staging deck," he said, and then disappeared.

Terraformers crowded the staging deck as the dusters returned from their third run over the planet. When I couldn't find my two friends among the others, I headed for their transport. The levator was active. I jumped in, exited onto the deck without breaking or bruising limbs, and headed for the control room. As I walked down the central corridor, one of Arthen's claws reached out from an opening and pulled me into an alcove. Jesel sat in a high-backed seat that seemed to envelop her. A mirror-smooth black reflective helmet completely covered her head; I saw no openings for her eyes, nose, or mouth.

"She'll suffocate in that," I said more to myself.

"It is a VR Conduit," Arthen said. "Permeable to oxygen but shielded from all surrounding sensory noise."

"What is its function?"

"It serves as a control conduit to the monitors," he said. "From here, Jesel can access all their data, their shielding and propulsion systems."

"How does she direct them?"

"By voice and by eye motion."

Jesel pounded the panel in front of her and shook her fists. I assumed that she cursed as well, but none of her colorful language made it through the conduit.

"Is something wrong?"

"Yes."

I waited for an explanation, and when I realized it wasn't forthcoming, I pushed Arthen, and he elaborated.

"Jesel cannot access one of the surface units on the western coast that she deployed today. We are not certain if data collection is corrupted or if the transmission signal is blocked."

At that moment Jesel slapped her right hand into the side of her helmet. A previously invisible seam opened up, and the conduit split at its middle like a round fruit. She impatiently worked it off her head as it continued to open and set it down on the counter before her. "If Broca makes even one comment about this, Arthen, I swear I will feed quatril juice to that decshil!"

"What is a decshil? And what is quatril juice?"

Jesel noticed me for the first time. "A decshil is something you never want me to call you, healer. And quatril juice is something I'll feed you if you ever make me angry enough to call you a decshil."

I nodded, realizing immediately that that was all the explanation I needed.

"Could you access the monitor?" Arthen asked.

She shook her head. "I flew one of the low atmosphere probes over to check it out." She frowned, still shaking her head. "Something's damaged the external sensory array."

"What do you mean?"

"There's little left of it—just a crushed mass on the monitor's dorsal surface."

"What caused it?"

She looked at me and shrugged. "I don't know. We set it at the base of some coastal cliffs, right along a primary tectonic fault, specifically to measure seismic activity."

"Perhaps an earthquake dislodged some rocks, and they hit the monitor," I offered.

"I agree with the healer," Arthen said. "That is the most likely explanation."

"Yes, I thought so as well, but then the monitor should have detected the seismic activity prior to its damage."

"What can we do?"

Jesel got up. "We'll replace it," she said. "I've parked the low atmosphere monitor right next to it. All we need to do is go down and drop another low-atmosphere unit in the spot where we deployed the original one. Won't even have to land. Arthen can set it for a fly-by launch, and it'll find its way to the designated coordinates. We'll be back up here before the last of the dusters finish their third run."

"Perhaps Dal Broca won't even realize what happened," Arthen suggested.

"Better that he doesn't know—for his own sake. We just need to get the captain's permission to go planetside one more time. We'll tell him we need to make some adjustments to one of the units, which we can't do from up here. He won't care."

All three of us headed for Command, but Dal Broca intercepted us just as we left the transport. As he closed in, I could see a smile cross his lips. He ignored Arthen and me, his eyes riveted on Jesel. "Where are you going?"

"Why do you need to know?"

"Well, one of your monitors seems to have wandered off. I thought you'd like to know."

"Speak plainly, Broca. What do you mean wandered off?"

"One of your low atmosphere monitors is no longer at its designated coordinates. You didn't know, did you?"

"We'll take care of it," Jesel growled, pushing past Broca and signaling for us to follow her.

"Don't bother," Broca called out. "I told Anders and Borthax to fly by the site after they complete their third run."

Jesel whirled around and marched back to where Broca stood. "That's my monitor! I will take care of it! Call them off."

Broca crossed his arms.

"Call them off, Broca," she repeated, more forcefully. I prepared to intervene, noting that Arthen did the same on her other side. Broca shook his head. "We work on my schedule, not yours. You and Arthen have already put us behind, and I'm not waiting for you to cover up for your mistakes."

Arthen stepped forward to interpose himself between the two, but Jesel waved him off. "Anders and Borthax won't find it. I know where it is. Call them off."

"How do you know where it is? Tell me, and I'll relay the coordinates to them."

"How stupid are you, Broca? They're flying a duster. It's built for high-speed, high-altitude flight. Sigma Tau's lower atmosphere thickens like soup in places. They'll have a difficult time staying in the air. Call them off."

Broca's smile disappeared. "Your arrogance in the face of the current situation amazes me. You've caused this setback, Jesel. Your inability to keep track of your monitors has forced me to rely on others. I can terminate your contract here and now if I wanted to." He slid past Jesel, and as he walked away he threw back at us, "You are grounded until further notice."

We watched him disappear, then Jesel turned to Arthen. "When will your mother's quatril tree bloom?"

"In one planetary month."

"So the berries will be ripe in another two months."

Arthen nodded, and Jesel smiled.

"Why should Dal Broca fear quatril juice?" I ventured one more time.

Jesel turned her smile on me, a smile less comforting than unnerving. As my two companions headed for the lift, I called after them, "Shouldn't you move the low atmosphere monitor back to its original site?"

"Why bother," Jesel replied. "Let Borthax and Anders fly back and forth over the area a million times and never locate it before returning to thrash Broca far worse than I would have."

While Arthen worked on calming Jesel, I chased down Broca.

"The captain made a serious mistake in assigning you to those two," he said, driving his stiff frame through the corridors, his arms tense, hands fisting reflexively.

"He didn't assign me to them," I replied, jogging to keep up with the neobiologist. "I chose to follow them."

Broca swung his head to glare at me. "Then I need to revise my opinion of the captain—and of you."

"May I ask you a question?"

"Ask it," he snapped, picking up speed to outrun me.

"Are there any chemicals or biologics in your soups that can harm or infect a humanoid?"

Broca stopped so suddenly that I ran into his back. "Why would you ask that?" Broca's close brown eyes inspected me, searching for something I couldn't define.

"Anders came to me—" I stopped short. What could I say? That Anders lied about his arm injury and that I knew Anders lied because healers enter the minds of their patients? That, during the healing process, I saw—felt—some of Broca's soups leak onto the duster pilot's arm?

Red heat welled into Broca's face, and fury wafted off his body, swirling out to cling to my face and arms. Grabbing the collar of my coat he pulled me into the aura of his anger. The sour smell of hatred pricked my nose. "What did Anders say?"

"Nothing—" Master Yeh counseled me no less strongly against explaining the healing process than revealing the darker side of our talent for collecting pain. Both, he said, would lead friends to abandon us and enemies to pursue.

Broca eyed me closer. "Who do you work for?" he asked in a whispering hiss.

"Dal Broca, I was merely wondering if there were any contact toxins in your soups."

He released my collar and retreated a few steps to inspect me from a distance. "Well, of course," he replied more calmly. "The aerosolizing agents, the vector transport media, the inert carrier compounds—they are all toxic to some degree, even without the active killing agents. I never handle them without proper retardant gear." Broca's face tightened. "Has someone been tampering with my soups? Did Anders contaminate them?"

"I don't know," I remarked truthfully. My mind drifted, and though Broca's tense, cramped face continued to impinge on my sight, his lips moved silently, firing out cutting, staccato words I couldn't hear. Anders materialized in my mind, his serrated teeth set in those blood red gums grinning cruelly at me, taunting me, it seemed. He held up the cleaning rag, stained darkly in places with liquid. He, too, spoke without words.

I wondered then at the absence of the auditory sensory inputs during Anders' healing. Sensory holes sometimes occur, usually a result of wide interspecies differences between the healer and the healed, but I had never experienced such a hole when healing another humanoid. Could individuals consciously exclude sensory inputs from access?

"—report anyone tampering with my biologics," Broca's voice snapped back into my ears. "Do you understand?"

"Yes, of course." Like seeing a reflection in glass, the image of Anders' healing clung to my eyes for a moment longer then shimmered away, leaving me to stare directly at Broca.

His narrow gaze betrayed his dissatisfaction with my answer. "Everyone would like to see me fail," he replied, stepping closer and whispering. "They don't like us, healer. My failure is your failure—Earth's failure. And believe me, no one—*no one*—will protect us. And that includes Jesel and Arthen. You can help me swim or drown with me. Choose."

As he walked away, another question came to my mind, but as I turned to follow him, Jesel and Arthen appeared, whisking me away.

We sat and ate in the small galley, crowded with the dusting crews just returned from their third run. I noticed a change in the interpersonal dynamics this time: before arriving at Sigma Tau Beta, the terraformers had mingled freely; those who chose to stay away from each other based their choice solely on personal dislike. After the assignment began, however, I realized that they segregated themselves as if by nature—the dusters socializing and eating with dusters, the transport teams doing the same. The only one to bridge that gap seemed to be the captain; Dal Broca also dealt with both groups, but he neither socialized nor seemed particularly fond of either the dusters or the transport teams. Certainly no one cared for him, which was probably the only thing the two groups shared. As for Dr. Cra'taac, I never saw him outside of the medical bay. And Traevis—I had nearly forgotten him. I thought about it for a moment and realized that I hadn't seen him since the conversation we'd shared en route to the planet.

As I thought of Traevis and the captain's opinion of him, Dal Broca burst into the galley, shouting. "Where's Jesel? Where's Arthen? Get them down here now!"

"Stop ranting, Broca," Jesel shouted over his voice. "We are right here, if you'd shut up for a moment and use your eyes."

Broca whipped around and pushed aside the transport team sitting across from Jesel and Arthen. He leaned over the table at them. "Your contract is terminated! And yours, too, Arthen. Both of you are out!"

Jesel just shrugged. "Fine. Have the company send me my prorated salary."

Broca stood up, speechless, his lower lip quivering. He quickly recovered, though, and aimed another volley at her. "Salary? You'll be lucky to stay out of prison for murder!"

At this, all other conversations ceased in the room, and Jesel's face turned dark. "You're mad, Broca. The only murder I will commit is yours."

Broca smiled. "Not a chance, girl. Not after the Phelaan find you guilty of the premeditated killing of Borthax and Anders."

Jesel's speed amazed me: Broca's words still lingered in the air when she launched herself across the table, both fists clenched tightly and held straight out like battering rams. I expected the impact to render some of Broca's internal organs severely damaged, but her fists stopped only centimeters from the Earthling's abdominal wall. Jesel bellowed curses in several languages, and then I noticed Arthen grappling with her flailing ankles. Slowly, gently, he pulled her back into her seat.

By the time she was seated again, the torrent of rage had subsided. "Please explain yourself, Dal Broca," Arthen said calmly.

Broca's eyes never left Jesel as he spat out the words like discharging a weapon. "Anders and Borthax went down. Their duster crashed. Crashed! Looking for your mis-deployed monitor! I know you hated them, so what did you do? What did you do to get them killed?"

Jesel tried to rise but Arthen restrained her. She had been staring straight ahead until the accusation, when she looked up and met the Earthling's gaze. "You sent them down there, Broca—against my specific instructions. *You* killed them."

"How typical—not taking responsibility for your own mistakes, just pawning them off on someone else."

"You hypocritical idiot! You talk about taking responsibility when you ordered them down there and I warned you not to."

"Where was your monitor? Tell me! Where was it!"

"Both of you, shut up." Everyone turned to the entrance: the captain stood there, having risen up on his hind legs, his bulky exoskeleton taking up the entire doorway. He stepped in, casually grabbed Broca's shoulder, and moved him aside so he could stand in between the two warring parties.

"Captain, Borthax and Anders disappeared while searching for one of Jesel's monitors."

"Yes, Broca, I know; I am the captain. I received their distress call on the bridge." He turned to Jesel and Arthen. "It seems that they managed to trace the monitor's residual antigrav trail down the coast to the site of one of your tectonic monitors." He paused for a moment to let my friends consider his words before continuing: "Jesel, what was the low atmosphere unit doing heading for another monitor site?"

Jesel's face turned to stone, her jaw set, the maseter muscles tight, corded bundles at the angles of her mandible. I also noted the slight pupillary dilation of sympathetic output—the Phelaan humanoid equivalent of the Earthling fight or flight autonomic nervous system response.

"Thinking up a good lie," Dal Broca commented as the silence grew longer.

"Broca, I want civil behavior on my ship," the captain replied. "If you want to fight, take a shuttle planetside and do it there. Arthen, if Jesel refuses to answer, then you will tell me. Why was the low atmosphere probe out of position?"

Arthen opened his mouth to speak, but Jesel reached out and grabbed his shoulder. With a deep sigh, she began, lowering her eyes to the table: "The tectonic monitor halted communications. I tried to access its data files and failed, so I piloted the nearest monitor over to have a look."

"You had no authority to relocate monitors without my approval!" Dal Broca's eyes blazed, and he struggled forward to get at Jesel, not, I think, to physically accost her but simply to intimidate her as she sat under the withering silence of the captain.

The captain blocked his way and turned his attention to the Earthling. "Control yourself, Broca, or I will ask Cra'taac to brew up a sedative strong enough to put you to sleep for a planetary month."

Dal Broca, who crowded the captain's shoulder, backed away slightly. The captain's eyes remained on him until he stepped back a second and then a third time. Then he turned slowly back to Jesel. "Did you know that the dusters had not yet completed their third run?"

Jesel nodded.

"And you moved an active monitor, collecting data, to inspect a malfunctioning one?"

Jesel jerked her head up and to my surprise I still saw anger and defiance there. "I was on my way to ask your permission to drop down and deploy another low-level atmospheric monitor in fly-by," she said without a hint of fear in her voice. "It would've taken no time—except Broca sent a duster to find the one I moved."

Dal Broca opened his mouth, but the captain raised a pincer for silence. "What did you discover about the tectonic unit?"

"Entire sensor array smashed."

"Crushed—by falling debris?"

"Possibly—Arthen and the healer believe that, but the monitor detected no tremor activity just prior to failing. Captain, let Arthen and me go planetside and search for Borthax and Anders."

After a moment's pause the captain said, "Take the healer."

Dal Broca exploded. "They should remain here! Send others—send a dusting crew."

The captain waved an appendage in dismissal of Broca's words.

"We may need more than just healing," Jesel countered, "if they are still alive."

"Cra'taac remains here," the captain declared, shaking his head. "You get one chance. I'm not sending a rescue crew to save the rescue crew, right? That means emergency protocols in effect—everyone aboard must be capable of piloting the shuttle. Are you confident of the healer's skills?"

Jesel's eyes rolled over me briefly. She squinted her face to one side. "Yes, for what it's worth, I would say he has a greater than fifty percent chance of getting us back alive—but not undamaged."

I offered my own assessment: "Captain, without knowing the extent of their injuries, it would be wiser to send Dr. Cra'taac. I am sure he has more experience commanding a shuttle in an emergency."

The captain turned a multifaceted eye on me. "He does not. Cra'taac is an arrogant insect. He needs a map just to navigate the ship's corridors. I requested another physician, but the company sent him. Jesel, Arthen, get down there, pick up Borthax and Anders, alive or dead, and come back."

As the captain made to leave, Broca interposed himself. "Captain, I insist on choosing the rescue party. This is my project, and Jesel and Arthen should stay aboard the Colossus."

Jesel ignored Dal Broca, but I could see her fists clenched tightly. "Captain, will you set this decshil straight before I do it myself—the hard way."

"Jesel and Arthen's failed monitor, Jesel and Arthen's solution," the captain said simply.

"Captain, this is my project."

The captain turned abruptly to Broca. "Broca, this is my ship; I am the only one who gives orders."

Dal Broca stepped back, but refused to back down. "I will accompany them, then," he said.

"You step one foot onto my ship," Jesel growled, "and I will eject you above the atmosphere so you can make entry on your own."

"Don't threaten me, girl," he shot back.

"Broca, you will stay here," the captain said, laughing in his raspy way. "And if you don't, I will choose someone else to take your place."

Broca scoffed. "You have no authority over me, captain. The Phelaan Syndicate hired me; only they can let me go."

The captain made a strange rotating motion of his forelegs—perhaps a shrug. "Do what you want, then, Broca. But when Jesel throws you out of an escape hatch without an SOS jacket, consider yourself fired. Now get out of my way."

FIVE

On this trip I was certain that I would not pilot the ship. My role was to stay well out of the way and hope that Borthax and Anders would not require my talents—and if they did, that my talents would suffice. In fact, I barely made it aboard, leaping under the levator just as I heard the aft engines powering up. Jesel had set the emergency access unit on high vacuum again, so it spit me out into a painful heap on the cargo bay deck. By the time I rose stiffly, we had already lifted off the staging deck, and I felt the thrust pushing at my back as we accelerated forward. I struggled against the bouncing jolts as we launched out of the Colossus Impendor and dropped precipitously into the outer atmosphere of the planet. This was not the smooth, perfectly laid out flight plan of a navigation tube: this was the abandon of emergency, the heedless drive of improvisation, where speed outweighed all other considerations.

As I slammed back and forth in a corridor, I knew that if I didn't find a place to strap in, the trip would pulverize my skull and internal organs. Unfortunately, the jarring ride had confused me: I lost my orientation and finally decided to just lie down in the corridor. My left jaw grew numb, and I heard Arthen's voice in my left ear. "Healer? Can you respond?"

"Yes, I am here—somewhere," I mumbled as the ship banked sharply to port, sending me sliding down into the left wall of the corridor.

"You must strap in soon," Arthen said urgently. "Once we hit the lower atmosphere, the trip will become more turbulent."

"I don't know where I am."

"You are in the living quarters corridor," he replied. "My cubicle is nearest to you. Go quickly and lock yourself into one of the emergency seats in the wall by the entrance."

Somehow I crawled to the next break in the seamless wall, managed to raise myself up enough for the entry monitor to recognize my presence, and then fell through the door as it opened. Clambering up, I released the emergency seat, pulled myself into it, strapped myself down, and collapsed.

The tingling in my jaw woke me up. "Yes?" I slurred.

"You are alive," Arthen's voice shot directly into my brain.

"Yes."

"You may now join us in the command center."

"As soon as I can." The ship no longer bucked and dived through *g*s and negative *g*s, yet I was reluctant to give up the safety of the seat. I waited until I felt the haziness lift from my brain and clarity of thought begin to return. During that time I tested my senses, making certain that everything worked. As I began to feel normal again, I recognized a familiar odor in Arthen's quarters—Jesel's distinctive scent. I smiled: the thought of them together from a strictly anatomical and physiological standpoint still intrigued me; the thought of them together from a strictly personal standpoint made me happy.

When I finally managed to reach the control center, I found the navigation unit dormant. As I had suspected, Jesel piloted on manual. She deactivated the shields protecting the viewing ports and nodded me over to one of the circular windows: an ocean of bright green-blue, white flecked with cresting waves, silently rolled on below us, so close it seemed that I could reach down and skim the surface with my fingers. Just over our heads, the dark gray undersides of thick clouds formed an unbroken ceiling.

"We are heading south along the western coast of our continent," Jesel answered the question forming in my mind.

"Do you Phelaan possess telepathy?" I said jokingly.

"What? Mind reading? No, we don't. It's just that Earthling minds are so simple and predictable."

"All Earthlings are not alike," I replied, sensing Jesel's still brewing anger with Dal Broca.

"Jesel does not mean to insult you," Arthen answered. "She still feels anger toward the terran Dal Broca."

I laughed at the thought of the synchronicity between the insectoid and myself. "No offense taken." Wanting to change the subject and not let the tension rise with silence, I casually asked the nature of a new hologram I had noticed—a blue, hazy oval coruscating somewhere ahead of the piloting sphere.

"That is the dusting cruiser's emergency transmission beacon. Jesel follows it."

"Why not just head for the tectonic monitor?"

"Because we don't know where Borthax and Anders crashed on their way to intercept it." Jesel's tone had softened considerably. She even looked up briefly from the piloting sphere to eye me and nod—an apology? just an acknowledgment of my presence? I didn't know the meaning, but it didn't hold anger as far as I could tell. "Better to start off from the last place we can be certain they visited," she continued.

"The original location of the low atmosphere monitor?"

Jesel nodded.

"Can you tell if Borthax and Anders live?"

Jesel shook her head, but Arthen answered. "The dusting cruiser's beacon dampens the personal sounding flares implanted in each of us. The beacon's energy source is designed to transmit into deep space through dense atmospheres; the sounding flares emit only a local signal. First locate the ship, then send a rescue party to search for survivors, so the logic goes."

That I understood. I watched as we banked left into the coastal region of the continent. The blue beacon dropped below us, and Jesel circled overhead, looking for a landing site.

"Arthen, locate the working monitor for me," Jesel said, gazing at the holographic image of the planet's surface skimming under the ship, while I craned my neck forward to watch the actual vegetation blur past the view ports.

"One hundred fifty kilometers due south," he announced.

"There!" Jesel exclaimed, pointing to a wide straight line of cleared forest in the holo-image. We skirted the nearer edge, so I could look out the view port and see it ahead of us— a wide swath of burned and broken vegetation running in a straight shot due east into the continent. It ended abruptly, and there I could see something flashing in the early morning light.

"Why is the beacon behind us when the crash sight lies over there?" I asked, pointing at the devastation line.

"The beacon anticipates impact and jettisons itself," Arthen explained.

"All the better chance it will survive an explosive crash." I understood, nodding.

"I found a small clearing about a hundred meters north," Jesel said. "We'll land there and then head for the beacon."

"Shouldn't we search the wreckage first, in case they're trapped?" I asked.

Jesel had moved the ship over the landing site, hovered there, and nodded me over to her. I obeyed, and she gently rapped me on the forehead. "What do they teach you during all those years of training, healer? Nothing about survival—or common sense—I can see. Did you see the crash site?"

I nodded.

"That's a high energy impact scar. If Borthax and Anders remained aboard during the crash, there'll be nothing left of them to bring back."

I looked over at Arthen for an explanation.

"The crew automatically ejects with the beacon," he said.

"Ah. No use keeping the beacon intact if you don't do the same for the crew," I said.

"Now you're learning," Jesel replied, releasing our shuttle from hover mode and taking us down for a silent landing.

We headed for the levator tubes in the cargo hold but then took a detour through the living quarters corridor. "Wait here a moment," Jesel said, and ducked into her room. In seconds she returned, her hands empty. She looked at me inspecting her and grabbed me with both hands, turned me around and pushed me down the corridor. "Come on, no time for slow thoughts."

The levator deposited us gently on the soft packed coastal sand.

Arthen drew forth a flat metal disk from an inner pocket of his jacket, held it up in his outstretched palm and spoke softly to it. The coruscating blue oval of the beacon appeared. "This way," he said and headed back along the starboard side of the transport and then into a dense stand of the tall, coconut-like trees.

One hundred meters through the trees, Arthen stopped before a black double convex disk approximately one and a half meters in diameter.

"That's the beacon?"

Jesel shook her head. "That's the recovery buoy. It protects the emergency beacon from just about any harmful atmosphere the universe can think up."

Arthen pulled out a short silver rod the length of my palm and spoke into the top end of it: "Captain, Arthen here. We have located the recovery buoy."

"Any sign of Borthax and Anders?" The captain's voice rang out as clearly as if he stood beside me.

"No visual confirmation of their presence, captain. I would like to deactivate the transmission beacon so we can track their personal sounding flares."

"Right. Acquire and confirm the beacon."

Carefully, Arthen laid the metal plate he carried onto the center of the recovery buoy. The disk turned a fluorescent blue that seemed to seep into the central core of the buoy. "Acquired and confirmed, captain."

Silence for a few moments, then the captain answered. "Transmission beacon's signal acquired and locked. Go ahead and deactivate, Arthen, and find them quickly."

"Yes, captain." He replaced the com link in his pocket and laid a claw on the small disk with which he tracked the beacon. "Dormancy," he called out, and immediately the cobalt blue color retracted into the handheld disk, which then turned a slate gray. He picked up the disk and retreated to where Jesel and I stood. "The beacon's deactivated," he said plainly, handing the disk to Jesel.

The Phelaan humanoid held it up and called out "Activate sounding flare tracker." Two small dots appeared within the holo-image. "What is their location?" Arthen asked.

"Due east," she replied without looking up, her eyes riveted to the screen.

"How far away are they?" I asked.

Jesel frowned as she looked up at me. "I don't know."

"What do you mean, you don't know?" Arthen asked.

"Well, their signals are moving away from us!"

"How fast?"

"Three or four kilometers an hour—not fast."

"How are they doing, physiologically?"

Jesel touched the screen over one of the two dots. A list of data too minute for me to read appeared in one corner. "Borthax's vital signs are stable," she said, scanning through the information. "Hemolymph levels look normal, perhaps slightly decreased. Probably some small cracks at his joint unions causing minor leakage."

I sighed with relief. I had little experience healing insectoids—a fact I hadn't revealed to the Phelaan when I convinced them to hire me. I expected that a terraforming operation posed some inherent risks to the crew, but I expected they were well established and precautions were taken to minimize their occurrence. Desperation had forced me to take a gamble, and this proved to be the best paying, safest gamble I could make at the time. "What about Anders?"

Borthax's information disappeared, and Jesel touched the other dot. She skimmed the readings that scrolled down the scanning disk and shook her head. "Not so good," she said. "Vital signs—" she shook her head more. "Temperature elevation, rapid respiratory rate and heart rate . . ."

"His tachypnea and tachycardia may be due to his fever," I offered hopefully, more for myself than for Anders or anyone else.

"Peripheral perfusion's sluggish." She looked up at me. "He's bleeding—already lost five to ten percent of his blood volume I'd estimate. Nearing shock."

Shock—the word triggered reflexes in me that felt as innate as pulling one's hand away from a fire. How many patients had I healed who had fallen into shock? Surprisingly few, I realized, though not because I hadn't seen my share of natural disasters or casualties of war. But when patients fall into shock, their pain disappears; they no longer have need of my services. And I had yet to develop the skills to heal more than pain. In shock, the body systematically shuts down, turns off the nonessential machinery in a desperate attempt to preserve the vital organs, primarily the circulatory system and the brain.

Most humanoids suffer from cardiogenic shock and hypovolemic shock—the first a result of the failure of the heart to pump, to perfuse the body with oxygen and remove the cellular waste products generated from the process of maintaining life; the second, and more common kind in my experience, results from acute blood loss, leaving insufficient volume for the heart to pump—and therefore insufficient oxygenation and waste removal. It all comes down to the same thing—not enough nutrients perfusing the tissues and too much waste building up.

During my extensive studies of other races, I developed familiarity with other forms of shock: the Aquabiotica of Panus Three suffer from neurogenic shock when their peripheral nervous system shuts down or is in some way disrupted. The Aqua—vaguely similar to the mythic Earthling mermaids—have no blood and no vascular system; they do possess a highly intricate peripheral nervous system underlying their skin, which generates oxygen from the surrounding water and disposes of waste directly into their aquatic environment. The Uio experience psychological shock brought on by intense experiential trauma, with or without significant accompanying physical harm. The acute mental trauma causes shock and rapid decline to death as surely as a blaster pistol's discharge into my abdomen would kill me.

"We need to reach them soon," I murmured.

"Are they still moving away from us?" Arthen asked.

Jesel nodded. "Their pace has slowed a bit, though. It doesn't matter: they're too cumbersome to carry back here. We should take one of the utility sleds."

"No," I said adamantly. "We cannot waste time going all the way back to the ship. We need to find them now!"

I noted the surprise on the faces of my two companions. For a moment, I thought I had risen in their estimation and that they might in fact follow my recommendation. Then Jesel smiled and shook her head. "We get one of the utility sleds and track them on it."

I waited in the clearing with Arthen and the recovery buoy while Jesel headed back to the transport, saying something about malish displays of dominance and chuckling to herself. She returned shortly, although it felt like half a day. She jumped out, indicated the flat bed for me to sit in, walked around and sat in the passenger's seat while Arthen took the controls and headed in the direction Jesel pointed as she followed the sounding flare images on her scanning disk.

The forest immediately closed around us as we headed east and away from the shoreline: the trees grew shorter but packed themselves more densely, their trunks sprouting in a panicked array, angling in all different directions—some even twisting about each other in a strange dance upwards to the sky. On foot, we could have more easily navigated around the trunks. On the sled we constantly rammed into the trees and had to pick our route more deliberately, making detours around clumps of trees so tightly grown that they seemed to arise from a single, massive base. Other times we had to back up and try another way as we encountered a seamless wall of plant life.

Slowly—entirely too slowly for my peace of mind—we moved closer. I watched over Jesel's shoulder as the sounding flare icons on her scanning disk dropped closer and closer to the larger oval green icon on the screen that represented the sled. When we reached within one hundred meters of them, I waited for the slightest break in the unending overgrowth of trees. It came shortly thereafter—a widening of the ribbon-thin trail we had followed for perhaps four hundred meters. Making certain that the sled would not crush me against the nearby tree trunks, I grabbed the side of the bed and catapulted over the edge.

I gauged the distance to the ground poorly, missed my footing, and began to slide under the sled. Desperately I kept hold of the railing of the bed, righted myself, and ran alongside the transport. Jesel briefly looked up from the scanning disk, frowned, and turned suddenly to her right, catching me in the corner of her eye. "Hey! Get back in the sled!"

Arthen immediately slowed down, and I found my opportunity. I jumped in front of the sled and took off into the woods, following the thin but well-worn trail, which reminded me of the deer paths on Earth.

"Get back here, now!" Jesel called after me, but I knew she couldn't catch me. She and Arthen would remain on the sled, and they would just have to join me. The engine of action had finally woken and was driving me forward. It was reckless, perhaps, but that's one of the oddities of life, and certainly of my profession: there are moments when we sublimate our own instinct for self-preservation in order to aid another, recognizing—not consciously or unconsciously, but in the super-subconscious—the connection between ourselves and others. Master Yeh told me that the greatest philosophers of all the galactic races understood this fundamental truth—he called it one of the great universal laws—of the seeming paradoxical duality of our distinctness as unique individuals overlying an inexplicable but undeniable connectedness with all other life, regardless of distance or time.

I broke through a tangle of vines and stopped. Borthax and Anders lay before me in a jumbled pile. Borthax at first seemed to be sitting on top of the humanoid—only one of Anders' arms and both legs below the knees were visible around the bulk of the insectoid.

Borthax mumbled something. I looked at him and realized that he was shielding his companion. He mumbled again, and I noticed one appendage outstretched. I reached for it, thinking he wanted a hand up, and immediately froze where I stood.

In his claw, Borthax held a gray metal tube by a black handle—a blaster aimed at me. I stepped back slowly and stood still. Borthax faced me, but I couldn't tell if his eyes registered my presence. "Borthax, it is the healer. I have come with Jesel and Arthen to rescue you and Anders."

After a moment of silence, the insectoid mumbled a third time and lowered his weapon. Jumping forward, I helped guide him down to the ground. I looked at the two terraformers lying beside each other.

The sled ground through the vegetation behind me, but the sound registered only peripherally. My attention first went to Borthax because he was clearly alive. I quickly scanned him as I had done routinely with thousands of other life forms on medical ships, in planetary healing institutes, and occasionally, on battlefields. I noted multiple scorings, some deep, some superficial, tracing randomly across his carapace. One of his right appendages hung at a strange angle, the shoulder joint torn and steadily leaking small amounts of hemolymph. Tracing down the length of the damaged appendage, I discovered the claw was crushed in an open position. Otherwise, the insectoid appeared intact, although I realized his impaired speech and level of consciousness could signify either exhaustion or a serious head injury.

Satisfied that Borthax would survive without my immediate intervention, I turned to Anders. As soon as I saw him, I knew he was beyond my help: erratic breathing, quick and shallow, followed by long pauses, then a single deep breath and more rapid shallow ones; pale, mottled extremities; several long actively bleeding gashes on the lateral aspects of arms and legs; a deep spreading bruise over the left iliac crest and lower left abdomen. I grabbed his hand—thready pulse. I placed my palm over his right chest, the location of the heart in his species: his was beating too fast.

"Grblck!" is what I heard out of Jesel's mouth behind me, and though I am still not certain of the translation, I knew it was a curse.

"What happened to them?"

I answered Arthen's question as I continued my primary survey of Anders. "They either fell from a great height, found themselves under a landslide of very large, sharp rocks, or were attacked by something quite vicious."

"Attacked! Attacked by what?" Jesel shot back. "Arthen, are there predators on this planet?"

"I cannot say for certain, Jesel, because, like you, I did not examine the flora and fauna data on Sigma Tau Beta except for the target species. However, logic dictates that carnivorous species would likely evolve on a planet with such biosphere diversity. Of course you recall the expression *species evolve to fill the niches that exist*; well—"

"Shut up, Arthen! Look, Borthax the slug carried a blaster. Hand it to me. If Sigma Tau grew some big nasties and Broca failed to warn us, I swear I'll unload this entire energy clip into him. Help the healer; I'm going to scout around."

I felt Arthen's bulk drop down beside me. "Healer, what can I do to aid you?"

I felt the growing distention and firmness of Anders' abdomen. "Does Anders' species have spleens?"

"What is a spleen?"

"An immuno-filtering organ."

"Yes, they do."

"Where is it located?"

"The organ you describe lies in the lower left quadrant of the abdomen, well protected by the hip bone."

"Not if the pelvis is fractured," I replied. "Anders fractured his left pelvic bone and ruptured his spleen equivalent; I am certain of it. His abdomen is rapidly filling with his own blood: he's bleeding to death."

"Perhaps the transport's medical kit will prove useful. I have it right here."

"Not unless Dr. Cra'taac is in it," I laughed harshly. "Anders needs blood volume, vascular repair, and immediate surgery."

"No Dr. Cra'taac and no vascular repair tools," Arthen replied. "But I do have wound sealant and oxy-gel."

Oxy-gel. Every battlefield medic's dream. Oxy-gel starts as a very low viscosity liquid; when injected into damaged blood vessels it rapidly perfuses the extremities and transforms into a highly stable gel, replacing lost blood volume, slowly releasing oxygen to tissues while absorbing carbon dioxide and other wastes, and tamponading closed any torn vasculature.

"Measure out four auto-inject vials and hand them to me one at a time."

Within seconds, Arthen dropped a palm-size autoloader into my waiting hand. I searched in Anders' left axilla for his subclavian artery equivalent. I found it, or what I thought was it, stabbed the short needle through his pale mottled skin and manipulated the loader in and out. After a few tries, the autoloader beeped, signifying that its tip had located the lumen of a blood vessel. In less than three seconds it unloaded its contents into the artery. Almost immediately I watched the bleeding halt from the gashes on his left arm.

Three more times I repeated the procedure, the last two unloading the oxy-gel into the femoral artery equivalents in his legs. By the time Jesel returned, I had Anders' peripheral wounds temporarily repaired.

"Have you healed him?" Jesel asked.

I looked up at her, after what seemed like hours focusing on Anders. She stood over the two duster pilots and myself, Borthax's blaster pistol held out in her right hand, sweeping it back and forth as she eyed our surroundings.

"No," I said simply, still staring at her.

She stopped her vigil and gazed at me. "No? What have you been doing since I left?"

"Trying to keep him alive. He's in shock and beyond my aid as a healer. Right now he's beyond pain."

"What about Borthax?"

"I'll get to him. He's not seriously wounded and will live without my aid. No more questions, please. We are wasting time. Bring the sled in closer. We must move Anders as carefully as possible."

"We'll take care of it. Come on, Arthen."

I nodded, watched them disappear into the woods behind me. With one last look at Anders, I turned to his insectoid companion. I took him in, the whole of him, then closed my eyes and formed a mental picture of Borthax. When my breathing fell into the rhythm of his breaths, when my heart slowed to the pace of his multiple hearts, I reached down and grasped his injured right appendage.

Razor sharp images rapidly fell into my mind, too fast for me to process. Through the clarity of time and experience, I now realize that the problem arose from the nature of my bonding with Borthax: insectoid minds organize memories and thought patterns differently than humanoids, using a logic-based hierarchy grounded in both learned and genetically inherited cues. Since that time I have refined my capabilities with insectoids and know to realign my mind as well as my cardio-respiratory system prior to a healing. At the time, though, a dense compression of memories merged into one incomprehensible experience.

I struggled to pull out from Borthax's thoughts, as though caught in a thick and clinging mental trap. Slowly, with great effort, I drew myself back out of the tangle of memories. My vision cleared, and I stood beside his crushed appendage. Kneeling down, I scooped the thick white pain oozing from between the cracks in his exoskeleton into a large mound, packed it tightly, squeezed it down between my hands until it was of a manageable size, and then pushed it into my mouth, swallowing it.

I let go of Borthax's destroyed limb and sat backward on the ground. The duster pilot woke up briefly to look at me. He raised a working left claw and grasped my shoulder. I thought he wanted to say something, then he just sighed and lay back down. Jesel and Arthen returned, dragging the sled through the last bit of understory. "The path narrowed considerably in the last twenty meters," she explained.

I just nodded at the two injured duster pilots. "Please lift Anders carefully into the bed. And no jolting on the way back. I think the blood in his abdomen has actually tamponaded the bleeding from his spleen equivalent."

Jesel and Arthen looked at me curiously.

"The blood volume surrounding his injured organ has placed enough external pressure on it to actually prevent it from bleeding more. I think the oxy-gel in his extremities has helped as well."

"That's good," Jesel said.

"It's not good at all, but it's better than tearing it open completely. We need to avoid that if we want to keep him alive until we reach the Colossus."

Once they loaded Anders, all three of us worked to get Borthax—considerably heavier and bulkier—into the bed next to his companion.

The ride back to the transport seemed interminably slow. All of us remained silent, and to the few questions Jesel or Arthen asked of me, I replied with only a yes or a no. I could sense their uneasiness, whether with the serious nature of their comrades' injuries or with my unusual behavior I did not know. But none of that mattered to me—even the critical nature of Anders' injuries or whether he and Borthax lived or died.

My entire being focused on what I'd experienced when I bonded to Borthax. I still could not sort through and separate the individual images into a coherent pattern. When we reached the transport, Jesel jumped into the levator and then manually opened the hatch of the cargo hold. I supervised Anders' transfer from the utility sled to the small medical alcove. Arthen then drove the sled directly into the hold, both of us agreeing that Borthax was safe enough remaining where he lay.

"We'll need to use the sled to shuttle them over to the Impendor's lifts anyway," Jesel said as she closed the cargo bay door.

"Let's get going," I said. "We need to get them to Dr. Cra'taac as soon as possible." I remembered the ride down and quickly added, "But none of the tossing and banging around that we did on the way down here."

Jesel looked at me and smiled. "Going up will be far smoother than coming down," she assured me, then disappeared.

Arthen locked the sled to the transport deck and then secured Borthax to the sled. He walked up to me while I monitored Anders' vital signs. "Are you coming up to control?"

I shook my head. "I should stay here with the two of them; they are not stable enough to be left alone."

Arthen nodded, gazing at either myself or Anders—or both of us. "What happened to them, healer?"

"I don't know." And at that moment it was the truth. I strapped into the seat beside the sled and listened for the whine and jolt of ignition. The floor vibrated and everything loose in the cargo bay rattled as Jesel powered up the engines. I closed my eyes and reached out for the edge of the sled, hoping to find a handle, something to hold on to through the jarring takeoff.

SIX

Iremember Jesel's disembodied voice speaking softly in my ear like an ethereal agent of some ancient religious superstition, concerned about my well-being, asking about my charges, placing greater value in my existence than the universe would ever acknowledge. "I am fine," I admonished her numerous times. "Just get us to the Colossus quickly and safely."

Even feeling the crawling itch as the transport slid through the repellant field of the staging deck failed to loosen the coiling tension in my center. Something was wrong.

Arthen appeared in the medical alcove before Jesel had locked the landing struts. While I unslung my restraining belts, he unhooked Anders' sled from the wall-mounted monitors and engaged the anti-grav drives, swung the bed around, and directed it to the hold doors. "Jesel will open them from outside," he said to me.

I quickly scanned Borthax's vital signs before unlocking his sled and following Arthen. As we waited patiently for Jesel to open the doors, Arthen hummed. His entire carapace vibrated. Starting with his mouthparts, the harmonic thrumming spread back over his head and down the dorsal shell, extending through his appendages just before fingers of sound wrapped around to his ventral plates. Here the vibrations intensified dramatically, the slightly concave surface focusing and projecting the sound waves.

"You sound beautiful," I remarked. "A pity my soft body cannot make music like yours."

"We all possess talents unique to our species," Arthen commented through the continuous waves emanating from his body surface. "This we call transing."

"I have heard of it but never experienced it."

"You cannot," his voice ululated through the vibrations. "Insectoids possess an innate desire to connect with others. We abhor isolation and must constantly reaffirm our communalism— much like the humanoid drive to exert one's independence."

"I understand better than you realize," I countered.

"You cannot," Arthen insisted. "Can you imagine millions of individuals transing at once? Can you imagine standing where you are now, feeling the vibrations of a fellow member on the same harmonic pitch halfway across a planet?"

"The scope of experience fits the spectrum of perception," I replied, quoting my master. "Certainly I will never experience what you have, but the profound nature of the experience I can achieve in a manner suited to the limitations of my body and mind. As sentient creatures we possess one unique ability, Arthen—something that spans all races, all species: we can feel awe."

I reached out my hand. He tilted his head slightly in my direction and then after a pause, reached out with his right task appendage and placed it gently over the left temporal bone of my cheek. Skin, muscle, and bone resisted the transing for a moment; then, the vibration ran across my face. After a moment of numbness, I felt a tingle and then suddenly it shot down through my torso and out of my arms and legs. Everything shook violently, down to the cells of my body. Nausea rose up from my stomach at the same time that I felt control of bowels and bladder loosen. For one second my body was on the verge of exploding.

And then it was gone. The violence submerged into a uniform harmonic vibration. My body worked like a tuning fork, humming at the same frequency as Arthen. I could feel the sound bleeding into the metal deck of the hold from the soles of my feet. I closed my eyes and listened to my body sing.

"Find the voice suited to your structure."

My eyes opened; I stared at the wall of the hold. "How long have we been standing here?"

"Our transing lasted one minute."

"It felt like a lifetime."

"Then it was a lifetime."

"Thank you, Arthen."

Before he could answer, we heard the cargo bay's locking bolts shoot back, felt the initial grind of metal skidding across metal, and then watched the reinforced door rise.

Jesel stood alone on the ramp waiting for us. The sour downturn to her mouth and the tightness of her eyebrows indicated irritation, or worse—fury.

As soon as the bay door cleared her head, Jesel swooped in, pushing between both of us and grabbing the driving handles of Anders' sled. She tilted her head as though listening for a shadow of sound and then snorted. "You have time for transing, do you? Grab the foot of the sled and do some work."

The peace I felt from the special communion with Arthen must have heightened my sensitivity because Jesel's abruptness inflamed me more than I would have expected. "What have we done to irritate you?"

"Nothing you did," she said passing me. "It's Broca. He's waiting to interrogate you."

A twinge of muscle involuntarily constricted in my throat. "What did you say to him?" I called after her as she and Arthen trotted down the ramp.

"That you said Anders and Borthax were attacked."

As I nudged Borthax's medical sled out of the transport, the captain and Dal Broca appeared on the right, standing beside the base of the ramp. Jesel and Arthen steered Anders around the captain, allowing me to exit. Then, without a word to anyone, Jesel walked away, disappearing around the bulk of the transport. I tried to quickly pull in behind Anders' sled, but Broca jumped forward and slapped his palms against the front of the bed. I reluctantly throttled back on the antigrav drive, and the Earthling terraformer slid around to face me.

"What happened down there?" he demanded.

I stared at his face and with a magnetic snap, another image fell sharply into focus in my mind, something I had struggled to see but which had eluded me until that moment. That single vision hung before my eyes like a message I could not decipher.

"Healer, I want to know." Broca's stern, tight-lipped face reappeared.

I answered hesitantly. "I cannot say for certain."

He pressed his hands down onto the edge of the transport bed and leaned toward me. "Jesel said you thought they may have been attacked." He smiled with a sneering twist. "I want to know—in case I need to reformulate the soups to address any predators that might pose a threat to Phelaan settlers."

The captain interposed himself, forcing Broca to step aside. "How seriously are they injured?"

Medical information I rattled off with practiced ease: "Borthax has lost one task appendage, has another claw crushed and several cracks in his carapace, including a nearly fatal posterior skull fracture. Anders fell into shock sometime just before we located them: his injuries are serious, including significant blunt trauma to his abdomen, perhaps in a fall of some distance that fractured his spleen equivalent; significant blood loss; potential long bone fractures and multiple deep lacerations." Something occurred to me then. I looked around the staging deck. "Where is Dr. Cra'taac?"

The captain pointed a spiked task limb to the ceiling. "He returned to the medical facilities after Jesel described the injuries." He peered down at Anders. "He appears stable. You did well, healer—better I expect than Cra'taac would have done."

"Thank you, captain, but I am not a physician."

"They are overrated," he rasped, waving an appendage. "Take them up, and we'll see if Cra'taac can prove me wrong. Then"—he snapped a pincer onto the collar of my shirt—"I want you up in my office to explain what happened down there. Bring Jesel—and you as well," he finished, pointing at Arthen.

"Yes, captain," Arthen replied.

Arthen moved Anders toward the lift, and I followed. Broca skirted the captain, grabbed the drive handle of my sled, and tried to force it into idle. I resisted enough to keep it moving forward slowly, but the terraforming supervisor refused to quit.

"You haven't given me a sufficient answer," he insisted, gripping the drive fiercely and squinting at me bitterly.

Perhaps Jesel's insolence had put me in a uniquely undiplomatic mood, but I immediately raised my hand. "I have no time for idle questions, Broca. Either help me or get out of my way." Then, without giving him a chance to respond, I peeled away his fingers and shouldered him out of the way.

I made for the lift where Arthen waited for me. From behind, Broca's voice spiked in a soliloquy of anger. As we rose quickly in the lift, that single haunting image resurfaced, a wavering shadow in my mind's eye, like a reflection on shifting water. Freed of Broca's stifling presence, I searched my thoughts for its source, expecting it to represent a past healing for which I harbored some unresolved emotional ties. Particularly brutal healings leave seeds of psychic trauma that send buds to the surface of our conscious minds from time to time. Using tools of logic, healers eliminate those buds one by one, ultimately eradicating the offending source. But as I reached down to pluck this disturbing image from my mind, Arthen interrupted.

"Are you well, healer?" he asked.

I refocused my attention on the insectoid, and my mental fog cleared: I saw clearly the tether stretching from that persistent image to another insectoid—Borthax—and the terrible reality behind the STB operation opened up before me. Secrets appeared like locked boxes set in rows, knowledge of their presence but not their contents now mine. Fear uncoiled at my center.

"Your face contorts in pain. Were you injured planetside?"

I forced a smile. "No, Arthen, thank you for your concern. I am not injured. Just the pain from thinking too hard."

"The pain from thinking too hard," Arthen repeated. He nodded. "An expression to illustrate, not to relay actual pain," he said rhetorically. "Jesel uses such statements quite frequently."

I nodded.

"May I inquire as to what thoughts are causing you pain?"

Arthen's innocent question transformed my fear into suspicion.

Who knew the truth of what was happening on STB? Did Arthen know? Was he a spy for the Phelaan Syndicate? Who better to watch me than someone I had come to trust? And if Arthen knew, then Jesel surely knew as well.

"The dusters—Borthax and Anders," I said finally.

"For their health—yes, of course," Arthen nodded, "but you kept them alive for the duration of the journey back here. You were successful in your duty. You have no reason to feel concern for them: they are now Dr. Cra'taac's responsibility."

I smiled at the terraformer and momentarily forgot the dilemma I faced. "Arthen, you are correct in the strictest sense of the word *duty*. Nevertheless, in practice, for healers, duty rarely possesses such clear-cut boundaries. Perhaps this is one of the instances where humanoids and insectoids see things differently: I will assume that your species views responsibility as possessing a well-defined beginning and end, yes?"

"Naturally. Without well-established boundaries, the actions of others will overlap with one's own, leading to conflict, resentment, and inefficiency—duplication of work and, at the same time, the risk of leaving other tasks undone. In the most efficient society, the role of one individual begins right at the moment or place that another's ends. Is that not so?"

"From the standpoint of efficiency, I imagine you are correct. But in humanoid society, as I am sure you are aware, being a member of the Phelaan Syndicate, one judges the roles and responsibilities of citizens on more than just efficiency. We all try to meet sets of standards—for actions and thoughts—some of which society dictates, and others the individual determines. So, yes, on one level my duty to save Borthax and Anders has ended. On another level, it has not: we live and grow by learning from experience. And so, as I prepare to hand over responsibility for Anders and Borthax to Dr. Cra'taac, I have reviewed what I did for them, what I could have done for them, and what I did not do for them. Perhaps the next time I encounter such circumstances, I will do better—be more efficient. Most duties in life, Arthen, are not just one duty but many duties. What I mean to say is that my duty to keep Borthax and Anders alive may be over when we arrive at the medical unit, but on the broader scale my duty to learn from them will not end."

"So their fate still consumes you—your mind—because your duty to their health includes learning from their injuries?"

I laughed. "Yes, Arthen, and you explained it far more succinctly than I did."

The lift doors opened, and my attention immediately returned to the two duster pilots. I whisked Borthax down the hall and into the medical unit, Arthen behind me with Anders. Cra'taac was nowhere in sight. My face flushed with rising anger. Arthen maneuvered Anders' bed into one of the treatment bays and locked it. Immediately the sensors registered the humanoid's vital signs. I glanced at them quickly—poor but stable—and turned immediately to Borthax.

"The utility sled will not interface with the medical bay," Arthen explained.

"Unstrap him, and we can lift him onto one of the medical tables."

"I can take care of that," Dr. Cra'taac said, walking out of the back room. He gazed in Arthen's direction. "You are dismissed." Arthen bowed and turned to leave.

I grabbed the shoulder of Arthen's foreleg. "Where can I find you?"

"I will first help Jesel clean up the transport and refuel it. Then we will check the data stream from the biologics monitors, including the new low-level atmospheric that we dropped on our way back here. Then we must meet with the captain."

"The rescue taxed me considerably. I will need to replenish myself before sitting down with the captain."

Arthen nodded a claw. "Jesel and I will wait for you in the galley."

He left, and I turned back to Dr. Cra'taac.

"You are dismissed," he snapped before I could speak.

Ignoring his order, I began a formal medical summary: "Anders requires removal of his spleen equivalent, repair of his vascular injuries, setting of fractured bones and closure of his external wounds. Accommodations should also be made for the eventuality of infection, given the serious nature of the injuries he sustained. Borthax will need reconstruction of his distal right upper appendage, growth stasis applied to his severed limb and—"

"Cataloguing the terraformers' injuries and treatment modalities is unnecessary," he interrupted, a singularly rude action in all insectoid cultures when conversing with individuals of equal or greater status. Cra'taac was sending me a clear message: *you are inferior.* "I understand your role," he continued, "and I will take care of their needs."

"I will observe, then," I countered. "In case you need an extra pair of hands."

He waved his four task appendages in my face. "I am not deficient in hands and will have no need of yours."

Refusing to back down, I remained where I stood, and the doctor seemed content to ignore me. He began the process of rebuilding Borthax's crushed exoskeleton but, surprisingly, did little for Anders other than running diagnostics and replacing fluids. He seemed more interested in analyzing tissue samples than trying to save the duster pilots.

When the urge to push aside the doctor and initiate care overwhelmed me, I stepped out and headed for the galley, knowing that any insubordination on my part would have given Cra'taac an excuse to kill me.

Arthen and Jesel sat beside each other in the galley, which was otherwise unoccupied. I pulled out the seat across from them and looked down at a familiar plate of squirming brown.

Jesel's smile betrayed her cruel pleasure. "Arthen told me that you were hungry, and I know how much you love Phelaan dishes."

"Thank you," I said as brightly as I could and, spiking a wriggling mass onto the fork, shoved it into my mouth, all in the hopes of erasing Jesel's triumphant expression.

She seemed unimpressed by my efforts and watched me intently as I chewed and swallowed. "Eat up," she encouraged me, pointing to the plate. "Remember, salty early, sweet later."

A few more mouthfuls satisfied her, and Jesel's face hardened suddenly. "Arthen and I were discussing the legal grounds for killing Broca."

"No, Jesel," Arthen said quickly, raising both task limbs. "You proposed it, and I have delineated reasons against it."

Jesel nodded. "That is called a discussion, Arthen."

"A discussion requires that each party remains willing to give consideration to the opposing view."

"Well, I cannot help it if your rigid insect mind refuses to consider my option."

Arthen forced air through tight mouthparts in a squealing protest. "You are accusing me of intransigence?"

Jesel did her best to suppress the laughter I could plainly see rippling across her lips.

"Arthen, Jesel is playing a joke on you. We all know she is the stubborn one among the three of us."

Jesel pouted her lips in mock disappointment. "Aren't you ashamed of your insect-like lack of humor, healer?"

"Why do you want to kill Broca now?"

"Why?" Jesel slapped the table and sat up, all the playfulness having instantaneously evaporated. "That fool has known there are predators on the planet and never bothered to tell us!"

I believed Jesel's incredulity because I had come to realize that she was a poor liar; or, rather, she never bothered to lie, choosing instead to tell the stark truth with very insect-like conviction. Nevertheless, out of necessity, I retreated from our friendship. Trust others and die—both Jesel and Arthen had counseled me not to trust them. I studied Jesel's face in a brief respite from her interrogation while she spoke to her insect lover. Our forays down to the surface of STB had already stimulated increased pigment deposition in her skin: the ultraviolet radiation had turned her face and hands almost as brown as my own. When she looked back at me, I had my question ready. "How do you know that predators live on STB?"

"Because you said Borthax and Anders were attacked," she replied, waving her hand at me.

"I didn't say they were attacked. I merely speculated that it was a possible explanation for their injuries."

Jesel stared at me in silence long enough that I retreated to searching through my food for an exceptionally fat worm to eat. When I glanced up, her humanoid eyes remained fixed on me like rivets.

"What?" I whispered meekly.

"You know they were attacked," she said plainly, her eyes refusing to relinquish their grip. I tried to look elsewhere, to ignore her, but I could not move.

"Arthen, why would the healer deny what he knows to be true?"

"Why would you ask me when all I can do is speculate? He sits in front of you. Ask him."

"Well?" she raised her hands expectantly.

"I cannot give you answers," I replied truthfully. "But somewhere the information must exist, yes?"

"The initial survey reports," Arthen replied.

"Why don't we look there, then?" I said quickly.

Jesel finally unlocked her eyes from mine and eyed Arthen. "We could access them from the library."

"The company will have locked them."

Jesel stood up and waved away Arthen's concern. "Since when did that stop me from examining files?" She cornered her eyes at me. "Arthen and I will find the surveyor's report, and then we will know what Broca knows." She leaned over the table and stared at me, closing her humanoid eyes for added emphasis. "Then we will meet in my quarters and find out what you know—before speaking to the captain."

The two terraformers left me to finish my meal and to stew in my own thoughts, but I had already decided on a course of action. What Jesel didn't know was that I, too, wanted to know what I knew. Only that single vision appeared to me from Borthax's healing. As much as I concentrated, I couldn't decipher any more. It occurred to me that seeing Broca, and later Arthen, had triggered the memories and that if I reconnected with Borthax perhaps the indecipherable healing would reorder itself in my mind.

As the lift dropped through the ship's artificial gravity, I considered what lie might convince Dr. Cra'taac to grant me access to Borthax. I hadn't decided on one when I entered the medical suite— to find Borthax lying on an open treatment table, unattended. A tracheal oxygenator snaked into one of his respiratory spicules on his ventral carapace, and an autoloader connected to a pump was drawing out his hemolymph, filtering it and re-injecting it. Nearby, Anders lay on a mobile treatment bay under a blue semitransparent dome of light. The activated sterility field crackled and brightened as I stepped closer, dimming the humanoid's form inside while repelling the potential threat of infection that I posed. I slid between the two injured terraformers and peeked into the adjoining room—no doctor.

Cra'taac had left his only two patients alone—both seriously injured. The captain would undoubtedly label the ship's doctor incompetent, or at least negligent, in his duties, but then I wondered if the captain might prefer it that way. What Anders and Borthax knew—and what was locked in my head, coded and indecipherable—someone on board the ship might consider inconvenient and dangerous.

Dr. Cra'taac's absence gave me an opportunity to remain hidden from suspicion, so without further consideration, I returned to Borthax. I glanced at his unmoving head and his lidless stare, then I reached for the crushed remains of a task hand. Memories cast into me on the first healing reshuffled themselves. Images flashed by more slowly, sorting themselves into a time-sequence that I could follow.

SEVEN

I watched as Anders stumbled out of his evacuation cocoon, tripped over the lip of the unit, and catapulted onto his face. I drummed my abdomen with all four of my task appendages. "Shut it, you!" he mumbled. I continued to laugh, watching him shake off the dust and pull himself up. "Sorry if I can't handle the g-force deceleration like a good bug!"

"You're defective, Anders—just like the healer."

Anders reached around behind him and worked something hidden there. He swung his arm around and pointed a blaster at me. "I'll make you defective, and then we can be twins." The blaster wandered over my body, strayed to one side and discharged several times—pwhunk, pwhunk, pwhunk. Vegetation sizzled behind me; woody limbs cracked and fell, crashing through the lower canopy. The olfactory pores edging my upper limbs vibrated with the burning smell.

"Put it away—don't want the captain to know we brought along contraband."

"Listen, you just crashed a duster, stupid! He's not going to care about a blaster. You just lost your entire pay for this job—for the next three jobs!"

"Count yourself in that, too, mole!"

"I wasn't piloting. The emergency beacon will document that you ran us into the ground."

"And the same beacon will register your flawed navigation. You directed me right through that jet stream and the downdraft disabled the propulsion units."

"Fine—call it even for now. We can argue later. Have you contacted the ship?"

"Unsuccessful—I boosted my com signal to maximum and it still bounces back off the lower atmosphere. We must rely on our personal sounding flares."

Anders scratched his cheek with the barrel of his blaster while *he eyed the massive wreckage scar. "We're both going to lose limbs once the captain gets hold of us. At least yours will grow back."*

"We can blame that fool Earthling for sending us on this ridiculous mission."

"You're right: it was Jesel and Arthen's monitor. They should have come down and found it themselves." He walked into the dense tangle of the forest.

"Where are you headed? Anders! We should collect any gear that survived the crash!"

"We've got to move out of range of the beacon," he said through the trees. "It'll swamp out our sounding flares."

Salvaged gear bounced against my dorsal carapace. I estimated that I carried twice Anders' weight with my two upper task appendages, leaving my two lower ones to chop a path through the heavy fronds and dangling vines that closed us in a prison of greens, blues, and reds. "Now you see why I prefer desert planets," I said.

"Stop complaining, bug," Anders grumbled from behind.

"I will—when you carry your share of the gear, mole!"

"Okay, I'll tell you what. Drop the gear here. Set up camp"—in my corner eyelets, Anders' flickering form peered into a small visiscreen—"we're far enough from the rescue beacon signal, and I'll search around for something to eat."

"We have emergency rations. We don't need any native food. Besides, we don't know what's safe and what's poisonous."

Anders snapped shut the cover on his signal unit and smiled at me, pocketing the device and pulling out the blaster he had stuck under the elastic band at his waist. "Borthax, stop being such an insect: show me some of that initiative that got you discharged from the military and sent out on terraformer duty."

Half the salvage dropped to the ground from my open claws while the heaviest containers I slung in a great spray at Anders. He dropped to a crouch and cocooned himself, cursing with each successive blow from the equipment I threw at him.

"*Listen to me you soft-bodied, neuro-impaired dender, no one knows about my past, and I don't want anyone to know.*" *I took one step for him and stopped.*

He lay on the ground with the missiles of equipment scattered about, pointing the blaster at me. "*I've worked with Phelaan for a long time, Borthax—I know what its like to live with insects. You bugs respect one thing, and I'm willing to use it if you step any closer.*"

"*You are right, mole,*" *I said, reaching a lower task hand into the secure pocket of my jacket and pulling out a blaster.* "*Who do you think will survive this fight? Go ahead, I'll let you fire first.*"

He started laughing, dropped the weapon and slapped the ground hard, sending up small breaths of dust. "*Come on, Borthax, help me up. I wouldn't tell anyone about your past—they couldn't think any less of you than they do now. Come on, help me up!*"

I transferred my blaster to an upper task hand and reached down with my lower pair and pulled him off the ground. He rapped me on the shoulder, slapped away the dirt from his clothes and bent down to snatch up his weapon. "*Just make camp here, all right?*" *He examined his gun, eying down the exit port into the barrel and digging away a mark on the outside with a fingernail.*

"*Don't kill anything,*" *I replied.*

He shook his head at me. "*You're such an insect. Eat rations if you want. We've got one to two days down here—first they have to realize we've crashed; then they have to argue over what to do, if anything; then they have to argue over who will do what, if they decide to do something—and I am not eating those tasteless nutrition cubes.*"

"*We stay here until contacted.*"

He waved me off and stalked away into the trees, calling at me over his shoulder, "*Arthen has infected you with his standard policy garbage.*"

★ ★ ★

I sat by a fire's edge—the flames flickered and bent in a small breeze and a shadow dimmed the light for a moment. I looked up just as Anders formed out of the darkness. "Put it out!" he hissed.

Before I could move, he brutally kicked a boot toe into the ground, vomiting a large clot of dirt and roots into the heart of my fire. Flames squeezed out from the edges briefly, then the lid of earth smothered out the red to a gray billow of smoke.

I reached out with all four task arms, swiping at Anders' feet as he stepped around the circle, flicking dirt at the glowing rim of embers.

"Idiot! I'm cold. My hemolymph is gelling in my appendages!"

I caught an ankle with the dorsal spikes of one of my arms, and he jumped away. "Use your SOS jacket," he said, leaning down to rub his ankle.

My vision had shifted in the darkness, making use of spectra outside of the visual range of humanoids. The forest surroundings flattened: Anders, and all other objects for that matter, looked as if they existed behind a semi-translucent wall tinted black. Without motion everything was invisible unless I focused intently on a spot; visual acuity tied directly to motion, which highlighted the edges of objects in yellow or red, color dependent on the speed and acceleration of movement.

"The heating element of my SOS jacket has malfunctioned."

Anders' occiput and back outlined in red as he stood up. "Use mine then." I saw the darklight goggles strapped across his face, giant multifaceted lenses distorting his face.

"What's wrong with you? I can't fit into your jacket, and you know that. I've got four task appendages, idiot." Already I could feel my ambulation appendages stiffening in the cold. "Help me up. If I don't restart the fire, my limbs will freeze up."

"No fires," he said, raising his blaster at a sound in the darkness.

"Have you eaten something native? Your neural functioning is sub-optimal, even for you."

"There's nothing wrong with me, but there's a lot wrong with

this place." His left hand pushed out of the film of blackness and threw down something at my ambulation appendages, crossed underneath my body. I reached forward and raised it up in one pincer while my other three task arms examined the object, collecting information simultaneously. A picture emerged immediately of a long pole of wood, smooth and lacking bark, with an oblong piece of stone lashed to one end using dried vines—a triangular shape with sharpened edges created by meticulous, repetitive striking that chipped away flakes of the hard material.

"A crude weapon," I concluded, dropping it in front of me. "Is this what you have been playing at, Anders, while I sit here freezing? If you must hunt, use your blaster to kill food. I give you permission."

He dropped down next to me, crossed his legs and laid his blaster in his lap. He stared into the mound of my once-fire, smoke still clinging to its top. "I didn't make it," he said.

"What do you mean?"

He stared at the dirt, spoke to it with machine-like precision. "I saw a few of them poking around the emergency beacon. They ignored me as I approached. I fired the blaster into the trees above their heads and most of them fled except for one. It raised the spear and charged me. I shot it."

"What are you talking about?"

"The natives."

"There are no sentients on this planet—it's fallow."

Anders shook his head like a slow pendulum. "No." With his fingers, he bracketed his darklight goggles and adjusted them on his face, pulled them out then pushed them back into place. "No," still swinging his head side to side. He looked over at me. "No."

Pain gripped me, sucking me backwards. Anders shrank, shriveled and twisted, then was gone. "Stop!" I gasped, dropping against Borthax. The light in the medical unit was startling after the jungle's darkness.

The crushing hold on my right shoulder picked me back up, and instinctively I twisted about, seeking the source of my pain. Traevis' four eyes stared at me, his face placid and unemotional, as though he were holding a piece of equipment. "What are you doing?"

"My job," I whispered through the pain fragmenting my mind.

Traevis closed his humanoid eyes, then released his grip. Immediately, I stepped away from him and palpated my shoulder, searching for a fracture.

"You are friends of the terraformers Jesel and Arthen," he stated blandly.

"No," I lied, standing up once the throbbing subsided and I was certain that a bone mender was not required.

Traevis reopened his humanoid eyes, and the light blue striated irises stared intently at my face, probing at my misstatement, before slowly descending along my body. "Dal Broca searches for you at this moment. Why?"

"I don't know."

"I do." He pointedly gazed down at Borthax before continuing. "He believes you suspect."

"Suspect what?" I snapped, regretting it immediately. Defensive instinct revealed my lie, destroying any chance of convincing Traevis that I was ignorant of the ship's secrets. I needed to escape—wanted to run—but Traevis held me like a predator. If I struggled or showed fear, he would kill me. So I waited quietly for the mysterious Phelaan to dispense fate.

"He believes you suspect what I suspect," he replied after a long, considered silence. "That he oversees an illegal terraforming operation."

I said nothing.

"We must talk," he said, and motioned for me to follow him. We slipped out of the medical unit and headed for his quarters. "It is the only place on the ship that I am certain is clean of surveillance units," he said quietly, waving his palm across the scanning plate.

His room was small and empty—no bed, no chairs, no table. In the very center of the room he had placed a circular black mat woven from a soft fiber, and on this he indicated that I sit. He chose to squat in front of me as I folded my legs beneath me. I shifted to find a comfortable position and winced when I pushed off the floor with my right hand, having forgotten the shoulder.

"I am sorry for the injury," he apologized. "I saw you standing over Borthax and thought you intended to kill him."

"Healers do not kill," I replied. "The Healing Order forbids it," I elaborated, expecting that he, of a partly insectoid culture, would understand the principal of abiding by laws. When he failed to respond, I appealed to the humanoid side of his nature. "I worried about Anders and Borthax. I am merely a healer, not a physician: I was checking on them—to be sure that my treatment planetside had been adequate."

"They will not die because of your efforts," he said, "whether adequate or not." Then he briefly covered his insectoid eyelets in a sweeping motion of a long-fingered hand, as though splashing water on his face to cleanse it. "You have heard the ship's rumors that I am a spy. Well, I *am*—sent by the Phelaan Syndicate to observe and report."

The tension twisting inside me loosened a bit: if Traevis meant to kill me, he would have done so and not bothered to confess first. But I wasn't ready to trust him. "Observe what?"

"Observe the terraforming operation for illegal activity," he said. "The Syndicate had reason to believe that STB was not the ideal terraforming site portrayed by the company."

"On what basis?"

Traevis raised his hands in a universal humanoid gesture of ignorance. "Perhaps the initial survey team's report." He leaned forward. "You have seen it?"

"The survey report? No, of course not," I laughed at the absurdity of the thought. "I am less than nothing on this ship, Traevis. I am the defective, so labeled by Dr. Cra'taac."

He smiled. "Yes, of course. Perhaps Jesel and Arthen have seen it. You have spent time with them."

Even though recently I had withheld trust from my two friends, I was not ready to reveal their intentions to Traevis, whose line of questioning made me nervous. "I doubt it," I answered firmly, not wanting hesitancy to arouse suspicion. "They are terraformers: they do the job they are paid to do and no more. That is my opinion of their ethic."

"Then we are left with suspicion and no evidence," he sighed, getting up and pacing in a regular geometric pattern, reminiscent of a spider laying out its web. "We must have evidence," he emphasized fisting his hands.

"You," I corrected. "I am just a healer. My duty lies solely in the role of adjunct to Dr. Cra'taac."

"Your role is to help save lives," Traevis countered, stopping his pacing design. "If by your action or inaction others risk injury or death, then you have failed in your duty."

"What can I do?"

"You can tell me what you know about the illegal terraforming operation on STB, so that I can stop Dal Broca and the captain. They are leading this conspiracy."

I felt a noose suddenly tighten around my neck. Whether knowingly or by chance, Traevis had struck at the heart of my dilemma: as a healer, I had a moral and ethical duty to preserve life. But whom could I trust?

As I silently debated, Traevis approached and sat down in front of me. "STB possesses an evolving intelligence." Simple, matter-of-fact, words spoken with certainty.

"You know this?"

On his placid, unreadable face, a hinted smile subtly peaked the corners of his lips. "I deduced it through a logical series of eliminations. I have no evidence, though."

"Can you not access the initial survey?"

"No—the company owns it. Restricted access—company officials only." His blue eyes narrowed slightly, the pupils dilating eagerly. "Why? Would that help me?"

"I don't know," I replied honestly.

"What do you know?" He laid a long-fingered hand gently on my left shoulder. "Healer, if STB harbors an intelligent species, I must know—to protect it."

The tightness constricted my throat. For a time I couldn't speak even if I chose to do so. I closed my eyes and centered myself, followed my breath, and relaxed. *It is only life*, Master Yeh's voice spoke to me. *Do not fear it. Do not fear to act.*

"They are humanoid," I said finally. "Early sentient, tool makers, hunter-gatherers, possibly having developed a rudimentary spoken language but almost certainly at a pre-writing evolutionary stage."

"You have seen them?"

"No, but Arthen and Borthax have."

"How can you be sure?" Traevis lightly squeezed my arm, as though detecting my hesitancy. "We need tangible evidence, healer."

"When I healed Borthax, I saw them," I replied. "I am certain of it."

Traevis frowned, so I explained. "As part of the process of healing, a healer enters the patient's mind and experiences the events surrounding an injury or illness through the patient's sensory apparatus. When you found me, I was reconnecting with Borthax to reorder in my mind the images from the initial healing. Before you broke the connection, Anders showed a crude weapon to Borthax—evidence of the primitives."

"Good, that's all I need to know." Traevis stood up and reached into an outer pocket of his flak jacket.

I jumped up as the blaster's handle appeared, Traevis' long fingers wrapped around the shining black metal. Spinning around, I leaped for the doorway but immediately dropped like dead weight to the ground. Through the agony, I looked up at Traevis holding the blaster in one hand and my right shoulder in the other.

He smiled down at me, laughing cruelly.

I cursed myself. *Fool!*

"Relax," Traevis said, easing his grip on my shoulder, which allowed me to hear him over the pain roaring in my ears. He displayed the blaster. "This isn't for you," he said. "It's to help me protect Borthax and Anders. First, I needed to know if they could bear witness against Broca and the captain. What about Jesel and Arthen?"

"They don't know anything." I said it without thinking and suddenly realized that I believed it. They were safe—trustworthy.

"Don't tell them anything. As far as I am concerned, everyone aboard this ship is guilty—except for you and possibly Dr. Cra'taac. You are the only non-terraformers on this ship, aside from me. Broca runs the operation, the captain runs the ship, and both of them lead the terraformers."

He released his grip on my shoulder, took the hand I held up for assistance, and pulled me back to my feet. "Wait in your quarters until I can secure Anders and Borthax. Then I will contact you."

"And then?"

He pushed me towards the door. "And then we will escape."

As the entrance panel slid open, I said over my shoulder, "The captain has a cache of weapons."

Traevis looked up at me. "What? Where?"

"In an accessory passage added to the staging deck's outer skin, behind the scavenged and junked transport hulls. I saw three thermal cannons and six heavily armored personal action suits."

Traevis smiled, briefly closing his humanoid eyes. "Good. They may prove useful. Now, get back to your quarters and wait for me."

Had I completed my training with Master Yeh—to my satisfaction and not the Healing Order's—I would have obediently followed Traevis' orders. Training instills in us a sense of duty—of obligation—and in my experience meeting other healers, that translates into a degree of passivity. This is not to say that we allow the dictates of others to overrule our core principles—to act with compassion, to avoid harming others, and to never use our skills as a coercive force—but barring any such affronts to our guiding mandates, healers generally do what they are asked to do without question.

I was not so built—or, as I suspect now, that inclination to attend quietly and without protest to the demands of others never fully established itself in me, due to the premature termination of my apprenticeship. As it was, I ignored Traevis' plan and headed straight for Arthen's quarters. The door was locked, so I requested access. "The healer," I responded to the security request.

"Denied," it stated crisply.

Curiosity flashed through my mind, but I was intent on speaking with my friends—to warn them. When Jesel's entrance refused me access as well, my growing unease surfaced. Had Traevis miscalculated the security of his room? If the captain and Broca had heard my conversation with the Phelaan spy, then they would be after me. On a ship they knew well, with the aid of the terraforming crew, they would have little difficulty tracking me down and killing me, far from the regulating eyes of the Phelaan Syndicate and the protective influence of the Healing Order. I would become another easily forgotten casualty of the highly dangerous terraforming profession.

While foolishly standing outside Jesel's quarters, I weighed my options. Jesel and Arthen might have locked themselves in their quarters, or they could have been somewhere else on the ship; searching for them would decrease my chances of escape. On the other hand, if I waited in my quarters for Traevis, the captain and Broca would have no problems picking me up and quietly disposing of me.

For a moment I considered my responsibility to Anders and Borthax, but I quickly dismissed it. Traevis had taken on that task, and there was little I could do to defend the two injured duster pilots. If they were killed, that left the limited knowledge I possessed as the sole evidence of the sentients, and their survival was paramount.

I needed to save myself, leaving Traevis, Jesel and Arthen to rely on their own survival skills. Having resolved to fully test my piloting skills, I turned to head down to the staging deck and found Dal Broca blocking my way. He sneered at the shock on my face.

"What business do you have with the terraformer Jesel?"

I improvised, suppressing as best as I could the anger driving me to punch my fellow Earthling. "Jesel requested that I help her clean up the transport after finishing in the galley."

"And you came straight here?"

"Yes—with a few errands on the way."

"Such as?" Dal Broca's question shifted his lips just slightly, transforming his sneer to an expectant grin. He knew something about my recent activities. The question was how much.

"Visiting the medical unit to check on Anders and Borthax." If Broca knew of my conversation with Traevis, he would have to pull it out of me. "Jesel and Arthen were not in the shuttle," I added quickly, "so I looked for them here."

Broca took the bait to change the subject. "I found them in the library unit."

"Good," I said, turning around to leave. That's where I'd expected them to be, if not in their quarters.

"They're not there," Broca replied calmly.

I looked over my shoulder at him. "Where are they, then?"

He nodded to the entrance to Jesel's quarters.

As I stared at the door trying to work out what was going on, Broca continued. "They are under confinement."

Tension I had worked hard to conceal tightened my lips. "On what charges?"

Broca cocked his head as if surprised that I didn't know. "Attempting to access restricted information."

"The captain ordered their confinement?"

Broca's smile shifted again, and he slowly shook his head. "I did. They work under my authority, not the captain's." He paused a moment to nod. "Jesel's quite an expert at extracting information from locked sites. She would likely have gained access to the information she sought had I not fingerprinted the files." He stepped suddenly closer—too close—and stared at my face, searching for something small and hidden. "Were you not aware of their activities?"

Broca was looking for the lie, but hiding the truth, patently antithetical to the Healing Order's teachings, had become quite easy for me.

"I try to keep myself out of illegal activities," I replied, thinking of the terraforming project on STB. Hiding the truth behind another truth was technically not a lie, I told myself.

"Communication with incarcerated individuals is a crime as well."

"I was not aware of that."

Broca stepped back. "You are now," he said firmly, before walking past me and disappearing into the maze of hallways.

Broca's warning impressed upon me the urgency of escape. With that in mind, I made for the galley to collect as much food as I could carry without raising suspicions, having no idea if the transports' onboard supplies were intended to accommodate long trips. Luckily, the ship's mess was empty, so I needed no excuses for why I was rifling through the storage bins, pulling out packages and shoving them into my pockets. With arms loaded, I reached the entrance just as the captain appeared, blocking my way. He stood on his lowest ambulation appendages, which raised his round bulk to fully occlude the exit, and silently inspected everything with his insectoid stare. "Are you preparing for a molt?" he said finally.

Before I could speak he answered his own question. "Humanoids do not molt, do they?" He leaned precariously forward, forcing me to step back for fear that he would overbalance and fall over, crushing me. "Perhaps you prepare to hibernate, yes?"

"No," I replied. "Healing drains me of energy." *Avoiding criminals trying to kill you takes a great deal of energy as well*, I thought bitterly.

"You should cook the food before consuming it."

"Dr. Cra'taac gave me only enough time to pick supplies. He said I can prepare them in the medical unit while I work."

The captain's mouthparts canted downward at the corners. "He still requires your assistance?" the words hissed with derision and a subtle undercurrent of surprise.

"Yes," I replied and stepped forward, hoping the captain would interpret my impatience as the urgency of medical need and not the fear that truly squeezed at my chest.

He refused to give way. In fact, contrary to my hopes, he raised a task appendage and pointed to the galley behind me. "We will talk now."

"The doctor expects me to return soon," I protested weakly, knowing that the captain would not release me.

"Let the doctor exercise whatever skill he possesses," the captain replied, stepping into the room and forcing me to retreat.

For a moment, when I moved aside to allow him to pass, the exit lay clear. An impulse to run jolted me for a second and was gone—despite his size and lumbering nature, the captain could move quickly on his four ambulators; I wouldn't reach much beyond the corridor before he caught me. A small black spot in my mind suddenly expanded, covering vision and blotting out hope. My chance for escape had evaporated.

He took a seat at a table and waved a claw for me to sit opposite him. I dumped the contents of my arms onto the table, leaving alone the packages bulking my coat. I dropped into the chair he had indicated and waited for my sentence. I wondered if the talk was trial and judgment preliminary to summary execution.

For a time we sat without speaking, the captain forcing air through his oral aperture that he pulled in from venting spicules along the joining ridge of his dorsal and ventral carapaces. I listened to the low drone of air sucked into the spicules, like an ancient Earthling pipe organ in reverse, overlaid with the trilling vibration of his mouthparts. I was not familiar enough with the captain's culture to understand the meaning of his display—a meditative trance? A habit of individual nature, like Earthling humming? Or perhaps simply a signal of contemplation, of reflective consideration.

Or maybe preparation for killing me. I had considered all these possibilities when the captain finally spoke.

"What happened on the planet?"

The trilling had ceased, but the spicule drone continued, though considerably quieter, like an engine pulled out of drive into low idle.

"What are you referring to, captain?"

"I refer to the events leading up to the injuries sustained by Anders and Borthax."

"I am not exactly sure, captain." And that was the truth. The captain, I suspected, could detect a lie far more readily than Broca. Caution dictated that I avoid misstatements whenever possible.

"Do Jesel and Arthen know what transpired?"

"I don't know. I haven't spoken to them since the rescue. They've been confined to quarters."

The captain seemed unmoved by my probe. Then again, I had difficulty reading insectoid faces. Before the crash and the healing— at a time when the STB project appeared routine and legitimate— I had hoped that Jesel would teach me how to identify the subtle facial cues of insectoids. That time had never come, and now I was faced with an implacable enemy.

"We will have to wait until Anders and Borthax recover," I offered.

"Will they recover?"

I shook my head. At least I could speak truthfully about their injuries. "Anders was in shock when we found him. There was little I could do except stabilize him. No doubt Dr. Cra'taac can save him, but we will have to wait and see how much brain damage he sustained."

The captain's high-pitched whistling response painfully stabbed into my ears. "You have greater confidence in the doctor than I do," he said through the grating whine. He stopped the painful sound abruptly. "Will he remember what happened?"

"Anders lost a significant amount of blood," I answered. "His brain took a heavy hypoxic hit, but I can't say how much of the damage is reversible. However, in general, humanoid brains tend to partition recent memories into highly oxygen sensitive areas. Even mild disruptions frequently lead to amnesia for recent events."

"So likely he will have no recollection of what happened."

Was the captain relieved or dismayed to hear this? Was this a question or a statement? Again, I couldn't read the connotation in his voice—the nuances of speech that for humanoids allow a single spoken word to convey two opposite meanings, and an entire spectrum in between, depending on how it is delivered. To me, most insectoids spoke without any inflections. In this case, though, I had Traevis' information to help me: I knew the captain was relieved by the news, and I predicted easily his next question.

"What of Borthax?"

"He sustained significant trauma to his appendages and had a serious posterior skull fracture, but overall his prognosis is far better than Anders. He will recover"—and, answering the hidden question I knew lurked in the captain's mind, I added—"and I see no concern for memory impairment. He will remember what happened."

The tenor of the spicule humming shifted to a faster more excited frequency. The captain's trilling resumed as well, but at a lower, melancholy pitch, rolling slowly up and down in a wide, arcing ellipse, straying close then drifting away, only to return on a rising wave.

"Thank you, healer," the captain said finally, and got up. Without another word, he left the galley.

As I watched him go, I realized with horror what I had done: I had saved myself but ensured Borthax's death. I jumped up, leaving my supplies scattered on the table, and ran for the emergency exit—a ladder contained in a shielded tube that extended through the crew levels to the staging deck—not wanting to wait for the lift.

Jumping out at the crew quarters deck, I searched for Traevis' room. He needed to know that the captain intended to kill Borthax and probably Anders as well. The bland gray door slid away as my hand passed over the identification eye. I stepped through the entrance and stopped. Someone had carelessly kicked aside the central mat, bunching it up against the wall, and in the middle of the floor lay Traevis' SOS jacket. I walked in so the door would close, hiding me from the corridor. Closer inspection showed long deep sear marks tattooing the jacket. Round holes blasted through fabric designed to resist the void of space pockmarked the coat, and through these a dark congealing liquid had sprayed. Around it lay small pools and droplets of the same substance, the surface drying into a wrinkled skin over the liquid below. Looking up I noted the telltale scorch lines of blaster fire—and knife-edged grooves cut into the wall that didn't fit the pattern of any familiar weapon.

By the look of it, Traevis was dead. But I had to be sure. He was now my only hope for escape. I needed to find him if he was still alive. Standing up, I bent down and carefully inched toward the entrance, scanning the floor for a blood trail. I discovered nothing until the door itself opened up with my proximity. Just beyond the worn line of the portal's endless travel line I saw a small drip of black/blue.

★ ★ ★

In the medical unit, Borthax lay where I had left him. Anders was nowhere to be seen—nor was the doctor. I went straight to the storage bins and began pulling them open, sorting through the contents.

"What are you doing?"

I whirled around. Dr. Cra'taac stood in the opening into the back room. I didn't hear him in the back and assumed that he was out. "I'm looking for a molecular sorter."

Cra'taac loudly snapped all four of his claws. "How did you know I have a molecular sorter?"

"I saw you earlier using one to analyze a sample from the planet."

With his stilted mechanical gait he scuttled around Borthax and came closer. "They are unavailable. They are all in use."

"All? Why do you need more than one?"

"You are irrelevant," he clicked and turned around.

He meant that information is wasted on me. I wasn't about to give in, so I invoked the one thing that would get Cra'taac's attention. "The captain asked that I bring him one."

Cra'taac's head spun around 180 degrees. "The captain asked for one?"

I left the medical unit with an extra molecular sorter the doctor just happened to find and returned to Traevis' room, approaching it carefully, watching for the captain or the seeming ubiquitous Dal Broca. The drop of blood had dried flat onto the metal deck, but with the sample scoop I lifted an edge and fed it into the sorter. After a moment, the unit squeaked, and the results appeared on the screen—Phelaan humanoid blood.

The cleansers on board the ship removed all contaminants from the atmosphere and the surfaces of the crew decks over time. That meant that even small amounts of blood dripping on the deck would aerosolize as the cleansers' vacuums periodically filtered the air. With the sorter on continuous sampling, I followed a concentration pattern of Phelaan blood spun into the air from minute spots on the floor too small for me to see and trace.

The trail led me down from the living quarters through the engineering level, passing into the staging and maintenance decks to the lowest level of the ship: the sludge hold, as it was called, served as a flushing reservoir for waste the cleansers could not eradicate, ballast when the ship encountered low gravity atmospheres, and general disposal site for whatever the ship's crew wanted to get rid of without incurring fines for illegal dumping in regulated star systems. In general, ship crews cleared their sludge holds into space just before entering hyperspace, thus preventing tracking of their dumping but creating huge swaths of floating waste, some of which formed hazardous trash belts around planets.

I expected our sludge hold to be relatively empty, since we were circling an unregulated fallow planet and the crew could dump directly into space without fear of prosecution. A magnetic lock secured the trapdoor recessed into the deck at the end of the walkway; the bulky, crude metal disk, larger than my palms placed side-by-side, spanned the edge of the door and the surrounding reinforced frame. The lock possessed no keypad, manual disengagement handles, or even a keyhole. Searching the floor and the surrounding walls, I saw no control panel. The molecular sorter eagerly peeped that the blood path led straight to the sludge hold portal.

Dropping to my knees, I peered down through the square window in the center of the trapdoor. In the meager light from overhead, a surface flickered and flashed intermittently—liquid, I realized, shifting back and forth, catching the sparse light rays slipping down through the small portal. I pulled out a small mobile light source that I carried and shone it down through the window, pushing my face down beside it. Something floated in and out of view, perhaps six meters below me.

I pressed my face closer to the transparent barrier and shifted the light in frequency with the movement to keep the object continuously illuminated. With the correct rhythm found, inspection confirmed my initial suspicion: in the waste floated a body wearing a terraformer's flak jacket; the head was gone as best as I could tell, but estimating the height of the individual based on my best guess for the distance between us, the body belonged to Traevis.

I cut the light, deactivated the molecular sorter, and stood up. A dreamy lightness floated my thoughts. I needed to return the sorter before Cra'taac went looking for it and discovered the captain had no knowledge that he required it.

Without knowing why at the time—and even now failing to understand the motivation behind the action—I navigated through the ship back to Jesel's quarters. Had Traevis' death dislodged me from rational consideration of my position? Had I accepted the improbability of escape, and therefore had emotional need driven me to seek comfort in the moments before death? Whatever the truth, Jesel's door stood before me.

I laid my palm over the red panel light by the door and spoke: "The healer requests entry."

After a moment, the buzz altered pitch, and the door slid back.

Surprised, for a moment I stood still, peering inside. Jesel lay on her resting cot while Arthen sat beside her on a low platform, all four of his ambulating appendages folded beneath his carapace.

Jesel looked up, shielding her eyes from the corridor lights, recognized me and waved her hand indicating a low voice. "Don't stand there announcing it to everyone," she hissed. "Get inside!"

She moved aside to let me sit on the bed.

"I have to talk with both of you," I said with as much urgency and as little panic as I could manage.

"Have you heard about us?" she whispered.

I nodded. "Dal Broca was lurking outside your quarters when I tried to get in earlier."

Jesel squinted at me. "How'd you get in this time?"

"I don't know. I asked for entry, and it opened."

Jesel nodded with a snort. She seemed quite subdued, I imagined from the reprimand handed down to them by Broca and sanctioned by the captain. "That bastard Broca fingerprinted the survey archives."

"He told me—quite proud of himself for blocking access."

"Blocking access?" she laughed. "That fool didn't block anything. I knew immediately we'd been tagged. Arthen wanted to cut out immediately, but I told him to forget it. We'd been marked—no escaping that—so we'd get what we came for."

"You got the survey report? Here? With you?"

"Yes and no," Jesel whispered. Still watching Arthen, she leaned close to me and whispered, "I have the file on a data cube but the information remains encrypted and unreadable. It requires decoding equipment or an authorization code, neither of which we have."

Rocking away, she gazed at me briefly. "But there must be something good in there for Broca to come after us."

I wondered what she thought the survey hid. Looking at Arthen, I gingerly probed. "What do you and Arthen think it might say?"

"Information on some predator Broca failed to account for with his soups—that's what I think. She nodded her head at Arthen. "He disagrees. Says it doesn't make sense to terminate our contracts for something simple like a missed species."

"Terminate? I thought you were just confined."

Jesel's humanoid eyes betrayed her mix of emotions: those simple pupils, the tightening of the eyelids and eyebrows, conveyed so precisely her anger, confusion, frustration, and pain. "Confined, summarily terminated, and held for prosecution. Arthen took it hard—harder than me," she whispered suddenly.

"How could you know if there was a missed species?" They could if they were part of the conspiracy—but not if they were oblivious to it.

"Arthen lives by logic, reason, and fairness," she explained quietly. "He is the most honorable sentient I have ever met." She paused for a moment, and our eyes met. In that look I saw the love Arthen confessed and she tried to hide. Then she broke her gaze and looked at her lover sitting still beside us. "He could find no logical explanation for Broca's actions, considering we had advised him not to send the dusters to retrieve the biologics monitor and considering we retrieved both Borthax and Anders alive. Broca's actions alone I think he could have accepted, given my conflict with the Earthling, but the captain's silent acceptance of Broca's decree—" She shook her head. "Arthen has endlessly run through countless explanations but has come up with no reasonable conclusion. He is falling into psychic torpor."

Jesel spoke of an illness unique to insectoid and colony-minded species, but in many ways similar to the major depressions of humanoids, usually initiated by a triggering event. In most cases the catalyst involved the failure of the individual to adequately perform a required duty—and thereby failing the colony or the society—or the inability to place an event or consequence of an action in a logical frame of reference, the primary frame of reference for insectoid societies. After the triggering event, the individual becomes obsessed with correcting an action of the past, or understanding through logic, a random or illogical—rather, I should say alogical—result. Actions under both situations are futile, which only makes the individual more determined. As a result, the victim stops eating, resting, and functioning within the society. Essentially, he retreats first from his society, then from fruitful actions, and finally from life itself. Few reports I'd read described any reversals or cures once the individual received such a diagnosis.

"Since the Phelaan insectoids share a common culture with humanoids, who tend to act on emotions, I expected that Arthen and other Phelaan insectoids would be at lower risk for it."

"They are, healer, but they can still get hung up on thoughts or past actions. I didn't want to take the risk, so I convinced him to take a sedative to rest—only a small dose, just enough to curb his instinctual desire to over-think. He calls it humanizing him," she laughed quietly. "I tell him it's getting the bugs out."

"That's Earthling slang."

"Yes," she said, smiling weakly. "The only good thing to come from your planet."

We sat on the bed looking at the sleeping insectoid terraformer, and I gathered my thoughts. I had decided to trust them: I had no choice, but beyond that, their actions and the consequences confirmed their innocence. And hope reemerged for me. With their help, I might be able to escape.

"You should wake him," I started. Jesel looked at me, and my resolve strengthened. "You should rouse him—now. I have a solution for his logical mind that will clarify the events for him. It also requires that we act soon—immediately, in fact."

Without question, she retrieved an autoloader, replaced the half empty auto-inject vial with a different one that was full, then casually plunged the large bore reinforced needle into an auto-inject port implanted at the edge of one of Arthen's articulated abdominal plates. Almost immediately the terraformer rose from the platform, extending out his appendages and sitting back on the flat ridge at the lower aspect of his exoskeleton.

"Greetings, healer. Jesel, how long did I rest for?"

"Not very long, I'm afraid," she replied, pointing to me. "Blame it on the Earthling. He asked me to revive you. So, healer, what do you have to say?"

I looked at them both and sighed: "I can explain the captain's actions for you, Arthen. He and Dal Broca are involved in a conspiracy to hide the presence of at least one, maybe more, sentient species on Sigma Tau Beta."

EIGHT

"That bastard Broca!" Jesel fumed. She paced around the room, suddenly checked her course and headed straight for me, pointing an accusing finger at my face. "How do you know? Are you part of this? Have you seen the survey report?"

I gave way until she had me backed up against the wall. "During a healing," I said, "I see what my patients see in the moments leading to their pain and injury."

"And what did you see?" Jesel hammered at me.

"When I healed Borthax—a conversation between him and Anders. Anders described seeing the natives by the emergency beacon. One charged, and he shot it. He showed Borthax the spear it carried."

Jesel stood up on her toes and stared into my eyes. Her humanoid lids closed briefly, leaving her pair of multifacets gleaming in my face. She dropped back on her heels. "Is that all you have?" she asked.

Before I could answer, she turned around and looked at Arthen who strode up on his four ambulators. "That's not enough. We need stronger evidence."

Arthen reached out and grasped my left wrist with a claw. "Did Borthax see them?"

"I am not sure." The terraformers waited for me to elaborate. "Insectoid minds partition memories differently than humanoid ones—"

Jesel tried to hide her smile from Arthen by angling away her head, but her lover was not fooled.

"Jesel no doubt agrees," Arthen said, "but do not let her amusement distract you."

"Borthax's injuries required an extensive healing. If I can re-sort the memories in my head, I will better understand what Borthax experienced."

"How can you achieve this?"

"Briefly reconnecting with Borthax in the medical unit clarified the memory I described to you. I would have stayed longer, but Traevis found me."

Jesel's smile snapped away at the name. "The spy? He's part of it!" she snorted, restarting her circular pacing. "I'm surprised he didn't kill you right there."

"He's not part of it," I protested. "Actually, the Syndicate sent him to watch for illegal activity."

"I find that hard to believe," Jesel shot back. "Arthen, does that sound like the Syndicate? Doing the right thing?"

Arthen clicked his mouthparts nervously. "I have no insight into the motivations of the Syndicate."

"What?" Jesel rapped her lover's dorsal carapace. "This from the insect who protests nearly every government action."

"You exaggerate," Arthen objected weakly.

"It doesn't matter," I interjected, stopping the meaningless argument. "He's dead."

With silent curiosity, my two companions stared at me.

"Someone attacked him in his quarters. I followed a trail of Phelaan blood and saw his body floating in the sludge hold."

"Good," Jesel concluded, breaking off and cruising about the room again. "I never trusted him, whatever his purpose on this ship."

"He could have helped us escape," I countered. "He had a blaster."

"So do I," Jesel replied, pulling the weapon from her pocket. She turned it about in her hand, then proudly held it up for me to examine.

"The captain forbids personal weapons on board the ship."

Jesel looked at me as though I was a fool and then laughed. "And so naturally you believe we all follow such rules?" She shook her head and turned to Arthen.

"Where did you get the blaster?" I asked.

"It's Borthax's."

Jesel and Arthen gazed at each other. As they communicated in silence, I sat down on the bed, relieved, feeling the tension rapidly seep out of me.

"The captain could not know of this," Arthen finally said.

"Wake up, Arthen," Jesel retorted. "He accepted Broca's punishment of us without question. The captain hates Broca, so why would he bow to his wishes without protest?"

"I cannot believe the captain would engage in such illegal activities."

Jesel waved him off. "You're missing the point. We both trust the healer: STB possesses evolving sentient life-forms. That takes STB off the terraforming list. And still here we are, terraforming the planet."

Arthen clicked his mouthparts. "The healer's argument would explain the damaged monitor: evolutionarily immature sentient species generally view alien or unfamiliar objects as a threat and would likely attack them. We can now assume the sentients targeted the monitor's sensory array."

"Yes, yes, I'm glad that your logic is satisfied," Jesel replied impatiently. "But there are more important things to focus on, Arthen." She sat down on the bed and cradled her head in her hands. "Broca knows about them," she concluded sullenly.

"Let me propose, for the sake of argument," Arthen countered, "that Dal Broca remains unaware of the sentients. This would explain both the continued presence of the natives despite several duster runs and the lack of illness or death of humanoid crew members such as yourselves exposed to high levels of Broca's soups."

"Let me propose," Jesel shot back straightaway, "that Broca's incompetence fits better: he screwed up his soups and failed to eradicate the indigenous population. Maybe they have proved more resilient than he expected, or he simply miscalculated." She got up from the bed and kicked the toe of my boot. "As for illness and death in the crew members, there's no guarantee that he didn't include some slow acting toxin that will kill us ten or twenty standard solar years from now, long after we've been and gone from STB and worked enough other terraforming jobs to mask any responsibility on his part. And then all witnesses will be dead."

"He did say that he needed to reformulate his toxins to account for remaining predator species," I added. "What I cannot understand is how he could fail to eradicate the one species of absolute necessity for the success of this illegal operation."

"Because he's an idiot," Jesel replied.

"Such personal attacks provide no useful input," Arthen admonished. He ratcheted his head to face me. "I would speculate that he either failed to account for indigenous genetic strength or he has chosen slant eradication."

"Slant eradication?"

"If he's chosen that route, I'll kill him." Jesel leaned over me and closed her humanoid eyes. With her insectoid eyelets staring at me, she said, "I wouldn't put it past an Earthling to choose a slow, painful genocide."

"So now terraformers practice genocide," I replied calmly. "Earlier you and Broca bristled at my suggestion of the same."

"Not terraformers!" Jesel snapped. She jabbed a finger at me. "Broca is not a terraformer. He's a criminal."

I sat back and smiled. "I've been having a difficult time distinguishing between the two."

Jesel reached for me, but Arthen, who had moved closer during our escalating exchange, intercepted her grasping hand in one of his claws. "No more arguments," he hissed, the first and only time I witnessed his anger. "Constructive discussions only. Wasting time on irrelevant arguments will only ensure our deaths."

He held onto Jesel's arm until his lover's tight face loosened and the tension in her shoulders relaxed. Addressing me, he said, "Slant eradication is used only in extreme circumstances with species that prove highly resistant to multiple attempts at elimination through genetic, chemical, and even radioactive toxins. Terraformers consider it a last resort."

Jesel circumvented me and wandered the room. "Slant killing involves eliminating all food sources for a particular species and waiting until they starve to death." She looked at me, and I recognized the pain in her face, grief one feels upon hearing of a tragedy that, although not experienced personally, could have been, had circumstances chosen a slightly different course. "It would explain why we haven't been affected by Broca's soups. There's no need to kill them off immediately, anyway." She held Arthen by the shoulders as he shuffled past her. They stared at each other. "Someone's going to have to clean the planet of evidence that they existed."

"The soups do have an effect," I countered. "On some of us at least." My companions turned to me, and I explained. "Liquid from one of the dispersal canisters got on Anders' arm. He requested that I heal him of the pain. I couldn't tell if the substance simply burned him or whether a biologic had infected his skin."

"Probably both," Jesel answered.

Arthen clicked his task appendages in consideration. "Your points provide a stronger argument than mine," he conceded. "We all agree then that Broca has knowledge of the sentients."

"He has more than knowledge," Jesel fumed. "He's directing the operation. He has access to the initial survey data. He's studied it, and obviously it contains information that he doesn't want others to know. Why else would he fingerprint the files and order us confined without explanation?"

"He gave an explanation," Arthen argued. "Attempting to access restricted files."

"Not attempting," Jesel smiled. "Succeeding."

"He does not know that."

Jesel waved off Arthen's correction. "The captain's a party to it as well, because he knows about everything on this ship." She turned to me. "Who else?"

"Borthax and Anders," I said, "but I believe they had no knowledge prior to their encounter with the natives."

"Possibly," Jesel replied. She rubbed her forehead and looked up at me. "Then again, they may be in on this—illegal terraforming pays well because of the risks—and may know who else is involved. We need to know what they know."

"The captain plans on killing them," I said. "He suspects the dusters know something—"

"—and even if they don't, they are injured," Jesel interrupted. "It would be easy enough to eliminate them without raising suspicions."

"Then we have to save them," I said.

"Not necessarily," Jesel said looking up at Arthen. "We can't wait for them to recover enough to interrogate them. We need to know now what they saw and what they know. The healer can reconnect with Borthax, clean up his memories, and then we can escape. Leave the dusters."

"I cannot do that," I protested. "The Order forbids consciously withholding aid to those in danger. We must warn them at least."

Jesel laughed. "Warn them? Anders is in shock and Borthax unconscious. How should we warn them—leave a note on their clothes so when they wake up—"

"The healer is correct," Arthen interjected. "We cannot leave them."

"Why not?" Jesel protested.

"The healer's memories will be insufficient. We will need Anders and Borthax as direct witnesses when we bring charges against the company."

"You would risk your career for the sentients?"

Jesel shook her head. "Nice of you to think so highly of us, but no—Arthen and I risk our careers if we do not expose them. The law states that the first to bring charges for terraforming an off-limits planet will not be subject to prosecution or to license revocation; those who subsequently come forth will be considered accomplices to the crime."

"What Jesel failed to mention is the considerable reward for those who bring the charges, if the perpetrators are successfully prosecuted—a sizable percentage of the penalties exacted on the companies and individuals prosecuted."

"I completely forgot about that," she steamed. "Let's get back to business. We need a coherent plan."

"Might I suggest it?" Arthen said. "First, we must hide the survey data: if it is found on us, we will be killed immediately."

"Agreed," Jesel nodded. "Where should we put it?"

"I suggest we transfer it to the memory of a surface monitor and then use the VR conduit to steer it into hiding. We can access it later." Arthen twisted to face me. "While Jesel and I are so engaged, you will reconnect with Borthax to re-sequence your memories. In case we cannot save them, the information you possess will serve as our primary evidence."

"How are we going to get Anders and Borthax out of the medical unit?"

"Leave that to us," Arthen replied. "We will take care of them after hiding the survey data. After you complete the reconnection process, wait for us in our transport."

"We will need help if we are to escape," Jesel said quietly. She had a task, and her mind worked furiously on implementation; a cool smoothness of her face and a determined furrow of her brows had replaced the jaw-tightening anger.

I shook my head vigorously. "I do not trust anyone else."

"Who said anything about others?" Jesel retorted. With that, she displayed Borthax's blaster.

"One blaster might help, but not enough," I said skeptically. "Not enough to get us and two wounded dusters safely off this ship."

"Well, how about two blasters? I have my own—for my personal safety, being the only falish on this terraforming mission. It's in the small utility hollow beside the bed in my quarters on our ship. Pick it up when you reach the ship and wait for us outside, in case we are pursued."

"What about the captain's store of weapons?"

Jesel laughed. "Hallucinating again?"

"I thought you knew about them."

Jesel stopped laughing and sat up. "What are you talking about?"

"The thermal cannons and the armored personal action suits he has stored in a secret compartment on the staging deck."

Arthen's antennae fluttered nervously. "The captain has these items aboard the ship?"

"Yes," I replied. "I thought you knew about them and that's why Jesel attacked me when I argued with her about weapons on board the ship."

Arthen shifted his body toward Jesel. "Thermal cannons and PAS's would greatly increase our opportunity for success." The insectoid terraformer shifted to face me. "Healer, how did you manage to gain access to the compartment?"

"I just walked in."

Jesel's eyebrow hairs fluttered, as did Arthen's antennae. "You just walked in? You mean the door said 'Hello, healer,' and opened up for you?"

"No," I admitted. "The control panel wasn't connected at the time."

Jesel smiled and nodded at Arthen. "I knew he wasn't hiding a talent for beating security codes." She eyed me and shook her head. "That's not an option for us."

"What do you mean?"

"The control panel is certainly activated now—" Arthen said.

"—and the captain has likely booby-trapped the storage unit," Jesel finished.

"In most cases, they use an access panel that acquires and analyzes DNA," Arthen explained.

"The moment one of us touches that panel," Jesel added, "a hidden laser will fry us. No, we'll have to do with two blasters."

Jesel got up and pushed me toward the entrance, Arthen shuffling behind her. "I will not fire a weapon," I insisted.

"Then prepare to die," she said flatly, shoving me at the metal door, which slid away moments before I impacted it. She ducked her head out as the portal swished open, quickly looked both ways, found the hall empty and pushed me through. As she and Arthen headed in the opposite direction, she said, "Remember, healer, jump out of the nest if you want to fly."

I looked back at her, and she smiled—a tense, close-lipped smile I had seen her use with Arthen.

Dr. Cra'taac stood at the monitor panel of an isolation chamber when I walked into the medical bay. "I came to check on Borthax and Anders," I said as casually as my tense, adrenaline-heated body would allow. The doctor patently ignored me, so I walked up to Borthax, still intubated on the treatment table we'd placed him on when we brought him up from the transport. After one quick glance to make sure that the insectoid physician showed no interest in my activities, I reached down, grasped Borthax's damaged upper task appendage, and fell straight into his mind.

"The Terraforming Council will kill us for terraforming a planet with sentient life on it," I said, my mouthparts clicking furiously. My ambulators may have frozen in the cold, but my head surged with hot hemolymph.

"Someone on the ship knows about this, and they will kill us first."

"Then we must have proof."

Anders jerked his chin at the spear.

"That's not proof," I replied. "We need something they can't flush out an airlock or convince the Galactic Council that we fashioned ourselves to cause trouble. We need a specimen—DNA."

"There's one lying back near the emergency beacon."

"Did you kill it?"

Anders rubbed his forehead. "Yes, I think so. It didn't move after I shot it."

"Alive is better than dead, but we'll take what's readily available." I tried to rise, but my ambulation appendages had frozen

with the lack of movement in the cold night. "Help me up." Anders rocked himself off the ground, then lent me his one free hand—the other tightly gripped his blaster—and leaned back hard to pry me up. I unlocked my ambulators with my lower task limbs and stood swaying for an unsteady moment until the hemolymph thawed in my lower extremities.

My head ratcheted in a slow sweep. Anders pointed to my left. "The emergency beacon's over there." Raising my own blaster, I churned toward the coruscating red and yellow bars outlining the tree trunks.

"Why don't we just ignore them," Anders asked from behind me.

"You discovered that sentients exist on Sigma Tau Beta," I replied, slashing away giant fronds and low-standing bushes with the serrated edges of my task appendages. "Galactic law prohibits terraforming on such planets. A specimen will keep us alive and provide us a reward for uncovering an illegal operation."

"Someone on the Colossus already knows they exist, Borthax. A specimen won't keep us alive. It will get us killed. If the others can ignore them, then so can we. We say nothing, and we'll stay alive longer."

I ducked under a limb too thick to cut away. "If you wanted to overlook their existence you should have said nothing to me. You understand little about the insect mind."

"Insects don't all think alike."

"All insectoids believe that duty takes priority over individual needs or desires. The whole before the parts." The wall of vegetation ended abruptly. I stood at the edge of a sharp cut; radiant heat glowed and simmered in a shallow pool over the empty ground and stretched to the left like a long unnaturally straight river. The crash site. The emergency beacon stood out from the flat blackness to my right. I marched out quickly and stopped.

Anders squeezed past me and stared at the buoy, his head swaying back and forth to produce motion at the edges of objects and enhance resolution. "It's gone," he murmured, and walked forward.

"I will never understand the humanoid concept of individual morality."

Anders ran about the perimeter of the beacon, looking behind rocks, his blaster held straight out in his hand.

"Since when did you care about morality, Borthax?" he called back to me, shoving his blaster under the buoy's edge and then peering below. "You are one of the cruelest insects I know."

I scanned the ground systematically as I slowly advanced on the beacon. "Cruelty, as you put it, is an individual's judgment of an action or actions not expressly prohibited by law. Morality is a code determined by society, not a personal set of commandments held by each citizen as he deems them fit. That's why humanoid societies often self-destruct." On the near side of the buoy, I found biped tracks everywhere and long scraping marks leading into the woods.

Anders stood behind me, searching the forest with his blaster. I could just make out his eyes behind the dull glow of the darklight goggles. He turned his goggle-head toward me. "Phelaan humanoid culture has existed for millennia."

"Because insectoid structure has tempered the humanoid tendency toward chaos. I do not care about these creatures any more than you do, Anders. I care only for the laws protecting them. If the captain tells me that the Council made an allowance for their extermination, I will gladly help you kill them all right now, but until then we abide by the regulations."

I aimed my blaster at the forest. "They dragged your victim into the trees over there." I flexed all four of my task appendages. The movement and the heat of my exchange with Anders had warmed my hemolymph and lubricated the joints, easing motion and flexibility. "We may find others—perhaps collect a living specimen."

"They'll kill us to keep this secret. I'm not dying for these natives."

I could hear his steps bring him closer to me. The heat sweating off his skin pricked the prey sensors arrayed on my arms. "No moral restraints prevent me from killing you right now, Anders. Your self-preservation instinct smells like cowardice and irritates the olfactory pores on my carapace. Laws govern the universe; they govern you as well. You cannot switch them on and off at will."

I slid my body through the trees. "Stay close; my eyes pick up heat signatures more efficiently than your darklight goggles. Give me your blaster. I'll not have you shoot me in the back trying to fire in the darkness." Anders grunted in protest but handed me his weapon. I held both his blaster and my own and used my lower task arms to move aside the leaves and branches quietly. Using the motion sensors in my legs, I calculated our distance from the beacon, and when we had walked two hundred meters, the auditory pores along the lateral seams of my body vibrated. As we moved closer, the vibrations focused into ordered patterns with repeating units. "Your sentients are advanced enough to have language," I rasped to Anders.

We moved in silently. Heat signatures flared through the black film of trees. I stopped and crouched down; Anders joined me. Through a final layer of vegetation I could see a large open space. Perhaps ten meters away, a clump of figures formed a circle, their edges flamed in the red of motion. Occasionally one rose, pulling away from the others in a long trailing tail of heat, moved around the circle, and then melded back into the ring. I counted ten, but there may have been more, as they shifted constantly.

With my secondary task hands I dialed down the blasters.

"Give me mine."

"Be silent," I hissed. "I will stun one of them. Secure it for safe transport, then I will return your blaster. We keep the specimen hidden until we get back to the Colossus. I don't want an assassination party waiting for us on the staging deck." Working my third and fourth hearts, I forced warmer hemolymph into my ambulators, stood up and emerged from the forest. As I strode forward, the

heat signatures contracted, tightening into sharp edges outlining long-limbed humanoids. Hairy heads turned up to look at me from the ground.

I shot at the edges first, systematically firing on an intersecting path to drive the creatures together. The area before me exploded, yellow-red forms shooting off in a starburst; others lay motionless on the ground, their fiery bodies quelling slowly.

"Are you mad?" Anders ran past me and stopped a few meters away, parts of him shimmering in and out of the flat blackness when he turned his head one direction or raised an arm or shifted his body. He kneeled down beside the simmering bodies.

"You said one!" he yelled at me when I approached.

"We need some choice, so I gave us some choice." Five of the creatures lay on the ground. I looked up and saw a sixth crawling away. "They should all live, if I properly estimated the stunning dose."

"How do you know what they can tolerate?"

"Analyze, plot, and execute. I based my settings on comparably sized humanoids. If they live, it was adequate; if they die, it was too strong." The heat signatures of two had nearly faded to black. "I would say I overestimated their constitutional resilience."

Anders pulled at a native's waist, lifted the edge of something invisible to my eyes. "They use animal skins for clothing." He marched his hands up the creature's back to its neck, pushing aside thick mats of hair from the occipital scalp and leaning down to examine it. "This one's dead."

I pointed out a slight native nearby. A yellow glow still vacillated at its edges. "Take that one: it is definitely still alive."

Anders crawled between the others to the one I pointed out, and he turned it over, ran his hands over its face and chest. "It's falish, I think—much smaller than the others with facial hair and heavier musculature."

"Small size will make her easier to conceal."

He pulled out a roll of binding tape and began wrapping the creature's extremities. "Why do you think she survived when larger ones did not?"

I scanned the surroundings, suddenly aware that the natives who had escaped could return. I noted a haphazard clustering of squat shapes around us. "One of the others probably interceded, shielding her from a direct shot. Just enough blaster fire bled around the other to stun her. Stop asking questions, Anders, and complete your task."

Carefully, I approached one of the squat shapes, noted its domed top and a gaping hole in the side. My lower tasks swung side to side, pulling in the strong odor of the natives, which intensified as I drew nearer. I leaned into the hole, blasters first, then quickly retreated. "We found one of their communal living areas."

Anders looked up briefly, peering at one of the huts. "A village," he replied, then went back to wrapping the falish native.

"Yes, village, as you say—which means the others will likely return shortly. We must go now. You can finish later." I set off back along the path to the beacon, assuming that Anders followed. I heard him struggling behind me, cursing the body he dragged. I retraced our steps precisely with the help of my orientation organ, and soon clambered out of the clinging vegetation near the beacon. I waited patiently for Anders, but he failed to appear.

This time I blasted a path back through the undergrowth, not concerned about stealth. The village was still deserted when I returned in search of Anders. In my fury, I burned all the structures, saw flashes of hidden forms fleeing and chased after them, firing to kill and to clear the way. They moved faster than I anticipated, their bodies more flexible to slip through the dense growth and their knowledge of their land more intimate than my own. I assumed also, as I crashed through the forest, that overriding fear of unnatural strangers wielding deadly fires fueled their speed as well.

As I squeezed sideways between two tree trunks, they attacked. Large and small stones pelted me, bouncing away harmlessly; I fired at the forms closest, wielding the heaviest missiles. I killed three before the others disappeared into the darkness. I blasted two more as they ran.

The ground rose up along the side of a hill, and for a moment the vegetation thinned. I glimpsed a line of the natives heading into a cleft in the rock wall on the left. When I neared the spot, I stopped. My auditory pores picked up no sounds above the background noise of the forest. I ducked a look, saw a long thin passage between two high walls of rock.

I entered facing the opposite side, one blaster facing forward and the other facing backward. The passage curved back and forth for fifty meters then receded into an open space ten meters long and seven wide. Five mature natives with long hair curtaining their faces crouched over Anders' prone form. They stepped back from him when they saw me. As they made no move to attack, I did not fire but kept several eyelets on them while I knelt beside Anders.

He failed to acknowledge my presence with tactile stimulation, grunting with pressure applied directly to his sternal bone. His chest rose regularly, breaths shallow but unlabored. A large bluish knot protruded from his left forehead; I noted tears in his outer garments, slash marks with underlying lacerations of varying severity but nothing that appeared life-threatening. I reached under him with my secondary tasks, and while they were wedged there, my auditory pores vibrated. I had kept my eyelets on the five, and they had not moved. I shifted my head to the cleft through which I had entered—saw nothing. As I prepared to lift Anders, a fine mist of small particles dusted my antennae.

I gazed upward. The rock walls rose up forming a deep well, with the paling early morning sky visible above in the shape of a humanoid eye. Perhaps twenty meters up the near side a small niche appeared, and in it a large boulder. As it tipped forward I saw the heads of two natives who pushed it.

I fired on the five as they charged forward then slung my body over Anders. My visual cortex shut down for a moment with the impact, an unfortunate insectoid sensory reflex. Anders' body lay below the wall, and had the stone fallen unimpeded it would have crushed us both. However, an outcropping halfway down deflected its course, so it landed on my right posterior skull and dorsal carapace then rolled off, crushing the right primary task claw that held one blaster and severing the secondary limb below the second joint.

Immediately I shut down my second heart, the one that pumped hemolymph to my right thorax. When I tried to raise my head to the right, I heard a cracking and registered dimly the sensation of my shell peeling away from my inner skull. I lowered my head and slowly rotated it to the left until the lateral array of eyelets of my left eye could see the rest of the clearing. Gray movement—two creatures lay bloodied and broken on the ground; a third hobbled in a dragging circle, whimpering. A fourth appeared with a long spear similar to the one Anders had found. A long seared black scar ran diagonally across its chest. It sniffed at the wounded creature, then at the two dead ones on the ground and finally at me.

It made stabbing motions with the weapon, then tentatively stepped toward me. My left primary task appendage moved well without pain, so I raised it over and behind my head and carapace, trying to point it as accurately as possible. I waited until it got within three meters then fired. Just before the blaster discharged, the release clicked; in that instant, the native stopped and leaped out of the way. I watched the blaster deliver a fatal shot into empty space.

My assailant slid beyond my sight, and I panicked: flailing about, I shot wildly, hoping to catch him with a random blast. He reappeared very close, raised the spear in both hands and drove it hard against my carapace. It hit the shell and slid down, tracking into the first joint of my secondary task appendage on the right.

I yelled and fired repeatedly. One blast glanced off the polished stone spear head as the creature raised it to stab me again, the discharge blossoming over its face. It screamed, dropped the spear and toppled out of my view.

I woke up to the ground moving. It shifted under me, I heard a muffled sound, then recognized Anders' voice. "Borthax, get up. You are crushing me."

Anders pushed against my ventral carapace but had no chance of moving me. I flexed my ambulators, found them functional and dug my claws into the ground and slowly propelled myself off the humanoid. The stone still lay over my right tasks. "You will have to move it," I said, nodding at the boulder.

Anders stepped over me and examined my right side. He rubbed at his contusion and blinked up at the early morning sunlight. "Why do you think they left us?"

"Speculation is irrelevant at this moment. I have lost one task arm and the claw of a second is crushed; my carapace is cracked and my skull as well. I have contained the hemolymph loss as well as I can but I am likely to die of hypothermia and shock soon. Any more questions?"

Anders shook his head and turned to the stone. "It's too large for me to move."

"Can you lift this one end, lying on my arm? Just shift it enough to relieve the pressure: I may be able to pull my arm out."

"I will try, but I can manage only once, so you better take the chance when you see it." He rubbed the right side of his chest. "I think some of my ribs are broken. It hurts to breathe." He surveyed the stone, then cupped his hands below a chin of rock projecting out, leaned down and drove upwards.

I felt nothing. Anders groaned and drove harder. Still nothing. His feet began sliding backwards in the dirt, and I watched my opportunity fade. Then, I felt a slight release, and I pulled back hard. A tearing sensation worried me: I expected to pull away another amputated limb. Then it came free, Anders rolled aside, and I raised an intact arm, the claw severely crushed and the shell sheared away in places during the extraction. The blaster remained under the boulder.

"Help me up," I ordered. "I am unstable—unbalanced—with the injuries all on one side. In addition I have shut down the heart supplying the right half of my shell."

Anders dragged me up, and I pointed to the exit. He studied it for a moment and then turned to me. "They will ambush us as soon as we wedge ourselves in there. There'll be no hope of defending ourselves."

"Ambush or slow death by hemorrhage—I choose the first."

He beckoned with his hand. "Give me the blaster. I am in better shape than you are."

"I keep it, soft-body. Despite my injuries—which would have killed you—I am still better equipped to survive another attack, based on the weapons they utilize. You go first; I will direct you."

We squirmed through the rock cleft and struggled down the hill and through the burned village without being ambushed. Anders stopped to look at the destruction, but I continued on toward the beacon. "You burned it all," he said, catching up to me.

"You want to know why, I suppose. You moles always want to know why—never satisfied to act, always an explanation needed."

"I don't care about your reasons; I'm just impressed." He smiled and patted me on the shoulder.

"You approve then?"

"Wish I had done it myself. I suppose now you are ready to ignore them and get on with the terraforming."

"Your personal morality again. Somehow natives attacking intruders justifies extermination of those natives by the intruders—have I correctly explained your logic?"

"All right, I'll shut up, but we still don't have a specimen."

"First let us assure our own survival, then we can consider obtaining another specimen. If needed, we can collect the bodies of the ones I killed."

We entered the charred gap of the crash site slowly, alert for signs of ambush. "Perhaps we will be safer here, by the beacon. The natives may fear it now and stay clear." I lowered myself to the earth and leaned back against the large black saucer. "I must rest here. The activity has increased my hemolymph pressure, and I have begun to hemorrhage again."

"I will collect our supplies," Anders replied. "I will need the blaster. Hand it over."

I hesitated, then stretched out my appendage to him. He took the weapon and headed for our campsite. "Leave everything except food and the medical kit," I called out to him, and he waved at me.

★ ★ ★

I passed out and dreamed the frizzling echo of a blaster firing. The dream sound activated my visual cortex, which sorted through multiple inputs: the wide swath cut through the forest by the duster; the glaring heat of the midday sun falling directly on my ventral shell; small insects curling through the air; volatilized aromatic compounds in the supra-visual spectrum steaming off the surrounding vegetation. I again began to drift off to the sounds of the forest when another blaster discharge shook me. I grabbed the edge of the beacon, pulled myself up and lumbered into the forest in the direction of the campsite.

I crashed through the undergrowth and halted: a mass of the natives crowded the small area we had cleared. Others charged in from all directions; stones bounced off my carapace. For a second the writhing pack parted, and I glimpsed Anders stretched out on the ground, entangled with two motionless creatures. The natives closed around him again, wielding spears and heavy clubs; some had gauntlets fashioned of jawbones lined with sharp, barbed teeth.

Anders disappeared as the creatures collapsed upon him. I lowered my head, spread out my left tasks, and drove into them. The dorsal spikes on my appendages struck soft bodies, but a sharp *searing pain though my cracked skull overwhelmed me. Those in front gave way suddenly, and I fell forward, my ambulators losing hold on the earth. I levered away with my tasks, regained the ground and pushed up with my ambulators. Just as I rose, something struck me hard on my right side. One of the creatures held me fast and drove me to the left, my right arm pinned above my head. I reached around and plunged the dorsal spikes of my left claw into his face. He bellowed and released me. Anders' blaster flashed through my peripheral eyelets. I snatched the weapon from the ground with my left primary task and pivoted.*

A mass of them charged. I raised the pistol, but they hit me before I could fire. I fell over, and two of them lunged onto my left tasks. Another hairy one appeared behind them, raising an enormous stone to bring it down on my head. I twisted my claw inward and fired, sending the two backward into the third, who lost his balance and plunged away, dragged by the stone he held aloft. I blasted randomly around me, firing as fast as I could.

Suddenly, they disappeared. I called to Anders but he didn't respond. Keeping one eye on the surroundings, I examined the humanoid: he was breathing poorly and didn't respond when I shook him. I got up slowly and picked him up with my left secondary task, pulling, pushing, and sliding him onto my dorsal carapace, his limp arms dangling around my neck. With one functioning claw I managed to hold the blaster pistol and his hands. I could hear them behind and around us as I hobbled forward. Rocks and other sharp missiles fell around us. I turned and fired when pursuit brought them out from the cover of the trees. Over the ringing in my auditory pores I thought I heard the sonic boom of a ship approaching.

I detoured sharply left off the thin worn path and struggled through the heavy undergrowth. Another trail appeared as a slim break in the vegetation. I turned onto it and lumbered on as fast I could move. No more rocks or missiles came at us, but my suspicion of attack hadn't diminished. I turned to look back, and my left ambulation appendage struck something. I tripped, throwing Anders away from me. Somehow I held onto the blaster and prepared to fire at a sea of natives that I expected to wash over us. None appeared, and for a brief moment I lay back exhausted. My visual cortex wavered and then shut down.

I sat up suddenly and painfully. Something—a noise—had reactivated my eyes and my consciousness. I peered at Anders. I couldn't see him breathing. A shadow cast itself across my vision; something moved to my right. The natives had returned. I pointed my pistol and warned them off. One reached for the blaster, and I warned him again, tried to fire, but my claws locked. Then it spoke. I heard healer *and* rescue. *I lay back, and my visual cortex shut down.*

NINE

Borthax's mind slowly ebbed away from my own. I opened my eyes and removed my hand from the insectoid's claw in order to steady myself against the treatment table. Coming out of a healing often disoriented me, like holding my breath and diving underwater—too long in an alien, often hostile environment starves one's mind. After blinking away the black spots and dizziness, I looked around the room. Dr. Cra'taac had left me alone in the medical unit. I walked slowly to the door of the isolation chamber and pressed my face to the transparent viewing panel. Anders' vague form lay in the stasis cocoon in the center of the small circular room.

As my mind cleared away the shock of reordering the memories from Borthax's healing, urgency grew. With a quick glance at Borthax, I left the medical unit and made for the lift. My footsteps echoed in the empty hallways, and, standing silently by the lift access, I felt the column of air pushed out by the rising mobile chamber.

A sudden fear bore down on me as the lift approached, the whine of its propulsion turbines swelling rapidly. Traevis' warning of secret watchers chased me down the hall as I ran, imagining the captain and a team of armed terraformers emerging to confront me.

I flipped open the circular cover of the emergency ladder set in an alcove at the end of the corridor and dropped through the opening, catching my hands on the lip to stop a free-fall descent. Blindly I searched with my feet for the ladder rungs, found them, and pulled the entry portal closed before descending two levels to the staging deck emergency access tube and shimmying through it the way Jesel had taught me.

I stood in the shadows of the heavy curving bulkhead that partially obscured the tube entrance from the cavernous deck, watching and listening. When I heard nothing except the regular circular drone of the ship's engines, I waited a few moments longer. Something was wrong. I could feel it. Even during transit between job sites, terraformers worked on the staging deck. I had never found the impossibly large hold—the size and shape of a small asteroid—completely empty.

Ambush. The thought projected into my mind like a juggernaut, rolling over and crushing away all other considerations. I had no weapon to defend myself: I needed to get to Jesel's ship and find her blaster. Poking my head out past the giant metal structural fin, I could see a row of neatly aligned dusters. The transport was hidden somewhere in the distance. The dusters sat high on their landing gear, affording me no place to hide from view on the way to the transports and giving a clear shot to anyone kneeling on the deck floor.

I searched for Master Yeh's calming mantra and chanted it in my mind to release the growing tension. The tightness had begun to loosen when an electric jolt shocked my jaw.

"Do you have the blaster?" Jesel whispered in my ear at the same time that the signal booster warmed on my chest.

I huddled back into the darkness. "No," I hissed back. "I haven't reached the ship yet."

"Why not?" Jesel blasted back. "We don't have time, healer."

"The staging deck is empty," I replied, feeling the tension begin to rise again.

"Great! No one will see you. Get on the transport, pick up the blaster, and wait outside for us."

"The staging deck is never empty, Jesel. This is an ambush."

"Good. Flush them out before we get there. Hopefully you can reach the shuttle before they kill you. I've hidden the survey report, and we are heading down to medical right now. Out."

I suppressed the fury flushing up through my skin and focused on my next step. With a resigned sigh, I realized that I had no choice: if I didn't flush them, they would flush me. I pivoted around the bulkhead and ran along the wall, following its curving line past the dusters, wincing and ducking as I went, anticipating the distant pop of a blaster and the searing burn of the energy projectile hitting me.

With surprising speed, I reached the transport, the first in a line after the dusters, turned sharply left and slid under the squat bulk of its port side. I waited, panting for breath, for the sounds of running steps, of shouted orders, of the hunt, but heard nothing at first except the familiar low hum of the engines. Then I froze as another familiar hum appeared in the soundscape—the whirring of vacuum motors.

Slowly, I crawled to the edge of the ship's underbelly and peered up at the port side levator: someone had slid away the radiant heat shield of the access control panel and had activated the unit.

While the panel lights blinked green in my eyes, I frantically tapped open the communication line along my jaw. "Jesel!"

At first I heard only static in my ear. I called a second and third time. After a long pause, as I prepared to call again, Jesel answered. "Not now, healer."

"Yes, now!" I insisted as quietly as I could make it and still communicate the immediacy. "Someone's in the ship!"

"What do you mean?"

"The levator was active when I arrived—someone's in the ship."

"Leave there now," Arthen's voice crackled over the com. "The blaster is not a priority."

"Yes it is!" Jesel spit back. "Don't listen to Arthen. We need that weapon. Don't adjust the levator controls, go straight to my quarters, get the blaster and leave. Forget my ship. We'll meet you down on the maintenance deck."

"Did you get Anders and Borthax?"

"What's left of Borthax, but Anders—no."

"What do you mean? I just saw them. Cra'taac put Anders in the isolation chamber, and Borthax appeared stable before I left."

"Well, medical is destroyed now," Jesel said blandly. "Hemolymph sprayed everywhere, blaster impacts pocking the walls, even laser scorings across the floor. The isolation chamber door was blasted off, and the entire inside was incinerated. No time to talk. Just get the blaster."

Static buzzed in my ear again, and the signal booster cooled on my chest. I lay on my stomach under the transport, listening over the levator's vacillating hum for sounds of movement. How does one move silently, hide in shadows, become invisible? I knew nothing of stealth, realized that I felt like a prey species asked to enter the den of a predator.

Summoning what calm remained in me, I dug up everything I recalled from Master Yeh's teachings on focusing one's mind into a single point that could then cut through all adversity. Finally, I set myself before an image of my master and felt my body relax, my heart rate slow.

When I opened my eyes, I glanced across the floor of the staging deck, shimmied out from my hiding place and quickly jumped under the giant tube extending out from the side of the ship. The levator vacuumed me up into the hold, and I landed on my feet, grateful that my body had grown accustomed to the terraformers' systems.

Quickly, I skirted through the empty hold and hid behind the doors, peering up at the multifaceted eye in the center of the ceiling. No green glow at its core meant it was not activated, which meant no one in the control room could see me crouching inside the entrance. Relieved, I leaned against the wall and prepared to move. The lights flickered faintly, a diffuse halo around each one: I guessed that activation of the levator had automatically powered up auxiliary systems in preparation for the crew's entrance.

When I pivoted around to face the door, it beeped and slid away. The ship stretched and corridors lengthened as I moved slowly, stopping every three steps to listen for a voice or the sound of footsteps. I avoided the lift and the noise it would generate, choosing to climb up the auxiliary ladder one level to the crew deck. Jesel's door slid open as I neared it, and I jumped in and locked it.

A feast of disarray greeted me—clothes jumbled together everywhere, memory cubes strewn on the floor and on the work table, and boxes of equipment stacked around the room, the contents of some escaping out of the partly open lids. At first I thought someone had ransacked the room, then realized by the nature of the confusion that it perfectly represented Jesel's character.

Jumping onto the bed, I leaned across to the hollow on the right side, fishing my hand into its open mouth: I pushed my fingers through wadded underclothes, scooped out more memory cubes, pulled out coils of wire, a visi-screen, and a pair of storm goggles, then rapped my knuckles against the bottom without feeling the micro-studded surface of a blaster grip. Just as I grabbed the edge of the hollow to push myself up, I heard the door lock click.

I jerked up and twisted around. Someone was trying to enter. "Where's the damned blaster?" I hissed into the com unit.

"You haven't found it yet?" Jesel replied.

I dove down beside the bed and struck my hand into the left utility box, nervously glancing at the door, expecting it to open at any moment. "A sniffer mech couldn't find it in this mess." My fingers pushed down through more junk, an occasional memory cube, and many other oddly shaped objects that I couldn't recognize by touch alone.

"I'll be sure to keep my quarters clean from now on," Jesel replied with a sarcastic twist.

The muffled beeping of the door's access panel reached me, followed by a terminal click. "From now on won't matter. Someone's trying to override the security code." Desperately, I struck for the bottom, trolling for something familiar. My fingers brushed across a length of cool metal. I grabbed the barrel and inched my fingers back until I had found the handle. I grasped it firmly, pulled it out, and stood up, pointing the blaster at the door.

Nothing happened. The clicks had ceased.

"Well?" Jesel's exasperated query came through after a few moments of tense silence.

"I found it—finally," I said, not taking my eyes or concentration off the door. "And it seems like whoever it was has given up trying to get in."

"Then leave," Jesel snapped back.

"What if they're waiting outside for me?"

"Shoot them," she said simply. "Don't say hello, ask questions, or heal them. Just shoot and keep shooting until you are certain they're dead."

"I would advise that you wait briefly before you exit," Arthen's even voice came over the com. "Give them time to leave the vicinity or get frustrated and abandon an ambush."

"Thank you," I said, needing the confirmation of my own inclination not to run out firing haphazardly at nothing or, worse, running directly into the pursuer.

So I waited. No more clicks, no sounds from outside, only the steady electric murmur of the slumbering but activated ship. After ten minutes, blaster held just beside my right cheek, I released the lock and clung to the wall beside the opening door. A few seconds and I stuck out the blaster tip and pulled it back in. Nothing. Carefully, I looked out, down the hall, dodged back in, back out with a quick glance up the corridor and back in again. Nothing.

I slipped out, slid across the narrow passage and kneeled down, waiting for the door to close and the light from Jesel's room to disappear, hiding me partly in the shadows thrown by the dim emergency guidance lights on the ceiling. Still nothing to see. And nothing new or unusual to smell in the stagnant air of the transport. I reoriented myself to where I needed to go and slowly stood up.

As if recognizing my intentions, Arthen spoke through the com, his voice breaking the silence and startling me back to a crouch. "Don't use the activated levator," he advised. "Whoever is on the ship will now monitor it, if they suspect you are on board. Find the auxiliary unit in the secondary hold and exit from there."

Nervously I peered up and down the hall before answering. "Won't they detect the activation sequence?"

"Yes, but you will be out of the ship before they can reach you."

I changed course, going up the corridor and cutting down a connector passage to the other side of the ship before finding an aux ladder down to the hold level. The air in the access passage down to the secondary hold reeked of musty disuse. I wondered if the environmental filters had ever been changed; the smell was so potent that it made my eyes water. Using my forearm to wipe away the tears clouding my vision, I slid down the slippery corridor to the hold door.

"The environmentals need repair," I said, choking on the thick, dank odor as I reached for the access panel.

"There's nothing wrong with the environmentals on my ship," Jesel shot back. "You should know that."

I had to store the blaster in my pocket while I struggled to clear the growing flow from my eyes and at the same time punch out the security code.

"Jesel does all her own maintenance," Arthen reminded me as the hold door slowly slid aside.

"And something's leaking over the deck down here," I added as I stumbled into the empty storage bay. The horrible odor now burning my eyes originated from within the hold; it was so intense that I had difficulty breathing.

Vaguely I was aware of an instinctual fear warning me. I reached with a clumsy hand for the blaster, felt a rush of air pushing down from above and looked up just as something black dropped from above, slamming my head into the hard dimpled surface of the deck.

I remember the sensation of being dragged through corridors and over the thresholds of multiple doorways. My eyes gradually cleared as the watery discharge subsided, and my breathing eased as the musty air gave way to the not pleasant but not toxic familiar filtered ship atmosphere.

The dark unfocussed shape flung me onto the floor of a familiar place—the main hold. I recognized it as my vision and senses rapidly returned. Craning my neck up awkwardly to gaze over my supine body, I saw Traevis leaning on the doorframe, smiling. "What are you doing here, healer?"

The shock of seeing him passed quickly, replaced by overwhelming fear. "You're not dead," I whispered.

He nodded, his frowning smile that of someone considering a new or unfamiliar taste. "Thankfully so." The smile vanished. His hands tightened, and his jaw tensed. "What are you doing here, healer?" he repeated.

My arms and legs tingled where a moment before I had felt nothing. "My body feels . . . odd," I said aloud to myself.

"Ah, yes, that is my fault," Traevis said with an overly sympathetic smoothness. "The Phelaan possess a generally ignored vestigial stun organ that once produced a volatile agent used to incapacitate prey." He swept his long, spider-like hands across the pores patterning his face. "I had them reactivated and genetically enhanced: they produce a rather foul-smelling aerosolized compound that paralyzes—and in some cases, such as your own, alters the mental status of—targets. The odor is an unfortunate by-product of genetic modification, but I think it is outweighed by the chemical's functional advantages."

My arms had regained enough strength that I managed to push myself up to a sitting position. "Quite a useful asset in your line of work."

Traevis, who remained in the entrance, had rotated his right hip and drawn up his leg to the side, placing his boot flat against the opposite door frame, a position anatomically impossible for a humanoid without insectoid ancestry. For a brief moment, I thought I saw his face transform into a more brutal, angular visage, spiked and armored, and then it was gone, replaced by the familiar hard and smooth mixture of humanoid and insectoid. "What are you doing here, healer?"

I shook my head to clear the last wisps of confusion and distorted visions from my mind. "I—I was picking up some essentials for Jesel."

He rubbed his jaw while staring at me. "Really?" he said. "And how did she communicate her needs?"

"She told me," I replied honestly.

"And how did she do that if Broca terminated her contract and the captain confined her to quarters?"

I was caught. To give myself time to think, I rolled to the side, drew up my legs and worked my way up to a kneeling position. When I didn't answer, Traevis stepped into the room. The faintest breeze from his loosely flapping SOS jacket brought to my nose the pungent smell that had overwhelmed me in the aux hold.

"It seems that we will need to talk more."

My chest warmed, and Jesel's voice whispered in my ear. "Are you out yet?"

"Traevis, I don't have time for lengthy discussions."

"Traevis? I thought he was dead!"

"Tell me, if it wasn't your headless body floating in the sludge hold, whose was it?"

Traevis halted and reached back with one leg in a manner that appeared altogether insectoid to prop himself against the wall. "Anders."

"Get out of there, now!" Jesel bellowed into my ear.

"I concur," Arthen's calmer tone came over the link. "You are in considerable danger. Traevis has already killed Anders and seriously wounded Borthax."

Squatting on my haunches had begun to settle me, slowly driving out the fear of Traevis' surprising rebirth. "But I just saw him in the isolation chamber."

"A holographic projection," he said distantly, his eyes straying from me. "Anders' disappearance would arouse suspicion. Mine—less so." Traevis rose from his casual stance and fixed on me. "You were just in the medical unit?" His left hand disappeared into an outer pocket of his SOS jacket.

"Kill him—kill him!" Jesel yelled into my ear.

"Use the blaster," Arthen said. "Aim for his head and fire continuously until he is dead."

I felt my calm melt away, and instinctively shifted my right side away from Traevis to hide my hand reaching into my pocket for the blaster.

"Did you reconnect with Borthax?" The Phelaan took a step forward and closed his humanoid eyes. I wondered if this was his ritual before killing someone—shutting down his humanoid side and submitting to his logic and duty-driven insectoid inheritance: the executioner sharpening his ax in anticipation of the cut.

"If you want to kill me, you are welcome to: I gave Jesel and Arthen a disc containing a transcript of my healing."

"Hey! Don't send him after us!" Jesel protested into my ear.

Traevis withdrew his hand from the pocket. His large palm and spidery fingers obscured something smooth and gray.

"You are working for Broca?" I asked without thinking, feeling suddenly unencumbered by the prospect of dying.

The question struck Traevis oddly, impeding him like a wall. His humanoid eyes opened. "I do not work for the Earthling," he snapped indignantly. Shoving his left hand back into his pocket, he whirled aside and paced across the entrance. "I would never work for that fool," he continued, so engrossed in my inadvertent insult that he ignored me. "The company wouldn't find itself in this mess if it hadn't used exceedingly poor judgment in naming him leader of this project."

Fear jolted me awake, and like the prey that feels the restraining claw of its captor unexpectedly lighten, I stood up and pulled out the blaster.

Traevis stopped his circular migration two meters away and stared at me. "I advised them not to trust an Earthling with such a sensitive operation. Now I have to correct his mistakes." He noticed the blaster pointed at him, and a smile opened up slowly just as his humanoid eyes closed.

I swung up the blaster, aiming for the middle of his face, and fired.

In a blur of insectoid speed, the Phelaan assassin dodged the shot and charged. I fired a second time, searing the back of his hand.

Before I could get off a third shot, he hurtled down over me, the black SOS jacket blocking out the overhead light. He grabbed my wrist, squeezed and twisted.

The bones snapped under the strain, and my hand fell open. I lay on the floor again with the body numbness now rapidly dissipated by the searing pain of my broken wrist. Traevis picked out the blaster from my limp fingers and leaned back, grasping my collar to drag me up from the deck. With his humanoid eyes still closed, he tossed the blaster behind me and pressed the barrel of an unfamiliar weapon against my temple.

The cold metal pushed into the soft hollow of my right temple, just above the zygomatic arch. I could feel the circular void of the barrel's opening and my skin tenting up into the space. In a desperate effort to escape, instinctively I reached up with my left hand and tried to pry open the grip that held me steady and immovable. As my fingers slid over top of the hard tight skin of Traevis' hand, they encountered the wound from my poorly aimed shot. Instinctually, I probed its raw edges. I felt a gentle tug, followed by a distinct pull. Then an overwhelming magnetic force sucked me away into a long hidden place in my mind.

Someone screamed, heat seared my face, and sand swirling in thick clouds choked my nose and mouth as I breathed. Something fell against me. I opened my eyes, and sand invaded. I tried to rub away the sting but everything was so dry. I had no tears, my eyeballs grinding through the grit as I moved them. I coughed out sand and more entered than I expelled. More screams cracked, fluttered, and died in the brutal winds. Squinting carefully, cupping my hands bedside my eyes, I managed to see a form lying to my right. Around me other huddling forms swayed silently. With a wail, one collapsed.

A sharp, stabbing report struck through the confusing mix. I bore the pain of the sand and looked for the source of the sound. A dark shape quivered in and out of sight, then materialized out of the sand storm. First I recognized the blaster rifle, then the uniform. Military authorities. Head, body, and arms were encased in storm suits. I'd seen them before, marveled at how they repelled sand, the burning rains that dissolved metal and every other toxic atmosphere our planet could throw at aliens unfit to live here.

The rifle swung back and forth firing again, the blaster melting red holes in the dense fog of dust. Each time the rifle fired, one of the swaying forms exploded, and at the instant it disintegrated, before the sand could sweep in and erase it, the air was pure and clear in a perfect silhouette of its shape.

One by one my friends and family died around me, and I felt with each blaster discharge a piece of my existence crudely cut away.

Something struck my side, toppling me. Suddenly I felt my heart beating—in a rush to get somewhere it seemed—frantic, impatient. Life slowly faded from the edges toward the middle, until only my eyes and ears remained, the last windows of consciousness in my wavering house of flesh. A head appeared in my vision and descended slowly.

Traevis' smiling face peered down at me. "You missed one," he said, and someone replied nearby, too muffled by a roaring I had not noticed before.

"No—leave this one alive. If he manages to live he can serve as spokesman for our intentions." I watched Traevis retreat, eventually consumed by the contracting darkness. If I closed my eyes I didn't know it.

★ ★ ★

The roaring in my ears rolled fiercely toward me, and I waited patiently for the waves to strike, knowing somehow that they would never reach me. Instead, the gathering storm passed over me and flung itself fully upon Traevis.

Our minds snapped apart suddenly. I was prepared—how many thousands of times had I felt the pull at the back of my mind and then the sharp cutting break?—but Traevis was not, could not have been. And in that rare twist of fate when the tide shifts unexpectedly, the advantage swayed in my favor. I tore the weapon out of Traevis' stunned grip, twisted it around awkwardly, and at the same time threw my right elbow up under his jaw.

He recovered quickly and reached for the weapon but moved a second too late. My thrust overbalanced him, and he stumbled backwards.

I pressed the firing stud, and a solid blood-red beam erupted from the end of the weapon, burning a knife-edged line through the bulkhead curving above me, missing Traevis' head by a hand's breadth.

The Phelaan sprang onto the wall of the hold, scurrying on all fours to sit poised just above the closed entrance. He reached down with a spindly arm, breaking the plane of the access field just as I fired again. The second beam caught the unfastened collar of his jacket, fragmenting the discharge over his back and head. He swung down as the door slid back and leaped through as it closed behind his airborne body. I caught a glimpse of his SOS jacket smoldering before he disappeared.

I struggled to remain standing, still pointing the weapon at the door while the afterimage of our connection dissolved, and waited for the Phelaan assassin to charge back in and kill me. The hollowing nature of adrenaline subsided, and I was left alive, having expected to die: what chance was it that in the entire galaxy, I would have healed someone who had suffered at Traevis' hands? I remembered the healing, but that no longer mattered. Sometime in my past I had collected a debt, and now, at a time that otherwise would have punctuated the end of my life, I'd repaid the debt, and in doing so, hid a bit longer from death.

I looked up at the ceiling of the hold, at the distinct scar etched into the bulkhead, down at the blunt-nosed, drab gray barrel of the weapon I held, and back up at the closed door. The Healing Order would not prosecute me for returning the pain to Traevis. I had done it unwittingly, and yet, had I known that I carried pain created by

the Phelaan assassin, I would still have returned it to him. The real-
ization that I'd been prepared to kill Traevis struck me harder than
the pain of my fractured wrist. Something unpleasant crept over my
skin, as though I had fallen into an oily poison that clung to me, seep-
ing slowly inward. Nausea curled itself through my stomach at the
thrill of anger and defiance I felt—the desire to run out and hunt for
Traevis, to disintegrate him with his own weapon.

I wanted to throw down the pistol; instead, I picked up Jesel's
blaster, dropped it into my coat pocket and walked out of the room,
firing red beams in wide protective arcs across my path in case
Traevis chose to ambush me.

No ambush. Relieved, I retreated to the cargo hold and jumped
into the levator. As soon as my feet hit the deck I dropped and rolled
under the ship's side. I came up in a crouch, weapon raised.

"Get down!" Jesel growled.

The surprise flustered me. I looked left, right, bent down and
peered along the rows of ship underbellies. Multiple pincers grasped
me from behind, forced me down and pulled me under the shuttle's
edge. Arthen deposited my folded self between his spiny carapace
and Jesel's soft body.

"Are you trying to die?" Jesel hissed through her clenched teeth.
She lay on her stomach to my right, staring at the staging deck.
Without looking at me, she said, "How did you survive? Arthen here
was certain that you'd be dead but insisted that we pick up your
corpse."

"Technically that is not true," Arthen protested. "What I said
was *the healer's chances of survival have diminished considerably
since Traevis' appearance.*"

"That's what I said," Jesel argued. "That you expected the healer
to die."

"I did not give him a zero chance," Arthen replied calmly. "I simply stated that the possibility was infinitesimally small."

"I took Traevis' weapon and injured him," I whispered.

"Very improbable," Arthen replied.

"And very true," I countered. Something caught my eye, terminating the discussion. Legs. From behind the underside of a duster three ships away I had spotted legs running, disappearing behind a fin of the staging deck's supporting bulkhead on the left. "You should have waited for me in the maintenance deck."

"Arthen wanted to pick up your body," Jesel laughed, pointing her blaster in the same direction as the legs I had just seen. "Besides, Broca has mobilized the crew to find us and kill us. We had to blast our way onto the lift from medical. It's only a matter of minutes before they find us, if they haven't already done so." She turned suddenly on me. "My blaster! Did you—"

"Jacket pocket."

She dug around in my right pocket and slid out the blaster. Immediately she handed it into one of Arthen's claws.

Arthen pointed one of his task appendages to the right, where I caught of glimpse of four pairs of legs silently advancing between the ships. One by one the pairs cut to the right and disappeared. "They are flanking us," he whispered surprisingly well. "Broca aims to block access to the emergency shaft at the far end of the deck, thus limiting exit options."

"He means to force us back onto the shuttle," Jesel agreed. "No doubt Traevis booby-trapped it—probably an overload device linked to the engines: as soon as they power up, the fuel regulators will flood the engines and *boom!* unregulated thrust in a confined space makes for a large explosion." She shook her head. "I've seen it before; not because of an assassin but because of an untidy shuttle pilot who refused to do his own maintenance. Why do you think I accepted responsibility for maintaining these shuttles? Because I liked the job?" Jesel grimaced. "No! Because I don't trust one of these moles or insects to fix my ship—not even Arthen."

I looked at Arthen in surprise, and he nodded. "I know not to touch her engines—or anything on the ship if it needs repairs. I tell her, and she gets it done."

"Come on, we've been talking too much." Jesel's eyes narrowed as she looked at me. "This Earthling's chattering has infected us." Then she smiled and clapped me on the shoulder. "Arthen and I will provide covering fire. You will need to drag Borthax to the far end of the staging deck. Find the emergency shaft and climb down to the maintenance deck. We'll be right behind you."

I heard a rush of feet clanging on the floor, and Arthen fired regular pulses to the left. "They aren't waiting to flank us!" He trilled. I heard the whir and thunk of blasters charging and discharging, and red blobs of energy sprayed across the deck in front of us, impacted on the ship's side, and dropped a smoking shower of sparks from over our heads.

Jesel fired to the left several times and then scrambled forward, exposing her torso to aim and shoot down the line between the ships to the right.

"Jesel! Get back!" Arthen screeched, reaching out a free task appendage to hold her ankle and prevent her from crawling out farther.

I raised up my head to look through the wedge of space below the shuttle's belly and above the curve of Jesel's buttocks. Three pairs of legs advanced slowly down the lane between the shuttle and the neighboring duster. A few times Jesel's shots hit the legs and dissipated.

"They've got military grade dispersal shields," Jesel gritted. "Part of the captain's weapons cache, I bet."

I remembered my weapon, raised it above Jesel's back and fired through the small window of space. The continuous red beam cut a burning line through the invisible shield, fragmenting it into flying shards. Someone shouted, and the legs retreated, one pair toppling over.

"What?" Jesel whipped her head around, wedging it over her left shoulder to stare at me. "Where did you get that?"

"I took it from Traevis."

"What is it?"

"I don't know. He had it, I wrested it from him and shot him with it." For the first time I looked closely at the instrument and realized how odd and unfamiliar it appeared. "That's all I know."

"You fired an unknown weapon?" Jesel's surprise at my apparent stupidity acted like a magnet, drawing her back down beside me.

"I wasn't really thinking about whether I recognized the make and model," I replied indignantly.

"You realize that you could have just as easily shot yourself."

"Traevis trying to kill me preoccupied my thoughts."

"Give it to me," she demanded, holding out her left hand. Dutifully, I handed it to her. "Here, you keep this." She handed me Borthax's blaster.

Jesel rotated Traevis' pistol one way then the other. She shook her head. "What the hell is it?" she asked Arthen, handing him the weapon so she could devote her attention to our stalkers. I dropped Borthax's blaster back into her open palm.

Arthen flipped and rotated the object with mathematical precision, smoothly exchanging it between task appendages and prehensile orbital fimbriae and major antennae, gleaning visual and, I imagined, olfactory, electromagnetic, and other extra-humanoid sensory data. "A plasma weapon," he concluded.

"Impossible," Jesel retorted. "You can't make them that small."

"I thought plasma weapons were only ship-mounted," I added.

Arthen chittered impatiently. "Humanoids never cease to amaze me with their contradictions. You proclaim that your illogical thinking patterns breed innovation, and at the same time you hold onto rigid belief structures even when data disproves them."

Jesel muttered something untranslatable in Phelaan and discharged two rounds from her blaster at a cluster of spiked ambulation appendages that appeared under the duster in front of us. "Plasma weapons will cut through anything," she huffed. "Traevis' pistol destroyed the dispersal shield, but why didn't it burned a hole through that decshil's leg and the hull of the transport behind him—if it is a plasma weapon?"

"Under the correct circumstances, it should," Arthen replied bluntly. "We assume plasma weapons require large energy sources—"

"—they do," Jesel interrupted, scanning the deck for movement.

"Large ship-bound weapons meant for interstellar warfare require large energy sources. But a small one, used for close proximity fighting—or assassinations—would require a much smaller source. Any number of galactic races specializing in technology miniaturization could have secretly designed and built this pistol— perfect for killing through bulkheads or reinforced ship decking."

"We've already established that it cannot breach hulls," Jesel gritted.

"And I was no more than ten meters from Traevis when I hit him," I offered. "The beam scattered."

"Did you hit him or his clothing?"

"I hit the collar of his SOS jacket," I conceded.

"Then my theory remains intact," Arthen piped, enthusiastically. "If this weapon's components are based on standard plasma weapons, then the beam intensity will be inversely proportional to its length. This dial here"—he pointed to a large disc on the side of the barrel with a ridge bisecting it—"will set the range. A short beam will concentrate firepower while a longer one will sacrifice beam intensity for distance. Though based on the sole observation of one discharge, I am confident that Traevis set the weapon on maximum range, fortuitous for him: on any other setting, I believe the healer's shot would have proved fatal."

Arthen's logic sounded flawless to me. "I would agree with Arthen."

Jesel shot us both a look of savage defiance. "I just wanted you to make sure the thing wasn't gene-locked or booby-trapped!" She wrested the assassin's weapon from Arthen's claw and slammed down her blaster in its place with a force that would have broken a few bones in a mole's hand. "I didn't want it blowing up in our faces."

A nervous—and embarrassed?—sigh issued from Arthen's respiratory spicules all the way down his carapace. "It is neither genelocked nor booby-trapped."

"Good," she said, palming the weapon back and forth between her hands, weighing its feel. She finally settled it into her left hand. "The time for speculation and theory is over for us." She dialed down the weapon's range adjustor, then eyed us briefly with the same reckless smile she had just before piloting the shuttle through a precipitous drop into the atmosphere of STB. "Time for theory put into action."

In the time it took for Arthen to explain his understanding of the weapon, multiple sets of molish and insect legs appeared ahead to the right and left, some moving laterally, others tentatively forward—but all of them closing in on our position. Jesel chose the boldest group, sidling along the far side of the interposing duster. Picking a point directly above the mass of lower appendages, she pressed the activation stud: a fatter, denser beam of red cut cleanly through the heavy black hull, followed immediately by startled cries and a scattering of legs. An insectoid thudded to the ground, carapace smoking.

Without hesitating, Jesel turned the weapon on the others on our left and sent out a fan of red beams that cut through duster hulls and left seared black grooves in the Colossus Impendor's bulkheads.

"Arthen," she said, and without another word, Arthen grabbed suspension straps on a mass of junk behind him and began to crawl with admirable agility underneath the ship's hull to the starboard side.

I followed him while Jesel kept our attackers pinned down with intermittent fire from the plasma gun. Arthen popped up from below the ship and kept guard while I exited.

I inspected the nondescript mass that Arthen lugged and realized that it was what remained of Borthax.

"He is still alive," Arthen said to me while scanning for snipers.

"No appendages left, blaster patterns all over his carapace, but still alive."

"You insects are damned hard to kill," Jesel said as she flipped up from under the ship and led us toward the bow of the shuttle.

"It will work to our advantage for what we must now do," Arthen said.

"What is that?" I asked.

"First, get the hell off this ship," Jesel said, with Arthen nodding.

Jesel held up her hand for us to stop and be silent. She inched up to the end of the ship and peeked around the front. A volley of blasters fired immediately, forcing her back. Blindly she stuck the plasma pistol around the corner and fired randomly. "Go!" she ordered, nodding her head down the long open way to the rear of the deck.

With Arthen in the lead, dragging Borthax in the makeshift sling with his right task appendage and firing over his shoulder with his left, I charged down the straight avenue of dusters and shuttles lined up to either side. I heard Jesel firing the plasma gun at our rear.

Blaster discharges passed in black scorching lines over our heads and to the right and left. I ducked low to minimize the target, flinching as one red projectile burned the right side of my face as it passed.

I could see the back wall of the deck when Jesel yelled "The captain!"

I turned around and looked down the long straightaway. The captain stood in the open doors of the lift, partly obscured by drifting burn clouds. He carried a short, thick cylinder fashioned of long gray black tubes set in a circle. One claw clasped a heavy black handle suspending the length of the cylinder, and his other task appendage seemed to cup the back end of the object.

He pointed it straight at us, and the tubes blurred as they began to spin. A deep rhythmic hum echoed through the ship, and Jesel dropped to the deck. I watched, mesmerized by the spinning and humming.

"Bore laser!" she yelled, just as the spinning cylinder ejected a heavy red pulse that arced through the air, landing against the far side of Jesel's shuttle. A hammering vibration that I felt through the deck floor preceded a visible shock wave that rippled the air, followed by a concussive explosion that struck me like a moving wall, knocking me backwards and then rolling over my body, pushing at my clothes and plucking at the hair on my skin.

"Get him downside!" Jesel screamed over the torrent of sonic waves fragmenting on walls, deck, and every object they contacted. One of Arthen's claws snapped down on my collar and dragged me backwards. More explosions and sonic concussions passed over us.

We came to the end of the staging deck, and Jesel reached down and pulled up the circular cap covering the ladder tube leading down to the lower levels. She shoved the plasma gun into the opening then peered into the circular hole. She waved us over, then jumped through. Arthen slipped Borthax down through the opening; then he pulled me over and carefully lifted me up and fit me feet first into the emergency chute.

By the time Arthen closed the portal on the storm of rhythmic blasting, I had regained my orientation and felt well enough to stand.

The level just below the staging deck served as a maintenance and storage area. A cluster of dusters stood side by side nearest to us with the remaining three transport shuttles across the deck in close proximity to the lift.

"You don't plan on escaping in one of these?" I asked, looking at a duster as we passed.

"No," Arthen replied, dragging Borthax behind him. "The dusters have only enough room for the pilot and the navigator. Of course, there are the canisters below the wings. They are meant for biological and chemical agents, but they are quite large—enough room for both you and Borthax."

"I prefer to remain inside the hull of a ship."

"Arthen and I would never put you in one of the canisters," Jesel replied, and then with a hard-edged glance at me she added, "unless you get me very angry."

"That is something I know to avoid," I said.

"At least your wisdom extends so far," Jesel muttered. "The canister suggestion was Arthen's attempt at humor. Do you approve of his timing, healer?"

"I can see the utility of humor during circumstances of severe stress."

She eyed me. "Arthen could not have explained it in a more insect fashion." She shook her head. "You are either devoid of humanoid emotions or have an insect ancestor in your lineage."

Jesel took us past the first two shuttles, saying "They need engine maintenance—minor tweaking, but I'm not taking chances. We'll take the best and leave the rest."

She walked around the nose of the third shuttle, examining its portside mid-engines, then headed to the stern and inspected the main engines. She nodded, slapped the hull, and turned to me. "You remember our trip down to rescue Anders and Borthax? Well, this one's going to be even better."

She nodded to Arthen who handed me his blaster. "Keep lookout," she ordered, then opened the port-side levator's access panel and punched in the activation codes.

I kneeled below the boxy snub nose of the transport and trained both blasters on the lift doors, expecting them to open anytime—to see the captain's bulk appear, bore laser ready to blow me apart. Could I even harm him with two blasters?

I heard the familiar whirr and felt the levator's vacuum tug at the tail of my jacket. A quick over-the-shoulder glance showed Arthen sidling under the levator's port and disappearing. Jesel beckoned me, and I backpedaled, keeping an eye on the lift until the short riser angling down from the ship's side obscured my view.

She dialed down the vacuum. "Put him in—gently," she said, indicating Borthax with the barrel of her pistol.

I dragged the silent insectoid close to the port, wrapped the sling loops around his body so they wouldn't catch on anything, then slid him the rest of the way under the levator. It snatched him up, and he disappeared. After recalibrating, Jesel pushed me under it.

"Not too strong—" was all I could get out before the rapid-entry port sucked me into the bowels of the ship. Fortunately Arthen had moved Borthax out of the way; normally my weight would not injure an insectoid, but Borthax's exoskeleton no longer provided a stiff, impenetrable shield. In the brief time that Arthen had dragged him across the staging deck and down into the maintenance bay I had surveyed the wounded insectoid; the blaster wounds had super-heated his exoskeleton, making it brittle and subject to cracking with even a minor impact from a soft-body like myself.

I stepped aside just in time: Jesel came hurtling into the cargo bay and landed expertly on her feet. Without a word she left the bay. I walked over to Arthen who unwrapped the sling loops and dragged Borthax away.

"I will take him to the medical alcove," Arthen explained. "I would ask that you treat his injuries—set him up with whatever he will require for atmospheric entry. The med-kit also contains a bone-mender you can use to repair your wrist."

I nodded. "I would be happy to remain with him."

Arthen shook his head. "Stabilize him and strap him in for the trip down to the planet, then come up to command. Your chances of surviving down here are minimal with what we are about to do."

"What about Borthax?"

"Look at him." Arthen waved his task appendages over Borthax's blackened carapace. "He survived loss of all six limbs and close proximity blaster fire. And despite his condition, he still has a better chance of surviving here than a soft-body."

I took his meaning and followed him to the medical alcove. Arthen hoisted Borthax onto the treatment table and then promptly left. The fingers of my right hand had begun to stiffen after the exertion of moving Borthax, and they were rapidly losing their usefulness.

So with one hand I quickly undid the sling and threw aside the wrappings to inspect Borthax.

He was worse off than I initially suspected. In fact, his carapace had been so thoroughly engulfed in blaster fire that at first I had difficulty identifying specific anatomical sites. As it was, Arthen had positioned Borthax's head by the display panel of the medical diagnostic and treatment unit. With my left hand I pulled out the vital sign monitoring sensors and placed them strategically around Borthax's brittle shell. I pushed a tracheal oxygenation/ventilation tube into one of his primary gas exchange pores and activated it: the unit snaked into the hole and descended into his main respiratory tubule. I carefully forced a hemolymph monitor and delivery device through a patch in his carapace that hadn't seen blaster damage. The vital sign monitor panels winked on, and I examined the data that spun into form on the screens over Borthax's head: he had lost a great deal of hemolymph, but ironically the blaster fire that amputated his limbs also saved him from bleeding to death by cauterizing the very same wounds they created; however, the low hemolymph meant less oxygen for the frondlike respiratory tubules to glean, and as a result his tissues suffered from steadily worsening hypoxia.

I quickly delivered ten liters of fresh hemolymph, set the tracheal tube to deliver high-oxygen content, mixed atmospheric gas and to ventilate at maximum capacity until his hemolymph pH stabilized. I strapped him in for the precipitous fall into the atmosphere, after which I searched for the bone mender.

I opened the box, pressed the activation stud, stuck my fractured wrist into the cylindrical injury definer and programmed it for a repair cycle. Immediately the cylinder collapsed onto my wrist, and I felt a sudden point pressure just distal to the fracture point on my radius. A second point of pressure rapidly followed at the adjacent spot on my ulna. Once the device had injected the bone mender matrix under the periostia of both bones, it expanded, and I pulled out my wrist.

Jesel's voice grated in my ear: "Get up here now unless you want us to scrape you off the walls of the med-alcove!"

"I am coming up right now." With a last check of Borthax, I headed out of the med unit.

"Strap in now!" Jesel ordered the moment I entered the tight command compartment. She sat in the pilot's chair, Arthen to her right in the navigator's seat. I jumped into the seat on the left and strapped in.

"Activate piloting array," Jesel commanded, and the holographic sphere with the ship at its center appeared. She gave me a quick, severe look. "We're lucky the captain hasn't shown up with that bore laser and dissected the ship," she commented, insinuating that my delay had given the captain enough time to do just that.

"We're not on the staging deck," I said, trying to deflect her anger. "How are we going to leave the ship?"

"The maintenance deck has emergency escape portals," Arthen explained. "Jesel knows the release codes because she oversees shuttle maintenance."

"Illuminate lines of control," Jesel called out. "Manual drive."

I looked up at her words. "Manual? Why aren't you using the autopilot and the navigation tube?"

"That requires a link to the main ship," Arthen replied, "which will allow them to track us."

I nodded as the mid and aft engines fired up. I watched through the main view ports as the side of the Colossus Impendor bent outward then retracted, revealing space. Suddenly I shot backwards into my seat as we accelerated through the opening. Jesel whipped the transport around to briefly face the terraformer vessel.

"Say goodbye," Jesel said, and then we plunged toward the atmosphere of Sigma Tau Beta.

TEN

We hit the outer layers of atmosphere as hard as if we had crashed into a solid wall. Without my restraints I would have flown through the view ports. "Was it necessary to take the most direct route into the atmosphere?" I asked casually.

Jesel concentrated so thoroughly on piloting the ship that I don't believe she heard anything I said. Arthen plotted various trajectories that displayed above the piloting sphere.

"No. No. No." As the trajectories appeared, Jesel just as quickly dismissed them, erasing the images from the holographic screen.

"Perhaps you can suggest a course and destination," Arthen finally said.

"We're heading for the duster's crash site," she said.

"Why?" I asked, as Jesel steered us into a shallower, and much smoother, descent.

"The why I understand," Arthen spoke up, "but you are heading toward the southern hemisphere and the crash site is on the western edge of the largest continent of the northern hemisphere."

"If I left our escape up to the two of you we'd already be dead," Jesel replied.

I watched her hands in the virtual control gloves manipulate the threads of energy arising from each fingertip and running to various parts of the ship's hologram.

"I understand neither why we head for the crash site nor why we take the route you have chosen," I said, mesmerized by the movements of her fingers, so beautiful and lithe—a graceful, sensual dance—and so much in contrast to Jesel's personality and demeanor, as if her hands belonged to an altogether different individual.

Jesel sighed in frustration. "The residual radiation of the crash site will shield us from deep scans better than the planet's natural radiation, and it is likely the last place the captain would expect us to go. As for my trajectory, they can track our engines' heat signatures and will see that we head for the southern hemisphere."

"But they will also track our change of course toward the northern hemisphere," I replied.

Jesel smiled without taking her eyes off the piloting sphere and the global projection monitor indicating our location in the deeper layers of the outer atmosphere. "Not if the engines stop producing heat signatures."

She systematically shut down the propulsion systems. "We will glide down through the dense lower atmosphere, altering course and making it more difficult to track us—to predict our trajectory."

"Glide using what? Those underdeveloped wings?"

Jesel smiled at me briefly. "Yeah, the risers. The lower atmosphere runs pretty thick. It should provide enough buoyancy to the stabilizers to let us glide for a bit—until gravitational acceleration overcomes lift and we plummet to our deaths."

"Your humor sounds very much like Earthling humor," I commented, and she made a gesture at me I did not recognize but understood all the same.

"No need to insult me just because you don't like my jokes," she laughed.

"You laugh when we will likely die."

"Terraformers expect to die at any moment, so we are happy when we don't," she countered. "Besides, I will keep the bow and keel thrusters on line to aid in maneuvering. They are too small for the captain to see on the Colossus Impendor's sensors. With my skill and a little luck, I should be able to land us near the crash site—if not right on it."

At that moment she spun the piloting sphere sharply to port, rotating it steeply forward, and we dropped like a rock. "Hold on!"

"Healer, what's the hull temperature?" Arthen asked as we rode down through the lower atmosphere.

I glanced down, trying to maintain consciousness as the gravitational forces increased. It took a few moments to find the correct display. "Hull temperature reaching the critical zone; core temperature stable at high normal."

We veered steeply to starboard then leveled off. "We crossed
north over the equator and picked up enough speed with the last
dive to carry us to the crash site without too much reliance on the
thrusters. I hope." Jesel gazed at the virtual image of the atmosphere
surrounding us—thick white clouds with the occasional break
below the ship giving brief glimpses of the planet's surface, still far
below us. "The weather pattern here favors us," she mused. "The
cloud cover will protect us from the visual scans Traevis and the
captain will resort to when they realize they lost our shuttle's heat
signature."

Intermittent breaks in the cloud cover revealed our steady acceleration toward STB's surface. "Now it gets tricky," Jesel said eagerly,
as I watched the waves on the planet's western ocean blur past the
hull of our ship. She pressed her fifth digits into the piloting sphere,
and I felt the keel thrusters fire and the slight negative gs as the ship
rose slightly. Her fourth digits manipulated the risers to give the ship
more lift. "Look there," Jesel said, nodding at the global projection
monitor.

I chose to look through the bow view ports and saw a black
line on the horizon in front of us. "Land," I whispered, and Jesel
nodded.

"We'll make it," she said.

"Still plenty of time to crash and die," I replied.

"Now you're sounding like a terraformer," Jesel laughed.

We passed over the western edge of the continent, turned south,
and with the aid of the keel thrusters stayed just over the treetops.
The wide burn path of the duster slipped under the ship just as we
began to descend into the upper reaches of the forest canopy. Jesel
banked the ship around sharply, and we lost altitude quickly. She activated the bow thrusters, and forward progress ceased completely.

As we plummeted down, she fired up all the keel thrusters, and
we slowly descended. She landed us at the edge of the forest nearest the initial impact site. "The radiation will be strongest here, then

it dissipates rapidly as the duster disintegrated." We unstrapped ourselves and stood up.

"You should check on Borthax," Arthen said to me.

I nodded, then stopped at the entrance. Something had nagged at me since we first departed the terraformer ship. "Why did we return to the planet? Why not head out to look for help?"

"We didn't have time to plot a course," Arthen replied. "The shuttle's hull is not designed for long voyages in hyperspace, limiting our potential destinations."

"Besides," Jesel interrupted, "the captain could easily follow us through hyperspace and destroy the shuttle. We have a better chance of hiding down here and waiting."

"Waiting for what?"

"Waiting for them to come down after us," she replied. "Waiting for the Colossus Impendor to leave or to blow up; waiting for the crew to mutiny; waiting for an opportunity to escape while they are busy fighting among themselves. Waiting for our time to die." She shrugged her shoulders and smiled at me. "Any more questions, healer?"

"One," I said, just to spite her. "How will you know what happens on the Colossus?"

"Passive sensors," Arthen answered. "They require no energy source, so the ship cannot locate us. They simply register energy or particle emissions. A ship the size of our terraformer vessel produces an enormous amount of waste energy, thermal and radiative, and a characteristic spectrum of particle effluent. We can easily track them from the shuttle."

"Healer, it's like this," Jesel continued. "An ant can see you because you are big and loud, while you might not see the ant because it's tiny and its movements are too quiet for you to hear them. It's all a matter of size. We are the ants. The captain and the ship—they are you."

"How long can we afford to wait? We have little food and limited energy supplies. They could wait us out and catch us when we make a run for space."

"I am sure there is something to eat down here. The sentients eat, don't they? And don't worry about fuel: we have enough for the three of us to last down here for months and still have enough to make a break for a nearby colony."

"We will not have to wait months, healer," Arthen added.

I looked at the Phelaan insectoid and then at Jesel, who nodded. "Things will play out much faster than that. Why don't you go check on Borthax while Arthen and I plot possible escape routes and discuss potential destinations?"

"I will check on Borthax." While I made my way down to the medical alcove, thoughts whirled around in my head—potential outcomes of a mutiny aboard the terraformer ship, the possibility of fighting planetside, escape plans, the fate of the sentients, whether the captain and Broca might order dusting runs with soups designed to kill us. When I arrived, I found Borthax still alive, his vital signs stable and improved from before we left the ship. He remained unconscious, but I could do nothing about that: the shock to his system likely threw him into a coma that I hoped would pass as his body recovered. The stumps of his appendages oozed here and there, and I recauterized them to stop the slow bleeding. With his hemolymph volume returned to near normal, his respiratory distress had resolved, so I dialed down the tracheal oxygenator to minimal settings. With continued improvement I expected to have him off the respirator soon. At least I felt a small portion of my tension disappear because of Borthax's improvement. I took the time to examine my wrist and found the deformity already beginning to correct. The matrix released a local anesthetic that made the bone remodeling process painless, I noted thankfully.

When I returned to command, Jesel and Arthen were arguing over a holographic image I had never seen before. "We can barely make Piraeus Four with the fuel we have," Jesel spat out. "How do you expect us to reach Hyanuth Six? It's another two parsecs away. We'll have to refuel somewhere."

"We must head for a non-Phelaan colony," Arthen replied calmly.

"No!" Jesel shot back, standing up. Her face flushed, and her fimbriae stood erect. "That's exactly what they'll expect!" She stood there for a few moments, breathing furiously. With great effort—I could see the concentration twisting her face—she composed herself and sat back down. "Look, Arthen, we cannot always follow the logical path. Logic means predictability. Predictability—in this case—means capture and summary execution. We must act in a way they will not expect."

"And if they gauge our unpredictability correctly? If, as you argue, we head for the nearest Phelaan colony, they could reach it ahead of us. They could be waiting for us, and we'll have no time to contact authorities that might be able to initiate an investigation if we are killed."

Jesel shrugged her shoulders. "That's a chance we will have to take." She tightened her lips and narrowed her eyes. "But the chance of them reading our game is still lower than the chance that they'll follow us to the nearest non-Phelaan outpost—or even have Phelaan agents waiting there for us."

She turned to me. "What do you think, healer? What option would you vote for?"

Air hissed out of Arthen's mouth—a derisive sigh. "When have you ever asked the healer his opinion? Normally you eschew his suggestions. And I do not ever recall a time when you asked for a vote on anything."

"We are all in this together," Jesel countered.

Arthen hissed louder. "And when has that stopped you from deciding a course of action for us all?"

Jesel turned on Arthen, not with the look of anger I expected, but one of hurt. "Have I been so shrewish? So much the falish mole?"

"At times, yes. But never as bad as the others say you are."

"What?" Jesel bellowed, standing up again. "Which others? Arthen, I want names! Do you hear me? I'll show them how molish I can really be." She stopped suddenly.

We both heard the odd ululating sound coming from Arthen. I began laughing with him. Jesel looked back and forth between us. Finally, she nodded her head sharply. "A joke, is it? Your timing is off again, Arthen. We have no time for humor."

"I take exception," Arthen replied. "The healer—he laughs at my joke."

Jesel snorted. "Malish of any race will laugh at a rock." She sat down, gazing hard at the hologram, which I recognized as a representation of the sector of space around STB. First a smile, then a laugh broke from Jesel. "I hate you both," she chuckled. "Now, healer, give us your opinion."

"You really want it?" I asked. "You weren't asking for it just to spite Arthen?"

"Don't start with me."

I raised my hands for peace. "Well, I have to say that I agree with Jesel. The captain and Traevis will expect us to head for the nearest non-Phelaan colony and avoid any Phelaan associated ones."

"You moles stick together."

"Arthen, that was emotional and illogical of you," Jesel said, reaching over and stroking the insectoid's antennae.

"Although," I continued, "if Traevis truly *is* an assassin, his job is to kill. He may predict that we will follow the unconventional path."

"Shut up, healer," Jesel said.

I shrugged and took the navigator's seat, leaving Arthen and Jesel to continue their argument on where we should head. I had not sat in the navigator's chair since Jesel first began teaching me how to pilot the ship, so it took me a few moments to recall what all the different displays registered. I found one hologram that I hadn't seen before. I recognized the image of STB with a number of smaller objects in orbit around her. The larger ones, I guessed, were her moons. Each one of them had a small symbol associated with it. That left a tiny unmarked object. "Is this the ship?"

Arthen took a moment out from his argument with Jesel to lean over and examine what my finger pointed at. "Yes, that is the passive monitor's tracking of the Colossus Impendor. It can only identify a unique emissions pattern; it cannot specifically identify a vessel. Hence, a nondescript, unlabeled icon on the hologram." I nodded, and he promptly returned to his argument.

As I half-listened to their discussion, the blue dot representing the terraforming vessel mesmerized me: I watched it circle the planet in high orbit, its movement smooth and unwavering, the pulsing blue disk harboring some deeper rhythm, as though it served as a true conduit connecting me with the pulse of the living beings moving about on the ship.

I closed my eyes and stretched out my senses. They felt tense and tight, like muscles long unused suddenly asked to move again. And they hadn't been used, really. I hadn't healed anyone in any significant way for quite a while, my brief encounter with Traevis hardly worth mentioning from a healing standpoint. As I pushed past the staleness, the aching, I suddenly saw in my mind the inside of the ship; whether I simply imagined it, I cannot say, even now. Images of the ship flashed by in no particular sequence.

I saw first the staging deck, a pair of terraformers standing by the nose of a duster, others loading the canisters with Broca's soups; then a clot of insects and moles beside what remained of Jesel's shuttle; a humanoid punched the pad of the port-side levator's access panel; the maintenance bay appeared and then disappeared; the meal room—empty; the crew living deck, two armed terraformers standing outside one doorway, which somehow I knew was either Jesel's or Arthen's quarters; the captain closing a bag—at first I couldn't recognize the location, then I saw him whirl about and raise something in his hand that glinted, and as he turned I saw one of Dr. Cra'taac's diagnostic panels previously blocked by the captain's bulk. Everything faded for a moment, then the rapid shift of images proceeded again. In one I saw a figure in an SOS jacket walking away down a hall, the loose tails of the unsealed personal life support unit flapping with the speed of the movement.

The images halted abruptly. I felt a pressure building, forcing me backwards, accelerating and intensifying, finally expelling me from the ship, down through the passive monitor, and out of the blue pulsating disk. The force threw me back in my chair. I gasped as though I had been struck hard in the abdomen. I shook away the threatening darkness of unconsciousness.

"What is it, healer?" Arthen asked distantly.

Disoriented, I vaguely searched about on the panel before finding the holographic image of STB. Ignoring its satellite bodies, I caught the small blue disc in the corner of my eye, focused on it and watched it bloat, then rapidly dissipate, scattering like sand blown into the wind. I pointed to the rapidly disintegrating icon. "The ship" was all I could get out.

"The Colossus Impendor has exploded," Arthen stated simply. "What did I tell you, healer? Things will play out fast."

I looked at Jesel, my mind clearing rapidly. "Is that all you can say? The entire vessel has been destroyed. Who knows if anyone escaped."

"Let's hope that Traevis and Broca did not. As for the others— well, they took their chances, and they lost."

I felt a sickness grow in my stomach. "I need some air."

"There's nothing wrong with the atmospherics," Arthen replied.

"It is an Earthling expression, Arthen. It means that what has been said or done makes me feel sick, as though the air were poisoned."

Arthen thought on it for a moment, inclined his head subtly toward Jesel, and then nodded. "I understand. Please, however, do not leave the shuttle."

"Why?"

"We may need to move quickly," Jesel said, not in the least bit upset by my protest of her words. "If others escaped they might come after us."

"Can you not track them with the passive monitor?"

"No," Arthen responded. "The emissions from the drives of a shuttle or a duster hardly reach above the background radiation of the planet's atmosphere. Our passive monitors cannot hope to pick up such low-energy effluent."

"So we will just wait here until someone knocks on our front door?"

My two companions gazed at each other for a moment in silence, then Jesel looked at me curiously and said, "You know, we never thought about that. Arthen, I suppose we could set up some perimeter markers to alarm if a humanoid or insectoid comes within proximity of them."

"I shall program five, and the healer can help me deploy them."

I followed Arthen down to the cargo bay. On the way there we looked in on Borthax. "He is stable and doing much better."

"How soon will he awaken?"

"That I cannot be certain of—only to say that once he comes off the supplemental oxygen and his nutritional status improves I expect he will arouse."

"Good—we will need his testimony if we are to prove the case against the company."

The low-energy proximity markers were solid metal cylinders the length of my forearm with a single thick stake projecting from one end with a barbed tip. Arthen programmed each one using a magnetized metal plate he stuck to its side and on which he punched out numbers and symbols. When he completed the programming on one, he handed it to me. I carefully arranged the five in a carrying case set in the bed of one of the utility sleds. We jumped in and drove out of the cargo bay door, which Jesel quickly closed and locked from command. "Set them where I indicate, and I will keep watch," Arthen suggested, pulling out a blaster as he drove the sled.

The forest at the edge of the duster's crash site had been thinned by a combination of the impact and the intense heat. However, it appeared that the tree trunks possessed some degree of heat resistance and this, in combination with the high density of their growth pattern, shielded the trees only meters from the impact scar from nearly all damage. In fact, five meters into the forest I could see no signs of the destruction so close at hand. This helped the vegetation but hindered our progress, which Jesel regularly informed us of through our com links.

"How many monitors have you planted? Why is it taking you so long? If any survivors cut their engines on the way down, I will not hear them. You'll be on your own because I am taking off without you. I'm not risking my life for you two."

With each nagging hail, Arthen would shake his head and do his best to quiet her. "The forest density prevents rapid movement. We have two deployed and another three to go. We will let you know when we require your assistance. We realize that you will do your best to warn us if a ship approaches. However, in order for us to be most efficient, you must limit your contact with us, as it distracts from the performance of our task."

It took us half the day to plant the monitors and create a perimeter five kilometers across. We reached the last marker site, and I was beginning to show the strain of the work from the heat and humidity. Arthen directed me to the base of a particularly thick stand of very tall coconut-like trees. "Place it just in front of the nearest tree," Arthen called to me.

I examined the ground, kicking away loose debris hiding the soil. I toed the earth with the tip of my boot to make sure that I wouldn't strike a rock as I had with the previous two units. I grasped the last monitor mid-shaft, bent forward and raised it above my head. Just as I prepared to slam it into the ground, my implanted com unit flashed hot and Jesel's sharp voice grated in my ear. "Perimeter breach!"

Before I could answer, Arthen shuffled past me, rising up on his rear-most pair of ambulation appendages and with a secondary leg motioned me to silence. "Where?" he asked, his clicks transmitted into and translated directly by my auditory cortex.

"Between units one and two."

Arthen dropped down to all four ambulators and gently pulled the last proximity marker from my hands. "Get back to the ship."

I stood up, spun around, and stopped. The forest formed a wall of green around me—a thousand different plants creating an unreadable labyrinth with no markers.

"Here, take this." Arthen handed me the scanning disk. "The green icon at the center represents the transport. You are blue; I am red. Stay away from any black markers that might appear."

"How will you find the ship?"

"My positional sensory organs: they tie me to the shuttle as though we were linked by a cord."

"Stop talking and get moving!" Jesel ordered impatiently.

With a nod to Arthen, I snaked through the undergrowth, keeping my blue dot heading toward the larger green dot on the unit's screen. Trying to coordinate a two-dimensional primitive graphical image with three-dimensional reality proved more difficult than I anticipated: my movements followed the ambulation pattern of an intoxicated humanoid, making slow and inefficient zigzagging progress toward an unseen goal.

"Perimeter breach!" Jesel snapped into my ear.

Reflexively, I crouched down in a patch of thick-stemmed plants with malodorous funnel-shaped white flowers. Curling into a fetal position, I stared closely at the dark screen. Two black dots appeared to either side of me, moving quickly in a tapering fashion for the transport. "They'll cut me off!"

"Well, stop wandering about and run!"

"What if they have weapons?"

"They'll probably use them."

I took my best guess for the straightest route to the ship and ran. Dense, impassable thickets constantly forced me left and right, and I tried as best as I could to compensate. The ceaseless humming and barking of the forest disappeared under the throbbing of my heart and the rushing waves of my breathing. The ship refused to appear, and I was about to check the scanner when Jesel shouted "Stop!"

I dove into the ground, lying flat in the moist dirt. "They're just ahead of you," Jesel whispered. I didn't need to look at the monitor because the tremor of footsteps vibrated up into my skin.

"He's somewhere near," a voice said: the distorted, broken words seemed to spray out of a nozzle. I recognized the phase translocation created by a universal translator device, likely part of the protective headgear.

"He's heading for the transport," another, deeper showering voice replied.

"Should we kill him or use him as bait?" the first asked.

"Ransom," the second answered.

As quietly as possible, I pushed up to all fours and slowly lifted my head above the underbrush. A few meters ahead of me stood a pair of humanoids wearing two of the armored personal action suits from the captain's secret armory. Full helmets with visors hid their eyes, and a row of three mesh discs typical of standard universal translators covered the bottom halves of their faces.

The one on the right turned in my direction—an awkward but necessary shift of the torso, since the helmets abbreviated the degree of lateral head rotation. Just before I ducked back into the green, waist-high overgrowth, I noted the thermal cannon attached to the suit's chest scaffolding and folded neatly down along the side of the body.

"Damn, I can't see or hear anything with this helmet," one of them growled.

"Well, I'm not taking mine off," the other said. "Who knows what Broca dumped down here."

"Probably turn us into mush in a month."

Their laughter cut off abruptly. "Listen! He's coming."

The high-pitched whine of motors struck my ears, and I imagined a mechanical arm coming alive, raising up the thermal rifle it carried and eagerly searching for a target.

I didn't hear their prey so much as feel it—a rhythmic vibration pricking my skin. At first I thought it was a breeze quivering the crowded foliage against my skin. Then I recognized it, just as the pitch and intensity rose dramatically, jarring muscles and bones. Transing!

Something crashed through the forest to my left—I caught a brief flash of reflective black—followed by a spray of blaster fire.

"Shoot him!"

The transing peaked in an ear-shattering screech and then stopped.

The *ruum-thunk, ruum-thunk-thunk-thunk*, of a spitting thermal cannon pounded the air moments later.

I ventured a peek and saw the one with the cannon launching red thermal projectiles to the right. His companion stepped up and struck him on the helmet with the butt end of a blaster. "What are you doing? I wanted you to shoot him, not the whole damned forest!"

The cannon ceased firing, and the terraformer lowered the mechanical arm holding the weapon. "His buzzing interfered with the targeting system."

"Well, he's stopped making that blasted noise, so let's get him before he starts up again." Blaster Man pounded Thermal Cannon on his back, and the two ran after their prey.

As soon as they disappeared, Jesel's voice broke into my ear. "Hurry up! Arthen diverted those two so you could escape."

I stood up and ran a few steps before stopping. "That was Arthen?"

"Yes," Jesel replied impatiently. "Now get on board!"

"I can't leave him," I said and immediately took off after the two armored terraformers, Jesel yelling untranslated Phelaan curses into my ear. Unencumbered as I was by either weapons or protective gear, I easily caught up with the two terraformers, slowing down to avoid running into their backs. I quickly realized, though, that my former pursuers didn't know or care that I was behind them, either because of their forward-focused attention or the sound-dampening nature of the personal action suits. I followed them as closely as my courage would allow.

We weaved through the planet's crowding forest, and I lost all sense of direction, while Jesel's curses mingled with intermittent tremors from the thermal cannon. When the terraformer began firing more frequently, the residual heat wakes hit me like a series of hot showers.

We ran into a small, tight clearing, and the terraformers split right and left, then stopped. Through the narrow vertical wedge separating their bulky shoulders, I caught a glimpse of Arthen facing us, blaster raised, with a high impassable wall of bamboo-like trunks behind him. Without stopping to think, I charged forward and crashed into one of the terraformers.

"Hey!" A grunt, blasters fired, and I bounced off the humanoid's hardened shell and fell into the middle of the dirt ring. Blaster Man twisted his torso, angling awkwardly down to view me. He pointed the blaster at my head, I heard the quick whir of the generator before it fired, and I closed my eyes waiting for the flash, the pain, and the end. At that moment a powerful transing blast shot over me like a projectile, lifting the hair at the back of my neck and sending a tingle through my skin. I opened my eyes: sound waves formed an odd shell of vibrating distortions around my assailant. Suddenly, they penetrated the personal action suit: everything snapped into sharp focus, and there was a vacuum of silence followed by a harmonic frenzy that blew apart the armor.

A piece of the chest plate struck me in the face, knocking me back to the ground. The blaster-carrying terraformer lay at the edge of the clearing, his personal action suit disintegrated. His companion, who had been thrown against the trunk of a tree, quickly recovered, swaying a bit on shaking legs before steadying himself. His mechanical arm raised the thermal cannon and aimed it at me. Its gaping black muzzle quivered over me, then drifted away to my right. From behind me a blaster fired, but its projectiles skipped harmlessly off of my assailant's personal action suit. I heard the *ruum* and then . . . a *whirrr*, followed by a hammering *thrumm*. Like a curious beast, the thermal cannon turned to the sound, just as a red arc cleanly sheared off the mechanical arm. The terraformer spun around and pulled out a blaster. A second *whirr-thrumm* preceded another red arc that struck the humanoid in the chest and exited his back without distorting the arc itself.

I clambered to my feet. Arthen was still standing where I had seen him on entering the small clearing, his blaster now pointed in the direction of the red arc's origin. Grabbing his shoulder, I yelled, "Let's go!"

First I heard the crash, then, looking over my shoulder, I saw the captain break through the trees. His bore laser spun furiously. Even though his eyes seemed to look everywhere, I felt them focus on me. My skin itched suddenly. With a new transing from Arthen building behind me, I ran.

The *whirrr-thrumm* overpowered Arthen's vibration. The hammer hit the air, I felt an instant of sharply focused pain on the middle of my back, and then nothing.

ELEVEN

Iawoke in a swirling haze of sensations—auditory, tactile, and visual images all mixed in an amorphous mass of undefined experiences. Sounds sharpened and focused in my mind first. I couldn't make out words, only distinct, repeated patterns that I recognized as the voices of several individuals. Then words appeared from within the morass; soon I could follow sentences and then exchanges between speakers.

I opened my eyes and saw only dark blurs amidst bright blurs. Someone touched my shoulder, and it took my conscious mind a moment to process the tactile input.

"Healer, rest yourself." I recognized Jesel's voice. "The blaster temporarily blinded you—visual cortex overload. Sight will return a bit more slowly than the other senses."

"You heal rather rapidly for a soft body," another voice said, also familiar but not immediately identifiable. "I am impressed by the speed of your recovery. I shot you at less than a meter's distance."

Captured! I recognized the voice and tried to rise. A rougher hand held me down, and a third, familiar voice spoke to me softly. "Be still, healer. You are among friends." Arthen's words quieted me down. I lay back down, closed my eyes and slept.

★ ★ ★

When next I opened my eyes, I recognized the medical alcove of the shuttle. I turned my head left and saw Borthax lying beside me on the other treatment bed. Someone had removed the tracheal oxygenator. I noticed his breathing coming strong and regular, whistling through his primary respiratory pores.

"He awoke yesterday."

I turned to the right and saw Jesel standing a few meters away. She came over and stood beside me. "He was in a great deal of pain, so we opted to sedate him until we can get him to a proper medical facility."

"Help me up, please," I asked, and she grabbed me under both arms and pulled me up. "I feel like the shuttle landed on top of me."

"That's because I blasted you point-blank." The captain clicked into the room.

I felt the blood flush my face and my heart rate rise. He stopped beside Jesel and placed a claw on her shoulder.

"The captain had no knowledge of the sentients," Jesel informed me.

"You were lucky I had no intention of killing you," he said.

"Had he set it on anything more than minimal stun at that range, you would have been fried," Jesel laughed, cutting it off abruptly with a serious stare that mirrored my own. "The captain was not collaborating with Broca or Traevis."

"Or Cra'taac," he added.

"Dr. Cra'taac? He knew about them?"

The captain nodded. "He was the leader of the operation. I am still not certain he was even a physician. I always had my suspicions about him. A terraformer doctor who could not pilot? Hah! But that is irrelevant now. We must make plans for escape." He tilted his head just slightly to the Phelaan terraformer. "Jesel, now that the healer has recovered, I want you up at command."

"Wait!"

The captain and Jesel turned to me.

"You cannot leave me without an explanation. I want to know what happened."

"You deserve an answer," the captain agreed after a moment's consideration. "Jesel, go up to command. I will join you and Arthen shortly." Jesel nodded and left. The captain walked up to me. It was then I noticed the amputation of his left primary task—all that remained was a charred stump just distal to the first joint.

"Traevis?" I asked, nodding to his limb.

"Cra'taac." He laughed at the shock on my face. "You are naive, healer. You look for the simple explanation but not the logical one. Yes, Traevis was a spy and an assassin as well, but Cra'taac served as the principal killer. As I said, I never trusted him—especially after examining his instruments while he slept. I found the molecular sorters among his tools, not uncommon for a terraformer doctor to possess. We use them to test crewmembers' tissues for lethal exposure to the biologic and chemical toxins employed in the terraforming process. His sorter did have tissue from some of the terraformers, but it also contained unidentified samples. And I found genetic pattern comparisons in its data sink."

"I don't understand."

"I didn't either, at first. So I kept a close watch on Cra'taac. After you, Jesel, and Arthen went planetside to rescue Anders and Borthax, I found Broca and Traevis in the medical bay, in deep consultation with the doctor. When you returned, I knew from the dusters' wounds that something had happened down there. You concealed information—that I knew the moment Broca started pestering you about whom you had healed. Something down on the planet worried Broca. Traevis—he is a Phelaan and could hide killing his own mother. Cra'taac—he is an insect: he would think no more of killing his mother than he would of eating a meal. But Broca—his emotions betrayed them all."

"Why did you go along with Broca's dismissal of Jesel and Arthen?"

"I wanted Broca to think that Cra'taac had spoken to me—either threatened me to acquiesce or had offered me in on the conspiracy and that I had accepted. Jesel and Arthen—I locked them up for two reasons. First, to protect them: they were likely going to be killed along with the dusters, and keeping them in one place allowed me to watch over them, limit who had access to them."

"So you were the one who gave me access to Jesel's quarters?"

The captain nodded. "I temporarily transferred my release codes to you."

"And the second reason?"

"You knew something—something about Anders and Borthax, something about STB. You would not talk unless forced to. By squeezing those you trusted, I squeezed you. I needed to see how things would play out. Only then could I understand what was going on. Soon after you left their quarters, the two of them did as well, Jesel carrying a blaster. I knew then that the three of you planned to escape the ship. I guessed that Jesel and Arthen would try to take Anders and Borthax, so I headed down to the medical bay to confront them—to get answers.

"I arrived ahead of them and found Cra'taac systematically blasting Borthax. He had taken off three of Borthax's limbs by the time I arrived. What happened to Anders I cannot say."

"Traevis killed Anders," I informed the captain. "He told me."

The captain nodded and turned to leave.

"Why did you have a secret store of weapons?"

The captain stopped and slowly rotated back to me. "You thought that I would use the thermal cannons to eradicate the natives."

I nodded.

"A reasonable conclusion—but incorrect. I have been on both sides of mutinies, healer, and I have learned that if you prepare for a fight, you are more likely to avoid one. I have not risen to captain a ship without avoiding death and killing a few rivals along the way."

He raised his shortened appendage. "But even I sometimes suffer from arrogance. It will kill you more surely than your worst enemy. I was on my way to that very storage room when I met Dr. Cra'taac. I had little regard for Cra'taac, thinking him just a weak insect obeying orders. When I entered the medical bay and tried to stop him, he turned on me and took off this limb before I could react. He would have taken off my head had Borthax not struck aside the blaster with his last remaining limb. For his bravery, he lost that one as well, before I crushed Cra'taac's head with the bore laser I carried. Borthax had enough strength to tell me about the sentients on the planet before he lapsed into a coma.

"I understood, then, Cra'taac's use of the molecular sorter: the unknown samples were from the sentients. One of the other shuttle crews must have captured some and collected samples while they were setting up the biologics monitors. Cra'taac initiated the gene pattern comparisons between the terraformers and the pre-sentients—all moles. He was plotting the evolutionary potential of the pre-sentients based on established sentient species."

"If Borthax does not survive, this information will help prosecute the company."

The captain nodded. He held up a small disk. "I collected Cra'taac's data. The fool should have destroyed the evidence of his curiosity along with Borthax, but his own arrogance defeated him."

"And what of Broca? He must have known of this."

"Of course he did. Why do you think he got the position of operations leader? The company offered it to him because he agreed to ignore the existence of the pre-sentients. He surely read the preliminary reports on the planet. I assume that the company killed off all the members of the initial surveying group when they decided to eliminate the pre-sentients and terraform the planet. An A-grade planet like Sigma Tau Beta requires minimal expenditures for terraforming with maximal profitability to the company through colonization. A planet like STB makes a terraforming company—financial outlay occurs only at the beginning, during terraforming; after that, everything is profit."

"Does this happen frequently? The disregarding of life, the wanton destruction of species for profit?"

The captain shook his head. "Not so frequently as you might imagine. We terraformers are risk takers, but we are not fools—at least most of us. The majority of companies will not contract to terraform A-grade planets because in most cases, when they resurvey such a planet, invariably some species is found with sentient potential. The Galactic Council defines potential quite broadly, so it is quite easy to label a species as pre-sentient. The rewards are enormous, but one mistake and a planet like STB can destroy a company. They needed an unscrupulous leader, but not a criminal: terraformers with a history of criminal behavior, who are lucky enough not to lose their license, are watched carefully by the Galactic Council. No, they needed a respected terraformer whose personal stake in the project would coincide with theirs."

I understood then. "Broca was the first Earthling to lead a major terraforming operation. He stood to gain a galactic reputation with the success of STB's terraforming—"

"—or lose his career and serve on a disciplinary planet with revelations of the truth," the captain finished.

"He had as much to gain or lose as the company." I looked up at the captain, stared into his multifaceted eyes. "Do you think he escaped?"

"Broca? He did not. I sought him out and killed him. Then I headed down to the staging deck."

"Why did you shoot at us?" I interrupted, recalling the image of the captain standing in the lift doorway, the bore laser spinning up its energy, humming so melodiously.

"I did not," he continued. "I was burning brush."

I shook my head, not understanding.

"Clearing away the places that enemies can hide," he explained. "You needed to escape, so I helped by clearing out the medical deck. But I also needed to know who didn't want you to escape. Broca, Traevis, and Cra'taac certainly—but who of my crew could I trust? By aiding your escape, I forced their claws.

"Insects camouflage well, healer," the captain continued. "As long as they don't move, you'll never find them. Move and they are prey. You move first, and you are prey. I simply made them move."

"Why did you trust me?"

He picked absently at the stump of his amputated appendage. "You were not of the crew. You are a healer. Your integrity is without question."

An image of firing the plasma pistol at Traevis surfaced in my mind. I shivered at the renewed feeling of disappointment that I had not killed him.

"I followed Jesel and Arthen down to the staging deck after treating my wounds. When I arrived, I noted six members of the crew hiding behind one of the dusters and a larger group advancing toward Jesel's and Arthen's shuttle. They intermittently fired down the deck, and that is when I saw you retreating. Knowing, then, that you were not aboard Jesel's transport, I decided to eliminate my enemies—and yours. It may have seemed that I was firing on you, but it was only the angle by which you saw me targeting."

"Thank you, captain—for saving us."

"Do not thank me," he insisted. "I did nothing for your benefit— only to preserve my position."

"How did you escape?"

"Once I had seen you safely into the emergency chute, I continued the fight to prevent them from following you. Once sufficient time had passed for you to leave the ship, I retreated into the lift, set the bore laser on a continuous circular firing pattern and rolled it into the staging deck as I headed down to the maintenance bay. I jumped into one of the remaining shuttles and blasted out of there."

"And Traevis?"

He shook his head. "Traevis likely blew up the ship to destroy evidence and to eliminate all those who knew of the pre-sentients. I would assume that he survived."

"He always wore that SOS jacket as though he expected the ship to disintegrate at any moment."

"Perhaps that is what Cra'taac and Traevis planned all along," the captain mused. "After completion of the terraforming operation, kill all of us and destroy the ship and all evidence of the pre-sentient's existence."

"What about others?" I asked. "Other survivors."

"I don't know who else escaped," he replied. "Survivors are not my first concern. If Traevis lives, his first priority will be to contain the damage done to the project."

"What does that mean?"

The captain held up his remaining fore-appendage. "More questions will have to wait. We have the business of survival to address. Are you well enough to join us in command?"

"I am," I said, although still feeling somewhat lightheaded. "But what of Borthax?" I looked over at the nearly dead insectoid.

"Do not concern yourself with him. He may or may not survive, but we no longer need him with the data I gathered from Cra'taac's files."

"What I meant, captain, was should I remain here to tend to him?"

"You can do nothing for him. We have no time to delay if we are to escape. Jesel and Arthen removed the tracheal oxygenator, and he breathes well on his own. As Jesel said, we will keep him sedated until we can reach a proper medical unit."

I followed the captain up to the command deck, and as soon as we walked in, I heard an argument flaring between Arthen and Jesel.

Arthen recommended choosing the nearest non-Phelaan system; Jesel adamantly insisted on a Phelaan planet. The captain threw his support behind Arthen. Despite the odds against her, the Phelaan humanoid held the other two at bay.

I interrupted at the first lull in the battle: "Can someone tell me what we can expect Traevis to do, if he survived?"

Jesel answered immediately. "First, silence all survivors with knowledge of the pre-sentients. Second, contact the Phelaan Syndicate so they can send a cleaning crew."

"What is a cleaning crew?"

"Terraformers who specialize in correcting the mistakes of others," Arthen answered.

"But we *are* avoiding a mistake here."

Jesel scoffed. "Healer, how can you be so blind? The Syndicate knows about the pre-sentients. They want them erased. We didn't do it, so the cleaning crew will—and they'll erase us as well."

"The fringe of the fringe," the captain added. "They are all rogues, but some of them are the best surgical terraformers around—cutting out problem species without affecting the surrounding or interdependent species."

"But that's not who they'll send here," Jesel added.

I had an idea of the type of cleaning crew they would send. On other worlds I had heard of their counterparts—special military units, infiltrators, collecting agents. *Haksen'da.* The name itself raised the bile into my stomach. What hope did we have against a cell of legendary mercenary assassins? "What recourse do we have?"

Jesel laughed. "Recourse? Captain, our healer here sounds like the Galactic Council."

"So we will wait for a cleaning crew to arrive?"

"No, we will not wait," the captain replied. "You will leave with Jesel and Borthax in the transport and try to reach a non-Phelaan colony first. This is a company action, not the whole of the Phelaan Syndicate. As Jesel argues, we may find aid among regional governing councils that pull considerable weight in influencing outer rim policies; however, it is too great a risk to head into Phelaan territory."

"If we are not going together, then I prefer to stay here," Jesel said quietly.

The captain looked at her and shook his head. "You know why you and the healer cannot remain. If Traevis doesn't eliminate survivors, he will order them to begin planetside extermination of the native sentients. Arthen and I will begin the process of locating insectoid survivors and identifying those who were part of the operation and those, if any, who were not. The moles will have to fend for themselves."

I tried to understand the captain's words as something other than a sudden and unexpected racial bias, and in the process missed the remainder of the discussion. When I finally looked up, Jesel held tightly to Arthen's upper appendages. Her eyes were red, but I saw no tears. She said something to him in a low voice, then whirled around and pushed roughly past me.

She turned in the doorway and spoke to me in a slow, unusually regulated tone. "I am outfitting one of the sleds with supplies, healer. You have five minutes with them, then I will kick them off the shuttle."

MUTANT HORSE PUBLISHING

J.G.NAIR - AUTHOR

WWW.MUTANTHORSE.COM

Email: mhorse@mutanthorse.com

Visit our Mutant Horse Facebook page

The Healer Series

If you could wield retribution like a planet-crushing hammer, would you? Where would you draw the line between right and wrong? Good and evil? Small steps lead both to heaven and to hell, but would you know in which direction you were headed? Follow me, and I will show you the path I took...

The Healer Book 1: The Phantom Limb
(available at Amazon and at www.mutanthorse.com)

The Healer Book 2: The Tree of Pain (early 2011)

After she disappeared, I turned to the two Phelaan insectoids. "Captain, perhaps you can explain your decision. For the uninformed such as myself, it appears somewhat biased against the moles."

"Not somewhat biased, healer—clearly biased." He paused, and I made it just as clear by my stance that I would not accept acknowledgement without explanation. He nodded and continued. "We insects have a better chance of evading a Phelaan cleaning crew. If Jesel can reach an outpost, contact friends—and you, with the trust and respect due a member of the Healing Order, I will ask to go before the Galactic Council to plead our case—we might be able to delay Syndicate action long enough for Arthen and me to grow our exoskeletons to repel scanning fields. Given time, a new, denser exoskeleton will help us avoid ship-bound sensors, forcing a cleaning crew to come down to the surface to find us. However, the sensors will quickly pick out the humanoid terraformers, and the cleaners will rapidly eliminate them from the security of high orbit. And I will not hesitate to kill any humanoid crewmembers that we encounter." The finality of the captain's last statement served as a clear warning to me that the debate had ended.

"That is why you and Jesel cannot remain here with us," Arthen said. "Besides, Jesel is the best pilot of the three of us—four of us, no offense meant, healer."

True to her word, Jesel returned to the command deck, pushed past me, sat down in the pilot's seat and strapped in. "Get out," she said to Arthen and the captain. I looked at the two of them, and the captain proceeded out, grabbing the arm of my jacket with his one remaining fore-appendage. "Come, let us secure Borthax in the medical alcove. I believe this journey will be far rougher than your journey down here."

I could not conceive of a worse trip, and I did not want to think of it, but I understood the captain's excuse to leave Jesel and Arthen alone. Since Borthax remained sedated, I decided the wisest choice lay in re-intubating him with the oxygenator and setting it to auto: it would remain a passive system as long as Borthax breathed on his own and would activate only if his respiratory rate and hemolymph oxygen level fell below a preset value. While I took care of Borthax, the captain left for the cargo bay to look over the supplies Jesel had stocked on the sled. I had just completed setting the oxygenator's auto-initiate parameters when he returned.

"Arthen will join me shortly," he said.

"Thank you, captain." I turned to him and bowed. "May you find peace in your journey."

He nodded slightly to me. "Peace—I have never had peace, and I never will. I will die as every terraformer hopes to die—unknown and forgotten on some planet distant from civilization." He paused for a moment and though his eyes looked everywhere, I knew that his mind focused on me. His claws clicked when he addressed me. "I thought you a worthless addition to the crew, but you have proven vital: value comes as value needed. The universe has a design that negates all the plans we spend so much time creating. Good luck. I don't believe in it, but I will leave you with it."

I encountered Arthen on his way down to the cargo bay. He clasped my shoulder. "I will miss you," I said to him.

"You gave me knowledge to make me a smarter insect," Arthen recited the common insectoid words of parting. "Watch over Jesel. She may be a soft-body, but she possesses a shell as hard as any insectoid's."

Arthen followed the captain to the sled. I headed to command, expecting at any moment to feel the engines fire up and seconds later to feel myself battered around the rising ship. However, Jesel showed a great deal of patience and restraint, allowing me to reach command before lifting off.

I stepped in, and she called out "activate piloting array." That was the entire greeting I received. I took the navigator's seat, strapped in and braced myself. "Do you require my assistance?"

"Look for yourself," she said, followed by "illuminate lines of control. Manual drive."

As I turned to the navigation console before me, the ship

exploded upwards. The tremendous thrust forced the blood out of my head, and a black curtain dropped across my visual fields. I startled awake, grabbing at my chest. My heart raged with a fire that surely burned through my ribs and skin. Then I recognized the left jaw pain. Arthen's faint voice whispered in my ear: "Please, healer, rouse yourself."

"I am here, Arthen," I managed, rubbing the swelling over my left intercostal space to relieve some of the pain from the overheating com unit implant. The booster had reached its maximum.

"Jesel needs you at navigation. She cannot reach you, and she attempted to wake you with verbal stimulation."

"I am sure the verbal stimulation could have started wars on several planets."

I heard the faint hissing of Arthen's distant laugh. "I heard some of it. You are lucky she is strapped in and cannot reach you to initiate tactile stimulation."

"All right, stop babbling and get on with it," Jesel said aloud.

"My signal booster has reached its limit," Arthen said. "I wanted to say good-bye."

"Good-bye, Arthen."

His signal thinned and snapped away. Immediately the unit cooled on my chest, and I could breathe more comfortably. I gazed at the console in front of me: a transparent Sigma Tau Beta revolved on the main holographic projector with three blue navigation tubes arising from different places in its upper atmosphere and twisting off in wildly different directions.

"Jesel, why are there three navigation tubes?"

"Wait a moment," she said.

I heard her talking softly, then in a trembling voice she said, "I will remove an appendage to honor you." I recognized the expression as a common insectoid prayer to honor a dead or dying loved one.

"Yes, healer, what do you want?"

"Why are there three navigation trajectories plotted?"

"Because I haven't chosen which way to go yet," she replied calmly.

"I thought the captain said—"

"The captain no longer holds authority over me. It disappeared with the Colossus. I permitted him and Arthen to believe I would follow their suggestions because I tired of their arguments. Arthen knows in the end I will do what I consider correct."

"Why the secrecy?"

Jesel turned and gazed at me with her right eye. "No one needs to know where we are going, healer. The less we say, the less others will know. The less others know, the more likely we will live. Anything more?"

"Is there anything I can do?"

"Yes. You can transfer the navigation tube I choose to my piloting array—when I choose it."

"As you wish." We broke free from STB's atmosphere and still Jesel piloted the ship manually. I followed the course of our shuttle as a small blinking green icon on my navigation console, and I marveled at not only Jesel's piloting skills but also her uncanny inherent sense of three-dimensional coordinates. I knew we were most vulnerable in deep space, without the sensor-blocking atmosphere of a planet to hide us. The longer we flew without adhering to a standard hyperspace trajectory, the less chance Traevis or any other agents of the company could track us or project our intended course and destination. Still, without the aid of navigation, Jesel piloted the ship into space, spinning us back and forth between each of the three possible courses. I admired her innate talent to know exactly where each of her navigation tubes lay in relation to each other and to the planet.

When the time came, I transferred the tube she requested to her piloting system, and within moments we entered hyperspace.

TWELVE

On the fourth day of ducking and running—hovering in the gravitational lee of a planet or the scanner-scattering dust of an asteroid belt before shooting through space to another hiding place to wait again—Jesel came down to the medical alcove after landing our ship on some planet whose name I never learned. "I am going to the gaming facilities," she announced. "Stabilize Borthax, prepare all of our essentials for off-loading, then come and find me." She thrust a small case into my hands.

"What's this?"

She nodded at it. "Go ahead, open it and see."

I pressed the two catches on opposite sides of the box, and the lid's seal broke with a hiss. I raised it off and stared: Phelaan credits filled the container. The small gold, silver, and green coins formed a mound, all jumbled together. I reached in to touch them, and Jesel snapped the lid shut.

I pulled my hand back just in time. "Hey! You could have taken my fingers off!"

"Would serve you right," she said with a frown. "Play with your credits all you want. Don't touch mine unless I approve first." Her frown turned into a sly grin.

"How much is here?"

Jesel shrugged. "Two million—thereabouts."

I gazed at the resealed box and nodded. Then I looked at Jesel. "Why have you given me this?"

"Bring it with you when you come find me."

Suspicion began to form vaguely in my mind.

She must have caught the scent of my hesitancy because she continued after an exasperated sigh: "I am a clear target for thieves, healer. Look at me." She flourished her hands down from her head along her sides and twisted her hips demurely—or as demurely as a hardened terraformer could do. "A lone falish—carrying a sealed box?"

"A wolf in wolf's clothing," I muttered.

"What was that?" she bristled, her fimbriae stiffening into spikes, effecting immediate proof of my comment.

"One look from you and any thief with a grain of common sense or the self-preservation instinct will melt away into the crowd," I explained.

"You don't know this crowd. But you—a healer—they will not touch. Even here."

Unconvinced, I inspected her garb carefully, leaning down to one side then the other to discover what she might be hiding under her jacket. "Where have you put the blaster?"

Jesel laughed at me. "I am not carrying it, if that is what you are worrying about."

"Why not, if you are going to gamble? This planet, I would gauge, is relatively poor, and the poor live by desperate measures."

"I am not so foolish as to carry a weapon into a gaming establishment." She then tapped my forehead with one hand. "What are you thinking? These places utilize the latest screening technology and have as much or more firepower than the local military." She turned on her heel and walked out, calling over her shoulder, "Make sure everything is stacked by the hold entrance and ready to go before you leave. We won't have time to search for things when we come back here."

I did as she asked though it galled me to always follow her directions. Despite my many years with my egoless master, in the short time since his death I had managed to develop and feed an ego to rival any terraformer's. Perhaps I am exaggerating just a little, but it was there inside me, growing by the day. Still, I exerted some control over my thoughts and emotions and managed to push them down for the moment. I fed Borthax an extra slug of parenteral nutrition, a double dose of pain meds, and boxed and stacked all the essentials by the cargo doors in preparation for rapid off-loading. Anticipating that the company or Traevis would eventually discover us, during the four days since our escape from STB I had systematically run through the shuttle's manifest and located all the vital components necessary for our survival if circumstances required our rapid abandonment of the ship. I collected them together or at least tagged them if they were in current use and could not be stored; also, knowing Jesel and her reckless ways, I expected the worst. At least I thought that I did.

The small port in which Jesel landed the transport possessed one gaming establishment and as she had said, it was easy enough to find: like the houses of worship in some cultures, this facility dominated the center of the town. Larger by far than any other building, it rose five stories into the dust storm–blasted environment. Its domed and spired roof reminded me of the churches of Earth. Like an arena of the past, I could see several entrances located around the base of the building, and expected more located on the opposite side where I could not see them. As I neared it, choosing to follow the steadily growing numbers of individuals of numerous races migrating toward the nearest entry point, I stopped suddenly. Craning my neck up at the enormous structure now dwarfing me, I realized I had no way of finding Jesel: I imagined myself wandering lost within its vast internal maze until I either starved to death or Traevis and the Phelaan authorities located and summarily executed me while games continued around us unabated.

A reptiloid's face suddenly accosted me. He said something in an unfamiliar language: the suddenness of his appearance and the untranslated words briefly disoriented me. I stood there blankly. Those behind me waiting to enter cursed and hissed variously. A red tongue flicked out at me—that I recognized as a universal signal of impatience from a reptiloid.

"I am sorry, I don't understand, good malish," I answered in CombineSpeak.

The tongue flicked faster and his eyes constricted instantly to slits. Somehow I had insulted him. I knew that immediately and bowed slightly and stepped back, a standard reptiloid submission posture.

"I am falish, humanoid," the reptiloid replied in Combine. She examined my submissive stance—briefly fixing on my forehead where the Order had tattooed the healer's mark—and after a moment's hesitation, the tongue flicking slowed. "You'll live to your next molt."

I sighed with relief. She had granted me my life, which by reptiloid culture was hers to give or take for an insult such as mine. Nevertheless, I remained in submission.

"Your purpose, humanoid?"

"I am seeking my companion, a falish humanoid."

She grabbed my shoulders and pulled me forward to stand on a circular depression in the floor of the entrance to the gaming facility. She punched a few buttons on a metal plate she held and immediately I felt the prickling of a scan. "Falish humanoid—Jesel. Terraformer."

I had no idea how she could possibly connect me to Jesel through the scanner, and at another time I might have questioned her. This time I just nodded.

The reptiloid dragged me through the scanning unit and looked at the box I carried. Her tongue flicked. "Open it—slowly." She drew a blaster and placed it to my right temple.

The seals released, and when I opened it, the Phelaan credits shone dully in the sand-stormed air. The tension lifted from me: I don't know why, but I actually worried that when I opened up the box I might not see the coins in it. She looked at it, seemed satisfied, and nodded for me to close it. She waved the blaster for me to move on, and she headed for the next individual seeking entry.

"How do I find my friend?" I asked her, patting her on the shoulder and hoping that I did not insult her again by the familiarity of the touch.

"The bots will take you to her."

I accepted her word for it, though I didn't know to what she referred. Basically, she had the blaster, and I refused to test her patience. So I trusted to fate and walked into the facility. Almost immediately a small hovering upright cylinder flew over to me. "Jesel, terraformer?" it inquired in a pleasant nalish voice.

"Yes," I replied.

It dipped quickly forward twice—a nod of affirmation I guessed—and then took off. I followed it as closely as possible. We wove through a maze far more complicated than I had imagined—tables crowded with malish and falish of all galactic races, holographic simulators, combat pits, gaming cubicles, and encounter rooms with transparent walls for spectators to watch. The bot took me down several levels, across bridges spanning steaming pits with creatures moving about inside and cheering crowds leaning in precariously around the edges, then back up again until I had no idea of where I was, where we had started, or even if I remained in the same building into which I originally entered.

When finally the bot halted, I stood before a series of small tables arranged in a pyramid on the floor. Each table was large enough to accommodate only two individuals on opposite sides, facing each other. Before them lay stacks of transparent crystals of different colors and shapes, and each individual possessed an object built of separate joined crystals; the objects varied in shape, size, and color, but all of them seemed to lack parts, with those built by the individuals closer to the apex appearing more complete. The entire area buzzed with talk—from those at the tables to others standing near the pyramid's base waiting to join the game, to the spectators along the perimeter betting on the outcomes.

The bot nodded toward the middle of the pyramid. "Jesel, terraformer," it piped, then dipped and sped away.

I followed the line of sight of its nod and saw Jesel at a table in the very middle, pitted against a sizeable amphiboid, its green sticky body crowding the table and enveloping the seat on which it sat to the point of disappearing. Like the others at the tables, Jesel and the amphiboid bargained, exchanging the pieces that lay before them or pointing to a piece in their object, nodding, waving off, shaking heads. At some tables, heated arguments exploded. Often before the combatants could exchange blows, guards or security bots appeared and either pulled them apart and dragged them away or paralyzed them for several moments, gave them a chance to quiet down and either let them go back to the game or carted them off. As individuals disappeared—either through disrupting the gaming process or by bargaining away their built objects—members at lower tables advanced upwards to tables closer to the apex, their vacated seats taken by those standing by the base waiting to join. I saw all manner of bargaining wealth—credits, precious crystals, a matched pair of brown and green furred doas, even a ship, its holographic image held in the palm of a reptiloid's hand.

Jesel seemed thoroughly occupied by the game, and I didn't want to disturb her concentration by calling out to her, so I simply walked to the spectator's section opposite the apex of the pyramid, hoping that during one of the times when she looked up and scanned the crowds that she would take note of me. Certainly her eyes passed over me several times but she never once acknowledged me. So I sat quietly and followed the proceedings, understanding only what little I could deduce from watching. At one point, Jesel advanced to a table with a scarred and hard-looking rail of a humanoid. In contrast to his shabby appearance, his built object—a crystal sphere of nearly all blue—seemed almost complete except for a few missing segments and a few others with red, green or clear crystals. I noticed that he sat with his back to the apex and had not moved from that place since I'd arrived: he sat there and waited for others to challenge him. The challenge at the tables one and two tiers below the single table at the apex consisted of the opponents setting their built objects next to each other so they touched at one point. As soon as they touched, a conflict ensued between the objects, apparent from the intensification of the light emanating from the crystal pieces. The luminescence would rise in one and dim in the other, as though the first drew energy from the latter; eventually a winner rose in energy, permanently darkening the other. Sometimes this battle raged back and forth before a clear victor emerged; at other times, the moment the objects touched one dimmed, then went dead—sometimes the energy drain occurred so quickly that the losing object fell apart or exploded. When this humanoid won a challenge, he forcefully pulled from his opponent's built object pieces of blue crystal, with which he replaced the red and green crystals or filled in missing places in his sphere. The remainder of the losing built object he left for his opponent to take away and to reconstruct. At other times he collected crystals from those who chose to back down from a challenge they were certain to lose, permitting them to retreat to the safety of a table at a lower tier. This back and forth seemed a significant part of the strategy of the game: advancing when you felt you could win, retreating when you thought that you might lose, and patiently building a stronger built object in the lower tiers while waiting for someone to advance whom you could defeat. At the apex sat an enormous malish humanoid—so large, in fact, that he rivaled the bulk of the amphiboids, who are known for their tremendous girth. This humanoid sat calmly and watched the proceedings, his built object concealed in a cloth bag on the table. No one had challenged him since I had arrived.

When Jesel sat down opposite the thin humanoid, she immediately shook her head to his inquiry and indicated her built object—a shallow bowl of near-perfect green sitting upright on one edge and supported by two appendages of crystal, one reaching out from either side to contact the table so the entire thing looked like a disc with two legs sticking out. He pointed to the blue crystal foot of one leg and she waved him off. He insisted and she refused. His large, black, almond-shaped, pupilless eyes narrowed at her. *Jesel will strike him*, I thought at that moment; from where I sat I could see the set of her jaw. He smiled and pushed his sphere forward. I knew what he said: *give me what I want or challenge me*. Jesel simply sat and stared at him. And stared. The silence grew interminable—so much so that I felt my patience slipping. I actually stood up, prepared to intervene. I wanted to go from this place, and I had had enough of

Jesel's game playing. I would not let her risk our lives—Borthax's life—for her own amusement.

Something stirred in my visual fields, and I roused myself from my thoughts. Jesel had spoken and now waited for the humanoid to reply. He let the silence linger. Games. Posturing. I understood the combat for the best bargain. He finally raised two fingers. Jesel nodded. The humanoid pulled two crystals from the near perfectly green disc, leaving a gaping hole in the center of her built object.

Jesel said something to the malish humanoid, got up with her object, and turning around, weaved her way back to the very base of the pyramid and unceremoniously usurped the seat of an insectoid. Watching her fall to the very bottom tables of the game, I thought she would be furious, but she showed no anger, no signs at all that the move distressed her. Slowly she worked her way back up and by that time, the humanoid who banished her to the beginning had been eliminated by a phytoid with a red crystal tree, still missing a few branches.

Others then boldly advanced, but Jesel oddly hung back. Even I could tell at this point that there were times when she purposely refused a challenge, allowing her obviously more complete built object to lose pieces rather than challenge a clearly inferior creation. For some time I could not understand her strategy. Then I stopped watching her and watched the others. Soon, I saw her strategy, although I couldn't understand it: she traveled back and forth across the middle tables eliminating all the players there, except for one—the reptiloid with the ship as bargaining wealth. From my brief experience with this game whose name I didn't even know, I got the distinct impression that he was not a particularly skillful player. In fact, I realized that he probably would have been eliminated early on, had Jesel not been clearing his path of superior built objects.

When the reptiloid advanced to the second tier, Jesel moved forward after him. He sat on the apex side of the table, giving him the advantage in bargaining. Like the thin humanoid before him, he had built a sphere; however, his sphere seemed of poorer quality.

Although it was constructed only of green crystals, it was far less complete than the humanoid's. I had learned from watching the challenges that purity of form often won over purity of color. He knew that he needed to complete his sphere, and Jesel possessed curved green crystals in her bowl. He would challenge her oddly shaped built object.

Jesel nodded, and they placed their objects together, the reptiloid's sphere reaching into the shallow disk and contacting it at the center. To my dismay, I watched the sudden luminescence of her object immediately begin draining into the sphere. The reptiloid sat back and watched the flow toward victory, his tongue flicking out repeatedly. I looked at Jesel and noted the strange calm on her face. When I looked back at the built objects and her certain defeat I saw why: as the light drained out of her object, it seemed to shrivel, and as it did so, the legs broke contact from the table and curved inward with the collapsing bowel. To my astonishment and that of the reptiloid, when her object had shrunken adequately, the feet contacted the opponent's sphere like hands at the ends of encircling arms. The flow of energy continued to stream out of the disc and into the sphere, but then continued on into the arms. Slowly the sphere drained of its light, dimmed and went dead, the arms of Jesel's object glowing brightly, the whole of her built object looking like a belt with the flattened, shrunken disc as the buckle.

Jesel had won. The reptiloid continued to stare at his dead sphere, encased in Jesel's glowing green belt. She said something to him, and he broke his stare and addressed her, pointing to his object. She shook her head and pointed to his hand. He opened his palm, displaying the hologram of his ship, far larger and sleeker than our simple transport. She nodded to it, and he shook his head. She pointed to her shining built object, and again he refused. She turned directly to me and waved me over.

"Where's the box?" she said, when I arrived beside her. I produced the box, and she took it, setting it on the table. Then she turned back to me and leaned down. I had to squat to bring my face close to hers.

"Do what I say now, and do not challenge me later. Understand?"

I nodded, even though I didn't actually understand. I suppose my curiosity at what she planned overcame my internal filters for distorting the truth.

"First, take this—" She handed me a coin. "This will get you out of here fast. Go to the ship and unload only the essentials. Wait for me there. No questions, healer. Just do what I say."

"Should I leave now?"

She smiled. "No. You'll know when it's time to go." Then she turned back to the table.

"Uzuhr-zuddin," she started, addressing the reptiloid, "I won the challenge. I may take what I want."

"You may do what you want with my built object," he hissed in return. "Gotsoh says nothing about taking bargaining wealth."

"You lost," Jesel shot back. "I eliminated you. I control the bargaining now. I want the ship; you, I must assume, want to remain in the game to at least win back some of the wealth you bartered away to build that." She pointed to his dead sphere. "I am offering you my built object along with yours. You cannot possibly work with better tools if you want to win at gotsoh. No one ever gains the advantage of playing with two built objects."

"My ship is worth more than these," he countered.

Jesel sighed. "Fine. I will offer you what is in this box instead. But that's my last offer. You must take one, and I advise you to accept my original offer."

Uzuhr-zuddin's tongue flicked faster. "Show me."

Jesel unsealed the box and turned it around for the reptiloid to see. His pupils dilated. "Phelaan credits? How many?"

"How many does it look like?"

"Do not game with me, falish humanoid. How many?"

"Two million—or thereabout."

Uzuhr-zuddin nodded. "I will take the box then."

Jesel shook her head. "You act without honor, Uzuhr. You lost. Your ship was mine without any bargain, and I offered you a more than fair exchange. With both built objects you could have defeated the apex and won enough to buy five of those ships."

"You are right, perhaps," the reptiloid responded. "But still there remained a chance of my defeat. Here there is none. I will take the credits and go."

"You will take what's in the box and give me the ship in return," Jesel replied and then reached into the box and through the credits like they were air. In a slow, fluid motion, she stood up, at the same time drawing out her blaster from the container and pointing it at the reptiloid's head.

Uzuhr's eyes crossed as he examined the blaster's barrel four centimeters from the skull ridge of his forehead. I heard the buzz of the security bots surround us. I was too scared to move, afraid that any movement might be construed as aggressive and might instigate the bots to fire.

"Explain the situation, Uzuhr," Jesel said calmly.

"I will not. You are egg-fry, humanoid." Uzuhr spread his bright yellow and red throat sac defiantly.

Jesel shrugged casually, dropped the barrel and fired. The blast hit the reptiloid's throat fan, instantly inflating it like a balloon then shriveling it, a neat hole punched through the center with a starburst of charred black emanating from it. "Reconsider," she said, raising the barrel back to aim at his forehead.

The stunned reptiloid remained silent for a few moments, blinking away the fine dust from his blasted dewlap that had settled across his eyes. "I—I refused a fair trade," he stammered to the bots and the spectators that now surrounded us.

"Continue," Jesel encouraged him by setting the barrel against his skull ridge.

Uzuhr's tongue flicked with restrained rage. "This falish humanoid defeated me. She bargained with me honorably. I acted dishonorably, wishing to gain what I had no right to claim. Her actions were justified by mine."

The bots slowly retreated. I looked around, found them gone, and didn't wait another moment. I left the area quickly, stopping as soon as the gotsoh area disappeared from view. I pulled out the coin Jesel had given me and wondered how it worked. I turned it around in my fingers—no hidden catch, button, or activating device.

"I will take that, good malish," a voice announced. I looked down at a bot bent backwards looking up at me. An appendage snaked upwards and pointed at the coin. I handed it to the bot, which dropped the coin into what I can only describe as its mouth. It processed for a second then said, "Follow me, good malish," and sped off.

Somehow the exit path seemed like a straight line, so unlike the winding maze I took to reach Jesel at the gotsoh tables. Within moments, it seemed, the bot directed me to an unguarded door, bowed, and left. Without hesitating, I pushed through and found myself outside of the gaming establishment, beaten back by a dust storm that blasted my face and blinded me. I groped for my storm goggles, managed to find them in the inner breast pocket of my jacket, and put them on. Tentatively I opened my eyes to find the scene before me clear, as though the act of wearing the goggles somehow dispelled the sand storm. Of course, the storm still raged around me—I could still feel the sand blasting away the wrinkles from the exposed parts of my face and hear the howl of the wind in my ears.

I made my way back to our shuttle, entered through the levator and locked it down. At any moment I expected to hear a blast, feel the ship shake and through a rent in the hull watch the port authority constabulary pour in to arrest me. Silently I congratulated my foresight to catalogue and prepare all our essential equipment for quick off-loading. By the time Jesel arrived back at the shuttle, I had both transport sleds packed with all our important supplies and Borthax ready on the mobile medical gurney.

"Well done," she said with a laugh, inspecting my work.

"No thanks to you," I shot back. "Now there's no hope to escape quietly."

"That's right," she laughed. "The Phelaan Syndicate is bound to hear of my little show."

I unlocked the cargo hold doors and pushed Borthax to the entrance, deliberately forcing Jesel to step out of the way. "I'm glad that Arthen doesn't know about your betrayal."

Jesel grabbed my arm and held me still. She closed her humanoid eyes, and the stare of her insectoid facets hollowed me, a clear reminder of Traevis' preparations to kill me. "I haven't betrayed anyone," she whispered calmly.

Through the sweat and trembling of adrenaline, I managed to answer her. "You have sent out our location like a beacon across the galaxy. The company will descend on this place and capture and kill us, leaving Arthen and the captain where?"

"You'll see. Now link the sleds and follow me."

I pulled Borthax and the equipment sleds along behind me as I followed Jesel through the crowded and dingy narrow alleys of the port. She unlocked the docking bay where the reptiloid's ship lay, and the rising door revealed a battered hulk of a transport whose odd shape suggested that it was built piecemeal from junked ships.

"This is not the ship you won," I said, staring at the ugly monster. "Does it fly?"

"It does," she replied proudly, smiling.

"It isn't the ship visualized on his hologram."

"Of course not," Jesel said, taking the control box from me and guiding the sleds to the back of the ship. "I chose Uzuhr as a target because I knew he was faking. He looked too grungy, too third hatching, to have a high quality ship, but not so low that he couldn't afford to carry falsified papers on an expensive ship he doesn't own and a fine hologram to go along with it—a ticket into a high stakes game of gotsoh where major collateral is required. So while the company and the Syndicate are searching for the fine ship that he registered, we will escape in his piece of junk."

"And in payment he'll tell the authorities exactly what ship we're in."

"He won't inform authorities of anything. He'll let them believe we stole the ship displayed on his holo-unit." She paused in off-loading the supplies and sat down on the gunwale of the nearest sled. "He's not going to risk imprisonment and blacklisting from all galactic gambling shops by admitting to bargaining with false assets."

"But won't the port authorities register our flight plan?"

"Unlikely," she said, searching in the hold and finally pointing to a battered and scarred medical alcove. "Get that working and lock Borthax into it."

I inspected the unit, which seemed worthless. "It looks like junk no one bothered to throw out."

"It'll function long enough to transport Borthax to our final destination. Cannibalize whatever gear you took from our shuttle to get it running."

"So—about the port authorities?"

"Oh, yes—" She drove the sleds into the hold and winched down the bay doors with a whining, outmoded hydraulics system. "Uzuhr probably registered this ship under a false name, so there's no direct link back to him. Definitely defined it as scap. This is not an active ship's bay, didn't you notice? It's a storage bay—for keeping trash, supplies, spare parts, and junk—scap as we Phelaan call it."

"Scrap."

"What?"

"Scrap. That's what Earthlings call it."

"Interesting," Jesel nodded.

"So how are we to blast out of here?"

"It's still accessible for transit—for scap ships to load and unload. The opening to the sky is a bit tight, but I'll be able to navigate out without breaking too much off of the hull." She looked up at me and smiled. "Nothing too important at least."

We had left the planet behind and had entered hyperspace before I decided to address the other issue nagging my mind. Jesel, with either the telepathic abilities she denied or an acute insectoid sense that picked up Earthling emotional pheromones of which I was not aware, raised the issue first. "Something else bothers you, healer."

I felt my face flush. I prided myself on controlling all external displays of emotion—or thought so at least—and hated that cues of which I was not aware revealed the inner workings of my mind. Putting aside that one irritation, I addressed the more immediate one. "I could have been caught with that blaster and killed!"

"They might have tortured you a little, but they wouldn't have killed you." She smiled.

"I don't find your apparent lack of interest in my safety at all humorous."

"Healer, they never would suspect you. Me—they scanned me internally and externally."

"Internally? What do you mean?"

Her smile turned to a grin. "You don't want to know."

I shivered. "I suppose I have an idea. Just don't volunteer me again without first asking."

"I am sorry."

"Next: what were you thinking to shoot that reptiloid? You could have killed him at that range—in fact, I am surprised you didn't—and now every military unit in the sector will be after us."

"Hopefully."

"You've gone mad."

"Listen, healer, we can't hide from the company or from Traevis. If we stick to dark alleys, that's where they'll find us and kill us—out of the way, where no one will see them. That's what they want. They don't want the authorities looking for us because then the authorities are going to ask why—and why is not a question the company wants anyone asking."

"So it's better to be captured by dubious law enforcement officials for attempted murder."

"They won't capture us. But they will investigate—digging will make the company nervous and might force them to lie low for a bit. Take the pressure off us enough that we can find some help. Get protection for Arthen and the captain. Delay the company from sending a cleaning crew out to STB."

"And what about shooting him? Couldn't you have just threatened him?"

Jesel shrugged. "I had to project an image. A weapon is not enough in a place like that—especially to a reptiloid. He wasn't going to back down unless I shot him. They have thick, blaster-resistant skin. I dialed it down to low energy, wide-dispersal. When he spread his throat sac I saw my opportunity. I knew it would absorb most of the blaster's energy."

"You *are* mad. That was your plan all along, wasn't it? To get me to bring in the blaster, concealed in that box—"

"—Holographic shield—" she explained.

"—and then find someone with a ship to steal."

"I didn't steal it. I won it."

"How generous of you. I am sure he'll forgive you for his blaster burns."

"Oh, no, he won't," Jesel replied, seriously. "Remember his hatching name, healer. Zuddin."

"Why?"

"Because they're our blood enemies now."

"Thank you for embroiling me in a feud."

She smiled. "Anytime."

THIRTEEN

"Where are we headed?"

"Phelaan territory."

"Arthen and the captain argued against it."

"They are not here."

"They believed that the company has less to worry about from the authorities in Phelaan territory."

Jesel reclined in the pilot's seat and shrugged. "Possibly. But I can slip us into Phelaan sectors without using official transit lanes where we'll have to register. The company won't expect us to do something as foolish as this, so they'll monitor only the standard shipping channels, if they watch any at all."

"What about these other channels—the nonstandard ones?"

"There are too many of them to watch. Besides, I'm taking us to GauStegma."

"What is GauStegma?"

"The Phelaan home system."

I shook my head. "Every time I believe you are sane you do something to change my mind."

"They'll never look for us anywhere near GauStegma. It's truly insane to go there: the Phelaan Syndicate's governing body rules from there, and they most likely have a hand in this STB stuff—if not, they at least know about it. They'll expect us to submit the charges through the local governance council of one of the outlying colonies where central control is weakest."

"I thought that's what we planned on doing."

"We will, we will."

"How?"

"The planet furthest from GauStegma's star was designated early on as a strictly agricultural planet—minimal terraforming, minimal development. Just as a precaution in the event that food-producing colonies fell into the hands of enemies, the home-world would still have a source of natural resources. So, oddly enough, a planet within our central star system functions much like the independent systems at the periphery of Phelaan control—they are all pretty much ignored by the Syndicate."

"You have friends there who will hide us?"

Jesel stared at the piloting sphere in silence. I was about to repeat my question, thinking she had not heard me, when she answered. "Yes," she said so quietly I hardly heard it.

Jesel's piloting and navigation skills—or perhaps luck or the providential intervention of a divine life form in whose existence I didn't believe—helped us to avoid the Syndicate's agents, and soon enough we orbited the green planet at the far reaches of GauStegma.

"We don't have authorization to land," Jesel replied to my inquiry as to why we seemed to circle the planet endlessly. "So . . . we wait for a convoy."

Two days later, a stream of cargo vessels entered orbit, circled six times, and then streamed toward the planet. Jesel eased our ship into their vicinity, watched for a gap and smoothly inserted us into the smallest break in the regular intervals between convoy members.

I waited to hear the communications panel complain, signaling that someone had discovered our ruse and was calling our bluff. Amazingly, no one seemed to care.

"Surprising that none of the convoy ships noticed our intrusion."

"Oh, they did," Jesel replied casually.

"Why, then, do they not report it?"

Jesel smiled without looking at me, focused as she was on piloting the junk heap we called a transport. "Smugglers use this trick to avoid the authorities all the time."

"You are humanoid-insectoid symbionts. I was certain the insectoid nature would prohibit ignoring illegal activity."

"You are correct that we are preoccupied with the truth," Jesel admitted, nodding. "And that is precisely why we allow it: the majority of Phelaan citizens believe that the contraband laws are overly restrictive and impractical. Every Phelaan has bought something from a smuggler. Therefore, there is no moral obligation to uphold immoral—or just plain stupid—laws."

As soon as we passed through the monitoring stations—floating gates like enormous hollow eyes—in the lower atmosphere, Jesel steered us out of the convoy and north across the equator in low flight, skimming the treetops of green hills rising in rows and rows like ocean waves, across the mudflats of a wide delta at the mouth of a red-brown river curling and twisting through the green-blue carpet of a coastal forest and over the dry highlands stretching out from the leeward slopes of a coastal range of mountains. We turned west and hopped back over the jagged snow capped peaks and found the coast again, flying low over rocky shores with black sand and headlands jabbing like knives into a green ocean. We left behind the mainland and dropped so low over the water that occasionally a sudden high wave drummed against the belly of the transport.

"Are you concerned that we might be tracked?" I wondered aloud, leaning to a viewing port and eyeing the water just below us.

"No," Jesel replied, riding the rolling seas, dropping into troughs and pulling up as a wall of water loomed ahead, and then down again. "But it's the traps you don't expect that catch you."

In an hour's time, Jesel pulled the ship off the water's surface. Ahead I could see a long wide island edged by a ring of white sand and green forests rising to a spiny backbone of volcanic peaks. She circled to the opposite side of the island, whose appearance reminded me of the back of an Earth whale caught at the moment its mid-spine bends up out of the water as it surfaces and strikes back into the ocean depths.

She abruptly turned the ship into the island and dropped us into the water as we neared the shore, sledding us onto the sand. She expertly flung off both her restraints and headed for the exit while I struggled with the first of mine.

"Get Borthax ready for transport," she said over her shoulder as she disappeared.

I had become an expert at preparing patients for moving, so it took me little time to unhook Borthax from the ship's medical treatment bay and plug him into the mobile emergency sled's unit. In the brief time since our escape from the Colossus Impendor, my fractured wrist had healed, giving me nearly complete use of my right hand, which helped in preparing the wounded insectoid.

Jesel stuck her head through the entrance into the wrecked medical alcove. "Let's go."

I unlocked the medical sled, spun it around and navigated into the corridor and down to the aft cargo doors. The ramp led straight into the surf, waves washing all the way up to the lip of the bay. "The ship'll rust," I said jokingly to Jesel, who stood on the ramp up to her knees in wash.

She stared into the length of ocean reaching to the horizon's curve. On her back she carried an overfilled emergency pack, contents vomiting up from under the edges of the tented fabric closures, their lashings stretched to their maximum. Maneuvering Borthax's sled beside her, I stopped to follow her eyes to the blank horizon and to feel the chill of the water soak through my pants and down into my boots.

"That's the plan," Jesel said.

"What's the plan?"

"Rusting the ship," she answered, still staring into the rhythmic sway of the waves. "Time to move out of the way," she said and abruptly turned left, took three steps and leaped off the ramp into the water.

Having become accustomed to Jesel's cryptic moods, I followed her without delay and without further question. And, no sooner had I driven the medical sled off the ramp and carefully lowered myself into the chest-high surf, I heard the spinning groan of the ship's engines. With a jolt of adrenaline to help me push the sled through the surf, I managed to shift aside just as the engines spun around and fired, sending the ship backward off the sand and straight into the ocean. With the hold doors wide open, the ship sank within seconds, and the ensuing volume vacuum sucked water, waves, and sand downward behind the vessel.

Feeling the irresistible tow threatening to pull me to the bottom as surely as if a rope from the ship was lashed around my legs, I gunned the sled, shoved my arms down through the handles and locked my elbows. For a moment the whining motors smoked, and the sled slid backwards into the vortex behind me. Then, with a jolt, it broke the surface of the water and shot forward, slapping me against the waves. The sled's nose rammed into the sand just where the beach angled up from the water's edge.

I cut the motor, unhooked my arms from the handles and rolled onto my back, stretched out on the beach, exhausted.

"No time for relaxing in the heat," Jesel's voice said from above.

"You nearly killed Borthax and me," I snapped, my eyes still closed. "And I think I refractured my wrist because of you."

"No time for it," she said. I felt the toe of a boot nudge not so gently at my ribs.

"You can take care of Borthax from now on," I answered the boot, turning away, drawing up my legs and rising to my knees. I opened my eyes and looked at the calm waters, no indication of the ship except a single deep rut running straight into the water and two flashes of heat-melted sand where the reversed engines' exhaust hit the beach.

"I am sorry," Jesel said from behind me. "I—I wasn't thinking. It was foolish and dangerous."

I turned and looked at her.

Her face was red, and her humanoid eyes glassy. Our eyes met, and she looked away. "I should have delayed the engine thrust longer—told you what I planned." She looked up at me and said again, "It was thoughtless."

"Yes, it was," I replied. She reached for the sled controls, and I caught her hand. "I'll take care of it." Jesel stepped aside without complaint while I kneeled down beside Borthax and activated the diagnostics panel. A holographic image swirled into shape just above

Borthax's head. Remarkably, his vitals remained stable despite the trial of leaving the ship. I began a standard global assessment, visually scanning each of his major wounds for signs of infection, his amputation sites for oozing, and the joints of his carapace for evidence of dehiscence, but Jesel stopped me halfway through with a hand roughly squeezing my shoulder.

"We need to get off the beach."

My face flushed. Managing to suppress the angry response pushing at the back of my teeth, I gazed up at her.

She stood over me protectively scanning the headlands and both ends of the beach, a blaster in one hand and Traevis' plasma gun in the other. "The local compliance authority will have tracked us here. Standard procedure requires that they send out a team to investigate."

She peered down at me and smiled. "The compliance authority—the local security detail of the military—always follows standard procedures. They'll want to know our business if they find us."

"It will be hard to explain why our ship sank," I said, continuing my survey of Borthax.

"They won't find the ship."

"Don't you think the giant scar on the beach will make them suspicious?"

She shook her head. "Tide's coming in. It'll be under water in an hour."

Reluctantly—I was still in no mood to follow Jesel's orders, even if they sounded reasonable—I shut down the diagnostics and vowed to complete the global assessment later. Fortunately, the sled's motors functioned properly, even after overloading them to escape the sinking ship's suction.

Jesel led us straight off the beach and into the dense tangle of green growth edging the sand. Thick succulents sprouted like grass, crunching and snapping under our boots.

"They won't have much trouble finding us," I said, looking back at the wet trail we were leaving.

"Let them," she said with a bit more of the edge I expected from her.

We climbed the closest headland and dropped into a valley of tall trees with smooth grey bark that felt as supple as humanoid skin. Their wide, perfectly circular canopies held back the sunlight except for golden shafts that struck through small gaps, giving the under-story the appearance of a shaded cavern with bright columns holding up the green, semitranslucent roof.

Through the lowest point of the valley ran a shallow, fast-moving stream, and here the trees stood back from the banks so that the sun shone down in a long sheet of light, as though its impression on the ground created the waters. The air thickened, stiffened around us, and sweat budded over my face and bare arms and soaked through my shirt and pants.

We climbed a second headland and turned left, following the ridgeline toward a snowy peak in the distance, part of the spine of volcanic mountains I had seen as we circled the island in the transport.

"You don't plan on climbing that, do you?"

Jesel answered without looking back. "Why—did you break your legs on the way up here?"

I smiled to myself, feeling more comfortable with the hard-edged Jesel than the reflective, apologetic one briefly present on the beach. We needed a resolute leader, and I knew that I would never be one. Without Jesel's skill, intelligence, and gall we would have died on STB—or perhaps on the Colossus Impendor. With my anger evaporated, I followed Jesel again without question.

Just as the trail abruptly steepened, Jesel cut to the right and skirted along the mountainside. When we stopped bushwhacking and found the well-worn dirt trail I cannot recall, except to say that suddenly it was there, slowly snaking down the mountainside in gradual switchbacks.

Half the day had gone and the setting sun's mellow glow suffused the air when we stepped onto a ground transport passage, wide and paved. We walked no more than two or three kilometers before a transport vehicle approached from behind us. The insectoid driver stopped, looked once at Borthax, and without questioning why a Phelaan falish would be found in an isolated area with a critically wounded alien insectoid and an alien humanoid, he helped me set the medical sled safely in his cargo bed and made space in his cluttered cab for Jesel and me.

We passed through villages that hugged the roadside like teeth clamped down along the length of a silent black snake. Soon night darkened the sky and stroked the air with a cool breeze from the ocean; the road had turned away from its mountainous inland route and curled along the undulating shore. A green, glowing halo of light first appeared in the distance as I looked over the interposed waters of a bay. As we followed the shoreline of the bay, the glow grew more distinct, separating into thousands of individual lights from the single large mass I had first spied.

We entered the very edge of a town with brightly painted, square two-story buildings crammed together on either side, like obedient but eager children standing in rows. Jesel asked the driver to stop. He left us without a question—refusing Jesel's offer of compensation. We started along a road leading straight up a small hill and directly away from the water, weaving through a maze of narrow streets that baffled me, leaving only the ocean below as a recognizable point of reference. It was while I gazed over the water and the reflection of the town's lights wavering on its surface that Jesel stopped at the gate of a house. I shifted Borthax's sled into idle and inspected the building: painted a dark color obscured by the night, it consisted of several cubes set side-by-side, with the central one projecting out from the others and standing two stories high. Each square had one window in the middle of the front face, with a door replacing the window on the lower level of the entrance. A stone walkway wound from the gate to the door, and to either side I could see flowers blooming wildly in crowded beds.

"Bring him," Jesel said, pushing through the gate and heading for the door.

I pulled up behind her, and she banged harshly on the door.

After a minute, a light appeared in the window above us. I heard movement inside and then the door was pulled back, scraping on the entrance paving. A humanoid arm held out a lamp, illuminating us brightly and keeping the arm's owner in the dark.

The light suddenly dimmed, and a malish voice said "Jesel!" in a rush. He stepped out from the doorway and encased her in his arms. Jesel did not move, her arms locked to her side. He released her, and in the gentler light I could see the familiar long facial features of a Phelaan humanoid but little else.

They spoke closely so that even I couldn't hear what passed between them, though only the length of the medical sled separated us. After a moment, Jesel stepped to one side and waved me in.

The malish walked into the house, and I followed. Inside the door was a small foyer with stairs spiraling up just in front of me. Behind the stairs, I could see in the dimness from a drowsy overhead light a corridor leading back into the hillside. The malish placed a strong, heavy hand gently on my shoulder and pointed to the hallway, smiling.

I understood and expertly navigated around the centrally placed coil of stairs and into the back corridor.

"First door on the right," he said in a hard but friendly voice. From the sound alone an image appeared in my mind of the malish standing in the middle of the garden he'd created, looking across the ocean waters into a past cut by death and killing.

I turned the sled into a small room with a bed and a small window opposite. A door led off from the far end of the left wall. I steered Borthax to the foot of the bed and locked down the sled.

Jesel and the malish spoke outside in the hallway. Suddenly I felt exhausted; as soon as I lay down on the bed, I fell asleep.

I awoke with a start. Sunlight flooded in from the open window, through which a salty breeze also squeezed, swirling the thin pink and blue curtains and brushing locks of hair across my nose, making me itch. I rubbed at the tingling spots, combed away the inciting strands of hair, and propped up on my elbows. I could just see over the windowsill into the garden, through the swaying green stems of a row of cup-shaped blue flowers to the shining green sea. Looking down, I noticed that someone had removed all of my clothes and slid me under the bed covers.

Slowly and reluctantly, I got out of the bed and dressed. My terraformer clothes had been taken away, and in their place, I found a pair of heavy dark green pants, roughly woven of a thick but soft fiber. A white shirt of the same cloth hung loosely on my thin body. My boots sat in one corner, but next to the bed someone had prominently set a pair of crudely woven brown shoes, on the soles of which were sown rows of fibrous, ropelike treads.

The clothes, though rough and crudely made, felt comfortable, and surprisingly, so did the shoes. In the hallway, the aroma of warm food enticed me toward the rear of the house, down a narrow side passage and onto an open veranda sitting under a domed outcropping of hillside that served as a cover for half the space, leaving the other half open to the sky and the warming sun. Three circular tables of wood sat on the sea-polished stone cobbling, the one in the sun covered with plates of food. I sat down on one of the benches and surveyed the meal, recognizing a few of the dishes from the terraforming ship. Nevertheless, even the familiar ones looked and smelled more appealing. A single empty plate nestled among the laden ones, and this one I took and filled with food.

What I ate bore no resemblance to meals I'd had aboard the Colossus Impendor, including the rataan soup. It had no taste of fish, rather a fresh tangy bite that reminded me of citrus fruit from Earth. As I sipped at the soup from a cup, I heard a clicking behind me.

A falish insectoid entered the veranda from the same side door. Her round dark carapace and four short ambulatory appendages indicated Phelaan lineage. She raised up on her rear most legs, and I quickly pushed back from the table and bowed.

"No need," she trilled pleasantly. "Please sit and finish your meal."

"I am done, good falish. Thank you for the food."

"Oh, I didn't cook it," she laughed, a vibrating drumming against her ventral carapace. She scurried over and surveyed the table, running the dorsal surfaces of her task appendages over the food, collecting scents. Her antennae shivered as she smelled the food. "Tsulak is the preparer in the household."

"I don't know—"

"You met him last night," she interrupted. She picked out three small, red-shelled crustaceans from a dark red-brown stew and popped them in rapid succession into her feeding aperture. "He greeted you and Jesel."

"Yes." I remembered the vague outline of his face. "I'd like to thank him for the clothes and the food."

"You can—soon," she said, sitting down across from me and continuing to carefully pick out ingredients from the different dishes on the table. "Don't tell him that I am fishing," she whispered. "He hates it when I strip his dishes of the best parts." She leaned closer, and I joined her over the middle of the spread. "Says it alters the flavor and odor. I say they are meant to be eaten—and that's exactly what I am doing!"

I watched her use both task appendages simultaneously to choose items from plates on opposite sides of the table, deftly extracting what she wanted without disturbing the rest. Lekmana—I eventually remembered to ask her name—had walked her children to school and had just returned to see if I had risen.

"Tsulak insisted that I let you sleep. Rest heals most ills, he always says."

At the word *heal*, I stood up abruptly and turned to the house.

"Borthax rests as well," she said, like Jesel, able to read my mind. "Please sit down. He is stable and will live with or without your immediate attention. See here, Tsulak returns."

The malish humanoid appeared; his tall, strong frame filled the doorway, and when he moved into the courtyard his limbs and form flowed gracefully, as though he were swimming. In the sunlight his longish hair reflected black and blue. He smiled widely, showing bright white teeth, and enveloped my hand in both of his.

"Healer!" he exclaimed, as though my survival had been uncertain and now was assured. "So good to see you. Come sit down and eat."

I smiled at this endearing malish and obeyed, indicating the one empty bench at our table. "Thank you, Tsulak. I have already eaten. It was better than I have had in months."

He placed a long-fingered hand on my shoulder as he took the last place. "That's not so great a compliment with you coming off a terraforming operation." He leaned toward me and eyed Lekmana. "Has she been fishing?"

I hesitated, but he quickly shook his head. "No need for a diplomatic lie. I know she has. I can smell the ptis crawlers on her carapace."

My two companions laughed, and Tsulak reached out to hold one of Lekmana's claws.

"Where is Jesel?" I asked.

For the first time, Tsulak's face tightened along the jaw, and he closed his humanoid eyes. I recoiled just a bit, after my experience with Traevis, but quickly recovered, willing the tension down. From my time with Jesel and Arthen, I had learned to regard the Phelaan humanoid habit as a reflection of the desire to focus on insectoid logic, shutting down or minimizing the sometimes clouding nature of emotions. My question had placed an emotional strain on Tsulak that he wished to suppress.

"She has chosen to seek out the local authorities."

I nodded.

"You may speak freely, healer," Lekmana said. "Jesel informed us of what transpired on STB."

"We know about the sentients," Tsulak added brusquely.

"You don't approve of Jesel's plan," I surmised.

"No, we do not," Lekmana replied without hesitation. "She

insisted on going alone and refused to start with the regional governing council."

"Do you approve of her plan?" Tsulak asked. They both looked at me, and for the first time I felt a coolness in my hosts.

"Jesel hardly tells me what she plans," I said, "and she never asks my approval for anything."

"Typical," Tsulak said.

"But I do believe she intends to disseminate the evidence we've collected to enough local authorities so that even if the Phelaan Council eliminated us and ninety percent of them, a few would remain to transmit the data to the Galactic Council."

"Yes," Tsulak nodded. "She thinks that local authorities will protect her simply out of fear for their own lives."

"Is that reasonable?"

After a moment of consideration, Tsulak nodded again. "Yes. Regional and planetary governing bodies often scapegoat the locals to hide their own corruption and incompetence."

"Then the locals will regard the STB information like holding a bomb," I offered. "They cannot hide it, so all they can do is hand it off to someone else—someone weak like themselves."

When neither Tsulak nor Lekmana answered, I continued. "In that way, the locals will quickly spread the information, making it impossible for the company or the Syndicate to suppress knowledge of their actions on STB. It will eventually reach the Galactic Council, even if Jesel, Borthax, and I are killed."

"You seem to understand Jesel's mind very well, healer," Lekmana said.

Tsulak raised his head to look over us. "Where are the children?"

"In school, where else?" Lekmana shook her head—more of a rhythmic shifting of her thorax and head in opposite directions—and addressed me. "I never let Tsulak supervise the children alone. He would have them swimming every day instead of studying in school."

With mock severity, I shook my head at Tsulak, glad of the change of subject.

"Now wait a minute," Tsulak protested, the bite in his voice weakened considerably by his smile. "That story is over a year old." He turned to me to explain. "The children told me they had holidays, and I believed them."

"He never bothered to call the school to see if it was true," Lekmana added. "They missed a week of instruction."

Tsulak's smile widened. "We played at the beach the entire time. Lekmana's just upset because she missed it."

"How many children do you have?"

"Twelve, in three broods," Lekmana said. "A small pod, but we will have more."

"How long have you been together?"

"Ten years," they said.

I looked at the Phelaan humanoid malish and insectoid falish sitting across from me, and I saw a loving couple, bonded by time and offspring. Before the terraforming operation, their intimate connection would have strained my sensibilities, setting off the internal conflict experienced only by sentient beings, in which the self-perception of broad-minded tolerance strikes up against the reality of entrenched, provincial prejudices. The Healing Order, and my personal experiences as a healer, taught that life differs in its manifestation but not its essence, and the laws of the universe confirm that matter is simply a physical expression of energy; yet I could not have denied that the sight of a humanoid and insectoid couple would have felt wrong to me, despite the laws of physics. But that was before.

"Jesel and Arthen are fortunate to have such friends as you," I concluded.

Tsulak sat back and laughed while Lekmana snapped her pincers rapidly; I guessed this was one of the many options insectoids possess to display humor. "We are not friends," Tsulak said finally, "we are family."

My face flushed, and I stammered to reply.

Lekmana waved her task appendages over my face and head, a gesture of unknown meaning to me. "Did she not tell you who we are?"

"Of course not," Tsulak answered. "You know her—never one to explain anything unless forced to do so." He leaned forward and stared straight into my eyes. "Lekmana is Arthen's wife, and I am Jesel's husband. We are a quadrupel."

"When will Jesel return?" I asked, feeling the heat of anger sharpen my voice.

"No telling," Tsulak replied. "She only said that she would pass the information on to multiple local authorities."

"On the island itself?"

Tsulak raised his hands in a universal gesture of ignorance.

The sun had passed into the western seas and a steady evening breeze smelling of salt and sea life blew evenly over my face and through my moisture thickened hair when I saw Jesel's vague, shadowed form walking up the hill toward the house. She strolled leisurely in the center of the road. Without a word she made for the gate, but I stepped across the stone path to block her way.

She refused to look at me, kept her head down and attempted to skirt to one side and then the other. "Let me pass," she said roughly, her voice hoarse from either talking constantly or from breathing in the humid air.

"No," I said sternly. Two days had passed since my conversation with Tsulak and Lekmana, and I had remained vigilant by the front gate, waiting for her, leaving only for meals and sleep. In two days my anger had simmered, but on her return, her reluctance to talk stoked the flames again.

"What is wrong with you?" I asked, letting my fury snap out the words.

She looked up, and I could see the reddish bronze darkening

of her skin from prolonged ultraviolet exposure. "I am tired, that's all."

"I don't care whether you're tired!" I shot back. "What were you thinking to come back here! This is your family."

"Exactly." The single word escaped her mouth like a sigh given up as the only thing left at the end of a day carrying rocks up a hill.

"Don't you care about them?" Nodding over my shoulder to the house where the lights showed green and yellow through the windows. "You have put them all in danger—Arthen's wife, their children—your husband."

Jesel reached out with one hand and settled for clenching her fist when the frustration of exhaustion denied her my neck.

"You may have studied our anatomy and physiology, but you know little of the Phelaan culture, healer. They are already in danger. Punishment of an individual extends to those responsible for their training, their education—the life they led that brought them to the point of committing a crime. I had to warn them and get the information registered and out before the company sent collecting agents or *haksen'da* to eradicate them."

"*Haksen'da* are myths," I replied weakly, feeling defensive about how foolish I had been.

She pushed me aside easily and headed through the gate toward the house, saying as she passed me, "The dead they leave behind are not myths."

★ ★ ★

We stayed another night. Jesel spoke with Tsulak and Lekmana into the early morning hours while I was dispatched to prepare the children for school. The youngest crawled over the walls, using me as a perch from which to attack others scampering on the floor in mock battles, while the eldest argued bitterly over the order in which to add ingredients to make their breakfast, at the same time agreeing unanimously that any Phelaan dish I cooked would undoubtedly taste terrible. Still, the turmoil I was charged with taming kept me distracted from the deeper concerns irritating my consciousness.

By the time Jesel found me on the veranda, the children sat quietly eating the breakfast that I'd managed to create—pronouncing it awful, worse than something called peckel, and "the sweetest poison I ever ate"—and I stood by laughing, covered in minor puncture wounds, soaked in spots with urine and dabs of feces, and bleeding from multiple superficial lacerations, the result of errant attacks by small spiked appendages.

Jesel sniffed at me sourly. "Get cleaned up. We're leaving."

When I reemerged, cleaned of excrement and my wounds patched up, Jesel stood at the gate looking down the street and on past to the small white waves peaking silently on the green waters. Lekmana and Tsulak sat silently at one of the tables, holding hands and claws. The children had disappeared to school. The two at the table acknowledged me only with a blank look. I sensed that all emotion had turned inward for them; their hold on each other expressed it as clearly as if they had spoken to me—the desperate clinging when one is certain of falling off the edge of existence.

"I am ready," I announced to Jesel's back.

Without a word or a look back, she opened the gate and started down the road.

I quickly bowed to Tsulak and Lekmana. "Thank you."

Tsulak rose and shook my hand. Lekmana extended a task arm from where she sat, and I took it briefly. Then I chased after Jesel.

"Where are we going?" I asked when I caught up to her.

"Planetary transport station," she answered brusquely.

"And then?" I coaxed.

"To the interplanetary port," came the reply.

"And—"

She turned to me, and her face looked like a stone—hard, flat and expressionless. "To the Galactic Council."

"Isn't public transportation dangerous in our situation?"

"Let them kill us," Jesel replied with an eager defiance that worried me. "The information on STB will spread across Phelaan territory whether we live or die."

"You may want to die, but I do not."

"For a healer, you are surprisingly naïve," she said. "It's not a matter of wanting to die: I do not want to die, but I expect to die. You talk as if you neither want or expect to die." We stopped at an intersection, and Jesel looked down the cross streets before continuing. "Perhaps you need more training."

I accepted the insult silently because what she said stung with the sharpness of truth. Of course I expected to die, but I had acted as though I feared it—and perhaps I did at that time. "What about those on STB?"

Jesel's face darkened. "The sentients will be safe enough. The Terraforming Council will review Cra'taac's data that the captain collected and will immediately halt all operations there pending investigation. The question is whether Traevis got a cleaning crew there in time to kill Arthen and the captain. That I don't know."

"If we are irrelevant," I asked, "then why must we see the Galactic Council? Why not remain here with your family?"

We had reached the flat of the town in the strip of land between the water and the foot of the mountain. Phelaan citizens crowded the streets, and I heard the hum and felt the itching vibration on my skin of giant engines overhead. Transports cruised slowly above us, throttling down their massive engines in preparation for landing.

Jesel crossed the main traffic road and headed for the largest building I had seen in the town—a long, squat sand-colored structure—into which a line of Phelaan snaked. "We must register formal charges," she finally answered me. "Otherwise Arthen, the captain, you, and I will be charged along with the terraforming company."

Despite Jesel's confidence, tension still tightened across my face and abdomen as we passed through a gauntlet of armed Phelaan military personnel in the process of boarding the planetary transport. Once strapped in and in flight, I loosened the grip on my seat arms and considered the last several days with Jesel's and Arthen's family. Curiosity born of my profession finally forced me to ask the questions I pondered in my mind. "Jesel, what roles do Tsulak and

Lekmana play if you and Arthen—" I stopped, suddenly aware of the sensitivity of the issue.

Jesel's face flushed, and for a moment I thought she was going to cry. Instead, she angled her face away from me and focused on the floor of the ship.

I waited a short time for her to recover and then approached my thought directly. "I know you and Arthen were—are—lovers."

She didn't answer immediately. After a long silence, she asked "Did you figure this out or did Arthen tell you?"

"He told me."

"I thought so."

I bristled. "I am not as stupid as you think."

"I don't think you are stupid," she countered. "I think you are naïve. But you have survived this long, and that tells me some powerful force guards you—or you are unusually lucky."

I wanted to tell Jesel that no force guarded me—no god or superior being wasted its time watching over the insignificant actions of a creature so transient in existence as me—or her, for that matter. The irony of the situation held me back—the philosophical agent of the sublime realm of healing speaking out against the existence of a higher being, whose presence was defended by a terraformer who lived in a world founded on the stark realities of life, death, and dominance hierarchies.

Instead, I remembered what she once said to me. "Everything dies, Jesel. My time is still to come."

She snorted. "Your time came and went several times, healer."

"There's something I would like to know, if it would not offend you to answer," I replied, wishing to change the subject and avoid the question of god, higher powers, and the nature of existence.

"It's not the answering but the asking that might offend me."

We stared at each other for a long moment, and I noted just the hint of a smile curling the corners of her mouth. I took that to mean acceptance of the question I was going to ask. "Please tell me how, mechanically speaking, and why, physiologically and evolutionarily speaking, do Phelaan humanoids and insectoids mate."

Jesel looked out of a viewing port and smiled wistfully. I imagined she thought of Arthen then. After a few moments, she turned back to me. "The mechanics I will not describe. You don't need to know them from me, and if you are that interested you can access the Phelaan libraries for the anatomical explanations. But don't get any ideas: Phelaan falish insectoids do not mate with malish humanoids."

"You mean—"

She nodded. "Only malish insectoids and falish humanoids. And of course insectoids mate with each other to produce our insectoid offspring, just as humanoids mate to produce our humanoid offspring."

"Why then do insectoids and humanoids need to mate with each other?"

"We are symbionts," she said. "Phelaan moles and insects require each other to have offspring: a falish humanoid, when mating with a malish insectoid, stimulates an internal organ of his which produces a secretion that the malish then feeds to the falish humanoid. This hormonal substance is necessary for our eggs to reach their final stage of maturity. For the malish insectoid, stimulation of this gland, which can only be performed by a falish humanoid—the anatomy lesson I will not teach you—activates his sperm production, which otherwise remains dormant."

"So you mate out of necessity."

Jesel's eyes narrowed. "Are you implying that Arthen and I are lovers for practical reasons only? That we chose each other like buying cleaning solvents—we went looking for something we needed and chose the cheapest one we could find? Is that what you mean?"

"I mean to imply nothing, only demonstrate my ignorance. And I certainly do not mean to insult you or Arthen."

She continued to eye me suspiciously, then slowly her grimace disappeared. She nodded. "The Phelaan Syndicate is one people—insect and mole. We have many factions based on different political, social, and economic views but not racial ones. I am closer to my insectoid family than some of my humanoid family. We don't divide ourselves along racial lines. We cannot; we need each other to survive."

"Has no one ever tried to—to develop an independence from the other race?" I knew the question raised a dark specter whose shadow reached to all corners of the galaxy.

"Yes, long ago," she nodded. "It led to the Race Wars, and I'll not speak of them. The Phelaan Syndicate emerged after that, and they have held us together since then. No one wants to return to those times. Even though no generation still remains that experienced those wars, the trauma of that horror remains burned in the collective memory of my people. We will never again think of separating the two races. We are one."

"Does it bother you to know that the Syndicate may have knowledge of STB?"

"No. Governing bodies are naturally corrupt, even if the people who rule were not corrupt to begin with. The Syndicate may have saved us back then, but now they are like any other governing body—intent on their own survival. It's the people, the citizens, that matter."

"What do you mean?"

"Central governments are like poisoned waters, healer. Politicians—maybe they are good, honest, caring people. Then they enter the government—drink the water—and they become sick. They can't help but get poisoned. How long it takes depends on the good in them—"

"Their ethical constitution?"

She shrugged. "Something like that, I suppose. Stelthan pigs love mud. They can live for years as the cleanest of pets, grooming themselves constantly. But then, if they see mud—they can't resist. They will wallow in filth for the rest of their lives if given the chance."

Jesel raised her hand. "Healer, no more questions about our past. I have enough sadness to keep my mind occupied."

"I am sorry."

In my mind I tried to grasp the concept of Jesel's complicated family structure but quickly realized I needed more information. "You spoke of your humanoid and insectoid families. By that you meant what?"

"I mean the quadrupel. Arthen's and mine: his wife and offspring, and my husband and me. Don't you understand yet, Healer? Arthen and I love each other; he loves his wife and children; I love my husband; we all love each other. We are a family. Without Arthen and me, there would be no family."

I understood then. "Do you and Tsulak want children?"

"Yes. We all want humanoid children to join the quadrupel." She paused a moment, and I noticed the tears glossing her eyes. "Before I left, Arthen fed me the ouae juice. I can get pregnant now." She turned to me and wiped her face quickly. Unstrapping herself from the seat, she said, "I need to rest." She paused in the aisle and looked over her shoulder at me. "I cannot hide from the pain, healer." She sighed. "I have tried, and it doesn't work."

FOURTEEN

Jesel and I found transportation to the Galactic Council, where we submitted charges of attempted genocide. Later, Borthax testified from the hospital in which he was recovering. After the formal procedures to open an investigation, the Council released us.

Jesel and I promised to maintain contact, and I insisted that she let me know when she rejoined Arthen. I could not entertain in words my concerns that he might not have survived. She assured me that I could not rid myself of her so easily.

I encountered the Phelaan Syndicate several more times after that, and I sought out my two friends; several times I heard rumors of Jesel, but, by the time I could act upon the information, circumstances requiring my immediate attention pulled me away. Such is life: sometimes opportunity only exists as a dream in our minds. What we imagine as reality turns out, on closer inspection, to be an illusion, a mental mirage to help us cope with parting from friends or saying good-bye to a part of our lives. It was neither the first nor the last time I lamented my inability to keep my promises.

I don't for a moment believe in predestination or fate, but I have come to accept that each of our lives follows a certain course, a flow. Like a river may have a set route that nevertheless can shift in places given local influences—heavy rains, floods, drought, the influence and activities of sentient beings to manipulate its direction—we ourselves can alter the course. But the currents of life sometimes send us in directions we never intended or anticipated.

FIFTEEN

Several months after I left Jesel and the Galactic Council, I found myself back on Earth, finally ready, I believed, to resume the traditional life of a healer. I had seen and experienced enough of the darkness of the universe. I wanted to return to the path my Master had set out for me, and I needed to cleanse myself of the desire for retribution that had stirred a killing nature in me.

Within site of the Healing Order's central facilities, several hands from the crowd caught my shoulders and dragged me into a side street. In the shadowed light of the alleyway, several vague hooded forms surrounded me, speaking low enough that I could not make out the words or language. Just as I recovered enough from the shock of abduction to listen more carefully, they retreated, disappearing into the encroaching darkness. I stared into the silent, empty alley for a few moments and noticed a small black object sitting in the middle of the lane two or three meters away from me. My eyes grew accustomed to the darkness, and the object grew more distinct—a matte black, deeper than the surrounding darkness, as though a hole into space was pulled down and set in this narrow passage. Then the object unfolded, first an overly long jointed arm, then a second, followed by two legs that propelled the original transformed object into the air. A head finally separated from the top and the whole incomprehensible thing strode toward me.

Traevis smiled at me as though meeting a long lost friend. I recognized the SOS jacket he always wore. "We have unfinished business, healer."

"If you came to pay me what the company owes me, then I would agree," I replied. Time and distance had worn away my fear of him.

"You wouldn't want that payment."

"Then we have no business." I tried to sidestep him, but he blocked my way, being careful not to touch my bare hands.

"You are right. We have no business. The Galactic Council fined the company out of existence; the Phelaan Syndicate killed the company's officers who could have informed the Council of the government's involvement; and I escaped with my life."

"How unfortunate."

"I've been following you for the last month. Did you know that?"

I had no idea, but I said nothing.

Traevis smiled in reply to my silence. "I know so much about you now—what you like to eat, what you like to drink—how you sleep in your bed and how many times you wake up at night."

"Anything else you want to say, Traevis? Tell me quickly because I have business to attend to."

"I have never failed to complete a mission—"

"That's not true," I interrupted, unable and unwilling to hold back a triumphant grin.

"—until our encounter," he finished. "By rights you should be dead, but you are not." Then he did something I could not have anticipated: he bowed respectfully. "You possess a weapon of great power, healer—far more dangerous than anything I carry."

"It is not a weapon," I protested.

"Yes, it is, if you learn to use it properly."

"You mean abuse it," I snapped. "Healers use their powers to heal, not to kill. Never to kill."

"Never?" The wry smile that curled the edges of Traevis' lips infuriated me. "You nearly killed me—closer than anyone yet." With a fluid motion of his hand, he indicated the plasma burns on the side of his head. "You regret it, don't you, healer—not killing me?"

As I stepped forward and raised my hands, I knew that my actions were foolish and would end in my death. I didn't care, though: at that moment I wanted only to crush Traevis, to pulverize him like a clot of dirt in my fists and scatter the dust into the air. Master Yeh's face appeared then in my mind, with that rare look of anger mixed with disappointment. I focused on his face, quickly stepped back and quieted my breathing.

Traevis, it seemed, sensed my recovery of reason and

pushed again. "Have you ever thought of becoming an assassin? I know an amphiboid who could get you started, and with my recommendation—"

"I will never become like you," I replied resolutely.

"Don't be so certain." He shrugged casually. "You cannot deny the power any longer, perfectly camouflaged within the irreproachable selflessness of your profession. Don't forget that it saved your life."

A paralyzing horror swept down over me from its hidden perch in my mind. "You envy me," I whispered loud enough for Traevis to hear.

He nodded. "You possess a phantom limb—a secret talent of undeniable advantage—highly prized by assassins and our clients. Think of it, healer: you can collect the crimes of a sentient universe and wield retribution like a planet-crushing hammer. I will never be so proficient at killing." He bowed again.

"And I will never kill."

He laughed. "You wanted to kill me just a moment ago." He tapped his right temple then pointed at me. "Action is only one step from thought. How long can you deny the thought, healer? Shall I guess?" He closed his humanoid eyes and stared at me with his multifacets—briefly—then his pupils opened up again. "Only until your morality demands action. It begins like that with creatures such as you—the desire to erase evil often ends with the creation of it."

"Kill me now, and spare me from more of your words."

"I could," he replied calmly. "Perhaps microinjection of a slow neurotoxin that would kill you in five or fifty years, whatever I chose. Easily enough administered by a nanosyringe as I accidentally bump you while passing on the street. Or, more fitting—the spiraling *chi* torture, something I learned here on Earth."

After a pause, he shook his head. "Sadly, I only kill for payment, and I have searched everywhere for someone who would pay to see you dead. Apparently your life holds no value to others. And so I wish you good fortune, healer. May you achieve greatness in the future. And when you do, remember this: someone will always pay to see the powerful die." He bowed deeply, folded his arms into his triangular-shaped thorax, turned to the side, and slipped into an impossibly thin space between two buildings. "If you ever decide to choose our path," his words issuing from the crack into which he had disappeared, "let the universe know, and I will find you." The last words echoed back and forth through the narrow alley.

For a long time I refused to believe that the Phelaan assassin had influenced me. However, I never made it to the offices of the Healing Order that day. In fact, it took me many more years before I faced the Healing Council again and then under very different circumstances. Instead, I spent five days wandering the planet and finally boarded the first deep space transport I could find with an available berth. I felt the pull of a new current, but I didn't know where it would lead me.

ABOUT THE AUTHOR

After a bit of wandering through his twenties, Ja Man found his calling as a pediatrician. At present, you will find him playing the didgeridoo or designing alternative universes when not otherwise occupied tormenting children or avoiding trees with his mountain bike. He lives with a sizeable cat who refuses to reveal his true name and who claims, in his heyday, to have fought off foxes and large birds of prey.